THE

REDWOODS

BLOOD
PACT

BLOOD PACT

DAVID HAGBERG

A TOM DOHERTY ASSOCIATES BOOK
NEW YORK

BLOOD PACT

A Forge Book
Published by Tom Doherty Associates, LLC
175 Fifth Avenue
New York, NY 10010

www.tor-forge.com

Forge® is a registered trademark of Tom Doherty Associates, LLC.

Library of Congress Cataloging-in-Publication Data

Hagberg, David.
    Blood pact / David Hagberg.—First Edition.
        p. cm.
    A Tom Doherty Associates Book.
    ISBN 978-0-7653-2022-3 (hardcover)
    ISBN 978-1-4299-4883-8 (e-book)
    1. Thieves—Fiction.   I. Title.
    PS3558.A3227B56 2014
    813'.54—dc23
                                        2013025070

Forge books may be purchased for educational, business, or promotional use.
For information on bulk purchases, please contact Macmillan Corporate
and Premium Sales Department at 1-800-221-7945, extension 5442,
or write specialmarkets@macmillan.com.

First Edition: March 2014

Printed in the United States of America

0   9   8   7   6   5   4   3   2   1

FOR LORREL, AS ALWAYS

BLOOD
PACT

The HMS *Britannia* was Cunard's newest paddle wheel steamer to make the Atlantic crossing from Boston to Halifax to Liverpool, but she was primarily a mail carrier and not very well suited for her 115 passengers, who were stacked in dark, cramped cabins belowdecks.

Fr. Jacob Ambli, twenty-nine, a man just under six feet, with a broad face and youthful though intelligent dark eyes, emerged from the empty dining room aft of the funnel and went to the rail. He wore loose gabardine trousers and a thick sweater against the evening cold. If trouble were to come this night he wanted fighting room and flexibility.

It was just after eleven and the overcast sky showed no stars. Nothing was visible except for the faint luminescence of the ship's wake as it tumbled down the eight-foot waves. The horizon had been lost once night fell, lending an even greater sense of isolation than he had felt trekking across the American southwest deserts and mountains searching for Cibola north of the Rio Grande. A search that had been successful.

Ambli—who'd traveled from Mexico City three hundred kilometers overland by mule train to Veracruz, where he'd picked up a sailing vessel for Havana, and from there another sailing vessel to Boston—was less certain than ever that he would reach the Vatican with the blessed news. But praise be to God, he would persevere even though he was now certain that men who wanted to murder him were aboard this very vessel, and according to Fr. Jesus de Mijares, who had come with orders from His Holiness the Pope to expedite Ambli's return with the diary, would probably strike sometime in the middle of the night in the middle of the Atlantic.

They had met three weeks ago at the new Carrollton Inn Hotel in Boston, where the older, much bulkier priest with a frown that seemed to be permanently etched on his enigmatic face, had opened his arms in welcome—in public.

As they'd embraced he'd whispered in Ambli's ear, "Do you have the diary on your person?"

"Yes," Ambli said, reaching inside his coat pocket, but de Mijares stayed his hand.

They were in the lobby and they went outside where de Mijares, who was also dressed in a long, dark frock coat instead of his clerical robes, produced cigars. When they were lit, the two priests walked along the front of the hotel's interconnected row houses, the morning thick with heat and humidity. "You are in grave danger from here until we reach Vatican City."

Ambli had worked and traveled under the name of Señor Roberto Gomez, as a surveyor and mapmaker from Barcelona under the service of the Spanish child Queen Isabella II, whose advisers, when she was only nine years old, had ordered the military expedition into the Spanish deserts of New Mexico in search of gold. They'd fought Indians, rattlesnakes, scorpions, poor food, scurvy, and most of all the relentless heat. "You know of my mission," he replied.

"Sí, and your devotion and your training, but I'm telling you that I was sent to protect you on the final leg of your voyage, which will be by far the most dangerous."

"With a man of the name Jesus on my side, I cannot fail."

"This is no laughing matter. It's the Voltaire Society and they never fail."

Ambli, of course, had heard of the organization, which traced its beginnings back to 1776, two years before the French philosopher's death. Voltaire, who had despised the Catholic Church—calling it neither holy nor Roman—had formed the society at the urgings of a group of wealthy businessmen and bankers in Great Britain and across the Continent to somehow curb the Church's growing wealth, by extorting its money whenever possible, and even resorting to outright theft when necessary: artwork, business ventures, buildings and land through complicated tax transactions, and shipments of gold from the New World.

But he'd never thought they were his real enemy on this mission. It was the Spaniards who wanted the seven cities of gold, which it claimed as its own. The modern-day Cibola was seven caches of gold and silver that the monks of Mexico City's diocese had stolen over a period of one hundred years from government shipments back to Madrid and Manila, and had transported the wealth via mule into the Norte Americano deserts through a place called the *Jornada del Muerto*—journey of death—where they hid it.

Spain wanted it back, thus Queen Isabella II's military expedition. But the Vatican claimed the treasure for itself, thus Ambli's assignment to join the search party, and record the trip in two diaries: one that was the true account of the mission, which he'd kept for himself as a secret, and which he meant to carry back to the Vatican, and the other a false account, showing wrong distances and cleverly altered directions. His diary led back to the seven caches of gold, while the expedition's official diary would lead nowhere.

Of the nineteen Spanish soldiers plus Ambli, who marched north six years ago, only two made it back to Mexico City, with only the false diary and some maps to show for their sacrifice. Ambli, who it was believed had been killed by Indians on the return trip, had instead hidden for five days in the mountains near Querétaro about two hundred kilometers north of Mexico City until he figured it was safe to return and make the arduous trip back to Rome.

Quite a few people were out and about, despite the heat and humidity, and Ambli shook his head. "I meant no disrespect, Father, it's just that I'd always assumed that the Society was of no consequence in these modern times."

"No disrespect was taken, but you are wrong about the Society. Spain may be our enemy in this business—though that in itself is hard to believe considering Isabella's devotion to Gregory—but the real danger to us is, and has been for the last fifty years, the Society."

Gregory was Pope Gregory XVI, and Ambli was shocked by de Mijares's casual mention of the name of His Holiness. But he decided on the spot that he still had much to learn. He'd been chosen for the assignment because of his youth, his strength, his energy, and his intelligence. And, he thought now, perhaps because of his naivete. Before the priesthood he'd been a farmer and a mason but after his ordination he'd been trained as a surveyor and mapmaker, never dreaming that the far-seeing Vatican strategists had selected him to go to Mexico to search for the gold—simply because he would endure and would never question his orders.

"Do you think that they will try to assassinate me here in Boston? Why not before, in Mexico when there were many more opportunities? I don't understand."

"First they want the real diary, the one you carry with you."

"How could they know or even suspect something like that, unless they got hold of the expedition's official diary?"

"Because they killed Pedro Rodriguez and Luis Zapatero, the only two soldiers to return alive. And when their bodies were finally discovered no diary or maps were found."

"But how do you know this?"

"I was there. I followed the four Society agents from London."

Ambli was startled and a little afraid. Reflexively he looked over his shoulder. "Four of them," he muttered.

"Only two now," de Mijares said. "And maybe only one by the time we reach the mid-Atlantic."

Ambli had bit off the obvious question—how two Voltaire Society agents had been eliminated—mostly because he didn't want to know. Except that he'd understood, by some basic instinct at that moment, that Fr. Jesus de Mijares was a dangerous man. And just then a very good friend to have so close at hand.

And for the three weeks in Boston de Mijares had never left his side, which had been fairly easy because the only time they left the hotel was to take their morning constitutional.

The real oddity, in Ambli's mind, had come in the beginning of the second week when he'd thought of something just before going downstairs for lunch and he'd opened the door to their adjoining rooms without first knocking.

De Mijares, stripped to his waist, and wearing only his trousers but no shoes or stockings, was on his back on the floor, his knees drawn up, and his hands clasped at the nape of his neck, doing what he'd later said were called sit-ups. Sweat streamed down his face, and glistened on his hairy barrel chest.

"Pardon me," Ambli had said, embarrassed, and he started to back out, but de Mijares called him back.

"It's all right, I'm nearly finished."

"I don't understand," Ambli said. De Mijares was obviously expending a great deal of energy, but for no apparent reason. Physical labor to accomplish something—plow a field, build a wall, dig a well—he could fathom, but not this.

"I need to keep my muscles in tone," de Mijares explained.

Ambli shook his head, still not comprehending.

"Keeping fit is one of many requirements of my Order."

Ambli spread his hands.

De Mijares stopped what he was doing. "The Knights of Malta, surely you have heard of us," he said. "The Sovereign Military Order of St. John of Jerusalem of Rhodes and of Malta? SMOM—Sovereign Military Order of Malta?"

All of a sudden it came to Ambli and he involuntarily stepped back a pace. At various times since the Crusades in the eleventh century they'd been called either healers for Christ—helping care for the poor and sick pilgrims to the Holy Land—or Soldiers for Christ—taking on military operations for the Church. Most of them were nurses but some, like de Mijares, were Knights in armor in the field to do battle.

Standing at the rail expecting trouble at any moment, Ambli recalled that conversation, and his revelation. He'd been frightened and yet drawn to the priest who'd been sent to offer his protection.

He suddenly got the strong impression that someone was watching him, and he turned abruptly. Fr. de Mijares stood in the dining room doorway, one hand raised on the doorjamb, only the outline of his figure clear in the darkness.

"Father, you startled me," he said.

"Do you have the diary on your person?" de Mijares demanded weakly. Something was wrong with his voice, as if he were in excruciating pain.

Ambli started forward, but de Mijares stopped him.

"Stay at the rail. Do you have the diary?"

"Yes."

"Throw it overboard."

"No."

"Now, before it's too late," de Mijares cried. He looked over his shoulder and all at once he was shoved violently to his knees on the deck, the back of his head erupting in blood.

Before Ambli could move a muscle two men sprung from the dining room, stepping around de Mijares, who was now on all fours. One of them carried a short club, of the kind used to tap a beer keg. Both of them were small, five-five or five-six, and slightly built but they moved lightly, with the grace of cats.

"Good evening, Father, let us have the diary and you can return to Rome unharmed," the one with the club said, his tone reasonable, as if he had asked for some salt at the dinner table. He spoke in British-accented English.

Ambli stepped back until he was against the rail. "You have murdered Father de Mijares, why?"

"He's not dead yet. But he killed two of our companions. The diary for your life."

"My life is of less concern than my immortal soul," Ambli said, and he reached into his trousers pocket for the leather-bound diary.

Before he could pull it out to toss it overboard, the man with the club was on him, smashing the billy into his forearm, breaking both bones.

Ambli started to cry out, the pain intense, but before he could utter a sound the second man clamped a powerful hand over his mouth. Together the two of them forced him to the deck, pulled his broken arm back, and removed the diary from his pocket.

"You won't understand, but the treasure you found has another use. It is something many times more important than the corrupt Spanish government, and certainly even more important than the Mother Church in Rome."

Ambli was a large man, but he was helpless as the two men easily lifted him off the deck and rolled him over the rail into the sea. The dark, incredibly cold water closed over his head and by the time he clawed himself to the surface, Fr. de Mijares's body was hitting the water.

The last human being Ambli ever saw was the man with the club, tossing it overboard, the look of cold triumph recognizable even at a distance and in the dark.

Ambli had failed, but he had tried and he hoped that a merciful Jesus would accept him to His bosom; praise be to God.

PART

ONE

Present day

Sarasota, Florida

ONE

Sarasota was the center for the fine arts in all of Florida, with a bronze reproduction of Michelangelo's statue of David as its symbol. Kirk Collough McGarvey back at his desk at the University of Florida's New College, after too long an absence, stared out his window at the swimming pool–blue waters of Sarasota bay. Life had been easy here, but with an emptiness.

He wanted to be happy back teaching Voltaire to the bright kids in the semi-private liberal arts college, and yet he was without his wife who'd been assassinated, along with their daughter, when an IED meant for him went off right under the limo they were riding in.

And just this afternoon, his last class for the day finished, and his office hours over with, something else intruded on his thoughts. Some niggling worry at the back of his head; some red flag raised by his early warning system, which had been honed over twenty-five years working first as a field agent for the CIA, then rising to director of operations and for a brief stint director of the entire agency, and finally as a special operations officer, had been kicking into gear over the past several days.

At fifty, just under six feet, built like a rugby player he was in perfect condition in part because of the luck of the genetic draw, but also because of daily workouts in the gym, runs on the beach, and swims in the Gulf where he lived on Casey Key. He'd been one of the best field officers that the Company had ever known; a shooter in the parlance, which was well known in the business. What was not so well known, though it was rumored, was the number of people he had killed, or the heavy toll those ops had taken on him, physically as well as mentally.

That he'd been a killer and yet an academic fit him well for some odd reason. He was self-confident, intelligent, honest, and above all dependable. But he was a hard man in the right situation—made all the more decisive and deadly because of the manner of his wife's and daughter's deaths. In the old days he might have kneecapped an opponent to stop the man, but during the last few assignments he'd preferred the double tap to the head to make sure no one would be coming up on his six.

All in the past, he wanted to tell himself, though he'd thought about calling his old friend Otto Rencke who still worked at the CIA as its director of Special Projects to see if anything was in the wind. But rising from his desk and grabbing his briefcase he'd decided that he was being a little paranoid. In any event if something was coming his way it would show up when it showed up.

Later, he hoped, though over the past several months he'd become a little bit jumpy, even bored.

"Once a field agent, always a field agent," a former deputy director of operations had told him a number of years ago. It was the same guy who'd called him an anachronism, his skills no longer needed in the new order of things. Until 9/11 and the necessity to find and kill bin Laden.

He walked out of his tiny, book-lined second-floor office, the philosophy department all but deserted as usual on a Friday afternoon at the end of spring term and the start of summer break, and headed for the stairs. But he stopped, and glanced over his shoulder as one of the young teaching assistants came out of an office and went to the restrooms at the end of the hall.

He couldn't quite put his finger on what was bothering him. Maybe a car or a van parked in an unusual spot. Maybe a chance encounter with someone who shouldn't have been on campus. Maybe someone seated on a bench reading a paper who didn't look up as Mac passed. Maybe a motorcycle following him through the end of the green light, chancing running the red.

He went back to his office, laid his briefcase on the desk, and took a Walther PPK semiautomatic pistol, chambered for the small 7.65 cartridge, out of a locked drawer and put it in the front right pocket of his khaki slacks, along with an extra magazine of ammunition in his left. The pistol was lightweight, but compact and reliable. It was a spare, and a very old friend.

Locking up again, briefcase filled with notes for a new Voltaire book in hand, he went downstairs and headed for the faculty parking lot where he'd left his rebuilt 1956 Porsche 356 Speedster convertible in gunmetal gray with red leather. An indulgence since he'd come back to Florida, and one he knew that Katy would have loved.

His white Guayabera shirt was plastered to his back by the time he reached his car.

At that moment a very tall, whip-thin man, dressed in an obviously expensive European-cut charcoal gray suit, white shirt, tie knotted, shoes well shined, got out of a Lexus SUV and came over.

McGarvey looked up mildly and scanned the parking lot. No one else was out or about, nor had anyone followed him from his office. But he was alert, his senses humming.

"Dr. McGarvey," the man said as he approached. He spoke good English with a French accent. He was a head taller than McGarvey, his face narrow and pinched, his nose Gallic.

"Actually it's Mister," McGarvey said.

They shook hands. "Of course," the man said. "I am Giscarde Petain, and I have come from Paris to discuss the Voltaire Society with you. It is my understanding that you are something of an expert on the philosopher and his teachings."

"I've written a book, but I don't think I've run across any mention of a society."

"Not many have," Petain said. "Do you have a few minutes to talk, perhaps somewhere out of the sun?"

"Actually no. What do you want?"

"Your help. Before there are more killings, and before everything that we've worked for over the last two centuries is lost."

"I'm sorry, monsieur, but you've come to the wrong man," McGarvey said, and he reached for the Porsche's door handle, but Petain shot out a hand and stopped him.

"I need to make you understand the urgency of my being here."

McGarvey pulled his hand away and stepped back. "Turn around and spread your legs."

Petain didn't seem surprised. He did as he was told, and moved his arms away from his torso, understanding that he was going to be searched. "I am not armed."

McGarvey put down his briefcase and quickly frisked the man, finding no weapons. But he did find a French passport and when the man turned around he compared the photograph with Petain's face. They matched, and McGarvey returned it, but he was sure that he'd never seen the man before, or noticed the Lexus in the past few days.

"You have two minutes to tell me who you are, how you know me, and exactly why you're here."

"My name I've told you. I am a businessman—a stockbroker actually, with the Euronext Paris, which was the old Bourse before we merged with the markets in Amsterdam, Lisbon, and Brussels."

"I know the market."

"I learned of you by your reputation in certain intelligence circles. I have friends in the DGSE who when I made inquiries told me that you once lived in France, and had been of some service."

The DGSE was the Direction Générale de la Sécurité Extérieure, France's external intelligence service. While the organization wasn't exactly in love with him, his sometimes presence in the country over the past few years had been tolerated.

"And specifically we need your help to locate a diary that was stolen from us ten days ago."

"You said killings."

"Yes, starting in eighteen thirty-eight, the latest three days ago in Zurich," Petain said. "And there is no reason for us to suspect they will stop now."

"Who is the they?"

"The Catholic Church, we think. More specifically a faction of the Knights Hospitaller."

This group, including the Sacred Military Order of Malta, which was supposedly the militant arm of the Knights, McGarvey had heard of, though he'd never had any dealings with them. But his interest was piqued. "A nearly two-centuries-old war between the Vatican and your Voltaire Society. Why me?"

"The Vatican knows your name as well as I do because of your involvement several months ago involving property they believe is rightfully theirs. With the diary missing, you're next."

"Someone wants to kill me?"

"That likelihood is very high, yes, monsieur."

"Who, specifically?"

"I have a story to tell you first, though you already know many of the details."

TWO

□

McGarvey brought the Frenchman back to his office in the Department of Philosophy building, the hallways deserted.

They sat across the desk from each other, Petain's coat still buttoned properly, and it didn't seem as if he was sweating. "I won't take much of your time," he said. "But we do need your help."

"We?"

"I represent the Voltaire Society, which is prepared to pay whatever fee you may ask for. But time is of the essence and as I told you outside, my life is in danger as is yours."

"By your coming here."

"Yes, and by your involvement in an affair in Southern Texas involving a lost cache of gold that legend has was hidden by Spanish monks from Mexico City."

"It never existed," McGarvey said. But a lot of other people had believed it did, including María León, an officer in Cuba's intelligence service—who was one of Fidel Castro's illegitimate daughters—and had been willing to kidnap Otto Rencke's wife and commit murder to find it.

"Oh, but it does, as do four of the other seven," Petain said, and he let it hang for a long second or two, as if he'd expected McGarvey to argue the point.

The operation with Castro's daughter had led McGarvey on a bloody chase from Havana to Mexico City and Seville and eventually to a desert site just across the Mexican border in Texas where a huge crowd of Cubans and Mexicans—many of whom were involved with the drug cartels—had gathered in search of a fabulous treasure of Spanish gold and silver. If it had ever existed it had been moved by the U.S. government to a vault at Fort Knox. But when that vault had finally been opened it was empty.

"Let me give you a little more of the background so this will make some sense to you. In seventeen seventy-six, two years before Voltaire's death, the society was formed at his urging, by a group of businessmen—primarily bankers—in Paris, and eventually in London and even Rome. It was to be an insurance agency of sorts by which the major banks of every major European nation would safeguard each other's assets against coups, wars, inflations, market crashes, and even natural catastrophes. And fledgling democracies—such as your own."

"Never had anything to do with Voltaire," McGarvey said.

"It has more to do with him and his philosophies and his feelings about democracy than you might guess."

"To his way of thinking democracy did little more than support the idiocy of the masses."

"Consider his world—your revolution had just begun, and France would not be far behind. He actually thought that an ideal form of government was in fact a democracy tempered with a little assassination," Petain said. "Don't you agree?"

"No."

"But it has been your business for twenty-five years."

"If you've come to hire me as a shooter, you've wasted your time and mine," McGarvey said, and he started to rise, but Petain waved him back.

"The fund for our endeavors originally came from the four charter banks and from the personal wealth of the dozen founding men, but since the mid-eighteen hundreds the money has come from the seven caches of gold in your southwestern desert. Voltaire himself thought the idea to plunder the treasure that the Vatican believed was rightfully its was rich—which was his word—though it was many years after his death before we were able to find it."

"I'm still not understanding why you're here."

"Spain also believes the treasure belongs in Madrid. Catholic monks had been siphoning off gold and silver that had been bound back to Madrid through Havana, or to the far east via Manila. So two military expeditions were sent north from Mexico City to find what had already become a legend. The first disappeared, no trace of the men ever found. But the second in eighteen thirty-eight was stronger and better equipped. Even so only two soldiers managed to return with maps and a journal of their trip. The locations of the seven caches had been found and marked on the maps and in the journal, and even a few gold coins and silver bars were brought back."

"I was at the archives in Seville and nothing was mentioned about any journal or maps."

"That's because they never reached Madrid. Our agents killed the two soldiers and took all the evidence."

"And this is what has been stolen from your bank vault?" McGarvey asked. "You need a private detective, not me."

"The maps and journal were fakes, as we suspected they might before. But one of the members of the Spanish expedition was the surveyor and mapmaker. His name was Jacob Ambli, and he'd been sent by the Vatican as a spy. It was he who drew the false maps, while he kept the real journal, in which the actual locations were pinpointed.

"Five days after the two Spanish soldiers were eliminated, Ambli made it back to Mexico City and from there to Veracruz where he took a ship to Havana and another to Boston. He was met there by another man sent from the Vatican to protect him, and save the journal."

"SMOM."

"Oui," Petain said. "They boarded the paddle wheel steamship *Britannia*, bound for Liverpool. But both men disappeared overboard."

"Your agents?"

"Oui. We couldn't allow the journal to reach the Vatican. If the Church—or Spain for that matter—had known where the treasure was buried all of it would have disappeared, and either been squandered to prop up the corrupt government in Madrid or used to build dozens of gold-encrusted cathedrals around the world. A useless waste, then as well as now."

"The Voltaire Society got the diary, and over the past hundred and eighty years or so, you've dug up at least three of the caches and used the money for what?"

"For good, I can tell you that much."

"Spare me," McGarvey said, getting to his feet. "Now if you don't mind, monsieur, get the hell out of my office."

Petain jumped up. He was distressed. "Please, you don't understand."

"Your society committed murder to grab this journal, and now someone has stolen it, and you want me to get it back for you. As I said, you need a private detective."

"Jacob's diary, and it was in a very secure vault in Bern. We need you to find it because both the Vatican and the Spanish government have been searching for years, and the point is they're still searching."

McGarvey opened the door. "You've come to the wrong place. I'm not in the business of hunting for treasure."

Petain handed him a business card. "You cannot imagine how important this is. If you change your mind call me anytime night or day." He stepped out into the hallway but then turned back. "My life is in danger, as are the lives of the other members of the Society."

"Send your own people to search for it."

"There aren't many of us left," Petain said. "In any event we are businessmen, not professionals." He hesitated. "My life is in danger, and so is yours. Not because I came here to talk to you, but because you came so close on the *Jornada del Muerto*. Be careful with your movements, Mr. McGarvey. Trust no one."

Petain turned and left.

McGarvey waited a couple of minutes before he got his briefcase and headed out. He didn't want to catch up with the Frenchman. Even if the fantastical story were true McGarvey wanted no further part of it. Otto's wife had been kidnapped by Cuban intelligence agents and held at gunpoint to force her husband to cooperate in a wild-goose chase that had ended badly, with a trail of bodies.

Useless.

He took his time walking the fifty yards or so back to his car, and when he reached it Petain had just gotten into his Lexus. Two students, a boy and a girl, were unlocking a couple of bikes from the rack nearby, and out of the corner of his eye McGarvey noticed a black Mercedes S550 with deeply tinted windows at the exit from the parking lot ready to turn toward the Ringling Administration Building and past it North Tamiami Trail—Sarasota's main north-south thoroughfare.

But the Mercedes was just sitting there not moving, not leaving the parking lot.

Everything was wrong.

Petain backed out of his parking spot and headed toward the exit at the same moment the Mercedes pulled out and turned to the right along Bayshore Road south toward the Ringling Museum.

"Get down! Get down!" McGarvey shouted to the students who looked up but stood there like deer caught in headlights. He tossed his briefcase down, withdrew his pistol, and headed on a run at a diagonal toward the Mercedes, hoping to reach the road and block it before it was past.

Petain's Lexus exploded with a tremendous flash completely engulfing it in flames, flipping it up on to its roof, sending pieces of metal and burning plastic flying outward. A split second later the boom followed by the immensely hot blast wave knocked McGarvey off his feet, singeing his eyebrows, car parts flying all around him.

The detached roof of the car, twisted and on fire, fell from the sky as if in slow motion, landing directly on top of the two students.

The Mercedes sped past, as McGarvey managed to sit up, giving him just an instant to catch the first three digits of its Florida plate.

He got to his feet, his ears ringing, his entire body numb. Stuffing the pistol back in his pocket he went to see if there was any possibility that the boy and girl could have survived.

A couple of aides and a woman by the name of Carolyn on the Ringling Museum staff staggered out the front doors, blood smeared on their faces. The blast had taken out several windows in the two-story building.

Other students and faculty came on the run from the direction of the bay.

Petain was dead, nothing of his body left intact, and the students at the bike rack were dead as well. None of them had a chance. And whoever had placed the explosives in the Lexus and had set it off hadn't given a damn what collateral damage they would inflict.

Staring at the burning wreckage of the Lexus, McGarvey was brought back to the morning at Arlington National Cemetery where he and his wife and their daughter had gone to the funeral of Todd Van Buren, their son-in-law who'd been assassinated. Driving away from the graveside ceremony, he'd followed Katy and Liz riding in an SUV that had exploded, killing them instantly.

He'd lost a lot of his ability to feel much of anything: compassion, remorse for the people he had eliminated in his work for the Company, and love for anyone or anything. And it had only been in the past few months, since the incident with the Cuban woman and the treasure that had been buried in the Texas and New Mexico deserts, that he had begun to get anywhere close to normal. Enough to read a book, see a movie, or watch a sunset over the Gulf of Mexico and not feel guilty about enjoying it.

Now this senseless thing. Petain had been at war. But the boy and girl at the bike rack were innocents.

A siren sounded somewhere in the distance and then another. The Vatican or the Spanish government or the so-called Voltaire Society or some fabulous treasure meant nothing to him. All that mattered was finding the people who had killed a boy and a girl. That he would do. Guaranteed.

THREE

□

Within a half hour the fires had been put out and the bodies of the students had been loaded aboard an ambulance, but it had taken much longer to find anything identifiable as human remains in the totally destroyed Lexus. And by six a crane had loaded the frame and other parts, including the engine block, onto a flatbed truck to be taken to the police garage where it would be examined.

A skeptical Sarasota police detective who knew something of McGarvey's background had briefly questioned him. "Any idea what happened here?" he'd asked. His name was Jim Forest, and he looked like a kid, with dark features and a wide smile. But he seemed to be good at what he did and McGarvey had respect for him.

"Not really. I was getting into my car when the Lexus blew."

"Didn't see anything, talk to anyone?"

"Saw those two kids get killed, and some people in the admin building cut up with falling glass. But it could have been a lot worse if it had happened a few hours earlier."

Forest shrugged. "Trouble does seem to follow you."

"Not anymore," McGarvey said. "I'm retired. Just here teaching kids a little philosophy."

The crowd had mostly thinned out by now, and the flatbed truck driver was securing the Lexus's chassis, leaving only a couple of police cars plus the crime scene investigator's panel truck. McGarvey, drinking a cup of coffee someone had brought over, leaned against his car.

"Why do you suppose I have this hunch that whoever was in the Lexus came here to talk to you about something?"

"Sometimes even good cops get it wrong."

Forest shrugged. "Thanks for the compliment, if that's what it was. But I think you're lying. And I don't like it."

McGarvey tossed out the rest of his coffee. "Are we finished here?"

"For now. But let me know if you're leaving town anytime soon."

"Sure," McGarvey said, and he got into his car.

"You're up to something. I can see it in your eyes. It's a specialty of mine, reading people."

"Let me know if you catch the bad guys."

"Bad guys?"

"The ones who planted the explosives in the Lexus. Semtex. You can smell it."

Back at his two-story home on Casey Key, just across the island's only road from the Gulf and less than a hundred feet up from the Intracoastal Waterway, which ran ten miles or so north to Sarasota Bay and fifty south to Fort Myers, McGarvey got out of the shower, and as he toweled off he padded to the sliding glass doors that looked down at the swimming pool.

Forest was right, trouble did follow him. Always had. At first because he'd been ordered to do things, but in the past several years it was because his reputation had caught up with him.

Wrapping the towel around his middle, he went downstairs, where at the wet bar in the family room he poured a snifter of Remy Martin XO, and walked to his study, where he powered up his computer and phoned Otto Rencke on encrypted Skype.

The two of them had a long history together, all the way back to a couple of operations in Germany and Chile in the early days when Rencke was nothing more than an archivist for the Company. But since then they'd become close personal friends. Otto, who was a genius and an odd duck, had married Louise Horn, almost as brilliant and odd as her husband. When McGarvey's daughter and son-in-law were assassinated leaving Audrey, their two-year-old child, an orphan, Otto and Louise had adopted her, which in McGarvey's estimation was a perfect fit. They were odd people—always had been—but they were loving and kind.

Nowadays Otto, whose specialty was computer operations, was the

CIA's chief of Special Projects, and Louise, who had been a chief photo analyst for the National Security Agency and now did freelance work for the CIA, lived in a two-story colonial in an all-American suburb outside of Washington, where the chief purpose in their lives had become McGarvey's granddaughter.

Rencke picked up on the second ring, his long, almost always out-of-control frizzy red hair tied up in a neat ponytail, which was Louise's doing. Her project after they'd gotten married a couple of years ago was to clean up her husband's act. Now his jeans and sweatshirts were usually clean, he wore boat shoes instead of unlaced sneakers, and he'd stopped eating Twinkies and drinking heavy cream. Lately he'd seemed happier than McGarvey had ever known him, though he'd lost none of his genius, or his almost preternatural ability to see and understand things. Nor had he lost his almost constant boyish enthusiasm.

"Oh, wow, Mac, you weren't hurt? You're okay?"

"You heard about the car bomb on campus?" McGarvey asked, though he wasn't surprised. A number of years ago, Rencke had put a tag on him. As long as he knew where McGarvey was, his computers would sift through every available bit of real-time information on that location.

"Of course. But you weren't just a bystander."

"No."

"Didn't think so. What do we have coming our way this time?"

McGarvey hesitated for just a moment. Early in his career he'd tried to distance himself from everyone he loved—even going so far as to leave his wife and child. He wanted to protect them from the bad people he'd had to deal with. He'd lived with the constant worry that someone, someday would retaliate against him by hurting his family. Which had happened, but not for the reasons he'd worried about. The bomb at the Arlington cemetery had been meant for him; their deaths had been an accident. In any event, Otto was a CIA employee, and he and Louise had always understood the risks.

"The guy in the Lexus that took the hit was Giscarde Petain. And he'd come to ask for my help with something having to do with a group called the Voltaire Society."

"Just a sec," Rencke said, and less than a minute later, he was back. "Okay, I'm getting thirteen million plus hits—everything from the Voltaire Society of America, which promotes what they call the spirit of enlightenment, to the University of Denver student honors organization. Lots of French philosophic and scientific groups, and even a Bible study organization in Geneva. None of them sounds like anything someone would be murdered for."

"Anything on Petain? He gave me a business card that lists him as a vice president of special accounts with the International Bank of Paris."

Rencke chuckled a half minute later. "Your reach is getting wider. I have more than forty-four million hits, but nothing that specific. There's the ABC International Bank of Paris, and the International Bank of Paris and Shanghai. Is there an address?"

"Just a phone number that I haven't tried yet."

"Checking," Rencke said, and he was back almost immediately. "The phone is an accommodations number, with an automatic message to leave a name and contact information. No e-mail address?"

"Just the number."

"Give me a minute," Rencke said, and this time his fingers flew over the keyboard and when he looked up he shook his head. "Lots of Giscarde Petains in Paris, but none associated with any bank whose name is even close to the International Bank of Paris. Nor am I coming up with that name in connection with any of the thirteen million Voltaire Societies."

"How about the Company's database?"

"I checked that first, along with the FBI, NSA, Homeland Security— everyone in town, plus Interpol. Not a thing, Mac. This guy under that name does not exist."

"Let's try Jacob Ambli, or Father Jacob Ambli."

Again Rencke shook his head. "Nada."

"Try him in the time frame of eighteen thirty to eighteen forty something. Mexico City."

Rencke suddenly laughed. "As in *Jornada del Muerto?*"

"Ambli was supposedly a spy sent by the Vatican to hook up with the second Spanish military expedition to search for the treasure."

"We came across some of that in the archives in Seville, but only two soldiers made it back to Mexico City, and I don't remember the name Ambli. And both of those guys had been found robbed, and killed. No maps or journals."

"According to Petain, Ambli was the expedition's surveyor and mapmaker. It was the Voltaire Society who killed the soldiers and took their diaries—which were false. Ambli, who'd kept the real diary, made his way to Boston where he was met by another man from the Vatican. But both of them were killed by the Society and the real diary was stolen. Jacob's diary."

"I'll check, but a lot of this stuff—if it exists—will probably be pigeonholed in some dusty library somewhere. Probably in Seville, or more likely in the Vatican Secret Archives. A lot of luck getting to either of them for any information. I'll try, but why, Mac? It's just a fairy tale."

"A fairy tale that got Petain murdered," McGarvey said. "He came to me because a friend at the DGSE recommended me, and because he knew that I'd been involved with the search a few months ago."

"What'd he want, specifically?"

"Jacob Ambli's diary, which the Society had hidden in a bank vault in Bern. Someone stole it. He wants me to get it back."

"The diary with the location of the treasure caches?"

"Seven of them, of which, according to Petain, only four are left."

"What happened to the other three?"

"I didn't ask, and he didn't say. I told him I wasn't interested."

"And he told you that the diary was of extreme importance and that your life was in danger," Rencke said.

"Something like that," McGarvey said. "He left my office, got into his car, and before it got ten feet it disintegrated."

Rencke was suddenly serious. "Like Katy and Liz."

"Yeah. And two kids who happened to be nearby were killed. I don't give a damn about finding some diary or going on another treasure hunt. I want the bastards who assassinated Petain without caring about any collateral damage."

"I understand," Rencke said. "Anything else?"

"Might be a long shot, but a black Mercedes S550 was stopped at the parking lot exit, and it took off just a second or two before Petain's car blew up. Florida plate, but all I got was E or F and seventy-six or maybe seventy-eight for the first three. But it got out of there in a big hurry."

"Any idea who was inside? One or two people? Men, women?"

"Windows were too deeply tinted to see anything."

"Bumper stickers, dents, dings?"

"None that I saw."

"I'll check into it. But get some rest, *kemo sabe.*"

McGarvey nodded. "How's Audie?"

"Missing her grandfather."

"The semester is just about over with. Soon I can get free I'll come up for a visit."

"Promise? She's been asking about you."

"Honest injun'," McGarvey said. It was one of Rencke's bon mots.

"I'll tell her," Rencke said

McGarvey was seeing Petain's car going up in flames; he could feel the heat on his face and arms, see the piece of metal falling on the kids. He broke the connection and sat back with his Cognac, his vivid memories of Katy and Liz dying in the explosion at Arlington playing in his head, over and over.

F O U R

□

The Casey Key rental was a luxurious two story, with a formal dining room, library, snooker table, huge gourmet kitchen, sitting room, solarium, living room done up in bright nautical prints, and a formal staircase leading up to six palatial bedrooms, three of which looked over the Gulf and the others over the ICW.

Captain Emilio Miranda, thirty-six, whose work name was Juan Fernandez, came to the head of the stairs, and held up for just a moment to listen to the near absence of sound, before going down.

He was a slightly built man, more wiry than thin, with wide-set very black eyes, a dusky Spanish complexion, thin lips over which was a pencil-thin mustache. This evening he was dressed in jeans, sneakers, and dark T-shirt. He was a dangerous-looking man, which in fact he was. In his eighteen-year career as a field agent with the Centro Nacional de Inteligencia, the CNI, which was Spain's central intelligence service, he had run successful operations, some of which included deaths, in the United States, Canada, Great Britain, Australia, and New Zealand. His parents had both been English-language professors at the Carlos III University in Madrid, and subsequently his command of the language was nearly as good as that of his native tongue.

He crossed the main entry hall and went back to the small service kitchen that opened on the multitiered patio and pool. Donica Fonesca, dressed in a black bikini, was tossing a salad to go with some baguettes and a large plate of cheese. She'd already laid out a couple of bottles of Mourvedre, a nice Alicante red.

She was tall for a Spanish woman, with short black hair that revealed a long slender neck, pretty shoulders, and a more rounded than usual figure for a Flamenco dancer, which had been one of her covers. At twenty-six she'd never married, nor had any ambition for a family, though she'd never been shy about taking lovers—not since an affair with her college math teacher. She was a lieutenant in the CNI who along with lieutenants Felix Huertas and their second-story man, Alberto Cabello, made up the mission team. She was almost certainly having an affair with Huertas, but as long as it didn't interfere with their orders, Miranda didn't care.

She turned and smiled. "I hope you're hungry, I've made plenty. Some wine?"

"Okay," Miranda said, and he sat down at the counter. "Why the swimsuit?"

"I'm going in the pool after we eat, I expect that we'll have some company." She poured them both a glass. "I'm glad I wasn't there today," she said.

"It wasn't pleasant, but you're right, we may have the other problem coming our way. Señor McGarvey was right in the middle of it, as we suspected he might be."

"Was he injured?"

"Alberto said he thought the man was on the ground, but we were moving too fast for him to be sure. In any event McGarvey is home. He just finished calling a number in Berwyn Heights. Encrypted Skype but the angles were wrong this time, so we didn't get much."

"Our Washington Bureau thinks that his friend Otto Rencke lives there."

"That's my assumption, but except for the town the number was blocked."

Donica thought it over. "We suspected that Petain would come to see him sooner or later. It was only a matter of time before he left Paris, and no one was surprised that he came here, given McGarvey's recent history—and the little theft from Bern."

"We still don't know who pulled it off, or even what was in the vault."

"Jacob's diary?"

"We can't be certain," Miranda said.

"The analysts in Madrid are being overcautious, don't you think? The diary is the only logical possibility. Now we simply wait for Señor McGarvey to make his move and follow him."

"If Petain came to ask him for help."

"He did."

"That's another supposition," Miranda said. "Wishful thinking."

Donica was vexed. "I don't understand."

"We thought that Petain would come here to talk to McGarvey, to ask him for help. All we can say with certainty is that the Frenchman did come here, but we didn't have the chance to bug McGarvey's office so we have no idea what they talked about."

"What else?"

"I don't know. Maybe information about the *Jornada del Muerto*. But just because we thought Petain was coming to ask McGarvey for help finding the diary, doesn't mean that's what he did."

Now Donica was frustrated. "Then why did we kill the man? Why did we take the risk?"

"Because those were our orders, my dear."

"The Society will send someone else."

"Perhaps," Miranda said. "Or perhaps McGarvey will go in search of the diary, leaving us to follow him."

Donica went back to her salad making.

"Where are the others?"

"Alberto went down to check something on the boat, and Felix is wandering around outside. Or at least I think he is." She looked up. "What about the two students who were killed?"

"What about them?"

"From Señor McGarvey's profile he comes across as an honorable man."

"A contract killer."

"He is a teacher, Emilio. Maybe he cares more for his students than you think he does. Maybe collateral damage means something to him."

Miranda scowled. "Sentimentality has no place in this business."

"They were innocent kids. You said so yourself."

"I said they were in the wrong place at the wrong time." He shrugged. "What's done is done. From this point we concentrate on McGarvey to see what he does."

"What if he stays put?"

"Then our job here is finished. We pack up and go home."

Donica stopped what she was doing and looked at him, an odd expression in her eyes. "But you don't believe that."

"No," Miranda said. "I too studied his profile. If Petain asked for help unraveling the mystery, it's exactly what Señor McGarvey will do. It is in his nature."

"And the deaths of the students? Won't that give him pause?"

"On the contrary. Their deaths—senseless to his way of thinking—will spur him on." Miranda shook his head. "Señor McGarvey will make his move, and it will be sooner than later, I suspect."

FIVE

☐

McGarvey dressed in a pair of shorts and a T-shirt, went downstairs, and in the kitchen tried to figure out what he wanted for dinner—or even if he wanted anything to eat. He was unsettled not only because of the students' deaths and how they had died, but about Petain's story.

He'd always tried to keep as low-key as possible, below as many radars as he could. But his name had been front and center in the public's eye because of the business with the Spanish treasure just north of El Paso, and the huge crowd of Mexicans and Cubans that had crossed the border to claim it. But it hadn't ended until the second confrontation, this one at the Fort Knox federal gold depository, with another crowd, mostly of Cubans—these people expats living in Miami. Both times there'd been no gold or silver. No treasure.

Yet in the end Rencke had considered that there might be some truth to the legends. And so had María León, a colonel in the Cuban intelligence service.

The computer in his study chimed. It was Otto.

"You've got trouble coming your way," he said, barely contained excitement in his voice.

McGarvey switched off the light. "From the beginning," he said.

"The Voltaire Society exists and so does their bank in Paris. And oh, boy, what a fight those guys have been having with the Vatican and with the Spanish government."

"Is María León involved?"

Otto was taken aback. "Has she contacted you again?"

"No. I was just thinking about her."

"She's not involved this time, at least her name hasn't popped up. But the fight I'm talking about started in the early eighteen hundreds and has been going on ever since. And it's intense, Mac. Honest injun'."

"The Spanish treasure?"

"The one that everyone but you and I believe exists. Not only that, I found out that the Voltaire Society's bank has actually been in existence since seventeen seventy-six when it was chartered by six businessmen who each put up the equivalent of one million dollars."

"How did you find that out?"

"Through its transactions. At first they were on paper, of course, and only two actual documents exist in our Library of Congress from records of a Richmond, Virginia, bank that went under in eighteen sixty-five. Two money transfers that took place before the Civil War. In each case for the same amount: five million dollars, from the International Bank of Paris."

"For what reason? Who was the payee?"

"The treasury of the United States of America. But that's not all. The transfers came two years apart—one in eighteen forty-four, three years after Jacob Ambli and his diary disappeared, and in eighteen forty-eight. Time, if we're to believe Petain, for the Society to reach New Mexico and retrieve some of the silver and gold."

The story was far-fetched and coincidental, and McGarvey told Otto just that.

"I don't believe in coincidences any more than you do," Rencke said, and he sounded excited as he did whenever he had the bit in his mouth. "But Petain told you that besides propping up banks in Europe, the Society used the money to help fledgling democracies. Maybe they foresaw our Civil War and sent money to help."

"To a bank in Richmond, the capital of the Confederacy?"

"The Confederacy didn't really exist at that point, and who knows, maybe someone in the Society had a sense of humor, just like its name-sake Voltaire had."

"Doesn't make any sense," McGarvey said, and yet there was a certain symmetry to the idea. Petain had come to him with his fantastical story and he was assassinated.

"A lot of things don't make a whole hell of a lot of sense, Mac. And here's another one for you. I ran the partial tag number you gave me, and came up with a hundred seventeen hits. Tampa, Miami, Jacksonville,

Tallahassee, even one in the Keys. But the most interesting was for Juan Fernandez from an address just off the Calle Ocho in Miami. Little Havana. But Señor Fernandez only exists in a few places—Mercedes Benz of Miami, the dealership where the car was purchased for cash three weeks ago, and the Florida Department of Motor Vehicles. But no Fernandez lives at the address on the title. The man doesn't exist in Miami. And the only other place his name pops up is for a three-month rental on Casey Key, right next door to you."

"Fernandez is a work name," McGarvey said, not terribly surprised.

"Be my guess. Probably the CNI. I'm working their mainframe in Madrid now, but this guy most likely is a NOC, so he'll show up only as a coded entry somewhere that only his case officer would have access to." In the parlance a NOC was an intelligence agent working in the field with No Official Cover.

"These people are team players, so there'll be more than just him."

"Exactamundo," Rencke said. "Have you seen or noticed anything over the past few weeks? Met the neighbors? Been invited over for drinks? Anything like that?"

A good-looking girl in a bikini at the pool. She'd waved, and he'd waved back. A guy doing something with a small Boston Whaler center console at the dock. Another guy at a second-floor balcony—or maybe the same guy from the boat. Nothing unusual. Yet thinking about it now, maybe they had sent up an alarm; they were nothing out of the ordinary for Casey Key this time of the year, yet they were new.

"Three, maybe four people. Didn't seem as if they were trying to hide."

"And?"

"I don't know," McGarvey said. "But I'm going to check it out."

"Watch yourself," Rencke said.

McGarvey switched off, and upstairs he got a pair of night-vision binoculars from the hall table at the balcony sliders and took them back to the master bedroom, one side of which looked across at the house next door. He'd taught Katy to use them when she wanted to look for night feeding birds.

Lights spilled out onto the pool deck from what he thought was probably a kitchen. Other dim lights were on in other parts of the downstairs, but all of the upstairs windows were dark.

He watched for a full five minutes, but saw only one dark figure appear briefly at one of the open first-floor sliders and then disappear. Someone was home, but no one was in the pool or down at the dock by the boat. Nor could he spot movement at any of the upstairs windows or balconies. Nor could he detect any signs of surveillance equipment; cameras, parabolic dishes, microwave antennas.

Setting the binoculars aside, he got dressed in jeans, a lightweight dark long-sleeve pullover, and boat shoes. He took a 9 mm version of the Walther PPK from a drawer in his nightstand, screwed a silencer on to the end of the barrel, checked the load, and pocketing a spare magazine of ammunition, stuck the pistol into the waistband of his jeans at the small of his back, and went downstairs where he slipped out of a side door out of view of the next-door house.

SIX

□

Donica had just finished laying out a bowl of blackberries, blueberries, strawberries, and raspberries over which she had poured some Lepanto, a mild Spanish brandy from Jerez, when Alberto Cabello came to the doorway. He was twenty-four, thin, almost anorexic with long black hair and the eyes of a night cat. He was dressed in a bicycler's black spandex shorts and top.

"He is on his way over," he said in Spanish. His voice was soft, his manner unhurried.

"In English, please," Donica corrected automatically. "Are we talking about Mr. McGarvey?"

"Yes."

"Where is Felix?" Alberto asked.

"He just went upstairs to surveillance."

"Make yourself ready, but stay out of sight unless the need arises."

"He must suspect something. Perhaps his friend in Washington discovered your work name. It is no coincidence that he is coming here at this moment."

"Is he armed?" Donica asked.

"I don't know, but he's dressed in dark clothing."

Donica shrugged. "I suspect that he is no different than any American male," she said. "I'll go out to talk to him." She took off her bikini top, her breasts small and firm.

"Maybe not," Alberto warned. "Don't provoke him."

"That's exactly what I'm going to do."

Cabello had disappeared into the darkness outside, and Miranda took a 9 mm Steyr GB pistol and silencer from a drawer in the kitchen desk.

He'd always favored the unusual Austrian-made semiauto because it was very light—less than one kilo unloaded—carried an eighteen round magazine, and could be disassembled in under six seconds. All their weapons were fitted with silencers.

"I thought we needed him alive," Donica said.

"The need to keep you alive is greater," Miranda said. "And make no mistake, this man is dangerous. He is a killer."

"So am I."

"You are an amateur by comparison. And too ambitious."

She was hurt, though it was true she was ambitious. When she'd first joined the CNI her primary training officer, Lieutenant Martinque Cordona, had skirted around two issues: The first, would she be willing to make a kill without hesitation, with no remorse? And the second, would she be willing to use her body if need be?

Donica had smiled. "Of course," she'd said.

"Then you will go far, my little dove," the lieutenant said.

That evening Donica went to his room where they made love. Within less than twelve months, her training completed, she went on her first assignment, posing as a high-priced call girl in Paris to seduce a German diplomat at a meeting of the G7. It went well enough that two weeks later the German resigned as finance minister, unable to stand up to the CNI's blackmail demands. It was the outcome Madrid had wanted.

The good news was that Donica became a superstar overnight, but the bad news was that overnight she got an overinflated opinion of her own worth.

"You're right, of course," she told Miranda. "But before you start shooting let me see if I can calm him down. He's better to us alive."

"What will you tell him?"

"I'll improvise."

"It's not necessary. It was only important that Petain came to see him. Finding that out and eliminating the man as a threat was our primary mission goal."

Donica waved him off. At the open slider she flipped on the pool lights, but not the overheads, and outside she grabbed a towel from the cabinet and draped it over her shoulders before she padded across the patio to the water's edge.

For several long seconds she stood unmoving, aware of the picture she made, and smiling a little because of it. But then she heard a noise to her right and she turned as the American appeared at the edge of the darkness. He had a pistol in his right hand, a silencer on the muzzle.

"Do you mean to shoot me, or is this a simple robbery?" she asked.

"Who are you, and what are you doing here?" McGarvey asked.

His manner and tone of voice seemed languid. "I think it is I who should be asking those questions," Donica said. She smiled. "But you are my next-door neighbor. I've seen you in your backyard. On the dock."

"Where are the others?"

"If you mean Juan, I think he's somewhere in the house. We're getting set to have a light supper. Won't you join us?"

"The Mercedes registered to Juan Fernandez was involved in an incident at New College today," McGarvey said, and he stepped into the light and stopped five feet away.

Donica wanted to back up, but she stood her ground. "Put the gun away, Señor McGarvey, we are not your enemy. In fact we're after the same thing as you are."

"She is telling the truth," Miranda said from just inside the house. "We mean you no harm."

McGarvey pointed his pistol directly at Donica's head. "I won't miss at this range."

"There is no need for violence."

"Listen to him," Donica said, but McGarvey cut her off.

"Why has the CNI sent a team to watch me, and why did you kill the man at the university?"

Donica could see directly into McGarvey's eyes, and all of a sudden she felt cold. "He's an intruder, Juan. Shoot him. We will be within our rights here in Florida."

"Because the man who came to ask for your help was the enemy," Miranda said. "Yours as well as mine. Had the situation been reversed he would not have hesitated to kill either of us."

"What about the two students who just happened to be there?"

Donica could see McGarvey's jawline tighten, but she also spotted Alberto in the darkness behind a palm tree across the pool. "Too bad for them," she said. "But then Americans are used to drive-by shootings and bombings."

Miranda reached around the corner of the slider and pulled off a shot, but McGarvey had already stepped left, and he fired three shots at the house, turned and fired two shots over his shoulder at Cabello across the pool, and disappeared into the darkness.

SEVEN

□

Moving fast, and purposely making a fair amount of noise, McGarvey headed toward his house, but then doubled back and quietly made his way through the darkness to the front of the next-door property. Keeping close to the side of the building he threaded his way through the expansive landscaping—bushes, pineapple palms, several fruit trees including two very tall ones bearing avocados and mangoes—until he reached the driveway.

Besides the woman and the man in the house, McGarvey was fairly certain that there were at least two other CNI operatives on the property. They'd been expecting him, which meant they had a surveillance operation going on, watching his moves, listening to his phone calls and possibly even his encrypted Skype conferences with Otto. The pistol fired at him from the house had been silenced. They expected trouble but did not want to involve the local authorities if at all possible.

Somehow they'd known that Petain would come to talk to him, and they had waited until it had happened. But it made no sense that they would kill the man in such a public way, when it probably would have been easier and a lot less messy to assassinate the man in Paris before he came here. Except that they had *wanted* him to bring his request. In effect they wanted the same thing from McGarvey that Petain had come to ask for—help finding the diary stolen from the Voltaire Society.

The Spanish government believed the treasure was buried in New Mexico, and after nearly two hundred years they were still actively searching for it. But unlike the Cuban government that thought it could somehow negotiate for a part of the gold and silver, Madrid wanted the entire prize, and had sent agents to kill for it.

Which begged the question that if Petain had been telling the truth about the missing diary—and there was no reason for him not to have told the truth—who had taken it? Not the Spanish, maybe the Vatican. But that possibility raised the question why had they come here, and not to the Vatican?

The black Mercedes was parked in the driveway, the doors unlocked. McGarvey slipped behind the wheel and opened the glove box, which contained nothing more than the service and owner's manuals, plus a contract from Mercedes-Benz of Miami in the name of Juan Fernandez at the fake address off the Calle Ocho.

A garage door opener was clipped to the visor. McGarvey pressed the button and got out of the car as the garage door started up. He left the car door open and sprinted past the front entryway to the opposite side of the house where he held up just around the corner.

A half minute later a slightly built man dressed in what looked like black spandex appeared at the open garage door. He was armed with a pistol, the big silencer tube visible even from where McGarvey stood in the shadows.

"The bastard's not here," the man said over his shoulder to someone in the garage. "Maybe he's left."

"It was a trick," a man replied. "He's gone around back again."

The slightly built man turned. "We have to get help for Emilio," he said, and he disappeared inside.

McGarvey waited a full ten seconds, about as long as he figured it would take the two men to return to the pool area, before he stepped around the corner and hurried to the open garage door, where he paused for just a moment to make sure one of them hadn't stayed behind.

But the garage was empty, the house silent.

It would not take them long to realize they had indeed been tricked, only this time they would most likely split up, one covering each side of the house.

McGarvey went to the service door that led into the house and listened for a second or so, but hearing nothing he opened the door a crack. Some-one toward the back of the house was talking, his voice low but urgent. The woman interrupted, her voice louder, her tone even more urgent, but McGarvey couldn't make out the words.

Everything since the explosion had been nothing more than an exer-cise in futility, as far as he was concerned. These people had killed Petain, and they meant to kill him to find or protect some diary. But he was focused on the senseless deaths of the two students in the parking lot. He wanted to know why this team of CNI operatives didn't care about inflicting that kind of collateral damage. In his estimation they were no better than common thugs; terrorists of the same stripe as al Qaeda.

Slipping inside to what was a short service hall that led straight to a large pantry, McGarvey closed and locked the service door—unless one of them had a key no one would be coming up on his six—and headed toward the back of the house.

EIGHT

☐

Donica was on the tile floor just inside the sliders to the pool, holding a bath towel against the wound in Miranda's chest, blood spreading under his shoulders and head. He was pale and obviously in pain, but he hadn't lost consciousness nor had he lost his wits.

Cabello and Huertas had come around from the front of the house, but they'd looked over their shoulder when Emilio had ordered them to find McGarvey.

"Alive if possible. But I don't want any more casualties here. We're getting out as soon as possible. *Hacer comprender?*"

"*Sí,*" both men said.

"I think he means to come inside to finish what he started," Huertas said.

"Not against four guns," Miranda disagreed. "He's a killer, but he's not a fool. Our primary mission of taking Petain out has been accomplished. But if you can run McGarvey down before he gets back to his house—which I believe he means to do—you might be able to reason with him."

"At gunpoint?" Huertas asked.

"It's something a man such as he would understand. Now, fly away and do as you were trained to do. With finesse."

"We need to call a doctor for you," Donica said when the two men were gone.

"We're not compromising the mission," Miranda told her.

"You'll die."

"If the bullet had hit anything vital I'd be dead by now."

"There's a lot of blood."

"Nothing arterial," Miranda said. "I told you that McGarvey was a dangerous man. A killer. Just the sort we need to help us."

"Impossible," Donica protested. She was not in love with the older man, but she'd been on three missions with him, and she had developed a great deal of respect. "This situation has no upside unless McGarvey is eliminated."

"We need to reason with him. Apologize for those two kids. He's been involved in operations where he caused the same sort of collateral damage. And his wife and daughter were killed in an operation that was meant for him. He understands mistakes."

It all sounded crazy to Donica. She felt as if she were losing her mind. "At what cost? How important is this diary? More than our lives?"

"Yes."

"I'm just supposed to stay here and let you die?" she asked, and she could hear an hysterical note creeping into her voice. She wanted to cry. "This is crazy. Everything has changed now. The kids at the school. You. The bastard is stalking us, and if he's as good as you say he is we won't have a chance unless we surrender."

"Prison," Miranda said.

"I don't care, Emilio. I'd rather go to jail than die. We'd be exchanged sooner or later as political prisoners."

"No. We have the blood of the two students on our hands, and they have the death penalty in this country."

"Then call our handler in Madrid. Tell him what has happened. Ask what we need to do."

"I already have my orders. The fact that the Voltaire Society knows about him, and was willing to send a man from Paris to talk to him, makes McGarvey potentially the most dangerous man to Spain."

"Then call for help to kill him."

"First we'll try reason," Miranda said. "The soft touch."

It was as if she was in a slow-moving avalanche; she knew that it was coming, she could hear it, feel it, and she knew what it would do to her, to them all, once it reached them. But she couldn't convince him. He wouldn't listen.

"It's my duty now, since you are incapacitated, to call for instructions," she said. She could hear the desperation in her voice. "I don't want you to die like this."

Miranda's expression softened. "I know about your brother. Nothing you could have done to save him."

Sudden grief nearly overcame her. "I promised our parents."

"I saw the police file. He was shot running from a robbery."

"I could have stopped him. He was only fifteen."

"Sí, but you can't save the world."

Donica lowered her head, her eyes closed, tears welling up. It wasn't fair.

Miranda suddenly rose up on one elbow with a grunt, the pistol in his hand.

"Don't," McGarvey said from the hallway.

Donica opened her eyes and looked up at the same moment Miranda fired one shot, the bullet plowing into the edge of a kitchen cabinet, and McGarvey fired back, hitting Miranda in the forehead, killing him instantly.

NINE

Felix Huertas, who'd taken the north side of the house, had reached the open garage first and tried the knob but it was locked. He was a trim man of thirty-five, whose movie-star good looks and black slicked back air and aquiline nose had earned him the nickname of Rudolph—for the twenties movie star Rudolph Valentino. As he started to back off he was sure that he heard something very soft, but unmistakable. Someone had fired twice. Silenced pistols, maybe the same caliber.

A moment later Donica cried out in pain, and Huertas's gut clutched.

Cabello appeared at the garage door. "No sign of him on the south side," he said.

"He came this way and locked the door from the inside. But he's got Donica."

Cabello started to turn away, but Heurtas stopped him.

"It's probably already too late. He has to know that we're out here somewhere and he's waiting for us."

"But it's Donica."

"I know," Huertas said, his heart aching, but at this point he had no idea what he should do.

"Are we just going to stand here?" Cabello demanded. "Or maybe run away like frightened schoolchildren?"

Huertas, who was number two on the mission, had the second of two sat phones. He called their handler, who was at a CNI safe house in Washington. "We have been compromised," he said.

"What is the nature of it?" the senior agent asked. Huertas did not know his identity, nor had Miranda.

"Our primary target is down."

"Yes, we know this."

"Señor McGarvey has become a problem, for which I need immediate instructions."

"Since it is you calling, I assume that Emilio is dead or incapacitated."

"Sí," Huertas said, and he quickly related everything that had happened since the car bomb exploded not only killing Petain but two students, and McGarvey's interference here.

"Is he still on the property?"

"Yes."

"Are you alone?"

"I have Alberto."

"Your primary mission is to kill Señor McGarvey, after which you will dismantle the surveillance equipment and physically remove every memory device. No traces must be left. Is that clear?"

"Emilio thought that McGarvey would listen to reason."

"Shots were exchanged," the handler said. "It is too late for reason. Kill him and get out of there. No other considerations. Do you understand?"

"What about bodies?"

The handler did not hesitate. "Leave them."

"They'll be traced to us."

"That is not your consideration," the handler said, and he was gone.

For a long moment Huertas listened for other sounds from inside the house, but there was nothing.

"What are our orders?" Cabello asked.

"We are to kill Mr. McGarvey, destroy the surveillance equipment, and leave," Huertas said. Donica had been nothing more than a frolic, but he did care for her, and he hoped that she still lived. Emilio, on the other hand, had been a mentor from the start, almost a big brother.

"We'll take the same way around back, catch the bastard in a cross fire," Cabello said and started to turn away again, but again Huertas stopped him.

"Goddamnit, wait a minute. If you run back there blindly and get into a shoot-out, you'll end up dead."

"What the fuck do want to do, Rudy? Stay right here in the garage where it's safe?"

"No, you little prick, but this time you're going to use your head, and not make the same mistake Emilio made, by opening fire on the bastard. The guy is a pro, and we're going to treat him as one."

"What do you want to do, talk to him? Get him to see reason?"

"That's exactly what I'm going to do, and when he shows himself you're going to shoot him dead. But we're going to move slowly and with care."

TEN

□

McGarvey stood at the entrance to the poolside kitchen, listening to the sounds of the house, and of the young woman kneeling next to the dead man. She was sobbing, the noise mostly at the back of her throat, her narrow shoulders hunched, the nipples of her small breasts erect.

There were at least two other men on the property and it wouldn't take them long to figure out that whatever was going on was happening at this end of the house.

"Why did Spanish intelligence send you here to spy on me?" he asked.

Donica didn't look up or reply. She stared at Miranda's eyes, which were still open, his mouth twisted in a grimace of pain and surprise. Blood had stopped leaking from the wound in his chest.

"What do you people want with me?" McGarvey said.

She shook her head. "He wanted to talk to you."

"He shot at me by the pool."

"To protect me."

"Spare me."

Donica looked up, grief stricken, yet there was something else in her eyes. "We came to ask for your help."

"You came to kill a man who came to ask for my help, and in the process you killed two innocent young people."

Donica looked at Miranda's face. "He was sorry for it."

"The man you killed told me that he was from the Voltaire Society. What do you know about it?"

"Nothing."

"You were briefed. You've been here, watching me, for at least three weeks. You were expecting Petain to come to see me, and your mission brief was to kill him. Why? What is the Voltaire Society to the Spanish government?"

"You know damned well what it is. They want the same thing that we want—what's rightfully ours."

"The Vatican might have a different opinion."

"They stole it from us," Donica flared, but still there was something else going on.

"Your people stole it from the natives."

"In exchange for civilization."

McGarvey stood in the relative shadow at the end of the corridor from the formal dining room. The pool's underwater lights were on, but the patio deck was in darkness, and the surrounding landscape was in even deeper shadow. "The Cubans want a piece of it."

She laughed.

"What do you know about Jacob Ambli's diary?"

"I don't know what you're talking about."

"According to Petain the Voltaire Society has had it since the mid-eighteen hundreds. But someone stole it from a bank vault in Bern. He was sent to ask for my help finding it."

Donica said nothing.

"Supposedly it has the directions to four caches of gold and silver in southern New Mexico."

"Seven," Donica blurted angrily, but then, caught out, she looked away.

"You know damned well what I'm talking about," McGarvey said. "But if your people don't have the diary, who does? And why were you ordered to kill Petain in such a public way?"

Donica looked at Miranda's face and she hung her head. "I'm just a field agent. I follow orders."

"Orders to kill Petain. What about me? What orders were you given?"

She looked up. "We wanted to find out what Petain told you and convince you to help us instead."

"What made you think that would ever happen?"

"The Society is your enemy, we aren't."

She was stalling for time, of course. McGarvey stepped a little farther back into the corridor. By now the other two CNI operatives had to be just outside. "The police are on their way, maybe we'll wait and you can explain it to them."

"You did not call them."

"A friend did."

"Señor Rencke at the CIA? But if you'd wanted the police to become involved you would have talked to them after the explosion. But there've been no warrants issued. No one is coming here."

"A witness gave them a description of your car and the tag number, registered in the name of Juan Fernandez. They'll trace it here, just like I did. I was faster because I have access to better computers."

"Cristo!" Donica suddenly cried. She fell forward onto Miranda's body at the same time someone from just outside in the darkness called out.

"Señor McGarvey, we want to talk to you. No more shooting."

Donica suddenly rose up, Miranda's pistol awkwardly in her left hand, and began firing, the first three shots going wild.

McGarvey fired one shot, aiming it at her left shoulder, but at the last instant the woman moved in that direction and the bullet crashed into her neck just below her chin.

She sat back, dropped the pistol, and raised both hands to the wound, but she was drowning in her own blood and she knew that there was nothing to be done. She opened her mouth to say something, but couldn't speak.

"Goddamnit," McGarvey shouted. "What's wrong with you people? All this for some treasure?"

ELEVEN

Huertas was just left of the open slider, his back pressed against the stucco cement block wall, his pistol in both hands raised to chest level. Cabello was a couple of feet away, his pistol also up.

The night was very still, only the sounds of the pool pump around the corner.

"It is more than just the money, you must know that," Huertas called. "It's our cultural heritage. That's all we want."

"A heritage that your people stole, and now five more lives have been lost because of it," McGarvey replied. "When will it end?"

"The start will be here, tonight, if you will listen to me," Heurtas said. "You cannot believe how important this is."

"There was no real reason for this. The gold and silver, if it exists, is buried on U.S. soil. Your government can make a claim through the court system, just as it has done in the past. There was never any need for what happened today."

"We can't simply turn our backs on the situation and walk away."

"That's exactly what you're going to do."

"If we refuse?" Heurtas asked.

"Then you will die here," McGarvey said.

"Or you will die, Señor. And perhaps you might ask yourself why."

"The two kids at the college."

"This is not your fight," Heurtas said. He took a quick look around the corner then ducked back out of sight. Donica was down, next to Emilio, her chest covered in blood. He had an instant vision of her two months ago back in Madrid while they were training for this operation. They'd taken a room in a hotel off base because no one was supposed to be together during an assignment, but they'd not been able to keep their hands off each other.

The part he loved most about her were her long legs. Now they were bent at the knees. She had been kneeling when she'd been shot and she'd fallen backward. The image was more obscene in his mind than his vivid memory of her long legs spread for him.

He began to feel genuine hate.

"Think about it, Señor, I beg you," he said. He turned to Cabello. "Get the boat ready." They had a safe house on Siesta Key where they'd left a car and papers for an emergency just like this one tonight.

"What about our equipment upstairs?"

"It's mostly encrypted, and the laptop is set to erase if anyone tampers with it."

"What about Doni?"

"She and Emilio are dead."

Cabello was moved. Like Huertas he had a crush on her. "We're just going to run off, and let the bastard get away with it?"

"No," Heurtas said, and he took another quick look into the house. McGarvey was nowhere to be seen. "Señor McGarvey, I'm still willing to talk if you are."

"Throw your weapon down where I can see it," McGarvey said.

"As you wish," Heurtas said. He reached around the corner and tossed his pistol on the floor a couple of feet away from Donica's body.

"Tell the other man with you to do the same."

"He is gone."

"Bullshit."

"I sent him to your house to wait in case we couldn't resolve our differences here like gentlemen. If you return alone he'll know that I'm dead and he will kill you."

"Why are you telling me?"

"To convince you of my sincerity."

"Right," McGarvey said. "Show yourself."

Huertas turned back to Cabello. "Give me your gun, and make the boat ready. I'll take care of McGarvey and then grab the laptop."

Cabello was doubtful, but he handed over his pistol. "Emilio said he was good."

"He shot Donica in cold blood, and I'm not going to let it go. Now get to the boat. If I'm not there in ten minutes, get back to Madrid and make your report. "

Cabello took off into the darkness on the other side of the pool to the stone path that led down to the dock that was just off the Intracoastal Waterway.

"Señor, I am coming in now," Heurtas said. "Unarmed, so do not shoot."

McGarvey didn't answer.

Heurtas stepped around the corner, the pistol concealed behind his back, and stopped just within the sliding doors. "Señor?" he called out.

A moment later a tremendous crash of breaking glass came from somewhere in the house. Heurtas turned on his heel and raced outside, around the corner to the south side of the house where he figured McGarvey had broken one of the big windows to make his escape.

TWELVE

☐

Standing across from the long table in the formal dining room, McGarvey had clear sight lines to the window through which he'd just tossed a chair and the corridor back to the pool kitchen. He didn't want to get into another shoot-out with these people, but he did want to find out the extent of their surveillance operation on him.

For now he was simply buying a little time. With the woman and one man down, he thought the other two operatives would tread with care.

Huertas appeared briefly just outside the shattered window. McGarvey stepped back into the deeper darkness of the room, certain that he was invisible to the CNI operator, who turned and looked away, and then ran off toward the south.

McGarvey went back out into the corridor and followed it to the main staircase in the front entry hall and hurried upstairs. He figured that whatever surveillance equipment they had in place would be in an upstairs room facing south, toward his house. But he didn't think it would take long for the pair of CNI operatives to realize that they had been tricked and come back.

At the top he hesitated for a moment, cocking an ear to listen for a sound, any sound that might indicate that there was a fifth or even sixth operative that he hadn't seen, waiting for him to charge blindly into a trap. But the house was quiet.

Pistol at the ready McGarvey headed left to the first open door, where again he paused for just a moment before rolling inside, and quickly swinging his aim right to left. No one was here, but it was the room used for their surveillance operation.

The sliding glass window was open to a small balcony, across from which was a perfect sight line to his house. The twin beds had been stacked one atop the other and moved aside. A long table in the middle of the room, well away from the open slider so it couldn't be seen from outside, held several pieces of electronic equipment. Among them was a small optical laser that could be used to detect vibrations on a window-pane from someone talking inside the house. They'd been able to listen to all of his telephone conversations.

Two low lux cameras mounted on short tripods were aimed at the house, along with what McGarvey took to be an infrared motion detec-tor, and two other pieces of equipment that might have been some sort of a telephone intercept system—one for landlines, the other for cell phones.

All of it was connected to what looked like a military-grade laptop computer that was powered up and at this moment displaying a split screen with four images—two side views of his house, another of the front entryway and driveway, and the fourth a view of the rear, looking down across the pool and his study window.

The last two were from cameras mounted outside, and it vexed him that in the last three weeks he hadn't spotted them, even though he'd had the growing feeling that something was coming his way, that someone was watching over his shoulder.

Maybe he was getting rusty after all. For a long time, especially after Katy and Liz had been killed at Arlington, he'd professed that he wanted out of the business. And just a few months ago he'd said as much to Otto and his wife Louise.

"I'm getting out," he'd told them. "It's over." But Louise had dis-agreed.

"What about the rest of us?" she'd demanded. "What are we sup-posed to do? Me and Otto?"

He'd had no answer for her.

"You have a gift, Kirk. Rare and terrible as it is, we need you."

"All the killing."

"All the lives you've saved. What about them? Or don't they count?"

"My wife and daughter were murdered because of my gift, as you call it," he shot back. "I'm done."

"What about your grandchild? Are you just going to walk away from whatever comes her way?"

"That's not fair, goddamnit."

"No it's not," Louise had told him. "But it was the hand you were dealt."

And here he was in the middle of something again, and he knew that he could not walk away from it; it wasn't simply because of the two students who'd been killed, it was because of who he was, who he'd always been.

Somewhere in the distance, down on the ICW, he thought he heard the sound of a boat motor starting up, but then it moved away, north perhaps, and was lost.

A portable phone was lying on the table beside the intercept equipment. McGarvey laid his pistol down, got a dial tone, and called Rencke, who answered on the first ring.

"The number is blocked, are you calling from the house next door?"

"They set up a surveillance operation. Laser aimed at my house, cameras front, back, and side, infrared detectors, what looks like telephone intercept equipment."

"Have you neutralized the opposition?"

"Two, but there are at least two others."

"How long before you have company?"

"Good question," McGarvey said. "Matter of minutes, unless I have to shoot someone else."

"Okay, all this gear has to run by something. Could be remote. Is there any sort of a computer nearby?"

"A laptop. Right now it's showing four angles on my house."

"Have you touched it, or anything else?"

"No."

"Don't," Rencke said. "And don't let anyone else near it for five minutes."

"No guarantees," McGarvey said, but Rencke was gone, and the split-screen images were replaced by a list of what appeared to be files, though they were in some script of squares, tiny circles, and other odd marks.

McGarvey picked up his pistol and went to the door, but no one was in the corridor, though he was certain it wouldn't take them long to figure out what was going on and come looking for him.

A cursor moved quickly down the list, and back at the top the first file opened. A screen of a half-dozen photographs of McGarvey coming out of Café L'Europe on St. Armand's Circle were quickly followed by many more screens of a dozen shots each showing McGarvey at New College, at Macy's, swimming in the Gulf, working on his sailboat docked in the ICW behind his house. Then the images began to process so rapidly he could no longer make them out. It was clear that the CNI had not only closely monitored his movements, but they had been very professional about it. He'd never spotted them.

The next file consisted of what appeared to be audio recordings that showed up only as spectrum readouts. Then a very large file of more than fifty gigabytes, possibly of videos, came up.

"Still there, Mac?" Otto asked, his voice coming from the computer.

McGarvey picked up the phone. "Yes."

"You don't need the phone now. Are you still okay?"

"So far. Did you break their encryption system?"

"Piece of cake. It's an old military one the Chinese developed about five years ago. But did you see the still shots in the first file?"

"Yes. They were watching me pretty closely, but I never spotted them."

"They probably double- and triple-teamed you. But this doesn't make any sense. Spain is not our enemy."

"They're looking for the gold and they're in a fight to find it before the Voltaire Society drains the piggy bank."

"The Vatican has to be right in the thick of it too," Rencke said. "And everyone is after the diary, which is why the Voltaire Society came to you and the CNI mounted the surveillance operation, and why in all likelihood someone from the Vatican will be or already is on your trail."

"Señor McGarvey," Heurtas called from the corridor.

THIRTEEN

☐

Heurtas stood next to the open bedroom door where they'd set up their surveillance equipment. He'd listened to everything the bastard Rencke told McGarvey and it made him sick to think that Emilio and Donica had died for nothing.

They knew about the Society, the Vatican, and even the diary, and on top of everything Rencke had apparently figured out how to hack their encryption algorithm and unless he was stopped the CIA would have everything.

"Sounds like you have company," Rencke said. "Hold them off for another fifteen minutes. I've run into a problem with their auto-erase function."

"Señor McGarvey, there is no way out for you. But if you come out with your hands above your head you have my word that you will not be harmed."

"I shot the man and woman downstairs in self-defense," McGarvey said.

"You were trespassing."

"You've been prying into my business for the last three weeks. Why?"

"We do not want to kill you, but we will if we must."

"Unless I miss my guess the fourth operator took off in a boat a couple of minutes ago. North, I think."

Heurtas had heard the boat start up and leave, but it was exactly what Alberto needed to do. At all costs he had to get back to Madrid and make his report.

"You miss your guess."

"What does the CNI want with me?"

"We can work something out," Heurtas said. "You can't imagine the danger. For all of us."

"Tell me," McGarvey said.

The bastard was stalling for time.

"I'm almost there," Rencke said. "Ten minutes and I'll have complete access to their files."

"I can't allow that to happen," Heurtas said. He saw no way out, and he was starting to feel a sense of fate: whatever was coming his way would come no matter what he did. For no reason he could think of he had another erotic thought about Donica.

They were on a field exercise, in which the two of them plus one other officer were supposed to infiltrate an actual air force base and place mock explosives around the communications center. At one point he and Donica got separated from the third officer—who they learned later had been captured. A couple of hours before dawn they were holed up in a storage space at the rear of a hangar used for helicopter maintenance.

A siren had sounded and from their hiding spot they could hear the sounds of a meter-by-meter search.

"They'll find us sooner or later," he'd said.

"At least they won't shoot us for spies."

"Do you want to give up now, save us the wait?"

She had smiled and he remembered the set of her pretty mouth, as she shook her head.

They made love, as quietly as they could, though Doni had been a moaner, and it wasn't until three hours later, when they were both too hungry to wait any longer, they came out with their hands up.

It was the best sex he'd ever experienced, because of the danger, he supposed. Had they been caught in the act they would have both been fired. But they hadn't been, and now it was a memory that he could never share with her.

"Are you listening to me?" Heurtas asked.

"Yes," McGarvey said.

Heurtas suddenly stuck his pistol around the corner and began firing, walking his aim left to right across the room.

FOURTEEN

McGarvey slid left and dropped to his knees as the barrel of the pistol came around the door frame and Heurtas opened fire. He'd heard the final desperation in the Spaniard's voice, and as he moved he fired four shots at the wall eighteen inches to the left of the open door.

Heurtas grunted something, and dropped the pistol as he fell backward with a tremendous crash.

"Mac?" Rencke shouted.

"I'm okay," McGarvey said, straightening up.

Heurtas was down on his back, a lot of blood welling up from a chest wound, and one in the side of his face just above his jawline. His arms were outstretched, the pistol he'd dropped just out of reach of his right hand. But he was alive, his eyes filled with pain and with hate.

"*Bastardo,*" he wheezed, and he tried to reach for his pistol, but McGarvey kicked it away.

"What was the sense of it?" McGarvey asked. "The one who left in the boat will get back to Madrid, if he's lucky, and tell them what? Mission accomplished? Petain is dead?"

A sudden look of intense terror came into the Spaniard's eyes. "Petain?" he said, coughing, and he went slack, his eyes open.

McGarvey bent down and felt for a pulse at the man's neck, but there was none.

Otto was calling his name, and he went back into the surveillance room. "It's okay," he said. "Are you finished with the download?"

"Yes, it only took a couple of minutes. I was stalling to give you some time to defuse the situation. What happened?"

McGarvey was tired. "Three people are dead up at the college, and three more are dead here. The cops are going to have a hell of a time figuring it out, and the trouble is I'm not going to be able to help them, because I don't know what this is all about."

"Hopefully there'll be something on the computer that sheds some light. But what do you want to do next?"

"I'm not going to let it go, if that's what you mean."

"I didn't think so. But sooner or later the cops down there are going to find the mess and make the connection between the car bombing and the bodies and surveillance equipment and come knocking on your door. So what do you want to do, *kemo sabe?*"

"I'll fly up in the morning and we'll go over whatever you decipher on the laptop."

"I'll send a plane; I don't think it'd be such a good idea right now if you flew commercial, in case the locals are keeping an eye on you."

"Make it seven at Dolphin Aviation," McGarvey said. "There's usually not too many people around at that hour."

"Don't push your luck, Mac. Get out of there."

"Do you want me to take the laptop?"

"No need, I'm going to fry it," Rencke said. "Watch yourself."

Before McGarvey could turn away the computer screen went blank, and the power light went out on it and all the surveillance equipment.

Pistol in hand, in case the fourth CNI operator had not left on the boat and was still somewhere in the house or on the property, McGarvey made a quick search of the other bedrooms, finding passports in the names of Juan Fernandez, Diego Cubrero, Rufo Tadena, and the woman Sophia de Rosas—who the man he'd killed downstairs had called Donica or Doni. The passport pictures matched the woman and the two men, only the fourth for Rufo Tadena was of a man he'd not seen.

More significantly was the fact he found only four sets of documents, four overnight bags, sets of clothing and toiletries in four separate bedrooms.

Pocketing the passports, he went downstairs and methodically made a search of the entire house, before he switched off the pool lights and stepped inside where he stood in the shadows for a long moment listening to the near absence of any sounds except for the call of some night hunting bird in the far distance. No boats were passing on the ICW, nor any car on the island's single road, and the only light was the glow in the sky to the north from Sarasota.

The real world seemed a long ways off just at that moment, the deaths at the university and the three here that he'd killed weighed heavily. Senseless, all of them, especially because he still had no certain idea of the why of it, except for a diary that was a century and a half old.

Taking care with his movements McGarvey went down to the dock where a twenty-three-foot center-console Boston Whaler with a big outboard motor had been kept on a lift. He'd spotted it a couple of times out of the water and covered when he'd been working on his own boat. But he'd never seen it in the water. It was gone.

The fourth operator had not bothered to grab his passport. It likely meant that they'd set up an escape hole somewhere not too far north where they'd left more documents and everything they would need to travel back to Spain without arousing the suspicions of any TSA agent. Covering their asses. Standard tradecraft.

McGarvey debated going after him, but it would only result in another shoot-out. To prove what?

He stuffed the pistol in the waistband of his slacks and headed back to his house, the expression in the woman's eyes as she knew that she would die stuck in his head.

FIFTEEN

☐

Cabello shut off the engine just at the ICW green marker 49A, and listened for the sounds of someone following him. In addition to the sailboat, McGarvey had a RIB dinghy with a big outboard that was perfectly capable of coming this far this soon. But nothing was behind him.

Less than three miles north of the surveillance house, he was just off Siesta Key where a series of red and white private markers showed the narrow channel to the docks behind six rental properties, all but two of them vacant because of the low season. One of them, a small bungalow, had been set up as their escape route.

"Make no mistake about it, Señor McGarvey is an exceedingly dangerous man," Major Pedrosa Prieto, their handler at Torrejón Air Force Battle Air Command outside Madrid, had warned them. "Tread with very great care, for he is a man supremely capable of killing you given the proper circumstances."

But they had not tread with care. Accidentally killing the two students had been a serious mistake on Emilio's part. Doni had been right; McGarvey had cared very much about the kids, so much so that he had refused to listen to reason about the danger he was in.

Because of it she and Emilio were dead, and most likely Felix too. Now it was up to him to get back to Madrid, though how he was going to explain losing their computer and surveillance equipment was beyond him at the moment.

He restarted the very quiet four-stroke Honda and slowly picked his way down the channel to *libertad*, freedom, what they called their escape route, stopping every fifteen or twenty meters to listen.

"Is he some kind of a hero, then?" Emilio had asked.

"More like an avenging angel," Major Prieto said. "I don't know all of the details, but apparently one of his first assignments for the CIA—a kill outside of Santiago, Chile—went bad through no fault of his, and his government left him hanging in the wind. When he got back home, his wife divorced him and he went to ground somewhere in Switzerland. From that point, for whatever arcane reason, Señor McGarvey became a champion of what were, in his mind, just causes."

"Don Quixote," Donica had offered, and everyone but the major had laughed.

"With respect, Lieutenant," he'd said.

All six houses were dark when Cabello tied up at the dock, bow and stern, not bothering with spring lines because if all went well he would be on his way to Miami within less than a half hour.

He took a rag out of the port coaming box right at his elbow and wiped down everything he'd touched--steering wheel, shift lever, throttle, key and key float—and headed across the sloping lawn to the house. Clean khakis, white shirt, dark blazer, and loafers were waiting for him in one of the closets, along with an overnight bag of toiletries and changes of clothing, plus a passport under the name of Castaneda Trujillo, a wallet with matching documents—driver's license, national health card, photographs of a nonexistent family, even a love letter from an old flame—and a Nokia cell phone with two dozen telephone numbers, all of them connecting to various CNI blind numbers that were answered by various recorded voices.

Up at the house he found the key under a potted plant and let himself in. Once he had the door closed and relocked he leaned back against it and closed his eyes. What an absolute cock-up. He knew that he was lucky to be alive, but he also understood that he was going to have to do a lot of explaining why the mission had failed so spectacularly.

They'd been trained as a team, but they'd also been through intensive drills in which one or even all of the other team members were down, in which case they would have to continue alone.

"Where are the others?" a man, or possibly a woman, with a high, soft voice asked in Spanish.

Cabello opened his eyes and reached for his gun.

"If you draw your weapon I will kill you," the person said in a reasonable tone.

Cabello could only make out the figure of someone very large on the other side of the small kitchen. The room was nearly pitch-black and he couldn't make out any details, except that he was sure now that it was a man and that his life was in immediate danger.

"Who are you?"

"My identity is of no concern. You have come here because there has been trouble. Where are the others? Dead?"

"Sí."

"Tell me the manner in which they died, and do not lie to me, Señor Cabello, I will know."

"Do you know about McGarvey?"

"Yes."

"He shot the others."

"Has he followed you?"

Cabello shook his head. "I don't think so. I was ordered to get back to Interpol to file my report."

"I said do not lie to me, Señor," the man said, and he fired one shot from a silenced pistol.

The bullet slammed into Cabello's left arm with an incredible bolt of pain. He cried out, clapping his left hand on the wound.

"I warned you, no lies."

"What do you want with me?"

"The truth. The Voltaire Society in the person of Giscarde Petain came to talk to Señor McGarvey, and your team killed him. Why?"

"He was our enemy."

"In what way?"

Cabello hesitated.

"Be quick."

"You have come this far, you know about our operation, I suspect you know everything else."

The figure moved closer so that Cabello could make out his features. He looked like a very large teenager, but with the calmness of a monk. He was dressed in black jeans and a black polo shirt.

"How close have you come? How close has McGarvey come?"

"We killed the Frenchman to keep the Society from learning the truth."

"Yes, the diary of Jacob Ambli. But your people do not have it and now it appears that Mr. McGarvey has declined to help in your quest. But he knows about it?"

"Yes, at least I think so. He made a phone call to a friend at the CIA and discussed the incident at the college."

"But your team has no idea where the diary is, or who may have stolen it?"

"No."

"Nor does Mr. McGarvey?"

"No," Cabello said.

The dark figure raised his pistol and a thunderclap burst inside of Cabello's head.

SIXTEEN

It was after ten, and though McGarvey was tired he couldn't shut down. Drink in hand he stood at the open sliders looking across his pool and down the sloping lawn to the gazebo that Katy had loved so much. But he had to keep reminding himself that even if she were here he wouldn't have been able to explain to her what had happened today. In fact he would have probably moved her into a hotel in town before the flight up to D.C. tomorrow morning.

He had taken another shower and slipped on a T-shirt and shorts. At this moment Otto would be sifting through the computer's memory that he'd downloaded, and possibly even hacking into the CNI's database in Madrid. Tomorrow they would have some of the answers—hopefully enough to begin with or to step away and let the police and the FBI handle the mess.

His phone rang, startling him out of his thoughts. It was Otto.

"Do you know a Sarasota PD Lieutenant Jim Forest?"

"I talked to him at the college after the car bomb. He was sniffing around, pretty sure that I was somehow involved. Why?"

"He's been parked down the road from your house for the past five minutes and he just now is pulling into your driveway."

"How do you know?"

"I haven't fried the CNI's surveillance gear yet, just in case the fourth operator decides to come back. Anyway I spotted the Chevy Suburban from the camera in front of your house, and ran the tag. Thing is, it's not a department car, it's his own."

McGarvey immediately thought of the Mercedes parked next door. "Could Sarasota PD have gotten the tag number and ran it the way you did?"

"First thing I checked, but there was nothing in their logs—leastwise not in their mainframe. Anyway, if they had anything they would have checked next door and found the mess. I can have a cleanup crew there first thing in the morning."

"Someone on the seventh floor might take notice," McGarvey said. The office of the CIA's director Walter Page was on the seventh floor in the Original Headquarters Building. The man ran a tight ship unlike a lot of previous directors who were only political appointees and not professional intelligence officers like he was.

"We'll see," Rencke said. He ran the Company's computers and he had more or less carte blanche, unless he did something totally outrageous.

"Keep tabs on the cops—the county guys too. If it looks like they're getting involved, I want you to back off."

"The Bureau has this. Sooner or later they're going to put two and two together and come knocking at your door. How do you want to play it?"

"Depends on who asks and what they ask."

"Watch your back tonight."

"Will do."

McGarvey hung up just as the doorbell chimed, and he went to answer it. He put the pistol in the drawer in the front hall table, flipped on the outside lights, and waited a few moments before he opened the door.

"A little out of your jurisdiction, aren't you?" he said. "Or is this a social call?"

"Let's say I'm here as a professional courtesy. Nothing official. May I come in?"

"Why not?" McGarvey said, and he led the lieutenant through the house to the pool patio. "Drink?"

"A beer would be okay."

McGarvey got a couple of bottles of Dos Equis with pieces of lime. They sat at a small table from where they could look past the gazebo to the dock and out to the ICW.

"Nice place you have here," Forest said. He was dressed in jeans and a short-sleeved pullover, a puzzled look on his face. "Thing is we don't generally get the kind of trouble we had today around here. It's out of our league, if you want to know the truth."

"Has the FBI sent someone from Tampa?"

"A couple of forensics people are going through what's left of the Lexus. And someone will be coming down tomorrow to talk to you. Thought you might like a heads-up."

"I'll be in Washington."

"I could hold you as a material witness."

"Tell Mullholland that I'll be checking in with Bill Callahan, he's the deputy assistant director for Counter-Terrorism." Lloyd Mullholland was the Bureau's special agent in charge of the Tampa office.

Forest smiled a little. "Pulling rank?"

"A little, but I have a couple of ideas I want to check out."

"Care to share them with me?"

"Wouldn't do you any good, believe me. Because whatever this was all about this afternoon will probably be a job for the Company, or at the very least Interpol. It'd be a waste of your time to get in the middle of it. To start with, the Bureau is going to take over."

"Like I said, they already have."

"So why are you here, Lieutenant?"

"Name is Jim. And I know that whoever the guy was in the Lexus came to talk to you about something that got him blown up. I'd like to know what he had to say."

McGarvey looked away for a moment, sorry that he was involved, and yet curious. "The guy's name was Giscarde Petain, from a bank in Paris, but we've not been able to find such a bank or anyone by that name involved with the banking business in Paris."

"We?"

"He came to ask for my help searching for something that he said had been stolen from a safety deposit box in an affiliate bank," McGarvey said, sidestepping Forest's direct question.

"What was it?"

"Doesn't matter, because I told him that I wasn't interested."

"But you were in the parking lot when his car blew up, with him in it. Now that must have gotten to you."

"The deaths of those two students got to me," McGarvey shot back. "Senseless."

"And you're going to fight back," Forest said. "I have a few connections too. Enough to know some of your background, including how your wife and daughter and son-in-law were killed."

McGarvey held him off. "I'm not trying to pull rank, but you're out of your league with this. Trust me; back off, let the Bureau handle it."

"I'm not going to back off, goddamnit! My daughter is a freshman at New College. It could have been her killed this afternoon. And I fucking well want to know what the hell is going on. What the hell might be coming her way next. Do I pull her out of school or can you tell me that she'll be safe? Absolutely safe? Your word as a father who's already lost a child."

It hurt. "They're after me now."

"You're going to run."

"I want them to follow me away from here."

Forest got to his feet. "Trouble finds you, McGarvey. Maybe it would be for the best if you didn't come back."

SEVENTEEN

□

The CNI safe house on Siesta Key was a winter rental in a group of similar properties. Since it was out of season the entire neighborhood was all but empty. It was why the Spaniard infidels had rented this place, and the bigger house on Casey Key, and after his initial search Fr. Dominigue Dorestos proved who they were watching and why they had found a safe haven such as this one so necessary.

His handler had warned him at the contact house in Rome that he should expect Kirk McGarvey to be somehow involved because of the Cuban intelligence service's search for the treasure. What had been unexpected was the presence of the man who'd come to the college, apparently to speak to McGarvey, and the CNI's reaction to the meeting. Previous to this afternoon the Spaniards had been content merely to watch the former American CIA director, presumably to see what his next moves might be. And especially to watch for someone from Havana to show up.

"This is a delicate situation, as you may well understand, Father," Augusto Franelli had briefed him two days ago. "The Voltaires have evidently lost something of great import. Very likely the diary. Our first guess would be Cuban intelligence—except we do not believe they have the expertise for such an operation. The Spanish do, but they have been sent to America presumably to either contact McGarvey or wait to see if the Cubans do so."

"Which would suggest that he might be the thief?" Dorestos asked.

"Not the man's style. Nor do we believe that even if the Cubans showed up would he agree to help."

Then this afternoon just after Dorestos had arrived here, Franelli had called his cell phone to advise him about the car bombing.

"Perhaps the man at the college was a Voltaire, come to ask for

McGarvey's help," Dorestos had said. "And perhaps it was CNI who destroyed him."

Franelli—a tall, ascetic man who'd been in the military arm of the Hospitallers since he'd left the Italian army's Ninth Parachute Assault Regiment as a captain eleven years ago—was silent for a beat. "Perhaps you are right."

"It would make sense, sir."

"So, it is something that you will find out."

"Shall I attempt to make contact with McGarvey to see if he knows of the existence of the diary? It might be important. Because if he does know, then mightn't he continue the search on his own?"

"That's not likely," Franelli said. "He would have no motivation. He's a reasonably wealthy man even by American standards, and after the business a few months ago with the Cubans first in Texas and then at Fort Knox, he was done with it."

"Not necessarily."

"Yes, necessarily. He went back to his home in Florida. When you find out exactly what the Spaniards are up to you will return here at once. Do you understand, Father Shadow?"

"Perfectly," Dorestos said.

"And what else you may have to do when you learn what there is to be learned? Because make no mistake, the infidel Spaniards are the enemies of the Church in this."

"Sí."

On the flight over from Rome to New York and then to Tampa where he'd rented a car, now parked in the garage, he'd had plenty of time to work out all of the ramifications of his assignment, especially what it would ultimately mean for the well-being and continued strength of the Church.

The treasure, lost for a century and a half, rightfully belonged to the Vatican from whom it had been stolen, and it was his job, as a defender of the faith, a soldier for Christ, to recover it, even if it meant he had to take a life or lives again. But only for the grace of God's glory, and only at the behest of the Jesuit's Superior General, who was known as the Black Pope because his robes were black by contrast to the white robes of his Holiness.

Standing in the deeper shadows a few feet from the man he'd shot to death he watched and listened for someone else to come, but the night was silent.

He recognized the man on the floor as Alberto Cabello, but his showing up here had come as a complete surprise. It had to mean the CNI had run into trouble this evening. Probably of McGarvey's doing, if the SMOM files he'd been allowed to read were anywhere representative of the man.

He phoned Franelli and explained what he'd found, what he had done, and his speculation that something must have gone wrong at the CNI's surveillance house.

"I can think of no other reason for Cabello to have shown up," he said.

"You may be right, but you must make sure that McGarvey has not agreed to work with them."

"Immediately."

"Under no circumstances must you allow an interaction with the authorities, especially not with the FBI who will almost certainly become involved because of the car bombing."

"I understand," Dorestos said.

"We need the information, and you are the only man who can get it," Franelli said, and Dorestos's heart swelled. "God be with you, my son."

"And with you, Monsignor."

Pocketing the telephone, Dorestos let himself out of the house, carefully locking up, and went down to the boat. For a long time he stood stock-still, in the deeper shadows, as was his usual preference, and listened to the night sounds.

Somewhere to the north, up island, he could hear music from one of the clubs, and out on the ICW a barge slowly glided up the waterway toward Sarasota. But there were no other sounds.

He got in the boat, started the engine, and slowly motored out the private channel and into the ICW and headed south, a slight, almost beatific smile creasing his boyish features. He was most happy when doing God's work.

EIGHTEEN

□

After Jim Forest left, McGarvey took his silenced pistol from the hall table, got a box of 9 mm ammunition and a cleaning kit from a locked cabinet in the pantry, and walked back to the poolside table where he got to work.

He laid out a towel, unscrewed the suppressor, and laid it down. Next he switched the pistol's decocking lever down to the safe position and ejected the nearly half-empty magazine, setting it aside. He cleared the chamber of the one round then, pulling the front of the trigger guard down and pressing it sideways, he jacked the slide back and removed it. He took the recoil spring off the front of the barrel and set it aside with the magazine and slide.

With care for a task he'd done a thousand times he cleaned the barrel of firing debris, and wiped down the weapon frame and all the parts with an oily rag. Once the pistol was reassembled, he removed the cartridges from the magazine, wiped it down with the rag, and reloaded it.

When he was finished he washed his hands at the kitchen sink, made a ham and cheese sandwich, and opened another bottle of beer and sat listening for boat traffic on the ICW, the loaded pistol on the table in front of him.

He'd been thinking about the fourth CNI operative who had taken the boat and headed north. It was possible, even likely, that the man would come back to find out what happened to his team, and perhaps try to finish the job here.

But after a half hour when only three boats had passed, all of them heading north, he took his pistol and went upstairs where he packed a light bag with a few toiletries and a pair of jeans, a shirt, and a few other things. Anything else he might need was at his Georgetown apartment, along with his go-to-hell kit that was stacked with a pistol, money in U.S. dollars, British pounds, and Euros totaling about ten thousand dollars, along with a half-dozen Krugerrands, several valid passports in different names, driver's licenses, medical insurance cards, untraceable credit cards, photographs of nonexistent families, even letters from friends. It was everything a man on the run needed to cross national frontiers and get lost for a reasonable period of time.

He had the same sort of kit here at the house, and he'd considered leaving it behind. But even though he would be flying up to D.C. aboard the CIA jet, he still had to get from Joint One Andrews Air Base to his Georgetown apartment, between which just about anything could happen.

The CNI had gone to great lengths to keep tabs on him, and deny him further contact with the man from the Voltaire Society, so it took no stretch of imagination to think that somehow they might be waiting to intercept him in Washington. And he never went anywhere under the sole protection of another man or men, another agency. Never.

He took the money and papers from the concealed floor safe in his walk-in closet and stuffed them into his overnight bag and took it downstairs to the garage where he put it on the front passenger seat of his Porsche.

Again he stood for a few seconds, thinking about what he was getting himself into, and exactly the why of it. He wasn't sure, except that he kept seeing the falling piece of burning debris from Petain's Lexus falling out of the sky onto the two students at the bike rack. They hadn't a clue what was about to happen to them. And it wasn't fair. Someone had to account for their senseless deaths; someone beyond the CNI team who apparently had been sent to stop him from making a deal with the Voltaire Society.

He'd never considered himself a do-gooder, assassins never thought of themselves in that vein. Yet the truly evil people of the world—the bin Ladens, the Hitlers, the Mussolinis, the Stalins—deserved to die. Or at least he'd come to believe that philosophy, though sometimes he'd had his doubts, his serious reservations that sometimes caused him nightmares. But in the end he was who he was.

An avenging angel someone, somewhere, had called him, only they hadn't meant it as a positive comment on what he did.

All the lights inside the house were off, and in the kitchen he turned off the pool lights and the lights on the gazebo and down at the dock, as well as the small, colored spots that illuminated the palm trees and other landscaping elements around the house.

He laid the pistol on the pass-through counter from the kitchen to the pool deck and set down on a stool inside the house to wait.

The phone rang at the same time he heard a boat coming from the north down the ICW, but he couldn't make out its lights.

The number was blind—out of area on the caller ID screen—and McGarvey answered on the fourth ring, waiting to hear the signal that the Blackburn Point Bridge was about to open.

"I hoped I'd catch you before you went to ground," Bill Callahan said. They were old acquaintances, if not friends. Callahan was more or less a by-the-book FBI assistant deputy director who'd considered guys like McGarvey renegades. Useful, he grudgingly admitted once, but a renegade none the less.

"What makes you think that I'm going to ground?"

"You were involved with a car bombing, and I'm assuming it was meant for you."

"Not this time."

"Our Tampa SAC seems to think you belong at the head of the list, and he wants to talk to you first thing in the morning."

"I won't be here," McGarvey said. "I'm flying up to Washington first thing in the morning." The Blackburn Point Bridge hadn't made a signal yet. "Are you at the office?"

"Home."

"How're Mary and the kids?"

"Just fine," Callahan said. He'd been there for McGarvey after the funeral for Katy and Liz even though the Bureau had him in custody. He was a family man and he understood Mac's pain. "Do you want to talk to me about what happened? The local police report has you as a prime witness, but they say that you told them nothing."

"They wouldn't have been able to do anything about it, and if they start to seriously poke around someone else will get hurt."

Callahan was silent for a beat, and when he was back he sounded resigned. "Why did I think that you might say something like that? I could have you pulled in, but I doubt if it'd do us much good."

"I'll come over to your office tomorrow, as soon as I can. I'm going to need the Bureau's help."

"With what?"

"Start by keeping your SAC in Sarasota. I don't want him poking around down here. You can depose me yourself. It's a long story."

"All your stories are long. I'll keep the SAC reined in for now, but what else do you want?"

"Time."

"Christ, Mac. Three dead so far. What the hell are you into now?"

The bridge had not signaled that it was opening, and McGarvey thought that he heard the highly muffled sound of an outboard motor at dead slow somewhere very close.

"I'll tell you tomorrow. You'll just have to trust me until then."

Callahan hesitated. "You've never lied to me."

"No, and not this time either."

"Tomorrow afternoon."

"I'll be there," McGarvey said.

He took his pistol and went upstairs to the widow's walk on the roof, where keeping below the railing so he didn't present a silhouette, he was in time to see a dark figure flitting from shadow to shadow from the dock next door up to the house.

In his bedroom he grabbed a pillow from the bed and one of his dark sweatshirts from a bureau drawer. Downstairs at the kitchen pass-through he stuffed the pillow into the shirt and propped it on the stool he'd been sitting on. He pulled the stool a little back from the counter so that it was in deeper darkness, then headed outside around the pool and down to the gazebo.

The fourth CNI officer had come back, as he thought the man might, and this one he did not want to kill. He wanted some answers.

ПINETEEN

□

Fr. Dorestos stood just outside the doorway into the pool kitchen of the CNI's surveillance house, all of his senses hyper alert for any sign that the killer—who he assumed was Kirk McGarvey—was lurking somewhere inside.

An attractive young woman lay on her back, her neck and bare chest covered in blood. The body of a man, also shot to death, lay a couple of feet away. The woman had a silenced pistol in her hand. A shoot-out had occurred here. But noiseless so as not to attract the attention of neighbors, though the house to the south was dark, and the one just to the north had only its outside landscaping lights on.

These people and their killer had been careful. Professionals, something Dorestos respected.

Taking care not to step in the blood, with his pistol, a SIG Sauer P226 9 mm with the Osprey silencer that reduced sound by a respectable 125 dB, in hand he crossed the kitchen and set out to search each room on the first floor.

A window in the dining room had been broken out, a chair lying on its side nearby. Dorestos glanced over his shoulder the way he had come from the kitchen. There'd been an altercation in which two of the four CNI officers had been taken down. He looked at the window again.

McGarvey had fled deeper into the house, to this room, pursued by the other officers, and he used a dining room chair to break a window.

To make it seem as if he had escaped. But it had been a ruse, because McGarvey had not been finished here.

Dorestos went upstairs, careful at the top to make certain no one was waiting in ambush. A body lay outside an open door in the corridor to the left. Even in the relative darkness he could see the blood pooled on the wood-planked floor, see the blood splattered on the wall across from the door and the damage to the wall next to the door frame.

Stupid on the part of the dead man to hide behind a flimsy plaster-board wall.

He remained standing stock-still in the dark for a full fifteen seconds before he made his way down the corridor, sure that whatever had happened here was long over with, and that McGarvey had come to find out what he wanted, got into a shoot-out, and left.

At the door frame he held up for just a moment before he rolled around the corner and swept the room with his pistol. After a beat he lowered his gun and stepped back.

The table held some sophisticated surveillance equipment all connected to a laptop computer. Laying down his pistol he booted up the laptop, which opened with nothing but a black screen, a blinking white cursor at the upper left corner. The machine's memory had been erased, probably automatically when McGarvey, or whoever, had tried to access it.

He gingerly approached the window and hanging back out of sight from anyone on the ground, he had an excellent sight line to the house next door—the one to the south that showed no lights, not even outside lights on the palm trees. McGarvey's. All the surveillance equipment was pointed in that direction.

Dorestos started to go when something in his peripheral vision caught his attention and he turned back. For a long second or two he didn't know what it was, until all of a sudden he spotted a small green light on one of the cameras pointed out the window.

Instinctively he stepped into a pool of deeper shadows to one side of the open door. The computer had been disabled, but at least one camera was still powered up. It came to him that McGarvey knew there were four CNI officers here, and that one of them had escaped—to the north—by boat. It was also possible, even likely, that McGarvey might be expecting the officer to return.

The priest saw the error he'd made. McGarvey had been waiting for the boat to return. It was possible that he'd heard it coming down the ICW to a low-slung swing bridge. But the tender had not signaled an opening.

McGarvey knew that someone had come back, and whoever was controlling the surveillance equipment was waiting for someone to show up next door.

Dorestos glided across the room and pulled the camera's plug, and methodically pulled the wires from all the other equipment. McGarvey might be alerted, but he would have to suspect that it was the fourth CNI officer.

Out in the corridor Dorestos stepped over the body, and at the head of the stairs phoned his controller. They used the Australian-based GSM Thuraya encrypted satellite network, immune to interception by any governmental agency.

"You must be at the surveillance location now," Msgr. Franelli said. "What is your exact situation?"

Dorestos explained what he had found, including the blank laptop and especially the live camera pointed at the house next door.

"The deaths are Señor McGarvey's work, without doubt," Franelli said. "And now he will be expecting someone to come for him."

"I do not believe that the Spaniards convinced him to help," Dorestos said, meaning no humor.

But his handler chuckled. "No. The question you have called to ask then is: What must come next?"

"Sí."

"At this moment Mr. McGarvey will be very dangerous, not likely to be approachable by any ordinary means, and certain that whoever comes his way this night means to kill him. But in this we might have a slight advantage."

"He cannot be convinced to help us?"

"Not tonight. But he will want some answers, which he figures you might have for him. It means that he will not want you dead."

"I don't understand, Monsignor. Do you want me to kill him, or try to talk to him? Perhaps I might surrender myself; go in without my weapon and with my hands up."

"No. At this point he must not know the Hospitaller's involvement."

"What then?"

"Listen carefully, because what you must do next will be extremely difficult and dangerous," Msgr. Franelli said, and he explained what he wanted. "A delicate but necessary illusion."

"I still do not understand."

"It is simple, Father. We still need his help, and he will give it to us in such a way that he doesn't know he has. You will drive him like a quarry to its hunter."

"What if the opportunity you suggest does not present itself?" Dorestos asked.

"Then you will create one, or you will have failed."

Pocketing his sat phone, Dorestos went downstairs to the dining room, and flattening himself against the wall peered out of the shattered window. The house next door was still in darkness, and he had to assume that McGarvey was now waiting for someone to show up. Probably the fourth CNI officer.

He had no earthly idea what he should do next that would fit with his orders, but he wasn't frightened. At least not of McGarvey, not even of death because surely there would be salvation for him on the right hand of God. Each time he went out on a mission he was given absolution from his sins by the unit's priest. But this time he'd been given Extreme Unction, which was usually reserved for a person in extremis—on the verge of death. At this moment it was a comfort.

Something moved in the nearly absolute darkness alongside a pair of cabbage palms. He couldn't make out a figure, but he'd seen a slight shifting of patterns. McGarvey was waiting there, at the rear of the house with a view not only across his pool deck, but of the rear of the Spaniards' rental.

Dorestos stepped back. McGarvey had set a trap for someone coming up from the dock, or across the backyard. Presumably whoever was monitoring the camera trained on the front of the house would have warned him if someone were to come that way. But that option was off the table now.

Letting himself out the front door he hesitated for only a moment between the Mercedes parked in the driveway and the open garage door as he tried to work out the meaning of the two facts. But whatever might have happened here earlier this evening made no difference now.

He made his way through a line of flowering bushes that separated the two properties, then hurried silently down the north side of the house to the rear corner overlooking the pool and pool deck.

From where he stood he could make out the two cabbage palms

where he thought he'd seen McGarvey, but from this angle nothing was there. It had either been a play of shadows or the CIA assassin had moved.

Keeping low and moving fast he darted fifteen feet to the relative safety of a grouping of three tall palm trees, hoping to draw fire, but the night remained silent. If McGarvey were out there somewhere he was biding his time, waiting to see. What?

Farther down the backyard a small gazebo just above the ICW, where a large sailboat was docked, a tender with an outboard motor out of the water on a lift was in darkness. It would make for a good firing position, though quite a long distance to the rear of the house for a pistol shot. But McGarvey's file warned that the man was reputed to be an expert marksman of "outstanding abilities," who should be approached with extreme caution.

Dorestos turned to search the pool deck and open sliders into what from here appeared to be a kitchen with an open pass-through to a counter with four stools on the pool deck. To this point he still had no idea how he would comply with his orders, until he suddenly saw the solution.

Something dark was seated at the pass-through inside the house. But the figure didn't move and it was crude, certainly not a human, though evidently meant to look as if a person were seated there. It meant that McGarvey was within firing range of whoever took a shot.

Dorestos suddenly sprinted back the way he had come, pulling off three quick shots at the seated dummy as he ran.

Reaching the corner of the house two shots smacked into the stucco concrete block behind him, but low enough so had they not missed they would have hit him in the legs.

Then he raced toward the front of the house, his mission for this night accomplished. He'd gotten McGarvey's attention.

TWENTY

□

The two silenced pistol shots at a distance of seventy feet were impossible even under the best of conditions, but McGarvey figured that he'd had a fifty-fifty chance of catching the CNI operator low, in the legs.

He waited for just a second or two in the lee of Katy's gazebo in case the Spaniard intel officer was waiting for him, but then ran to the south side of the house hoping to catch the guy in front.

It was clear the man had come back to finish the job. Presumably he'd stopped at the surveillance house and found his people dead, which made him a motivated man.

McGarvey's phone buzzed in silent mode in his pocket as he reached the front. He ignored it, holding up to take a quick look around the corner.

He was in time to see a ghost-like dark figure heading south through a thick line of orange, lemon, and lime trees next door. The agent was moving fast, but it was more than likely that he would pull up short or even double back and wait in the shadows to shoot anyone coming up on his six. For sure he had not been hit.

Across the street, which was the long, narrow island's only road, was a narrow strip of beach and the open Gulf of Mexico. Nowhere to run and hide. The Spaniards' Mercedes was in the driveway, but the agent had headed south.

McGarvey went next door to the Mercedes where he popped the hood, yanked off the engine's plastic shroud, and ripped out all the spark plug wires. He tossed them aside, closed the hood, and headed around to the rear of the house where he would be in a position to intercept the CNI agent if he tried to make it back.

At the corner of the house he looked and listened for any sign that the man was heading this way, but he could detect nothing, and he went down to the dock where the CNI's boat was tied up, the key in the ignition.

One way or another he thought it was reasonable to suspect that the man would to try to make it back here, either to the car or to the boat to make his escape north where there would be another safe house and transportation.

He took the key from the ignition and pocketed it, then headed south just above the waterline. It was at least five hundred yards to the Blackburn Point Bridge across to the mainland, and a fair hike after that back up to Tamiami Trail—Highway 41—which led north to Sarasota.

He stopped now and then to make sure that he wasn't running blindly into a trap. Once he thought he heard something just ahead, but four doors down from his house he came to one of the several compounds on the island that was protected by a high concrete block wall, only a wooden gate opening to a path down to the ICW.

Lights illuminated the property and McGarvey spotted smudges near the top of the ten-foot wall, and for just a second he puzzled them out, realizing all of a sudden that someone had climbed up and over. The man was large but he had to be very agile, an athlete. It was a feat that McGarvey couldn't duplicate.

He stepped aside, out of the likely path of a ricocheting bullet fragment, and fired a shot into the lock at the gate to no effect. The mechanism was made of case hardened steel as he thought it might be.

A slight scuffling noise came from the southern end of the compound and McGarvey was in time to see a dark figure at the top of the wall for just an instant before it disappeared. He fired on the run, knowing he'd missed.

At the corner he was again in time to see the CNI agent disappearing in the darkness. This time he did not fire. Instead he ran across to the next property, this one whose sloping lawn led from a long dock, up to a cantilevered infinity pool just below a very large house.

He stopped in the darkness for just a second, searching for movement somewhere up on the pool deck, but he was in time to see the dark figure leaping up the wall of the next compound to the south and disappearing on the other side.

The man's speed was nearly impossible. He was nothing more than a shadow.

McGarvey reached the walled compound and ran immediately to the southern side, where he stopped again to listen and to watch the top of the wall.

"We are not your real enemy, *signore*," a high-pitched voice, either that of a young boy or a woman, called from the other side of the wall. The accent was Italian, not Spanish.

"You tried to kill me," McGarvey said. He leaned against the wall at the southern corner.

"Merely to get your attention. I knew the dummy in the chair was a ruse and that you were hiding somewhere very close with the intention of doing me harm."

"Get my attention for what purpose? You're not with the CNI." If whoever it was came over the wall, McGarvey would have a clear shot.

"Be careful who you talk to. Someone else will be coming to ask for your help, but trust no one. Believe me, Signore McGarvey, I have taken a vow never to lie."

"I'll put my pistol down, and you do the same. Come out and we'll talk."

There was no answer.

McGarvey waited a full minute then started along the wall to the front of the compound. But no one was there; nothing moved in either direction on the road.

His phone vibrated again. It was Otto.

"You okay, Mac?"

"I've been chasing after the fastest guy I've ever met, and I think I've lost him."

"It has to be one of the CNI operators, because the one video feed I left open was shut down."

"I don't think so," McGarvey said. "He spoke to me. Called me *signore*. He said that he wasn't my enemy and warned me that I wasn't to trust anybody. And he said something else damned curious. He said that he'd taken a vow never to lie."

"SMOM—Sacred Military Order of Malta."

"That's what I figured. The Spanish government wants the treasure, and so does the Vatican, along with the Voltaire Society. So who stole the diary? Whoever it was wouldn't be snooping around here."

"You're right," Otto said. "So what's next?"

"I'm not sure. But I'm getting a little tired of people who talk to me getting blown up, or people next door watching my every move, or someone from the Church taking potshots, so I'm going to find out what the hell is going on."

A boat roared to life on the ICW a couple of doors away.

"Got to go," McGarvey said, and he headed in a dead run back north to the CNI's surveillance house and the boat tied up to the dock.

The boat that had just started came up the ICW at full throttle and was well past when McGarvey reached the CNI's boat. He jumped aboard and turned the key to start the engine but nothing happened.

He turned to check the outboards, but the fuel lines were missing. He leaned back against the back of the seat, and shook his head.

The son of a bitch was not only fast, he was good.

TWENTY-ONE

☐

Dorestos tied a loop of line from the stern of the powerboat he'd stolen to a cleat on the dock at the CNI's Siesta Key safe house, put it in gear at idle throttle, and pointed out toward the ICW. As it strained against the tether, he stepped up onto the dock and released the line.

The boat slowly made its way up the narrow private channel, hesitated as it touched bottom, but then broke free and the torque of the spinning prop gradually eased it to the south into the deeper water of the ICW. It was unlikely that the boat would be associated with this place, giving him an extra margin of time to get away.

Nothing had been disturbed in the house since he'd left earlier this evening, and once he made sure that no traffic was moving on the road, he opened the garage door and headed north in the Chevrolet Malibu rental car. He tossed the garage door opener over the roof and into the ditch beside the road.

In ten minutes he was off the island and heading to I-75, which would take him up to the Tampa International Jet Center where he'd rented the car from Hertz and where the chartered Embraer Lineage that had brought him from New York earlier today was parked, its crew waiting at a nearby motel.

He'd not heard another boat coming from the south, and he was reasonably certain that McGarvey wasn't following him. Nevertheless he changed lanes often, and kept glancing in the rearview mirror to make sure no one was on his tail, until he was on the interstate highway at Clark Road heading north.

He called his handler and explained what had happened.

"You're sure that you got away clean?"

"Sí."

"Then you have done a good night's work, and the fact that you actually spoke to him, I think bodes well. But tell me, Father, what were your exact words?"

"I told him that we were not his real enemy. And I told him to be careful who he talked to, and not to trust anyone."

"What else? Exactly."

"I said: 'Believe me, Signore McGarvey, I have taken a vow never to lie.' "

"Then he knows who you are."

Dorestos didn't see it at first, but all of a sudden he realized the mistake he had made. "He can't know that I am a Hospitaller."

"Perhaps not, but considering the scope of the issue he will have to guess that you are from the Vatican. It was an error on your part, Father, but not a grave one."

"I will make a penance when I get home."

"As you must, but it will have to wait. Where are you at this moment?"

Dorestos told him.

"Good. Your aircraft will be waiting for you in Tampa, but you are not returning just yet. First you are flying to Washington, where you will get a motel room under your work name, of course, and rent a car with tinted windows."

"Do you believe that Mr. McGarvey will be there?"

"A government aircraft is to pick him up in Sarasota at eight in the morning, almost certainly to take him to Andrews where you will be waiting to follow him."

Dorestos knew better than to question how the monsignor knew this as a fact, because the Church had people on the ground in just about every city large or small in at least all of the western world—both hemispheres.

"Somebody else will almost certainly try to reach him; in this you were correct. Perhaps the CNI, perhaps someone else from the Voltaire Society, perhaps someone from his own government because we have an idea where some of this treasure that rightfully belongs to us has gone, though we don't yet know why. So it will be up to you to find out who he meets with."

"Shall I intercept whoever it might be?"

"No," Msgr. Franelli said sharply. "You have driven him to act. It is exactly what I wanted. Now I want to know not only who he sees, but what his next moves might be."

"Do you believe that he will lead us to the treasure?"

"Almost certainly. And we will be there to take it from him when he finds it."

TWENTY-TWO

The CIA's Gulfstream touched down at Joint One Andrews under a cloudless sky a couple of minutes before eleven, and taxied directly into a hangar. McGarvey gathered his bag, thanked the crew, and walked off the plane where a young-looking master sergeant named Andersen in ODUs was waiting with a plain blue sedan.

"Welcome to Andrews, Mr. Director, may I give you a lift into town?"

"Just somewhere I can catch a cab."

"Main gate, sir. There's always a couple there. If not we can call for one."

McGarvey hadn't slept very well last night, nor had he gotten much rest on the short, bumpy flight up. He'd called Rencke on the way out to the private aviation terminal at SRQ and told him that no escort was necessary.

"No problem," Otto said. "Louise was planning on picking you up. Audie's staying home from day care and she wanted to come along."

Audie was McGarvey's granddaughter. And sometimes thinking about her, seeing her face in the photographs and videos Louise sent him made his heart heavy; she was the spitting image of her mother, Liz, who had been a spitting image of her mother, McGarvey's wife, Katy.

"Could be I'm going to pick up a tail, so I'm going to cab it to my place in Georgetown. Make it easy for them. But I don't want you or Louise in the line of fire. And it might be best if you sent Audie down to the Farm for the time being."

The CIA's training base for new recruits and for some missions was at a place called the Farm on the York River south of Washington. His daughter and son-in-law had been codirectors of training and Audie had been adopted by the entire staff. She'd been sent down to stay out of harm's way twice; once just after her parents had been murdered and again a few months ago when Louise had been kidnapped and Otto had been forced to fly to Cuba for the funeral of Fidel Castro.

"Okay, but not until she sees you first. She's practically going crazy, looking at your pictures and videos."

McGarvey had seen his wife and daughter murdered in front of his eyes when the limo they were riding in exploded. And thinking that Audie could be exposed to the same kind of danger sometimes drove him to the brink. Sometimes it was nearly impossible to think rationally about her. "I don't want to take the chance."

"She's our daughter now, *kemo sabe*," Otto said tenderly. "Which means we get the final say."

"I'll be a couple of hours," McGarvey said, not wanting to press the argument. But less than twenty-four hours into a situation six people were already dead, and he expected the body count to rise.

McGarvey maintained an apartment on the third floor of a brownstone in Georgetown on Twenty-seventh Street with a view of Rock Creek Park where he ran every morning when he was in residence. He'd bought the place as a refuge after Katy had died, and before he could face returning to their house on Casey Key.

He dismissed the cab a couple of blocks from his place, and walked the rest of the way. Georgetown was in full swing with a lot of tourists especially along M Street, which lent the place an anonymity. Nevertheless he tried to come in clean each time.

On the ride in from Andrews he'd sat in the front passenger seat from where he could watch his six in the door mirror, but if anyone had tailed him from the base they were very good. A blue Chevy Tahoe with deeply tinted windows had been interesting from the time they'd turned onto State 4 into the District, but then he passed and turned north on Twenty-third at Washington Circle.

Standing now on Dumbarton at Twenty-eighth, waiting for traffic to clear so that he could cross, he thought he spotted the Chevy passing through the intersection one block north, but he couldn't be sure. When it didn't show up in the next block, he put it down to jumpy nerves, thinking about Audie.

A Grey Line tour bus rumbled past, and McGarvey walked across the street, stopping for a moment at a corner shop selling magazines, water, and flowers, so that he could look at the reflections in the window. He was jumpy, and almost certain that he'd been followed from Andrews, but no one was behind him. And the Tahoe was gone.

Around the corner a half block away, McGarvey let himself into the brownstone, and used the stairs to reach his third-floor apartment. The building housed mostly professional singles or couples without children and Bill Tyrone, an older man who spent most of his time away on cruises in the Caribbean and Europe. He'd once told McGarvey that there were three women he met on most of the trips who had more or less adopted him.

"Why stay home alone when I have all that attention?" he'd said, laughing.

McGarvey's fail-safe, which was a small bit of black shoe polish just inside the door lock opening, was intact. Nevertheless he drew his gun, unlocked the door, and eased it open with the toe of his shoe. Nothing moved inside, there were no sounds, and he rolled around the corner, sweeping his pistol left to right.

But someone had been here. He smelled the subtle lingering odor of a woman's perfume, probably expensive, but so faint it was impossible for him to guess how long ago whoever had worn it had been here.

Closing and locking the door behind him he made a quick search of his small one-bedroom place, but so far as he could tell nothing had been disturbed. He glanced back at the door. Whoever had been here was a professional. They'd not missed the fail-safe, and yet they'd worn perfume.

At the window he looked across at Rock Creek Park with its jogging paths, single road, picnic benches, and the creek itself, which wandered down from the national Zoological Park, but nothing seemed out of the ordinary. Nor was traffic below on Twenty-seventh Street out of the ordinary.

But someone was there. He could feel it in his bones. Maybe the CNI or perhaps someone else from the Voltaire Society. Or the man with the high-pitched voice from Casey Key who'd called him *signore*.

He retrieved his bag from where he'd dropped it just inside the door and brought it into his bedroom, where he laid his pistol down and took off his jacket. It was early but in the kitchen he poured a stiff measure of Cognac, downed it neat, and then phoned Otto on his landline. Several years ago Rencke had come up with a back-scatter encryption system that could scramble both sides of a phone conversation even though the encryption equipment was located only at one end. It worked especially well with landlines.

"Are you at home or at the campus?"

"Home," Otto said. "Louise is here too. Is everything okay?"

"I think I picked up a tail, but whoever it is, is damned good. Check to see if there have been any private jets landing in the past few hours from Sarasota or any place within a few hours driving distance."

"TSA only allows forty-eight private flights every twenty-four hours, so it should be easy," Rencke said. "Who do you have in mind, the CNI?"

"I think it's the guy who got away from me on the key. He was good."

"The Hospitallers have the rep. Are you coming out here today?"

"Soon as I see Callahan. Has someone picked up Audie?"

"Later, after you get here. She wants to see you."

"Goddamnit."

Rencke said nothing.

McGarvey hung up and stayed leaning against the wall by the window for a long minute or so, trying to calm down. He'd never been really afraid of much except for the safety of his family; his wife and daughter, and now his granddaughter. He'd tried to insulate them by keeping his distance so when someone came gunning for him they'd been pretty much out of the line of fire.

But it had not worked to save Katy or Liz, and he was very much afraid that it wouldn't work to keep Audie safe and that one thought drove him crazy.

He called Bill Callahan at FBI's headquarters downtown and left a message that he was on his way, and then called the private garage where his Porsche Cayenne SUV was maintained and kept while he was out of town, and asked for it to be brought around.

TWENTY-THREE

◻

The dark blue Chevy Tahoe with deeply tinted windows was parked on Dumbarton and Twenty-ninth Street nearly two blocks from McGarvey's apartment. Traffic here had been light but steady for the twenty minutes Dorestos had bided his time, watching the images on his iPad's Internet connection. He'd stopped by a Wendy's to get a sandwich and a soda, and was eating now. It was cover. Everyone was in too much of a hurry to bother noticing a man sitting alone in a car eating his lunch.

As soon as he'd landed at Reagan National he'd gotten on a U.S. air traffic control restricted site that showed the traffic pattern for the entire country. Homing in on the Sarasota flight patterns north along the eastern seaboard he'd picked out the government Gulfstream flight to Andrews earlier this morning.

From there he'd brought up the Russian GLONASS GPS system, which had been recently augmented to display actual real-time satellite images of what their Federal Security Service—which was the renamed KGB—deemed as hot spots. Among them was Washington, D.C., and environs. The system was much like Google Earth only better because it was strictly focused as an intelligence tool.

He'd watched as the plane had landed and taxied to a hangar where a few minutes later a plain blue Air Force sedan came out and drove to the main gate where a man carrying a small overnight bag transferred to a waiting cab that immediately headed into the city.

The angles had been all wrong for Dorestos to make a positive identification, and the man had not looked up. But his build was right, and the aircraft that entered the hangar had come from Sarasota, which had to be more than coincidence.

He'd followed the cab at a safe enough distance that even a man of McGarvey's tradecraft wouldn't spot him, and followed him to a brownstone building, which still wasn't decisive. But he had time, and he had patience, things he had learned at the Instituto Provinciale Assistenza Infanzia, which was the Catholic orphanage in Milan.

His mother had been a prostitute who'd given birth to him in a dark alley and had left him in a garbage bin where a policeman had found him and brought him to the nuns at the Chiese San Fedele, from where after a medical checkup he was taken to the IPAI.

But he never fit in. He was too big for his age, he had a sullen attitude that he'd inherited from his mother.

From the age of around nine or ten he began slipping out of the orphanage after dark, where he met up with a street gang, who after an initial initiation of knives and clubs, which he passed, set him to work first as a second-story man because of his youth and his size. By the time he was thirteen—and adept at street begging, breaking and entering, and even strong-armed robbery of old women—he'd graduated by killing his first man for a few hundred lira.

No matter what, no matter the situations he found himself in, no matter the trouble he'd gotten into, each morning before dawn he slipped back to the orphanage where he was safe. The Church was the mother he'd never known, and he loved Her with all of his heart.

Fifteen minutes after the man had entered the brownstone building he came out at the same moment a metallic blue-gray Porsche SUV pulled up to the curb and a man in a black jacket got out. The two of them greeted each other.

The angle was low enough that Dorestos managed to get a tag number, which he ran, coming up with McGarvey's name.

A minute later a Ford Taurus pulled up, the man who'd delivered the Porsche got in, and they left.

McGarvey waited for a couple of minutes at the curb, as if he were expecting someone—the Tahoe, Dorestos had the nasty thought—then got in and drove away.

Giving McGarvey a head start, Dorestos pulled away and followed the Porsche to Pennsylvania Avenue, and into the city past the White House to the J. Edgar Hoover FBI Building, where the car disappeared.

For just a minute Dorestos was confused, until he cautiously drove past the Bureau's headquarters complex, spotting the entrance to the underground VIP parking garage. He'd taken a chance that the American knew he was being followed and had laid a trap. But the simple truth was that McGarvey had come to Washington to report to the FBI what had happened. He might suspect, though that was far-fetched, but he didn't know that he was being followed.

Half a block away he got lucky with a parking spot where he waited a full five minutes to see if McGarvey came out, before he turned around and drove back to Georgetown, parking a block away from the brownstone, and going the rest of the way in on foot.

This morning he was dressed in neatly pressed khaki slacks, boat shoes with no socks, a yellow Polo shirt, and a lightweight blue blazer, all American with a European flair of side vents on the jacket.

No one paid him the slightest attention as he let himself in to the brownstone's unattended lobby. Six mail slots were along the wall between the elevator and the stairwell, ground-floor apartment doors left and right down a short hall.

He studied the name plates, until 3A, which was for T. Van Buren, and he shrugged. McGarvey's tradecraft may have been legendary, but he was apparently a man of sentimentalities. A fool even. T. Van Buren was the name of his son-in-law who'd worked for the CIA, and had been assassinated in the line of duty. No one would come looking for the apartment of a dead man.

Dorestos easily loped up the stairs to the third floor, where he stopped a moment at the landing to listen for anything out of the ordinary. Sentimental or not, McGarvey wasn't a stupid man. If he'd had the slightest inkling that he'd been followed from Andrews he might have stationed a CIA officer or two here to keep watch. But if someone were here they were making absolutely no noise.

At the door to the Van Buren apartment, Dorestos studied the hinges and door frame, especially the lintel for a proximity device, and the threshold for a pressure plate that might be connected to a silent alarm, or perhaps a small, narrowly directed explosive device that would be effective only at close range to avoid collateral damage.

But he detected nothing until he took out a lock pick set and bent down to inspect what turned out to be an ordinary PLY205 High Security front entry lock, that was pickable by any decent operator. Only the mushroom pin might present some difficulty to an amateur, and for just a moment Dorestos was a little disappointed, until he spotted a minute trace of what looked like black grease, or perhaps ordinary shoe polish.

It had not been disturbed, nor would it have been noticed by anyone but a professional. A little better, he thought, though not much, and at this point his estimation of McGarvey's abilities had dropped.

Scooping up a bit of the black grease with one of the picks in his set, he used two others to pick the lock in under fifteen seconds, and once the door was open he replaced the grease from where he'd removed it, and stepped inside.

The apartment was neat, but a little dust had accumulated on top of the coffee table and the flat panel television as if no one had lived here in weeks or perhaps months.

But something felt out of the ordinary, and walking across the living room Dorestos pulled out his pistol. An overnight bag lay on the bed, but the bathroom had not been used, and in the kitchen an empty glass sat on the counter next to a bottle of Remy Martin.

McGarvey had come here only long enough to drop off his overnight bag, have a quick drink, and call for his car.

But someone else had been here too.

Dorestos raised his head and sniffed delicately. It was a woman's perfume, vaguely familiar. He'd smelled it the moment he'd walked in the door. But McGarvey had come here alone.

At the window he looked down at the traffic along Twenty-seventh, as well as on the Rock Creek Parkway, but there was no sign of McGarvey's Porsche.

Deciding that searching the apartment would probably tell him nothing important, but might alert McGarvey that someone had been here, he holstered his pistol, let himself out, and walked back to his car.

He phoned Msgr. Franelli. "I followed McGarvey to the FBI's headquarters building, and then came back to his apartment."

"I expected he would talk to someone at the FBI. He has friends there, and the Bureau is very much interested in the bombing in Sarasota. But tell me, Father, did you find anything of interest in the man's apartment?"

Dorestos told his handler about the fail-safe on the lock, and his decision not to carry out a search for fear of missing another booby trap.

"But someone had been there before me. A woman. I smelled her perfume."

"Describe it."

Dorestos was at a complete loss, and he said so.

"Break it down. Was it strong or weak?"

"Very faint, but distinctive. Perhaps something like orange or lemon blossoms, but not so sweet, and maybe something else—acid with sugar, maybe a woman's body lotion." Dorestos remembered something. It was at the back of his mind, a smell, a place, maybe a room. But he couldn't put his finger on it. "I don't know."

"Do you think that you will remember it if you smell it again?" Franelli asked.

Dorestos brightened. "Yes, Monsignor, without a doubt."

"You've encountered it before?"

"I'm not sure. Perhaps."

"Can you remember when or where? "

Dorestos racked his brain, but all he could dredge up was a small room, with a desk and two chairs. A nun was seated behind the desk and someone else, maybe a woman, was seated across from her. He described the scene as best he could to his handler.

"You were very young. Maybe two or three. And the perfume was Chanel."

Dorestos was astounded. "How can you know this?"

"The office was in the orphanage, and the woman was your mother, who came only once to visit you. She wore Chanel."

TWENTY-FOUR

McGarvey waited in the ground floor visitors' lounge of the FBI headquarters building for a full fifteen minutes before Bill Callahan, the Bureau's deputy assistant director for counterterrorism, finally came down to get him. He was a large, athletic-looking man in his mid-forties, who in fact had played football for the Green Bay Packers for a couple of years.

"Good to see you, Mac," he said. "And I'd ask how are you doing, but I already have a pretty good idea."

"Your people found out anything interesting yet in Sarasota?"

"Let's take a walk and get some lunch," Callahan said. He took the security badge from around his neck and put it in his jacket pocket.

"Fair enough," McGarvey agreed, and they walked out of the building, and crossed Ninth with the light where a half block away they went into the Caucus Room, which was an upscale steak house.

Callahan was known here, and the maître d' showed them to a booth near the rear of the main room, where he ordered a mineral water with a twist, and McGarvey a Pils Urquell beer.

"I won't ask the questions I'd need to ask in my office, and in turn you're going to tell me everything because besides the three dead at the university, we found three more dead in the house next to yours. We think that they worked for Spanish intelligence, and that they were running a fairly sophisticated surveillance operation on you."

"They were CNI, and there's a fourth one, possibly dead."

Their drinks came, but Callahan told the waiter they'd order lunch later.

"You killed the three, including the woman?"

"Yes," McGarvey said, and he went over the entire day beginning with Petain's visit at the college, though not what he wanted, until the arrival of Jim Forest the Sarasota detective. "Otto downloaded everything from the computer and then fried it."

"Yes, we found out right away that the hard disk drive had been cleaned out. I expect that you'll share it with us. But why, what the hell is going on that the CNI wants to keep tabs on you and if you're right, killed the Frenchman?"

"And the two students," McGarvey said.

Callahan nodded tightly. "Josh starts college in a couple of years, and he's been thinking about New College. Maybe not such a good idea."

"There was Kent State, and the high school at Columbine, and others. We can't protect them all the time."

"You know that better than most. So tell me what the hell is going on, starting with the Frenchman."

"He told me that he'd been sent by the Voltaire Society to ask for my help finding a hundred-and-sixty-year-old diary that had been stolen from a bank vault in Bern. It supposedly has the locations of seven caches of gold and silver buried somewhere in southern New Mexico, by Spanish monks from Mexico City. Actually only four, because three of them have already been emptied, and he warned me that my life was in danger because of what I already knew, or thought I knew."

Callahan sat back. "Go on," he said.

McGarvey almost felt sorry for the man, who after all was just trying to do his job in an increasingly difficult world. Pressure came not only from the terrorist organizations he was charged with finding before another 9/11 occurred, but from the White House that wanted only good news, especially in an election year.

"You know what I was involved with a few months ago in Texas and then Fort Knox. It's not over."

"Our file is still open, as is, I suspect, DO's." The DO was the CIA's directorate of operations, which had been peripherally involved with the situation that had started in Havana with Fidel Castro's death.

"Walt Page would like to see it closed." Page was the director of the CIA, and just as straight a shooter as Callahan.

"I'm sure he would. Are the Cubans involved again?"

"Not yet."

"Let's go back to the Frenchman who shows up at New College to ask for your help finding some diary. What'd you tell him?"

"That I wasn't interested, and that he needed a private detective. He gave me a telephone number in Paris, but Otto couldn't find out much except that if such a society existed, it was under the radar, except that a transfer of money was made to the United States just before the Civil War, apparently by the society. But why the payment was made, who accepted it, and what it was used for is still up in the air."

"Another treasure hunt?"

"Yeah," McGarvey said, a little troubled that he was letting the man hang in the wind, but he needed some time.

"That to this point has involved some French society—coincidental that you're a Voltaire scholar—and Spanish intelligence, for which at least six bodies have piled up, possibly a seventh. Anyone else involved?"

McGarvey had debated the next point, because he didn't know if it would help or hurt Callahan. But the man was one of the good ones in a very large pool that contained a lot of bureaucratic assholes. Washington was filled with them. Trouble is that it was hard to tell the good guys from the jerks until it was too late.

"The Vatican."

Callahan was taken aback but for just a moment. "I see. Because the treasure was brought north by Catholic monks from Mexico City. They want it back. But Spain doesn't want to share it. Nor does the Voltaire Society, who does what—write checks to us? Or sends the occasional shipment of gold and silver our way? And to this point it seems as if everyone is willing to kill whoever gets in their way. Does that about cover it?"

"Not quite."

"The Cubans. But you said that they're not involved this time."

"Not yet, but I expect someone will be showing up."

Callahan looked away, a pained expression in his eyes and knit brows and the set of his mouth. "I don't know if I want to ask, but I've known you for too long not to: What's your take on all of this?"

"I don't know, I haven't made any sense of it yet."

"Jesus H. Christ, Mac, by your own admission you've gunned down three intelligence operatives from a friendly nation—one of them a young woman. How am I supposed to sell the director on the notion that you shouldn't be arrested and buried somewhere? Give us the time to straighten out this mess?"

"Because you'd never get it straightened out that way. Believe me."

"Save me your hunches," Callahan said. "But from where I sit, apparently in the cheap seats, there is no gold treasure buried somewhere in New Mexico—nor was there ever any. It's nothing but an urban legend, no different than Area 51 at Roswell with alien bodies and spaceships. Ghosts, hobgoblins, time travel, warp drive—beam me up, Scotty. My kids are into it, and my wife watches all the paranormal shows on cable—not because they believe in any of that shit, but because it's entertaining. The problem is the bodies. The murders. Assassinations. Acts of terrorism, whatever you want to call what's happened in the past twenty-four hours."

"I need a little time, Bill. It's all I'm asking."

Callahan threw up his hands. "Why did I expect you were going to say something like that?"

"I'll keep you in the loop."

"Please do," Callahan said. He stood up. "If I were hungry I'd have the steak sandwich, it's pretty good for twenty-five bucks. But I'm not hungry." He tossed down a fifty-dollar bill, and started away, but then turned back. "Are more people going to die over this thing?"

"Probably," McGarvey said, and he regretted it deep in his bones.

TWENTY-FIVE

□

After speaking with his handler, Dorestos turned his attention back to the GLONASS real-time images on his iPad in time to catch McGarvey's gray Porsche emerge from the J. Edgar Hoover Building and head back on Pennsylvania Avenue the same way it had come from Georgetown.

He figured it was likely that McGarvey would either go back to his apartment, or probably cross the river either on the Roosevelt or Key Bridge and head up the George Washington Parkway to the CIA headquarters.

He was betting on the CIA, so he pulled away from the curb and drove down to M Street and turned right, away from where Pennsylvania Avenue ended, keeping one eye on the iPad.

Just past the touristy shops at Georgetown Park, and two blocks before the Key Bridge he got lucky with a parking spot and pulled over to wait and see where McGarvey, still in traffic, was going.

He was having a hard time letting go of the scent of the perfume, which the monsignor said was Chanel—the same scent his mother had worn. She was long dead by now, he'd found out that much, but until today he'd had no real memory of her. But now he could see her in that tiny office at the orphanage. He couldn't make out her face, or even her shape, only her general outline, but her scent stuck in his mind. It was comforting to him, and yet frightening, one of the unconscious reasons, he supposed, that made him want to get out of McGarvey's apartment without searching it. He was afraid of the perfume.

The loneliness and sense of abandonment that he'd felt until he'd joined the street gang came back at him strong. Had his mother not come to visit him, he suspected that he might have adjusted much sooner, and yet intellectually he understood that such thoughts were probably beyond the ken of a two-year-old. But he felt the sense of loss now deep in his chest, and he wanted to cry.

The naivete was long gone—knocked out of him on the street, and later when he was sixteen and woke up early in the morning with one of the older priests at the orphanage kneeling beside his bed.

"It is all right, my son," the priest had whispered. He'd pulled the covers away, and pulled Dorestos's pajama bottoms down.

"I don't understand," Dorestos said softly, but he had lost his virginity with the whores two years earlier, and he knew damned well what oral sex was all about.

One of the Catholic jokes inside the orphanage had been: "How do you get a nun pregnant? Just dress her up as an altar boy."

The priest gently fondled Dorestos's penis until it was erect and then took it in his mouth, the sensation pleasurable, and Dorestos relaxed and enjoyed it, coming quickly to orgasm.

When it was over the priest smiled. "Now that wasn't so bad, was it?"

"Bastard," Dorestos said, and he clamped his powerful hands around the old man's throat, and strangled him.

The priest, whose name Dorestos never knew, did not struggle, and after the light had faded from the old man's eyes, Dorestos got out of bed and put the body under the covers.

He got dressed, took his possessions, including a comb, a safety razor, and a few items of clothing and slipped out of the orphanage into the early morning hours, back to his gang without the slightest idea what they did or where they lived during the day.

McGarvey turned onto Constitution Avenue, and just past the Lincoln Memorial turned onto the Roosevelt Bridge, across the river where he headed north on the GWM Parkway that led up to the CIA in Langley.

Waiting for an opening in traffic, Dorestos pulled out and caught a break on the Key Bridge, reaching the parkway about a quarter mile behind the Porsche.

The first week had been tough. He'd connected with the street gang but they'd been following him each morning and when he didn't return to the orphanage they wanted to know who the hell he really was. They believed that he might even be a snitch for the cops, and when he told them what had happened and why he'd left, they'd sentenced him to death.

"We want no fags among us," the gang leader Cristobol had said, and he'd pulled a knife and came up from behind.

Dorestos sidestepped the attack and defended himself with only his size, his speed, and his instinct for survival.

When it was over, Cristobol's left arm broken, three ribs cracked, his jaw dislocated, and his right knee dislocated, Dorestos had run away. He snatched purses for money to eat, he slept under bridges, he ran away from the cops, and that fall he walked nearly fifty kilometers out into the countryside where he found a vacation cottage on Lake Varese very close to the Swiss border. No one would be back until summer, nevertheless the pantry was reasonably well stocked with canned goods, and a closet in the back was filled with several dozen bottles of wine.

He'd spent most of the winter out there, finally getting bored enough to walk all the way back to Milan, where the first night he'd been picked up by the police because he'd made the mistake of going back to the street the orphanage was on, merely to take a look.

The police had turned out to be from the Vatican, who'd been on the lookout for him ever since the murder. They did not hand him over to the local authorities, instead they'd brought him to the Hospitallers.

"You're just the sort of young man we've been looking for," his first instructor had told him. "You have finally found a home among people who respect and love you."

That was in Malta, and over the coming years he'd been trained not only in Catholic ritual—he'd been ordained a priest at the age of twenty—he'd been taught English, French, and German, how to shoot just about any man-portable weapon in existence—including the American Stinger and the Russian Grail missiles—hand-to-hand combat techniques in which his own body could be used as a lethal weapon. But most importantly they'd taught him how to think, how to reason, how to analyze.

He became an assassin, a tool for the SMOM. In all he'd successfully accomplished seven missions, but, as Msgr. Franelli had briefed him in Malta: "This is your most important assignment. Of supreme importance to the Church as well as to our order."

"I will not fail you."

"Of course you won't."

Dorestos took his eyes away from the iPad and nearly missed McGarvey, who'd turned off the parkway on Dolly Madison Boulevard just short of the entrance to the CIA, and he had to suddenly switch lanes to make the turn and still keep well enough back that he would not be spotted.

He called his handler, and told him the situation. "Perhaps it's a back entrance," he suggested.

"It's possible. But it's also possible that you have been spotted."

"I don't think so. Where else might he be heading?"

"Unknown," the monsignor said after a brief hesitation, and it was the very first time Dorestos had ever heard even the slightest doubt in his handler's voice. It was disquieting.

"I will find out."

"With care, Father. You understand what's at stake."

Not completely, Dorestos wanted to say, but he did not. "Yes, Monsignor."

The boulevard went directly through the small town of McLean, where McGarvey turned north on a side street and after a half-dozen blocks, turned left again and then down a cul-de-sac where he parked in the driveway of a pleasant-looking two-story colonial, in a neighborhood of similarly well-kept homes. A tricycle with a pink basket was parked on the walkway to the front door.

Dorestos pulled over a block away and watched as McGarvey got out of his car, and looked back toward the street that passed the cul-de-sac for a long moment, before he closed the door and headed up the walk.

He was a suspicious man, but Dorestos could not bring himself to believe that McGarvey had spotted him.

He made a U-turn and drove back to a gas station and convenience store on a corner that whoever coming or going from the cul-de-sac would have to pass. He bought a Diet Coke and a sandwich and sat eating his second lunch, debating if he should try to approach the house on foot.

TWENTY-SIX

Before McGarvey could ring the bell, Louise opened the door, a warm smile on her long, narrow face. She was tall for a woman—over six feet—and whip thin, but her eyes were her best feature, very large, very wide, very dark brown, and very expressive.

"Windows into a woman's soul," she'd once told Mac. "No artifice here. What you see is what you get." She and Otto were head over heels.

"Did you come in clean?" she asked, though she knew he had. She was just overprotective of Mac's granddaughter, Audrey.

McGarvey shrugged. "Who can ever be sure," he said. He pecked Louise on the cheek and she stepped aside to let him into the stair hall, and locked the door behind him.

Otto, his red frizzy hair neatly tied in a ponytail, was fairly jumping out of his skin with excitement. It had been several months since they'd seen each other, and he considered Mac more than just a brother in arms. Their lives were deeply intertwined, and they'd been through a fair number of battles, the outcomes of which had not always been so certain. Otto had been there when Mac had been wounded and lay fighting for his life in a hospital, and Mac had been there when Otto had been held in badland, forced there because Louise had been kidnapped.

Standing next to him, Audie barely came up to his waist. She was slender with her mother's blond hair and Katy's pretty eyes and delicate mouth. She bounced on her tiptoes, one hand behind her back, the other at her chin as if she was a miniature philosopher trying to work out a difficult problem. But she looked uncertain, and when McGarvey approached she shied away, closer to Otto.

"It's okay, he's your grandfather," Otto told her.

Louise was beaming, practically in tears. It had been more than a year since McGarvey had last seen Audie, and he was nervous that she would reject him.

"Grampyfather?" Audie said in a small voice.

McGarvey hunched down to her level a few feet away. "Do you remember me?"

"You brought me Piggy." It was a small stuffed pig that McGarvey had got for her. Otto said she loved it.

"Yes."

She smiled and came forward. "Did you bring me another present?"

"Next time," McGarvey said.

"It's okay, I forgive you," she said seriously, and she gave him a kiss on the cheek and a hug before she went back to Otto.

McGarvey straightened up. "She's beautiful."

"Yes, she is," Louise said, and she turned to Audie. "But now it's time to pack your bag and get Piggy, before Uncle Brax and Aunty Terry come for you."

Audie's eyes lit up. "I'm going to the Farm?"

"Just for a few days," Louise said.

The child bounced on her tiptoes. "It was so terrible good to see you again, Grampyfather," she told McGarvey, and Louise led her up the stairs.

"She's going to grow up just like her mother," Otto said.

"And like you and Louise."

They went back to the kitchen. "Have you had lunch yet?" Otto asked.

"A sandwich."

Otto opened a couple of beers and they sat down at the counter. "What'd Bill Callahan have to say?"

"The Bureau's not happy about the mess in Sarasota and next door to my house, but he's agreed to give me a little time."

"Marty stopped the cleanup crew, sorry," Otto said.

"Can't be helped," McGarvey said. Marty Bambridge was the chief of clandestine services.

"Did Bill know the guys next door were CNI?"

"He guessed and I confirmed it. Has it reached Page?"

"He talked to Medina this morning, who admitted that some of his people might have been in Florida on vacation." Eduardo Medina was the director of the Spanish intelligence service. "Page told him that apparently they'd caught burglars in the act and all three of them had been shot to death."

"What was Medina's reaction?"

"Nada. Just asked if their bodies could be returned."

"There was a fourth operator. Any sign of him yet?"

"He's probably out of the country by now, or is on the way out. Could be he made his report to his boss, which is why Medina had no reaction. Which brings us to why they were watching you, something they had to know was very stupid and dangerous. And don't tell me they expected you to lead them to Cibola in New Mexico."

"It's why they killed Petain," McGarvey said. "They knew that sooner or later he or someone like him would be coming to talk to me. And just like Petain they warned me that my life was in danger."

"From who and why?" Otto asked. "It doesn't make any sense. The treasure does not exist."

"Petain thought it did."

"Nor is there any such organization as the Voltaire Society. At least not the one the Frenchman claimed he represented."

"The CNI operators killed him for some reason."

"Nothing on their computer but you," Otto said. "Christ, we're all grabbing at straws. It's nuts."

The phone rang and Louise caught it upstairs.

Otto waited until she called down. "They're around the block," she said.

She came down with Audie and a small pink backpack, from which poked the stuffed pig's head, just as a Cadillac Escalade with government plates pulled in behind McGarvey's SUV.

Terry Sweeney, who was chief of security at the CIA's training facility, came to the door. She was a small woman, with tiny hands and a ready smile.

Audie ran to her. "Aunty Terry."

"Ready to come play for a few days?" Sweeney asked, and she spotted McGarvey and Otto, who'd come from the kitchen. "Everything okay, Mr. Director?" she asked.

"Things could start to get a little dicey around here," McGarvey said. Lying to someone in Sweeney's sensitive position was not done. The woman needed to know if something was coming her way, for the sake of the installation as well as the child. "Who'd you bring with you?"

"Braxton Ezell." Ezell was the director of weapons training. He'd retired from the field as a NOC—which was a field officer under Non-Official Cover—when his left hand and most of his right were blown off in a firefight outside of Vientiane six years ago.

"Good man," McGarvey said.

"Keep us informed," Sweeney said, and she took Audie's hand.

At the open door Audie turned back. "Good-bye Mommy and Daddy, and Grampyfather."

When they were gone, Louise locked up and they went back into the kitchen. "I'm not cooking, so how does pizza for dinner grab you?"

"Fine," McGarvey said. "You guys are doing a good job with her."

"It's easy," Louise said. She opened them beers. "So what happened in Florida—or rather what's the upshot? Otto's told me some of what went down, but not all of it."

"The Spanish treasure in New Mexico," Otto said.

Her left eyebrow rose. "Are the Mexican drug cartels involved again?"

"They were stung last time, I don't think they'll buy into it again," McGarvey said, and he went into some detail for her from the moment Giscarde Petain had shown up at New College.

"At least the Bureau is off my back for the moment."

"That's a good thing," Otto said. "But I don't think Marty wants to cut you any slack. He wants to talk to you."

"Page should be able to run some interference."

"Not likely. This is election year and no matter who wins, Page figures that he's out. I look for him to resign within the next month or so, and he's not going to want to leave the agency with something like this hanging over his head."

"Politics," Louise said with some distaste. "But I want to know more about the perfume in your apartment. Have you smelled it before? An old girlfriend?"

"I don't know, but whoever she was, she was a pro. The perfume was the only thing she left behind."

"A message?" Louise suggested.

"Could be."

TWENTY-SEVEN

□

It was nearly five, a couple of hours since the man and woman had shown up in a Cadillac SUV and had taken a child away with them. In the meantime Dorestos had driven around the neighborhood, coming to the edge of a strip of woods that bordered the rear of the house. Several picnic tables were set up just within a small park with children's swings and slides and monkey bars.

It was a weekday and the wrong time for parents with their kids to be here, and he'd parked and made his way through the trees to the edge of the property. But there'd been nothing to see, except for a large backyard, equipped with a lot of toys for the girl. A lucky child, he'd thought.

He'd stayed at the park for as long as he thought he wouldn't stand out, and then drove back to the gas station where he parked in the rear, out of sight of the clerks inside.

It was late at night in Malta but the monsignor had promised that he was available no matter the hour. "It will be as if you were praying to God, he has answers for those who need Him, whenever they need Him."

Msgr. Franelli answered on the first ring as he always did. "Was it the back gate to the CIA? I'd hoped to hear from you before now."

"He didn't go there. Instead he came to a house in McLean."

"Is he still there?"

"Yes, but I can find no information on the address, it comes up a blank in all of my search engines."

"Tell me what you have seen all afternoon. Every detail."

Dorestos told him everything, including the little girl who'd been picked up by a man and woman driving a black Cadillac Escalade with government plates, and about the woman who'd met them at the door.

"Describe this woman."

"Tall, thin, jeans, sweatshirt. The angle was fair, but I couldn't make out much more than that. She never came fully outside of the house, nor did she look up."

"Standard tradecraft, but I think you're on to something. Unless I miss my guess the woman is Louise Horn, who used to work for the National Reconnaissance Office, which puts up and runs the American constellation of communications and spy satellites. Her husband is Otto Rencke, the CIA's Special Projects director, and a close personal friend of McGarvey's."

"I'll wait until McGarvey leaves, and then go in to question them. It could prove valuable if Rencke is such a good friend. McGarvey will have told him everything."

"Rencke is a genius. Quite possibly the smartest man on the planet when it comes to encryption techniques and information retrieval and collection. He makes connections. If you went to him you would have to kill him and his wife. If that were to happen Signore McGarvey would hunt you down to the ends of the earth, and there would be nothing we could do to protect you. You will make no physical contact with Rencke or his wife."

"Such dedication."

"Yes," Franelli said. "For now you will merely watch. And when McGarvey leaves you will follow him wherever he goes."

Dorestos glanced in his rearview mirror as a dark gray Ford Taurus passed on the street and turned the corner toward the cul-de-sac. He got a very brief glimpse of someone behind the wheel, but no one in the passenger seat.

"Father?" Franelli prompted.

"One moment, please, Monsignor, there may be a development."

"Tell me."

"A car has just headed in the direction of Rencke's house."

"Government plates?"

"I couldn't make them out."

"Driver, passengers?"

"No passengers, but I think the driver might have been a woman. One moment, please."

The GLONASS image on his iPad was directed tightly on the house. He pulled back to a slightly wider view and spotted the Taurus stop at the curb in front of a house a half a block before the entrance to the cul-de-sac.

Now the satellite's angle was too high to read a license plate number, nor could he detect any reaction from the neighbors or anyone in Rencke's house. He relayed this information to the monsignor.

"This woman has not gotten out of her car? She's just sitting there?"

"Sí."

"Does she have a sight line on Rencke's house?"

"I don't think so, but she's in a position to intercept anyone leaving."

"I want you to get the license number."

"Sí, Monsignore," Dorestos said.

He switched his cell phone to the camera mode and headed down the street toward the entrance to the cul-de-sac. As he passed the Taurus, he beeped the horn, and as the woman turned around to look out the rear window he snapped a picture of her face and the license plate.

Circling around the next block, he pulled up again at the gas station, and called his handler. "I managed to get a photo not only of the license plate but of her face. I'm sending it to you."

Franelli said something that Dorestos couldn't quite catch, but then he was back. "Give me a minute while I check something. In the meantime are you in a secure position?"

"Yes," Dorestos said. He'd heard excitement in the monsignor's voice. It was out of the ordinary, and his heart sped up a pace.

Traffic was beginning to build, and three cars were getting gas. A McLean police car passed, but did not slow down. Finally the monsignor was back.

"The situation has changed. I have identified the woman, and I believe I know why she is there, though it is extremely dangerous for her. She must know it, which means she is in a position to help in the search."

"For the diary?"

"For the treasure."

"What are my orders?" Dorestos asked, and he had a feeling that he knew the answer. But ultimately it's why he'd been sent here; it was what he'd believed would come to pass.

"If the woman tries to make contact with McGarvey, I want you to kill her."

"It could create a problem in broad daylight."

"She'll wait until after dark, on the off chance that McGarvey will come out alone."

"And if he does?"

"I'll make that decision then."

TWENTY-EIGHT

McGarvey was watching the woods out one of the rear windows when Otto brought down one of his laptops and set it up on the kitchen counter as Louise was phoning their pizza order. He connected with one of his powerful search engines on the mainframe at the Original Headquarters Building, and within a few keystrokes he was inside the FBI's Tampa Office.

"What's on the other side of the woods?" McGarvey asked. They were vulnerable here to someone coming up that way. Especially after dark.

Louise hung up and came over. "A road about fifty meters away, a park there for kids, hardly ever used so far as I know."

"Have you guys set up motion detectors back there?"

Otto looked up. "I didn't think we needed it. This location is secure. No way someone is going to trace ownership back to us."

"Unless someone followed me here," McGarvey said. He'd been having the same feeling ever since he'd left Andrews, and especially after smelling the perfume in his apartment.

"Do you want me to call for some muscle?"

"I don't want to get the Company involved yet. There're too many legitimate questions that I don't have the answers for. And I don't want them looking over my shoulder."

"Anyway, Audie's safe," Louise said softly. "Thanks to your hunches."

McGarvey nodded. Every time he thought about her, he was afraid. But going to ground again like he had in the beginning in Switzerland, and most recently in Greece on the island of Serifos, had done nothing to stop the violence that had been inflicted on his family, and the danger that he'd placed Audie in by coming here today. With Otto and Louise it was different. They were trained intelligence officers who'd known the risks when they'd raised their right hands.

"Look," Otto said turning his laptop around. "FBI Tampa reports a body of a fourth CNI agent in a rental on Siesta Key just a few miles north of the surveillance house on Casey. Your doing?"

McGarvey looked at the preliminary crime scene report and the photos of the body of a man shot to death, lying in a pool of blood. "No."

"Who then? Your Olympian able to leap walls at a single bound?"

"That's exactly who I think it was. I heard a boat heading north."

"But why was this guy protecting you?" Louise asked. "He has a reason."

"If it's the Vatican they want me to lead them to the treasure."

"By finding the diary," Otto said. "But even if we went after it, we wouldn't have an idea where to start, except for the bank employees in Bern. Getting inside a safety deposit would have been next to impossible."

"Unless they had the passwords."

"If I had been in charge of security I would have demanded personal recognition in addition to some password. I'd want to know who I was opening a safe deposit box for. Especially one that had been rented for more than a century and a half."

"You're both forgetting something," Louise said. "All this depends on Mac actually taking the challenge and going after the thing. Neither of you really believes that any such treasure exists. So why go through the motions?"

"Because of the two kids on campus who were killed, for starts," McGarvey said. "And because of the Italian who shot at the stuffed figure I'd set up in the kitchen. He told me that he'd known that it wasn't me, but he took the shot anyway to get my attention. Which he did. And because the CNI put people on my case whose intention, when I broke in on them, was to kill me. Also because one of these days I'm going to miss. Law of averages."

Louise leaned back against the counter. "That's a cheery thought," she said. "How about a little something to brighten up your spirits?"

McGarvey nodded.

"We don't actually have to go looking for it, because the people who took it will find us once they think that we're in the hunt."

Rencke sat up. "Whoa, she's right. The Voltaire Society guy comes to you for help, which is actually what the CNI thought was going to happen, so they took him out. The Spaniards would have been happy to let you take the next step so long as you didn't look over your shoulder and spot them. The last thing they wanted was to take you out. But you forced their hand. At the very least the Society and the CNI are going to come back."

"So will the guy from Malta," Louise said. "You're the magnet. If that's what you want to be."

"I don't think I have much of a choice."

"Just a mo," Louise said. She went to the hall closet and when she came back she laid a compact Glock 29 semiauto on the counter next to Otto, and stuffed another in the waistband of her jeans. "None of us walks around unarmed. Just in case."

"You're not in this," McGarvey said, but they both looked at him.

The doorbell rang. "That was quick," Louise said, and she headed to the front stair hall.

"Too quick," McGarvey said, suddenly alarmed. He pulled out his pistol.

"The pizza joint is just around the corner," Otto said. "They come here usually twice a week, they know the way."

McGarvey went to the kitchen door just as Louise looked through the peephole. She pulled the pistol out of her waistband and holding it behind her back with her right unlocked the door with her left.

"Louise," McGarvey warned.

She glanced back. "It's okay, I think, but you're not going to believe this." She opened the door and stepped aside.

María León, a colonel in Cuba's intelligence agency, stood on the stoop, her hands spread away from her body, a tentative smile on her pretty face. She was thirty-six with a good figure. "I'm not who you expected," she said, her English quite good. She was an illegitimate daughter of Fidel Castro's and had been involved a few months ago in an elaborate plot to kidnap Louise to force Otto to come to Havana for Castro's funeral, in order to dig McGarvey out of hiding on Serifos.

Her father's deathbed request was for her to find McGarvey and ask for help finding the Spanish treasure, a portion of which Fidel thought belonged to the Cuban people. There were a lot of deaths, and in the end she'd been disappointed and had escaped back to Cuba. A one-million-dollar bounty put up by a well-to-do Cuban ex-pat in Miami was on her head. Her coming here like this was extraordinary.

She spotted McGarvey, gun in hand, standing in the kitchen doorway. "Are you going to shoot me, or let me in? It's been a tough trip."

Louise stepped back. "Come in, put your hands on the wall, and spread your legs."

María did as she was told.

Louise took the purse from her shoulder, and handed it to McGarvey, who came forward.

"What are you doing here?" he asked as Louise stuffed the pistol back in the waistband of her jeans and did a thorough job of frisking the woman, who wore a nearly transparent scoop-necked white blouse, designer jeans, and low-cut soft leather boots. Her long black hair was done up in the back, and she wore an expensive Rolex watch in gold.

"She's clean," Louise said, stepping away. She took the purse from McGarvey and dumped the contents on the hall table, a passport and lipstick falling on the floor. There was no weapon.

"The same thing as you, I suspect," María said. "Looking again for Cibola. I've come to help."

"With what?" Otto asked over McGarvey's shoulder. "I can call someone in Miami who'd love to know that you were here."

"They'd come up and shoot me to death, or maybe take me back to the Calle Ocho and put me on trial. For what, being a true Cuban patriot?"

"Spare us," Louise said.

María flared. "I didn't run when the situation became difficult. I stayed and fought for my country."

"Along with the Russians' help until they pulled out."

"Anyway, I thought that you might need an extra hand tonight."

"With what?" McGarvey asked.

"A big guy in a blue Chevy Tahoe, looked like the Marathon man," María said. "But don't tell me that you guys didn't spot him?"

Shots from a silenced automatic weapon slammed into the front door, and the narrow windows that flanked it, nicking María in the side of her neck.

"Down!" McGarvey shouted. He made it to the living room window in time to see the Tahoe disappear around the corner at the opening of the cul-de-sac.

PART
TWO

That night and the
following days

TWENTY-NINE

The sleek Hawker 4000 biz jet touched down at Jeddah's ultramodern new airport a few minutes after midnight and immediately taxied to a private hangar owned by Prince Saleh bin Abdulaziz, a third cousin in the Saudi royal family. Once the engines spooled down and the stairs were lowered, a man with a soccer player's build, and the fair complexion of an Englishman—and the rich Oxford accent to match— thanked the flight crew and, carrying only a Louis Vuitton leather bag, stepped down and walked over to the Bentley coupe that had been sent for him.

He was a Saudi, born in Riyadh, and he'd been first a pilot in the air force, then a captain in the General Intelligence Presidency, and finally on his retirement five years ago when he turned thirty-four, he'd become a freelance enforcer for the Royal family.

He was dressed this evening in a British lightweight summer pinstripe in dove gray, with a Hermes tie, and hand-stitched Brazilian loafers. He was something under six feet, and moved like a cat, sure on his feet but seemingly in no hurry. He'd learned his deceptive moves playing soccer at Oxford, where he'd been sent to study international politics and to learn to speak flawless English and French. His real name was Mahd Ibn Khalden al-Rashid, but outside of the country he most often went under the name Bernard Montessier.

The driver, a dangerous-looking fireplug of a man, who had in fact been al-Rashid's hand-to-hand combat and weapons instructor in the GIP, got out and opened the rear door. "Welcome home, Mahd."

"It is good to be back, but I don't suspect I'll be here for long." They spoke Arabic. "Will the prince see me this evening?"

"Yes, and he is most anxious. All went well?"

"To a point." Al-Rashid settled in and sat back for the ten-kilometer drive down the Red Sea coast to Prince Saleh's compound not far from Mecca. The aircraft and the car were luxuries he'd gotten well used to ever since he'd gone to work almost exclusively for the prince.

Saleh had never occupied any official post within the government, and yet his work, almost always done in complete secrecy, was perhaps the most important in all the kingdom—sometimes nearly equaling the oil industry itself. He was the Royal family's money man, who worked with the drug cartels in Russia, China, and most importantly in Mexico and Colombia, to launder tens of billions in U.S. dollars and euros every year. He also dealt with the distributors in a dozen countries around the world—the biggest share of that business coming from the States.

It was he, working through several intermediary firms, a few in the United Arab Emirates, a couple in the United Kingdom, and five in Germany and Switzerland, who as often as possible had a huge effect on the price of oil via derivative and credit default swap trading. Almost all of it was so complicated that the transactions were completely under the radar of the American SEC.

Which made him among the most important men in the kingdom, with the anytime ear of the king himself.

But with the kinds of deals he was involved with, he'd often had to use the talents of men such as al-Rashid, to convince a cartel leader or businessman or some high ranking government functionary to cooperate. It took blackmail, extortion, and sometimes assassination by bomb, poison, pistol, knife, and even garrote when the need for silence and for a splashy effect was required.

Al-Rashid was a primary source for the prince's secret intelligence issues, and therefore was highly paid and highly treasured throughout the kingdom though only a few men actually knew his name, or knew about his home in southern France.

Because of the hour, traffic was almost nonexistent on the highway inland across the desert and in less than fifteen minutes, the driver pulled down the long gravel driveway to a cluster of three low-slung buildings, which were barracks and a military administrative center, plus a guard tower that rose twenty meters above the floor of the desert. All of it was just inside a tall fence topped by razor wire, and an electrically operated gate manned by three guards armed with American-made Knight compact automatic assault carbines. Two of the guards came out, while the third stayed behind.

Al-Rashid powered down his window as they approached. "Good evening."

"Good evening, sir," the lieutenant said. They were expecting him, but the prince's safety was paramount and they trusted no one. "Step out with your travel bag, please."

Al-Rashid did as he was told, and his person and the bag were thoroughly searched. The gate was opened again, and an armored Hummer came out for him. His driver was directed just inside the gate where he was to park in front of the barracks, and wait for however long the meeting would take. It was SOP. Very few people ever actually got up to the prince's palatial compound, which was another five kilometers away. Those who did were thoroughly vetted and closely watched.

The main house was a three-story building of nearly fifty thousand square feet complete with a crenelated roof line, minarets at the corners, and a dozen fireplace chimneys—though there were no fireplaces in the house. The indoor pool was made of marble with gold fixtures including several bare-breasted mermaids spouting water from all of their orifices, which was one of the prince's many bits of humor that al-Rashid had found stupid: *Nekulturny*, as a Russian friend in the FSS had told him a couple of years ago.

At the house, a guard ran an airport security wand up and down his body, before he was escorted to a third-floor balcony at the rear of the estate where Prince Saleh was seated sipping champagne. The man, who was in his late forties and educated at Harvard, was obviously Royal family by his bearing. His color was dark, his nose prominent, and his lips and eyelids thick. He was not a pleasant man to be around, in part because of his temper, and in a large part because he thought that he was the smartest guy in any gathering in which he found himself. None of the other royals, including the king himself, bothered him about his attitude, because he made a lot of money.

The prince waved him to a chair. "What took you so long? A flight to Bern amounts to only a few hours, and you were given the passwords. Did you encounter any trouble?"

"None," al-Rashid said. "But as I've already told you there were certain other considerations."

"Yes, to save your precious skin."

Al-Rashid shrugged. "If you wish me to martyr myself, simply say the word."

The prince waved him off. "Did you get it?"

"Yes, of course."

"Of course," the prince shot back. He pursed his lips. "One day you will step over the line: Do you know that?"

"Then you will have to hire someone else. Only there isn't anyone as good as me."

Prince Saleh gave him a cold stare. "You said, other considerations. What considerations?"

"It's a matter of translation," al-Rashid said. He took the diary, wrapped in vellum, from his overnight bag, got up, and reached across the low table and handed it to the prince.

The book was about the size of a short novel, with thick leather covers containing a hundred parchment pages on which the priest Jacob Ambli had drawn maps and diagrams—some showing what appeared to be large mounds or hills, with buried entrances, others showing directions and distances complete with compass bearings on land mass features—as well as page after page of dense writing.

"At first I took the language to be Latin, but it is not that simple," al-Rashid said.

Prince Saleh handled the book with fascination and a great deal of care. He looked up. "What then?"

"I think that it's in a code of some sorts."

"I'll call in a decryption team."

"I would advise against it."

"Oh?"

"To advertise that the diary is in our possession would invite trouble."

Again the prince gave him a cold look. "What trouble?"

"A car bomb went off in Sarasota, Florida, killing a member of the Voltaire Society, from whose bank vault we stole the book."

"Who was responsible?"

"Spanish intelligence."

The prince shrugged. "Why Florida?"

"Presumably the Society representative went to ask Kirk McGarvey to find the diary. The Spanish were waiting for just that to happen, and they killed the Frenchman."

McGarvey was well known by Saudi intelligence. "Did he agree?"

"No. In fact he killed them all, and then disappeared."

The prince thought about it for a moment. "How do you know that the Society asked for McGarvey's help?"

"Speculation. But the timing was right."

The prince tossed the diary on the table. "So now what? As it stands this is worthless to me."

"Which still may be the case even if I manage to have it translated. At the very least this may be nothing more than an urban legend. But at the most the so-called Spanish treasure might amount to only a few billion Euros, all but inaccessible to us somewhere in New Mexico. Possibly in the middle of the military's White Sands Missile Range. A hostile piece of landscape."

The prince waved his hand out to the desert that surrounded them. "We are a desert people, Mahd. And don't turn up your nose at a few billion. Or keeping it from the Americans."

"Or from the Spanish, or the Vatican, or the Voltaire Society."

"Of which we don't know enough."

"Very well, my Prince, what comes next?" al-Rashid asked, though he knew exactly what it would be.

"Have the diary translated, at which time we will plan an operation."

"To retrieve the treasure?"

"No, of course not. I want merely to keep it from everyone else."

Al-Rashid sat back, stunned for just a moment, but then he smiled. "We'll need help, if I understand what you are suggesting."

"Yes," Prince Saleh said. "From the Iranians. There are certain back burner connections I have."

"You would be playing with fire."

"Indeed—if it comes to that." The prince laughed because of the allusion.

THIRTY

□

Louise went upstairs to watch from one of the front bedrooms after she'd bandaged María's slight neck wound. Otto took a position at the living room window and McGarvey and María went to the back of the house from where they could watch the woods. Everyone was in calling distance of one another.

Nothing moved out there, but McGarvey expected the shooter to return, though probably not until after dark.

"I only got a quick glimpse of the guy in the Tahoe, but he sure as hell didn't look like a Cuban to me," María said. She was armed with a lightweight 5.45 mm Russian made PSM semiautomatic pistol that was all but useless except at extremely short range. It had been taken from her four months ago, and Louise had given it back from the gun safe in the front closet.

"I don't think he, was Cuban," McGarvey said.

"Well, who is he, then? He didn't open fire until I showed up."

She was at the breakfast room window adjacent to the kitchen from where McGarvey was watching. "Anything out there?" he called up.

"Nothing yet," Louise said.

"He'll be back," McGarvey said, and he looked at María, who was staring at him.

"Are you going to tell me who he is, and what his gripe with me is?"

"It was you in my apartment in Georgetown. How did you find out about it?"

"I have my sources, you know that. Anyway, how did you know I was there?"

"Your perfume, though you did a good job with my fail-safe on the lock. But what were you doing there?"

"Looking for you," María said. "I knew that you'd be showing up either there, or here, after your little dance in Sarasota." She smiled a little. "It's Chanel, I wanted you to know that it was a woman who had come calling."

"How'd you know about this place?"

"I had Louise followed from the day-care center."

"When?"

"Two months ago."

McGarvey looked away to study the woods again, not exactly sure what he was feeling other than nearly blind anger. Several months ago Cuban intelligence operatives had kidnapped Louise from in front of the day-care center where she'd dropped off Audie. In the process the woman who owned the school had been standing at the open door, children behind her, and had been shot to death. The bullet could easily have missed her and hit one of the kids. Audie.

The whole operation from start to finish had been a cocked-up mess in which María and the Cuban intelligence service had hatched an insane plan to find and steal the Spanish gold just across the border from Ciudad Juárez, Mexico.

A good many people had lost their lives, and at least two dozen Mexican drug cartel spies and spotters had managed to infiltrate the United States and lose themselves in the country somewhere. INS was still looking for them.

In the end she'd gone back to Cuba, presumably to either go to prison or be executed for her role in the operation, yet here she was.

Nothing moved yet in the woods, and McGarvey turned back to her. "The gold doesn't exist," he said. "I thought that you had that much figured out."

"Not according to Dr. Vergilio," María said. Adriana Vergilio was the curator of the Archivo General des Indias, in Seville where all of Spain's records from the exploration and subjugation of the New World were stored. "Something happened a few weeks ago that got her excited enough to warn me that the CNI was on the hunt."

"For the gold?"

"For you," María said. "I didn't think they'd get very far, so I ignored her. Until the car bombing at your university and the shoot-out with the CNI operatives next door to your house." She shook her head. "I couldn't not come." She glanced out the window. "So who is this guy, someone from the CNI gunning for me now that I've come to offer my help?"

"You wouldn't believe me if I told you."

"Well, Dr. Vergilio thinks you know something, and so does the CNI. You must have talked to them. What'd they tell you, or what did they do that made you kill them? Last time I checked, Spain and the United States are not at war."

"They left me no choice."

"You're saying you shot back in self-defense? Who was the guy in the car bombing? One of them?"

McGarvey didn't answer. The entire situation was insane, and was already so out of hand that he couldn't think of a way in which it could be ended in any reasonable way. And yet he knew that he couldn't back away. In fact he'd just as soon put a bullet in María's brain for the danger she and her operatives had put Louise and Otto in, and for the danger his granddaughter was facing right now.

"Goddamnit, I'm risking my life to help you," María shouted.

"You're still looking for the gold, and nothing's changed—you're still willing to pull the trigger on anyone who gets in your way."

"Like the CNI on Casey Key? Was it them who planted the car bomb and killed whoever was—" María suddenly stopped. "Whoever it was had come to the college to talk to you, about the only thing the CNI was so interested in they set up a surveillance operation on you. When whoever it was showed up they killed him."

"And two students who were innocent bystanders."

"Collateral damage," she said indifferently. "But what about this guy gunning for me now? He's not Cuban or Spanish—I don't think. But what's his relationship to whoever got killed in the car bomb? Who is he working for?"

"Go back to Cuba, there's nothing here for you," McGarvey said.

"You need my help with the Spaniards. Especially with Dr. Vergilio. Believe me she's the key, but she won't talk to you. Especially not now."

"Maybe I'll call my friends in Miami to come get you," McGarvey said.

"First we have to get me out of here. But all I came for was Cuba's share of the treasure—if there is any—and I think you know by now that there are a lot of people willing to kill because they think there is.

Just give us a shot in an international court to convince the judges that one-third should belong to us."

McGarvey figured that since the Maltese operative hadn't come in by now, he'd either left or was waiting until after dark. But if he was coming it was because María had shown up, and just like Petain she'd come because she wanted to help find the treasure. It was another factor that the Vatican didn't want.

He went into the dining room, and before María could react he snatched the pistol from her hand. "Your purse is on the hall table. Leave now while you can. He's not going to come after you until dark, and it'll be through the woods. You'll just have to take the chance that he's not watching the front of the house."

"I'm not going to walk away."

"He's probably gone anyway, figuring that either one of us or a neighbor called the police."

"No sirens. Anyway, if he's CNI he's monitoring the police bands."

McGarvey's grip on his pistol tightened. What to do? Shooting her would be easy because of what she had already done to his people. She was a sociopath who didn't give a damn about anyone other than herself. Much like her father had been. She claimed that she'd come to fight for Cuba, but he was almost one hundred percent certain that she'd come to fight for herself, to secure her position in Havana.

And yet in a lot of ways she was an underdog. She'd never had a father, no family, no friends from what he'd been able to gather, and almost all of the people she worked with and for were men in a machismo society that tended to trivialize women, even ones in her powerful position. She'd had to fight for every single thing she'd ever had in her entire life, with no one to help.

She read something of that from his eyes. "Cristo! I won't have you feeling sorry for me. Shoot me if you must, but I don't want your pity!"

McGarvey lowered his pistol, and handed the PSM back to her. "I'm not going to wait for him."

He went back into the hall.

"What's up?" Otto asked.

"He's not coming in until after dark, which means he's holed up somewhere safe until then. I'm going to find him."

Louise came to the head of the stairs. "Watch your step," she warned.

"I don't think he wants me. He wants her."

María had come to the stair hall. "We already know that. What I don't know is who the hell he is."

"He's from the Vatican. The Malta Knights."

María laughed without humor. "Why didn't I think of that? They want the gold and they're just as ruthless as we are."

"Have you dealt with them before?"

"No. Have you?"

"Not till last night," McGarvey said. "Go back to the kitchen and watch the woods."

"What are you planning to do? Drive, keep a lookout, and shoot all at the same time? Two guns are better than one."

"I'm not planning on killing him."

"Maybe he has a different idea," María said.

The house was silent for a beat. "I hate to admit it, but she could be right," Louise said. "Otto will watch the front, and I'll stay up here. If you get yourself killed I'll never speak to you again."

"Get your keys, you're driving," McGarvey told María, and he went to the front door and eased it open.

A blue BMW five hundred series sedan came into the cul-de-sac, and pulled into a driveway of a house across the circle down as the garage door opened.

"The Abbotts," Otto said.

When the garage door came down, McGarvey stepped outside and got into the passenger seat of María's rental Taurus and she slipped behind the wheel.

"The Knights," she said. "They're good."

◻

THIRTY-ONE

Dorestos, on foot, had just come to the opening of the cul-de-sac when McGarvey and the Cuban woman came out of the house. It was unexpected, but it was going to make his job easier than trying to storm the house and not get killed in the process, especially without taking McGarvey out. Though he hoped that day would come.

He ran back to his Tahoe, and drove two blocks away to the McDonald's on Old Dominion Drive, in the opposite direction from the gas station. He parked in the rear, mostly out of sight from the road, and finding the number for the Fairfield Taxi Service called for a cab.

He stuffed the 9 mm SIG Sauer P226 in his belt at the small of his back. Next he unscrewed the long suppressor from the barrel of the compact Ingram MAC 10 and stuffed it in his belt and the two spare magazines of 9 mm ammunition into his jacket pocket. He held the submachine gun under his jacket with his elbow. It was awkward, but only had to do until he got into the taxi.

He waited in the Tahoe for a couple of minutes, then locked up and walked around to the front. A few minutes later the cab showed up and he got into the backseat, giving the driver the address of a five-story government building he'd noticed on the way in.

"The place is locked up by now," the driver, a Pakastani, said.

"I'm meeting someone in the parking lot."

The driver looked at him in the rearview mirror. "I don't want any trouble."

"Neither do I. That's why we're meeting there. So her husband won't find out."

The cabbie smiled. "I get it," he said, and pulled out of the parking lot as the gray Taurus passed.

Dorestos thought that he could make out the figure of a woman driving. McGarvey was in the passenger seat; riding shotgun as it was called. He was about to tell the driver to turn left at the next intersection, but the Taurus turned right, which would take them to the park in the woods behind the Renckes' house.

He'd been spotted in the Tahoe, probably by the Cuban, and she and McGarvey had figured that if an attack against them were to come it would be from that way. It also meant that McGarvey might have spotted the Chevy one too many times for coincidence on the way in from Andrews. The GLONASS real-time satellite system he'd used had made him sloppy.

Five minutes later the cabbie pulled into the nearly deserted Government Services Administration Satellite Office parking lot.

"She'll be in the back," Dorestos said, laying the MAC 10 on the seat and taking the silenced SIG from his belt.

The driver was nervous now but he did as he was told.

"There is no one here," he said.

"No," Dorestos said, and he placed the muzzle of the silencer against the back of the Pakastani's head. "Drive over to the Dumpster, and park."

The cabbie practically jumped out of his skin, his eyes wide. "Please, do not kill me. I have a wife and three children and my mother to support in Lahore. They will starve without me."

"I'm not going to kill you. I just want to use your cab for a few minutes. Won't take very long for the police to find it, if you promise not to call for help for one hour."

"Take anything you want, please."

"Just here," Dorestos said, and they parked in the relative darkness next to a Dumpster. "Get out of the car, and start walking away, around to the other side of the building. But whatever happens do not look over your shoulder."

"I promise."

The cabbie got out and started away. But Dorestos also got out and shot the man once in the back of the head from a distance of less than ten feet and the man went down hard.

"May God go with you, my son," Dorestos said, and he glanced up at the office windows, but so far as he could tell there were no witnesses.

He jammed the pistol back in his belt and, careful to keep the man's blood off his clothes, picked up the body as if it were nothing much heavier than a pocket edition of the Ordinations, carried it over to the Dumpster, opened the lid partway with one hand, and rolled the body inside.

He transferred the MAC 10 from the backseat, screwed the silencer on the barrel, and stuffed the weapon between the driver's seat and the transmission hump. He drove off toward the road that led to the park at the edge of the woods.

In his estimation his assignment thus far had made little or no sense. Of course he would never voice such an opinion to Msgr. Franelli; though he was still a little naive despite his experiences, he wasn't stupid.

McGarvey was the key, always had been according to the monsignore. The Society had sent a man seeking his help, and the CNI operatives had killed him. Otherwise it would have been Dorestos's job of work.

McGarvey himself had taken out three of the Spaniards leaving only the fourth.

Now the Cuban had come seeking help, and she was to be assassinated. From that point—should he be successful tonight—it would be a matter of following McGarvey and his friends the Renckes. But if that didn't work, if for whatever reason McGarvey decided not to pursue the search, there was always his granddaughter as a force multiplier.

The deeper he got into this assignment the more he'd come to realize that everything he'd been tasked to do had almost certainly been ordered under desperation. Which was the part that made no sense to him. A few billions in gold and silver and other artifacts were but a drop in the bucket to the Mother Church. And considering the risks, it could turn out to be a public relations disaster much worse than had arisen over shielding pedophile priests.

But he was a son of the Holy Church that had given him a meaningful life.

At the park he slowed down as he approached the short turnoff. The gray Taurus was there, as he thought it would be, but neither McGarvey nor the woman were in sight. Expecting an attack from this direction they had left the car, announcing they were here, and had gone into the woods to wait. It was bait, and it rankled Dorestos just a little that McGarvey had assumed it would work.

They would be hiding just within sight of anyone coming from the parking area. The woman was the bait and McGarvey would be some-where very close to her. But he figured that if they were smart they would have gone deeply enough into the woods to a spot where they could also watch the back of the house.

He parked just behind the Taurus, and stood for a long moment lis-tening to the sounds of the deepening evening. A car passed on the road, and then a pickup truck. When they were gone he raised his head and drew a deep breath through his nose. Perfume. The same as he had de-tected at McGarvey's apartment in Georgetown.

Taking the MAC 10, he walked away from the cab to the eastern end of the narrow parking lot and angled away from the road. Twenty meters in, he stopped again to listen for the sounds of movement somewhere ahead, but hearing nothing. He stashed the submachine gun in some brush and started back to where he figured they would be waiting for him. Only he was going to give them what would be a nasty surprise.

THIRTY-TWO

McGarvey stepped out from behind the bole of a tree at the edge of the Renckes' backyard and waved at Louise, who appeared in an upstairs window. He stepped back to where María was waiting and they put their heads together.

"If he comes this way, which I think he might, he'll want you, not me."

"You've already said that, but why? Does he think I'm a distraction?"

"Probably exactly that," McGarvey said, and he held up a hand. He'd thought he'd heard something to the left, in the direction of the park. But the slight noise, whatever it was, did not come again.

"Him?" she whispered.

"I'm going out about ten meters to the right, and you're going to stay here in plain sight."

She laughed. "I'm not going to let myself be a sitting duck. If I get the chance I'll shoot the bastard."

"I want him alive. He won't take the shot until he knows where I am."

"Then what?"

"I have a couple of questions for him," McGarvey said, and he cocked an ear to listen again, but there was nothing except street sounds. He started away, but María touched his arm.

"I'm putting my life in your hands," she said. "Again."

"You should have stayed in Havana."

"Not possible for me."

McGarvey's first instinct when she'd showed up had been to telephone Callahan and have the FBI arrest her. But he hadn't done that because it was likely that any search for the diary would lead back to the archives in Seville, and María was the key to open that door for him. And it also occurred to him that the Knights had sent someone from Malta to keep him away from Spain—who had a claim on the treasure. And had ordered their man to keep Cuba out of it. Which left only the members of the Voltaire Society, if they could be found.

A bullet smacked into the tree just inches to their right, and McGarvey shoved María to the ground with one hand as he pulled off two shots in the direction he'd thought he'd heard the rustle of bushes a few minutes earlier.

"I'm not your enemy, Signore McGarvey," Dorestos called softly. He was very close.

"Why did you come here?" McGarvey asked. The man was off to the left.

"To protect you."

"From a woman?"

"From the Cuban intelligence apparatus in Washington that she controls. Move away from her and I will solve that problem for you."

"Then what?" McGarvey asked. He motioned for María to keep her head down and he started away on hands and knees at right angles to where he thought the shooter stood.

"I will walk away and leave you in peace."

McGarvey rose up a few inches and tried to pick out a darker shadow against the darkness. The only lights were of the houses behind him, and of the streetlights along the road, but none of that penetrated very deeply into the woods. Nothing moved.

"But not me," María said.

"No," Dorestos said.

María fired three shots, the small caliber unsilenced rounds making small pops.

Dorestos immediately fired two rounds, silenced, but close enough so that McGarvey could make out the right direction, and he headed off to the left, not caring how much noise he was making.

María fired two more shots, and Dorestos fired again. This time María cried out in pain. She'd been hit.

The dark figure of a very large man darted impossibly fast from right to left about ten meters from McGarvey's position, and disappeared.

"María?" McGarvey called, but she didn't answer.

"She is dead," Dorestos said, this time very close.

McGarvey feinted left, and moving on the balls of his feet brought his pistol up, as the very large man—nearly seven feet tall, and built like an Olympic pentathlon athlete in his prime—stepped from behind a tree. He held a pistol pointed at the ground.

"I mean you no harm," he said, his voice high-pitched. But he wasn't out of breath despite the speed with which he'd moved.

"What do you want of me?" McGarvey asked, keeping his pistol trained center mass.

"Only to provide you the opportunity to do your job."

"Which is?"

"You know," Dorestos said.

"I'm retired."

Dorestos shook his head. "Not since those two children were murdered in the parking lot of your school."

"Were you there?"

"No. But I saw the images. I was given the report, and I know how you must feel."

McGarvey glanced over his shoulder, his aim never varying. When he turned back the man was gone.

"You owe that woman no allegiance." The man's voice came from the darkness to the left.

McGarvey remained where he was, the bole of a reasonably sized tree a few feet on his left. "The monks in Mexico City stole the gold from Spain, who stole it from the natives, including Cubans. Your church has no claim."

"It is viewed differently in certain circles."

"Leave me alone," McGarvey said. "Or the next time I see you I'll kill you."

"Find the diary," Dorestos said. "I'll be close." He was farther away, back toward the road and moving now.

McGarvey started after him, but after a few steps he stopped, and held his breath to listen. The night was silent until a car started up and drove off. The man's speed was incredible, almost supernatural.

Holstering his pistol, he turned and hurried back to María who lay on her back, gasping for air. Blood oozed from a chest wound. She was conscious and she looked up at him, her eyes fluttering.

"He's gone," McGarvey said. He placed her hands, one atop the other, over the wound. "Press down, it'll help."

She did it, and immediately her breathing came a little easier. "Why are you doing this for me?" she wheezed.

"Beats the hell out of me," he said. "I'm going to have Louise call for an ambulance. I'll be right back."

"I won't move," she said, blood seeping from the corners of her mouth. "You'll have to put up with me for the duration."

THIRTY-THREE

□

At Le Bourget airport outside of Paris, al-Rashid told his pilot, second officer, and a young, pretty attendant Alicia, to stand down, but to be ready at a moment's notice should he need them again. It was nine in the morning, the day a little cloudy, and compared to Saudi Arabia, very cool.

"As always, sir," Muhammad Saeed, his pilot, said at the open cockpit door. Saeed had been his squadron vice commander in the Saudi Air Force. They'd been together with handpicked crews ever since.

It was about money, of course, and prestige: working for al-Rashid was by extension working for Prince Saleh. Plus the freedom. Wherever they stopped, they were free to come and go and do as they chose, the only condition was that they were on call 24/7.

Al-Rashid, wearing a double-breasted blue blazer, white linen slacks, and an open-collar off-white shirt, took a cab into town, and checked in at the Inter-Continental, the understated hotel near the Tuileries Gardens where he always stayed when in transit through France.

Alain Baptiste, the day manager, came out of his office and shook hands. "It has been several months since we've last seen you, Monsieur Montessier. Welcome back."

"Thank you, Paris continues to be my favorite city."

"Will you be staying long?"

"One or two days, perhaps a little longer. It depends on business."

"The suite is yours for as long as you need it. Will you require the aid of Mademoiselle Frery?" The woman was the hotel's main concierge.

"Not today," al-Rashid said, and he shook hands again, a custom he'd always detested.

Upstairs he gave the bellman who'd carried up his two bags a generous tip, and when he was alone he ordered up a pot of tea with lemon, and a bottle of chilled mineral water. He took a shower as he waited, and when his order arrived, he took a file from his carry-on bag and opened it on the coffee table.

The man who'd gone to the United States to ask for McGarvey's help finding the diary was Giscarde Petain, who had been one of the senior officers of the small and highly secretive banking group known for the last century and a half as the Voltaire Society. To this point al-Rashid had been unable to find exactly what this group's avowed purpose was, except that it apparently had the means in place to find and plunder several caches of Spanish treasure buried in the desert of the American southwest. This apparently under the noses of the local authorities.

Saudi intelligence had come up with the proper banking codes for the safety deposit box in Bern, at a branch of the Berner Kantonal Bank on Schwanengasse, apparently from a contact inside the bank's main offices with strong financial ties to the Saudi Royal family through Prince Saleh.

Getting his hands on the book had been as easy as strolling into the bank and presenting his credentials and the proper passwords. The surprise had come when he'd gotten back to his hotel and tried to read the thing. It was in Latin, a dead language he was reasonably proficient in as were almost all Oxford graduates, but it was in a code that someone within the Voltaire Society would know how to crack.

The only lead to the Society was Petain himself, whose photograph had been identified by the banker in Bern as the man who'd come six months earlier with the proper passwords. He'd stayed one hour, during which time he'd required the use of a copy machine. When he was gone it was discovered that the copy machine's internal mechanism had been tampered with in such a fashion that no record existed of what had been copied.

Their contact did supply them with an address for Petain in Paris's upscale, though mostly commercial, Second Arrondissement, just a few blocks north of the Louvre, and only a short taxi ride from the Inter-Continental.

The banker's written testimony was included in the dossier. *"We are told that he has a wife, Sophie, and one boy, Edouard, who is thirteen."*

The only photographs had been taken from two surveillance cameras at the bank on the day Petain had shown up and spent the hour.

Al-Rashid sat back with his tea as he stared at the photos. Petain had appeared to be a tall man, slender, with a Gallic nose and angular cheek bones. In one he'd looked up at the camera, an almost arrogant sneer on his lips, as if to say that he knew something secret, that he was on a mission of importance.

Now the man was dead, killed by Spanish intelligence agents who had set up shop in the United States for the sole purpose of stopping the Frenchman from bringing a message to Kirk McGarvey, the former director of the CIA.

Intriguing, but the conclusion that al-Rashid had come to was that the CNI had failed, and that they would have been better served by capturing Petain and forcing the man to tell them about the diary and who he thought might have taken it from the bank. But of course the Frenchman could not have known about the banker friendly to Prince Saleh because al-Rashid's second task after retrieving the book was killing the banker.

And now Paris. Sophie and Edouard.

Al-Rashid finished his tea then laid down to sleep; the hours in the air over the past days through several times zones was tiring and he was exhausted. He did not dream. He never dreamed.

He got up around six in the afternoon, took another shower, then got dressed in the same blazer, but this time with a black Polo buttoned at the neck, dark slacks, and three-hole British-made black walkers, which were not only sturdy and comfortable, but reasonably fashionable, obviously expensive as was all his clothing.

He went down to the lobby a few minutes after seven. Baptiste, Mme. Frery, and the others who'd been on duty when he'd checked in were gone for the day and he passed all but unnoticed out the front doors where the doorman hailed him a taxi.

Madame Petain lived in a second-floor apartment facing the Rue Gaillon, as chance would have it, just a half a block from the Drouant restaurant and sidewalk café. He had the driver take him to the restaurant, passing the apartment, the windows of which were dark.

The restaurant was mostly full, but al-Rashid's French was perfect and the one hundred euro note he handed to the maître'd got him a sidewalk table from where he could watch the apartment building, including its front entrance.

He ordered a bottle of sparkling mineral water, and a demi of Pinot Grigio to go with an order of warm oysters served with caviar that was one of the restaurant's inside specialties, but from time to time might be served outside.

The problem he faced was not one of squeamishness dealing with the widow and her son to find the name or names of other Society members—one of whom would hopefully have the key to the diary's code—but of the possibility that she wouldn't know.

Her husband's body, or what remained of it, was being held for now in the United States during the murder investigation, but if Madame Petain were to die, the people who came to her funeral would likely provide a clue.

That possibility would take time, and could very well end up messy with him on the run from the French police. Neither outcome was particularly disturbing to him, except for the time it would waste.

His drinks came first, and shortly afterward his meal on the heels of which a taxi pulled up in front of the apartment building. A slender woman got out, followed by a gangly boy and they went inside. A minute later the windows of the second-floor apartment were illuminated one by one. Madame Petain and her son were home, and no one else was with them.

Al-Rashid took his time with his light meal, especially enjoying the saltiness of the caviar and the bite of the ice-cold wine. When he was finished he tipped well, got up, and strolled leisurely in the opposite direction of the Petain's apartment.

The fifteen minutes or so it would take for him to circle the block and come in from the other end of the Rue would give the woman and her son time to settle down, and him the time to make certain that no bodyguard or guards had been assigned to her by the Society.

THIRTY-FOUR

☐

María had been taken to All Saints Hospital on a quiet street not far from Georgetown University Hospital. It was the go-to place that the CIA and many of the other U.S intelligence agencies in the area used when discretion was important. She'd been stabilized overnight and since noon had been in one of the operating rooms under the care of Dr. Alan Franklin. It was three in the afternoon now. McGarvey and Otto sat drinking coffee in the third-floor waiting room. It had been a long night.

"Bambridge is going to raise all kinds of holy hell once he finds out she's here," Otto said. Marty Bambridge was the CIA's deputy director of the National Clandestine Services, and was a by-the-book asshole, though he did run a tight ship.

"He'll get over it. In the meantime we still don't know if she came up here on her own, or even what her situation is in Havana. She could be on the run."

"She's here to redeem herself."

"Probably," McGarvey said. It was hard for him to focus. He'd been here twice to have Dr. Franklin repair wounds, and again when his son-in-law had been assassinated. Remembering the look on Katy's face, and the overwhelming grief on their daughter's was almost more than he could bear.

"It's not the same, *kemo sabe*," Otto said, reading almost all of that from McGarvey's posture. "She's not your responsibility. She's an intelligence officer from a foreign nation that we don't have diplomatic relations with. She's killed people and she'll do it again."

McGarvey looked up, suddenly realizing what Otto was getting at. "I was thinking about Todd and about Katy and Liz, not Colonel León. Trust me. She came here and got herself shot up, not my problem. What

I need to know is why the bastard from the Church didn't take me out too."

"They want you to lead them to the diary. The one that supposedly doesn't exist that shows the way to Cibola that also doesn't exist. But the one that people are willing to kill for. And are willing to herd you toward finding it."

"But why me?"

"Because you came damned close a few months ago. And once you get the bit in your mouth you never let go."

"Not interested."

"Sure you are. When Kim Jong Il called, you went to help. Same as when Fidel Castro sent his daughter. Now you'll do it if for no other reason than the two kids who got killed on campus, just for being in the wrong place at the wrong time." Otto looked up. "Anyway you better decide what you want to do because Marty's here."

Bambridge barged down the corridor from the elevator. He was short and thin with dark angry eyes and thick black hair, and he moved as if his feet hurt, and that fact, along with everything else, surprised him. He wore a dark blue old-fashioned three-piece suit

"We expected you on campus to be debriefed yesterday after the mess you created in Sarasota," he said even before he reached the waiting room. "And now this."

McGarvey almost laughed. "You're going to have a heart attack one of these days."

"You listen to me, we've had enough. Bringing an enemy intelligence agent here is nothing short of unconscionable. I want her gone."

"Where to?"

A nurse scurried down the hall. "Please," she said sternly. "This *is* a hospital."

Bambridge turned on her. "You've admitted a woman with a gunshot wound. I want her moved immediately."

"She's in the operating room."

"I don't care—"

"You're an idiot," the nurse shot back. She turned to McGarvey. "Doctor Franklin is just finishing up. He says she'll recover with nothing more than a scar."

"When can she get out of here?" McGarvey asked.

"A couple of days. Maybe a week. Friend of yours?"

"In a manner of speaking," McGarvey said, completely out of his funk.

The nurse gave Bambridge another sharp look and left.

Bambridge sat down across from McGarvey and Otto. "Look, I'm serious about this, and I have Walt's backing. As soon as she's able to move I want her out of here. This is a place for heroes—American heroes."

"And in this case a wounded asset, Marty. She stays until she's ready to move under her own power. If she's transferred to another hospital or if you try to send her back to Cuba right now, the same guy who shot her will try again. And he was good enough to get past me."

"All the more reason to dump her. If someone wants to take her down, it'd be fine with us." Bambridge sat forward and appealed to Rencke. "She ordered the kidnapping of your wife during which a teacher was killed at the day school where your kid had just been dropped off. Do you think that she'd have any qualms about trying something just as nasty as that if she thought the need was there?"

"She released her unharmed after I went to Havana for the funeral and Mac showed up to answer her questions. It was a crazy stupid stunt she pulled, and people did get hurt, a lot of them."

Bambridge turned back to McGarvey. "What did you mean, asset?"

"I'm going to take her to Seville with me as soon as she's fit to travel."

"Not a chance in hell. After what happened in Florida you're not going anywhere near Spain. As it is the White House is all over us for an explanation because as it stands neither our government nor Madrid's has any idea how to handle this mess you created."

"I don't expect they do. But I'll make a deal with you. Send some babysitters over here to keep watch over her. There's a possibility that the shooter will try to get to her as soon as I leave."

"You're not going to Spain—"

"First I'm going to talk to Bill Callahan about Cuba's intel operations here in the Washington area. If Colonel León did show up to spearhead some operation I want to know about it before I provide her a cover. Could be the Bureau will arrest her as a spy and exchange her for one of ours in Havana."

"We're clean in Cuba for the moment," Bambridge said.

"What else?"

"At the very least Walt wants you to come out to Langley for a chat and a debrief. We have to figure out some response for the Spanish situation. They're accusing us of mounting a counter-intel ops that resulted in the deaths of four of their people. They mentioned your name."

"They were spying on me, and when I found out about it I went over to talk to them. They opened fire first."

"But you went over there armed."

"It would have turned out differently had I not," McGarvey said. "They were responsible for the car bombing at New College."

"We're interested in that event too. Like who the guy in the car was, and what was his connection to you?"

"Bring the babysitters and I'll come out to Langley to tell you guys everything. But I'll want Callahan in on my debriefing so I won't have to go over the same material twice. I don't have the time."

Bambridge was frustrated even though he'd gotten just about everything he wanted, except for María's immediate expulsion from the hospital. And McGarvey felt some pity for the poor bastard. He himself had worked briefly as the deputy director of the clandestine services, that in the old days had been called the directorate of operations, and understood the enormous pressures the man was under. Dealing with NOCs—who tended to be super-independent people—was like herding cats only with deadly consequences, not only physically but politically.

The Spanish mission to spy on a former DCI that had ended up in the deaths of four of their operatives was highly embarrassing to the Spaniards, who at the moment were depending not only on the EU for economic bailouts, but on the United States for serious financial help. It was one of the reasons, McGarvey supposed, that Madrid wanted a piece of the treasure. A few billions would help their bottom line.

"I'll have Callahan on campus at five," Bambridge said. "Walt's office. I'll expect you not only to show up but to cooperate."

THIRTY-FIVE

□

The evening had turned chilly and standing at the corner from the Petain apartment al-Rashid turned up the collar of his jacket and put a Gauloises at the corner of his mouth. He didn't have the habit, but he'd found that a man smoking a cigarette was a distraction. The cigarette itself became a focus.

He'd spotted the bodyguard behind the wheel of a white Citroën DS4 hatchback parked across the street. The driver's window was open and the man was smoking a cigarette.

Crossing the Rue he meandered down the street where at the parked car he checked to make sure that no one was paying any attention to him and stepped around to the driver's side. Music came from the restaurant and someone was singing some tune but terribly off-key.

The bodyguard looked up. "What do you want, then?" He was a very large man, possibly a Corsican hood, al-Rashid thought. They considered themselves bully boys.

"A light, monsieur, if you please."

"Fuck off."

Al-Rashid took the unlit cigarette out of his mouth and tossed it away. "Mind your manners, mate," he said.

The Frenchman, realizing that something might be wrong, reached inside his jacket, but al-Rashid clamped a powerful hand around the man's throat, cutting off his breath and the blood flow from his carotid arteries.

It took less than a minute for the big man's desperate struggles to subside, but he'd been constrained by the narrow confines of the small car and had not been able to fight back effectively.

Al-Rashid released the pressure. "Who has sent you to keep watch on Madame Petain?"

The Corsican began to regain his senses and he reached again for his pistol, but al-Rashid batted his hand away.

"Quickly, who has sent you here? Was it someone from the Voltaire Society? I need a name."

The bodyguard lunged forward, but al-Rashid clamped one hand around the man's neck again. Almost instantly the Corsican settled back, and al-Rashid released his hold.

This time the guard slammed a meaty fist through the window, but al-Rashid slipped the punch, shoved the man's head back against the headrest, and clamped a powerful grip around his neck. This time he did not let go.

"You are an ignorant *salopard*, and mine is the last face you'll ever see."

It did not take long for the Corsican's struggles to cease. A minute later his heart stopped, and thirty seconds after that he was beyond reviving.

Al-Rashid took the cigarette from the man's lap where it had burned a hole in his trousers, and tossed it away.

He looked around, but still no one had noticed anything untoward.

He searched the body, coming up with a wallet and French National Identity Card in the name of Ghjuvan Petrus, which was the Corsican equivalent of John Peters, along with an American-made Wilson tactical conceal .45 caliber pistol. It was only a nine-shot semiauto, but it was one of the most accurate handguns in the world. The pistol of a confident man.

Al-Rashid pocketed the wallet, but left the gun in place. He powered up the window, took the keys, and locked the doors. With no visible signs of an injury or a struggle, the man was just another drunk parked at the curb, sleeping it off.

A taxi passed, and when it was gone al-Rashid crossed the street and inside the entry hall of the apartment building pressed the button for 2A. Moments later Sophie Petain answered.

"Oui?"

"It is I, Ghjuvan from the street. A man has delivered papers for you."

"What papers?"

"Concerning your husband, madame. From the Society."

"I don't know what you are talking about. But leave them in the mail slot downstairs and I'll have my lawyer look at them in the morning. Good evening, monsieur."

She was lying. Al-Rashid could hear it in her voice, though he didn't know what she was lying about. "Please, madame, I may lose my job. I was ordered to bring these to you."

The elevator door opened. "Come up if you must."

Al-Rashid rode the elevator to the second floor and went to her apartment. The building was very quiet. He knocked on the door. "Madame?"

"Slip them under the door."

"They will not fit such a narrow opening."

"*Merde,*" Madame Petain said. She unlatched the lock.

The moment the door was open far enough for al-Rashid to see that the foolish woman had not fitted a safety chain, he shoved it the rest of the way. Pushing her aside before she could resist, he stepped into the apartment's entry vestibule, and closed and locked the door.

The boy appeared at the end of the short corridor into the living room.

"Edouard, telephone the police," the woman cried.

Al-Rashid shoved her against the wall, clamped a hand on her mouth, and turned to the boy, who stood rooted to the spot. "I do not wish to harm your mother, but I will if you attempt to call for help. Do you understand?"

The boy nodded. "Are you the man who killed my father?"

"No. But I know who did, and I need your mother's help to bring them to justice, *hein.*"

The boy nodded again.

"Do not cry out," al-Rashid told the woman, and she blinked her eyes. He took his hand away from her mouth and pulled her into the expensively furnished living room where he had her and her son sit together on the couch.

"You have brought no papers for me after all," Madame Petain said. She looked haggard. It had only been a couple of days since her husband's death and it showed.

"No, and forgive me for the little ruse, but I needed to speak with you about the Society, that your husband gave his life for."

"I do not know what you are talking about. My husband was a private equity banker, nothing more. I knew that he was traveling out of France on business, but I had no idea where until I received word that he had died in an explosion."

"Who brought you this news?"

"The police."

"The Sûreté or the DGSE?" al-Rashid asked. The first were the civil police, the second France's intelligence service.

"The man was from Interpol," Madame Petain said. She'd gotten her second wind. "You are not a bodyguard. Who are you to come to me like this?"

"You are accustomed to bodyguards. Who arranged them for you?"

"My husband, whenever he was away," she said defiantly. "Now I demand that you leave."

"Indeed I will, and I apologize for the trouble I have caused you, madame," al-Rashid said. "Where is your husband's office?"

"I don't know."

Al-Rashid laughed. "Does he take a taxi or the Metro or does a car come for him?"

"Go!" the woman shouted.

Al-Rashid was on her in an instant and he slapped her very hard in the face, rocking her head back. "Answer me, you silly woman, or I will kill you."

Madame Petain was speechless, and al-Rashid raised his hand against her again, but the boy cried out.

"My father's office is in the next block. He walks to work each morning. I followed him once."

"What is the number?"

The boy gave it to him.

The woman glanced toward the windows. She was frightened. "You have what you want, now leave," she said.

"Oui," al-Rashid said. He leaned down over her as if he was going to kiss her forehead; instead he took her narrow face in both hands and twisted sharply to the right, breaking her neck.

The boy scrambled backward over the couch and reached the front vestibule before al-Rashid caught up with him and broke his neck.

He stood for a long half minute listening to the near absence of noise in the building, waiting for someone to come knocking at the door to find out what the fuss in 2A was all about, or for the sound of a distant police siren converging. But no alarm had been raised.

He went back into the apartment and began his methodical search.

THIRTY-SIX

□

Washington's rush hour traffic was in full swing when McGarvey took a cab from the hospital out to CIA headquarters in the wooded hills across the George Washington Parkway from the Potomac River. The weather, which had been clear for the past twenty-four hours, had clouded up, the heat and humidity oppressive; a thick wet blanket had been thrown over the capitol and surroundings, deepening moods and sharpening the tempers of anyone out in it.

A guard came out, gave the cabdriver a temporary visitor's permit that would allow him to drive to the Original Headquarters Building, drop off his passenger, and immediately return to the gate, and then looked through the back-door window that McGarvey had lowered.

"Someone will be waiting for you in the lobby, Mr. Director," he said. "Welcome back."

"Thanks," McGarvey said, and on the short curving drive through the woods and around the main parking lot to the seven-story OHB a lot of memories, some of them good but many of them bad, came back to him in living color.

Everything seemed the same, and yet so much had changed, especially the technology that had been developed—and continued to be developed—between the Company and the National Security Agency. Otto had explained some of what they already had and what was on the near horizon—completely unbreakable quantum effects encryption that tied in with QE computers that could work a million times faster than current microchip machines, and were by many definitions either already on the border with artificial intelligence, or just across it. Holographic memories that could not only accurately display a current time and place, but could remember the past as well as predict certain future events.

"All sci-fi to you," Otto had said, not derisively. "But then you're a people person. You see things that no machine in the pipeline is capable of. Instincts, hunches."

"Sometimes wrong," McGarvey had told his old friend.

Otto laughed. "You ever heard of a computer that never makes mistakes?"

"Even yours?"

"Especially mine. Why do you think I keep tinkering with them?"

The weapons and weapons systems were changing too; his old Walther PPK, the stuff of James Bond movies of the sixties, had evolved to weapons that fired smart bullets that could be guided to change directions in flight to seek out and kill a target—such as a human being—that emitted infrared radiation. Pulse weapons that sent a high-pitched pulse of sound so sharply focused and yet so loud that a human target could be stunned to unconsciousness. And if the pulse energy were raised by a factor of only two or three the target's brain would develop an instantly fatal number of tiny hemorrhages. Or nearly silent unmanned drones carrying hellfire missiles that could be controlled from bases halfway around the world from their targets.

But all of that technology was of little use this time around because at issue was a mystery that had its beginning the moment Columbus had set foot in the New World and had discovered a native wearing a gold necklace.

Just as Donald Rumsfeld, the secretary of defense, had told reporters after the attacks on 9/11—none of our advanced weapons systems, our nuclear submarines and missiles and stealth fighters and aircraft carriers could have prevented this from happening.

Boots on the ground. Human assets, even if they only carried Walthers.

Bambridge was waiting for him in the very busy main lobby. It was quarter after five, right in the middle of the shift change. "You're late," he said, handing McGarvey a visitor's badge.

"Yes."

"What happened to Otto?"

"He moved Louise to another safe house."

"Where?"

"You'll have to ask him that. But thanks for sending someone out to keep watch on Colonel León. She could be important."

Bambridge was clearly frustrated. He wanted to lash out.

They went through the guard points and then left down the broad corridor to a bank of elevators. "She'll be discharged in a couple of days, but she won't be in any shape to climb over walls with you. We're going to send her back to Havana. She can recuperate there."

McGarvey didn't bother replying. From any realistic point of view Bambridge was correct. María León was no friend of the United States. She didn't belong here.

Walter Page was waiting for them in his office, along with Bill Callahan and Carleton Patterson, a slender white-haired man in his early eighties who'd been the CIA's general counsel forever. The only one missing was Fred Atwell, who was the new deputy director and who would almost certainly take over after Page left. He was a White House favorite, who'd worked as special adviser on foreign affairs to the current president but who'd campaigned hard to get his present job the moment Page had announced his intention to retire.

They all shook hands and sat around an oval coffee table after they got coffee from a silver service on a cart.

"Fred couldn't join us this afternoon," Page said. "He's in Ohio campaigning with the president."

"A good place for him to be," McGarvey said, and the others, even Bambridge, chuckled. No one liked the man. From what McGarvey had heard Atwell was purely a political creature. The man knew absolutely nothing about intelligence gathering.

"The ball's in your court, dear boy," Patterson said. Of the others in the DCI's office his was the most unflappable persona. He'd seen practically everything during his tenure. He and McGarvey had a mutual respect.

"Spanish gold buried in our desert southwest. Mostly New Mexico, maybe some in Texas."

"A fairy tale," Bambridge said. Page tried to hold him off, but he plowed on. "After the last debacle down at Holloman, we went through government records back as early as eighteen twelve. And I do mean with a fine-toothed comb. Some damned fine archivists were called in and did the work on a contract basis. Totally apolitical. Nothing was found. Not one piece of documentation that there is or ever was any cache of treasure brought up to New Mexico by disgruntled monks from Mexico City. Urban legend, every scrap of it."

"The Cuban government was and is still interested," McGarvey said.

Bambridge waved it off disparagingly.

"Spain is interested enough to send people to watch me."

"Spanish treasure galleons sunk off the Florida coast, or even out in the Atlantic around the Azores. Spain has a legitimate claim, which has been worked out in courts of law. We've been that route. But not on dry land in the United States."

"The Vatican is interested. They claim that the treasure belongs to the Church."

Page was interested. "Was it someone from Rome who was blown up in the car?"

"No. But the person who killed the fourth CNI operative—the one who was found in the rental house on Siesta Key—was almost likely from the Church. The Knights Hospitallers."

No one said a word. Even Bambridge was temporarily at a loss.

McGarvey explained what had happened at his house, and again in the woods behind the Renckes' place. "He eliminated the last of the CNI operatives, and he meant to eliminate Colonel León, warning me that she was spearheading a Cuban intel op here in D.C."

"Nothing is showing up on our radar at the moment," Callahan said. "Which brings us back to your Voltaire Society."

"I haven't heard of this wrinkle," Patterson said.

"The man who came to the college to see me identified himself as Giscarde Petain, said he worked for something called the Voltaire Society. Apparently it is a group of bankers who have been doing their damnedest to keep money away from the Vatican since the eighteen hundreds. Evidently it was something suggested by the philosopher just before his death. He hated the Church, and I think this was some sort of a joke—his parting shot."

"And this Petain came to you for what reason?" Patterson asked. No one else seemed to want to speak up.

"According to him the Church sent one of its Maltese operatives as a spy on a Spanish military expedition to what's now New Mexico to find and map the buried caches of gold and silver. Which he did as the expedition's surveyor and mapmaker. He kept two journals—one of them false that he gave to the soldiers when they got back and the other a true account that he kept to bring back to Rome. He was lost at sea, killed by the Voltaires who took his diary."

"Christ," Bambridge said, but again Page held him off.

"You have our attention, dear boy," Patterson said.

"The diary was brought back to Paris where it was studied, and then was locked up in a bank vault in Bern. Supposedly the Spanish expedition found seven caches of gold—the seven cities of Cibola—and since then the Voltaires have plundered three of them."

"And did what with the treasure?"

"I don't know. But Otto thinks they made at least one payment to a bank in Richmond well before the Civil War."

Patterson smiled. "Well," he said. He exchanged a glance with Page.

"The diary was stolen from the bank vault, and Petain was sent to ask for my help finding it," McGarvey said, and the momentary silence that followed was in no way surprising to him.

Page was first. "Mac, you have to understand the great deal of respect that this agency owes you, the thanks the entire nation owes you."

"The story is fantastic, Walt. I don't know what to believe myself. But the fact is the Spanish government, possibly the Catholic Church, the Cuban government, something calling itself the Voltaire Society, which has already given our government money, are interested enough to kill for it. And among the dead are two young college students who were killed while I watched, and I couldn't do a damned thing about it."

Page spread his hands. "What do you want?"

"Stay out of my way."

"I don't know if we can do that," Bambridge said. "There's to be at least a coroner's hearing in Sarasota."

McGarvey got up. The reaction was about what he'd expected, and he couldn't honestly blame them. The story was at the very least far-fetched. But the bodies were real, and someone would have to answer for them. He headed for the door.

"What will you do now?" Patterson asked after him.

"Find the diary," McGarvey said without turning back.

THIRTY-SEVEN

□

Giscarde Petain had been a careful man, a precise man. His walk-in closet, separate from his wife's, was in perfect order. Trousers left to right in color sequence, light to dark. His shirts all facing left, the same with his suit coats. His ties were on an ingenious rack, as were his shoes in their own—at least two dozen pairs. His hats were in boxes, and his sweaters were arranged in cedar-lined drawers. Even his stockings and linens were ironed and set in order.

Al-Rashid stood in the middle of the master suite trying to get a sense of the man, and by extension perhaps, of the Voltaire Society. The apartment was quiet. No noises from the rest of the building or from outside on the street intruded. This was a serene place. An inner sanctum. A castle keep where a man with his family under siege could maintain if not his personal safety at least his secrets.

He'd made a cursory search of the place, finding nothing but the man's super-organized closet. This time he started again in the living room, ignoring Madame Petain's and the boy's bodies, and looked for what he had missed. Perhaps the obvious.

An hour and a half later, after going through the living room, dining room, kitchen and pantry, three bedrooms, two and a half bathrooms, all the closets, and the laptop in the man's study, which yielded absolutely nothing except that Petain had a penchant for pornography involving very young girls all of them prepubescent, he found himself back where he'd started from.

Frustrated, he went to the broad windows looking down on the street, parted the curtains a little to watch the sparse traffic, but then let them fall and perched on the window ledge that was wide enough to be used as a seat.

The seat was loose.

Al-Rashid got to his feet. Everything else in the apartment had been in perfect order, nothing had been out of place. Now this. Either someone else—Madame Petain or the boy—had pulled the ledge up, or this was a booby trap; open the lid and the apartment would blow. But that made no sense.

Getting down on his knees he examined the length of the ledge and spotted what could have been two spring-loaded catches, only one of which was engaged. He pressed the other and the ledge rose up on hinges.

Inside was a narrow compartment about three feet deep, at the bottom of which was a leather-bound case about the size of a slim hardcover book.

Making sure that the case wasn't itself booby trapped, al-Rashid pulled it out and opened it. The thing was an ordinary iPad. He powered it up and the first page contained a couple of lines of what appeared to be Latin in the same sort of code as the diary was written in. Below that was a blank box, obviously meant for a password. But in the bottom right-hand corner was an address on the Rue Gaillon.

Al-Rashid looked at the body of the boy lying in the corridor. The kid had lied to him. The address he'd given for his father's office was different from the one on the iPad. It probably meant that Madame Petain had also known the truth not only about where her husband worked but what he did. She'd known about the Society.

After the boy had blurted out his father's address the woman had looked at the window. At the time al-Rashid thought that she was perhaps looking for help, maybe the flashing lights of a police unit. But it had been the secret window ledge compartment, which she'd opened and failed to properly close.

Turning off the iPad, he stuffed it in his belt at the small of his back, closed the ledge, and left the apartment, someone up the street still singing terribly off tune.

The Second Arrondissement along with the Eighth and Ninth constituted one of the city's most important business districts, where a great number of bank headquarters along with the Greek-styled building that had once held the Paris Bourse—the stock exchange—were located.

During the day the area was as busy as was New York's Wall Street, but at this hour of the evening only the restaurants and the Opéra-Comique concert hall were open, and the streets were mostly quiet, except for the occasional taxi or police patrol.

Al-Rashid headed up the street, arriving at the address on the iPad in five minutes. The boy had probably not lied when he'd said that his father walked to work, which was clever of him, mixing one truth with a lie. Made the story more believable.

The building was a very narrow three-story wedged between two commercial banks, solid with tall arched windows on the first. Only the Society's number on a brass plaque over a plain green door distinguished it from its neighbors.

A streetlight at the corner cast long shadows, but lent enough illumination that allowed al-Rashid to get a good look at the door as he passed. He could open the lock without a problem, but he would need time to first find and then disable the alarm system that certainly would be armed. But the chance that a car, likely even a police patrol, would pass before he was inside was too great for him to take the risk.

He turned left at the end of the block and around the corner on the street paralleling the Rue Gaillon he found a pass-through back to a narrow courtyard that had at one time been used as a mews with stables that had since been converted into million-euro apartments.

A few windows were lit, but for the most part the space was in shadows. The rear windows of the Society's building were protected by bars, and the sturdy-looking metal door was covered by a pull-down mesh security barrier.

Taking a small penlight with a red lens from his jacket pocket, al-Rashid studied the lock on the mesh, the track on which it was lowered and raised and the roller bearings at the top, but he could detect no signs of an alarm mechanism. Nor could he see any video surveillance equipment. The Voltaires likely thought that their almost complete anonymity was protection enough, beyond ordinary locks and probably a basic alarm system.

Using a pair of case-hardened steel picks that extended from the handle of a Swiss Army penknife, he opened the lock on the mesh gate in under twenty seconds. Looking around to make certain that no one was looking out any of the windows, he slowly eased the gate up against the stiff resistance of a long time of neglect. No one had come this way in months if not years. But the grease had not completely dried up and raising the gate had been nearly soundless.

Nor was any alarm mechanism visible around the frame of the door, and especially not on the hinges. This lock, however, was stronger and it took a full minute before he'd defeated it.

The rear vestibule was nearly pitch-black. The air smelled dry, musty, like an antique bookstore in Nice that he went to from time to time. Ancient. As if business had been conducted from this location for a very long time. A century and a half or more, al-Rashid mused.

He lowered the mesh gate then closed the door and made his way to a narrow corridor that led to the front entrance and stair hall. An umbrella stand was next to a tall mirror and hat rack that looked as if they should be in a museum.

One door on the right was open to a reception area with a secretary's desk and an IBM Selectric typewriter. A small two-drawer file cabinet was placed in a corner behind the desk, and two side chairs were placed on either side of the doorway.

The file cabinet was not locked, but both drawers were filled with file folders stuffed with blank paper, newspaper pages folded to file size and magazines, most of them French.

Al-Rashid stepped back into the stair hall and held his breath for a long moment to listen, and then to smell and try to sense the meaning of the building. The age of it. The purpose of the place.

He was not carrying a pistol. And in fact he rarely went out armed, he'd seldom found the need. If he were stopped by the police he could offer up his Swiss Army penknife, but nothing else. And in the rare instances when he needed to use force, he'd most often found that his hands were enough.

Nor did he feel any uncertainty now, except that nothing about this place seemed right. He felt as if he had walked onto a movie set that had been made to look real, but on closer examination everything was a sham, an elaborate prop.

He checked out the front window but there was no traffic, and he started up the stairs moving softly on the balls of his feet, already convinced that he was not going to find the name of a translator for the diary here. The Society, if it actually existed, which he was convinced it did, was not as simple as he'd first suspected. There was more here, though. A clue if he was smart enough and patient enough to find it.

Near the head of the first flight of stairs al-Rashid suddenly froze. He thought that he'd heard a slight noise just to the left three or four meters away, as if someone had shuffled his feet.

Al-Rashid waited for a long time, listening, trying to gauge what it was he sensed, until he realized he was smelling a man's cologne. Faint, and he could not immediately place it. But whoever was just around the corner was not making a noise.

"*Giscarde, mon ami, c'est tu?*" al-Rashid said, and he went the rest of the way up to the landing.

A very large man, possibly the twin of the Corsican in front of the Petain apartment, stepped out of the deeper shadows just a couple of meters away, illuminated from a reflection of the streetlight at the corner. He held a silenced pistol in his left hand. A SIG Sauer, boxy but effective.

"We were expecting you," he said in badly accented French.

"What is wrong?" al-Rashid said, moving closer, his hands spread. "No one tells me anything. Sophie and Edouard are dead, for God's sake. And now Giscarde does not answer his cell phone."

"What are you talking about?" the man demanded. He was alarmed.

"I don't know who to call. I don't have an emergency number other than Giscarde's and he does not answer."

"He is dead."

Al-Rashid let his shoulders slump, and his face fell. "My God, I didn't know. I've been in Switzerland following up a lead."

The Frenchman was suspicious. "Why did you come here, of all places?"

"I couldn't think of anything else. But I have information about the diary, and I need instructions how to proceed."

"Tell me. I'll see it gets to the right person."

The man had made a mistake by admitting he knew a Voltaire other than Petain. "I was told only to report to Giscarde."

"He's dead, Monsieur McGarvey, as you well know."

Al-Rashid laughed. "Do I look like an American spy, you idiot," he said. "*Merde.*" He turned away.

The Frenchman stepped forward. "Don't move."

Al-Rashid turned back and grabbed the pistol, his hand so fast that the man had no chance to react.

"All I want is a name and a telephone number so that I can make my report."

"Fuck you."

"Give me that much and I'll leave you in peace. Otherwise I'll shoot you in the head and find another way. But understand me, mon ami, this business is of supreme importance to the Society. We are under attack, and I will not permit someone to stand in my way."

The Frenchman hesitated, no longer sure of himself.

Al-Rashid pressed the muzzle of the pistol to the man's forehead. "One name is all."

"I report to Monsieur Chatelet," the man said. "Robert Chatelet." He gave a telephone number.

Al-Rashid stepped back as if he were leaving, but then turned when he was certain that he would be out of the range of blood spatter and pulled the trigger, driving the Corsican backward off his feet. He stuffed the pistol in his belt under his jacket then went downstairs and let himself out the front door after making certain that the street was empty.

Three blocks later he found a cab to take him to the Moulin Rouge nightclub, and from there another back to the Inter-Continental.

Chatelet was the vice mayor of Paris, and one of the leading candidates for president of France. A sharp critic of the United States, and one of the leaders of the Socialist Party, he nevertheless was a strong advocate of keeping the EU and therefore the euro intact, whatever the cost.

THIRTY-EIGHT

□

Otto and Louise had settled into an upscale three-bedroom condo just off Dupont Circle in the heart of Embassy Row that was used from time to time as a safe house for visiting VIP intelligence assets. Pulling through the iron gates onto the All Saints Hospital Compound around eight in the evening, McGarvey could see the look of resignation on their faces when he'd left them, and he'd felt for them. But in this business a normal life was never normal, and if you wished for something like that you would be disappointed.

"Wouldn't have it any other way," Louise had told him at the door after dinner. She'd made a pot roast with mashed potatoes and gravy, and even a loaf of bread machine whole wheat. It was her stab at normalcy.

Otto had gone into his temporary office where he'd gotten busy trying to figure out what the Cuban DC intelligence apparatus was up to. So far there'd been absolutely no reaction to María suddenly dropping out of sight.

A cleanup crew had gotten rid of her rental car and had repaired the bullet damage to the front of the house. And with Otto's help they made sure that the surveillance system in place would also keep a sharp eye on the neighbors' houses.

"It won't always be this way," McGarvey had told her, but neither of them believed it.

"For the foreseeable future," Louise said.

McGarvey gave her a hug. "Make sure he keeps his head down. I don't know about this one."

She'd smiled. "That's about as likely as you doing a sudden one eighty."

The hospital's iron gate was electrically controlled from a security station just inside the front doors. Entrance was by recognition only. The place was secure. There'd never been a breach in its forty-eight-year history, which this evening was something else McGarvey worried about. There was a first time for everything.

He parked in the rear and was buzzed through the door by Ms. Randall—Randi to her friends—the same nurse from this afternoon.

"Good evening, Mr. Director," she said.

"Don't you ever sleep?" McGarvey asked.

"Who has the time?" she said. "She's awake and had a light dinner, but she's insisting that she needs to talk to you."

"Where are the babysitters?"

"Pat is outside her room on four, and Ron is in security."

McGarvey caught a slight hesitation. "But?"

"I don't think their hearts are in it. I guess the woman is a piece of work."

"That she is," McGarvey said. "I'll go up in a minute."

"Yes, sir."

The ground floor was made up of a staff lounge, the pharmacy, a small but brilliantly equipped laboratory, the food prep area where the chef, sous chef, and dietician could prepare anything from Cream of Wheat to boeuf Bourguignon with truffled asparagus, and the security station. All Saints could handle as many as twenty-five patients, but McGarvey could never remember more than a handful at any time. This evening in addition to María León there were only four other officers—all of them CIA—who'd been transferred from Afghanistan via the hospital at Ramstein AFB in Germany where they'd been stabilized.

McGarvey went to the security desk, which was manned 24/7 by men who were weapons and martial arts experts—many of them ex–Navy SEALs. This evening the hospital's on-duty security officer, Steve Ellerin, had been joined by Ron Kutschinski, a Chicago ex-cop who'd worked as muscle for the CIA for nine years, ever since he'd been wounded on duty. He was a bulky man, and handy with his fists.

"Good evening, Mr. Director," Kutschinski said, getting to his feet. He'd been perched on the edge of the desk from where Ellerin had access to more than a dozen low lux cameras around the hospital and grounds. Anyone coming within a few feet of the gates would show up on the screens no matter what the weather was doing.

"Anything doing?" McGarvey asked.

"Just you, sir."

"Keep your eyes open, there's a good chance we'll have some company tonight."

Ellerin looked interested. "How do you see it, sir? A team effort? A loner?"

"One big guy, but I've never come across anyone faster. The bastard is like a shadow; now you see him, now you don't."

Kutschinski grinned. "He's a lucky bastard, then. Coming up against you, and still being alive and kicking."

"Keep that in mind," McGarvey said.

"Sir?"

"He's not lucky, just good."

McGarvey walked back to the elevator and took it up to the fourth floor. Dr. Franklin, who'd operated on María, had finally gone home after a thirty-six-hour stint, leaving only three trauma nurses on duty. But he and two other doctors were on call 24/7 should the need arise. The lab tech and cooks wouldn't be back until five in the morning, and except for the security team and five patients the hospital was empty, and very quiet.

Nurse Randall was waiting for the elevator to take her down to three, where the four wounded CIA officers had been moved after Dr. Franklin ordered María to be kept in isolation. "Just in case," he'd told McGarvey. "These guys were in pretty tough shape. I don't want anything bothering them."

"How's the patient?"

"Bitchy," Randall said.

Pat Morris, the other CIA babysitter, was sitting in the darkness in the visitor's lounge at the end of the hallway from where he had a clear sight line to María's room.

McGarvey walked down to him. "If something's going to happen it'll probably be after midnight."

Morris nodded. "He won't get past Elias." He'd been a Navy SEAL and his primary weapon of choice now was the same as then: a Heckler & Koch MP7 submachine gun with a suppressor, which lay on the coffee table in front of him. He also carried a standard SEAL 9 mm SIG Sauer P226 pistol fitted with a suppressor in a shoulder holster. His jacket was lying over the arm of a chair.

"Keep frosty, this guy is good."

"May I speak plainly, sir?"

"Yes."

"This assignment sucks shit, if you know what I mean. I don't mind putting my life on the line for one of our own, but from what we were told in our briefing this broad is a colonel in Castro's secret police."

"That she is," McGarvey said from the doorway. "But she's an important asset for the moment. The guy coming our way to take her out has some answers I need."

"She's bait?"

McGarvey shrugged. "If that's how you want to see it. Thing is I want him alive, if possible."

"If not?"

"His life is not worth yours."

"I hear you, sir," Morris said. Like many SEALs he was not a particularly large man, but he had the look in his eyes.

McGarvey went down the hall to María's room and knocked on the door frame before he went in. She was watching television with the sound very low. It was the Tchaikovsky violin concerto in D minor live from Avery Fischer Hall at Lincoln Center. At first she was lost in it, a look almost of rapture on her pretty oval face, until suddenly she looked up and scowled.

"I want to get the hell out of here," she said, her voice still a little croaky as if she had a bad cold.

"Not for another day or two. How do you feel?"

"Like hell, and not just from a hole in my chest. I want to know why pretty boy is sitting there in the dark at the end of the hall. Is he keeping me in, or trying to keep somebody out?"

"Both."

"He's coming back." She said it as a statement, not a question.

"I think so. But if he gets this far, which I don't think he will, shoot to stop not to kill."

María laughed harshly. "Give me my pistol and I can protect myself, or give me a telephone and I can have ten operatives who'll close up this place tighter than a gnat's ass."

"We saved your life."

"After you put me in jeopardy."

"You did that by coming back," McGarvey said, and before she could say anything else he held up a hand, tired of her bullshit. "He probably won't try to get in until sometime after midnight. By then the lights on this floor, including your room, will be out."

"Where will you be?"

"Close."

THIRTY-NINE

☐

The CyberCafe du Monde, a few blocks from the Jardin du Luxembourg, was one of the very few Internet cafés in all of Paris that was open 24/7. Seedy with a dozen old and slow computers, it was the sort of place whose clerks didn't give a damn why you wanted to go online. They only wanted their 2.80 euros per hour.

When al-Rashid, who'd found the place listed on his iPhone, showed up a few minutes after three in the morning only four of the machines were in use, three of them displaying kiddy porn.

He paid for two hours, took a machine near the back door, and when it was connected brought up the website for Agence France-Presse and entered Robert Chatelet, *histoire*. Every man had a vulnerable spot, an Achilles' heel, and al-Rashid figured that the vice mayor of Paris and the leading candidate for president of France was no exception.

For thirty minutes he plowed through two dozen speeches and position papers published on behalf of the *Parti socialiste*, the PS, when Chatelet had switched from the center-right Union for Popular Movement because of what was being called the growing Muslim problem, which had come to the fore when a law had been passed banning the burqa—the facial covering for women.

Chatelet's position had not been unique: France for the French, purity of the language and customs, individuals on the world stage. Second to no people, to no nation.

Switching to the AFP's photo archive, he scanned shots of Chatelet as early as December 2004 in one of a group dedicating the opening of the stunning Millau Bridge over the River Tarn in the Massif Central mountains of Southern France, and as late as groundbreaking for the Lavallette

Dam in Saint-Etienne in 2012, and La Tour Bois-le-Pretre, which was a public housing project at the edge of Paris later the same year.

Al-Rashid brought up France 24, the global television news channel owned mostly by TF1—which was akin to CBS in the United States—but its archives yielded little more than what he'd picked up from AFP, except that he saw and heard the man. Chatelet was typically French, more or less undistinguished in stature and looks, but with a lovely wife who'd been a minor movie actress and model. His voice was rough, that of a smoker, and his French, to al-Rashid's ear, was southern country, not at all refined.

But neither the politician nor the husband had made even the smallest of missteps, which after more than an hour of searching the Internet was the most interesting conclusion al-Rashid had come to. The man was lily-white. Too pure, too clean. It was as if he was either exceedingly careful, or extraordinarily lucky. No politician was that without sin.

He scanned the archives of *France Diplomatie*, which was a site hosted by the Ministry of Foreign Affairs, *Le Monde Diplomatique*, which was a left-wing monthly magazine, and even some of the English, ex-pat-oriented news outlets such as *Paris Voice*, *Radio France Inernationale*, *Expatica.com-France*, and the *International Herald Tribune*.

Until the *Metropole Paris*—which was a weekly that included pictures, cartoons, and the occasional bit of gossip. In a brief photo spread Chatelet was dedicating some Paris street project, and beside him was a tall, slender woman, beautiful, with luxurious hair, high delicate cheekbones, and full sensuous lips. She was identified merely as Mme. Laurent, an engineer in the city planning department.

They were holding a golden shovel, their hands touching, and Chatelet was smiling as if he were the cat who'd got the cream.

Al-Rashid brought up more photo spreads in the *Metropole* from 2009 until just a couple of months ago showing the two of them together dedicating various city public works projects. In one photo their hips were actually touching, and in still another she was standing slightly behind him to his left, an arrondissement manager just forward, and Chatelet was actually touching her ass. In this photo she was identified as Mme. Adeline Laurent, City Works Special Projects Manager.

Five minutes later, he was inside the public area of the City Public

Works Department, where he verified that a woman of that name did indeed work there, with an office in the *Hotel de Ville*, which was city hall. It was a prestigious location for the office of a simple city engineer, but then French politicians tended to keep their mistresses close at hand.

He ran into some difficulty when he went looking for her address in the city directory. Seven women by the same name were listed, but within five minutes he'd narrowed his choice to only one of them who had a place in the northwest corner of the Eighth Arrondissement a few blocks above the Boulevard Haussmann and across from the Parc Monceau, where even very small apartments listed for more than one million euros.

Al-Rashid backed out of the program, erasing his steps, and left the café walking all the way up to the Boulevard St. Germain where he was able to find a cab to take him over to the Gare d'Austerlitz, and from there another cab to within a block of the woman's apartment.

The streets were starting to come alive with service traffic—street cleaners, delivery vans and trucks, garbage collectors, road maintenance crews making minor repairs overnight before rush hour began.

A bakery was just opening when al-Rashid walked through the park and stopped a moment to light a cigarette. The street was fashionable without being overly ostentatious as many Paris addresses could be, the building was four stories and well maintained with her apartment on the ground floor at the rear, in all likelihood opening on a rear courtyard garden.

Crossing the street he passed the front entrance, which was flanked by tall windows made up of small square panes of lightly colored glass, and inside he spotted the night doorman seated behind a small desk just within the entry hall. The image was distorted, but he was certain the man was asleep. The doormen in places such as these were mostly for decoration and not for security.

Crossing the street again he bought the early edition of *Figaro* from a newsstand that had just opened and walked down to the bakery where he ordered a café au lait and a warm croissant with a small container of raspberry confit. He sat by a window from which he had an oblique view of Mme. Laurent's apartment.

Chatelet was a member of the Voltaire Society, which made it likely that he either had the key to translate the diary or he knew the person or persons who did. Mme. Laurent was in turn the key to the mayor.

Which was the next problem. Vice mayors of large cities, and Paris was no exception, usually did not travel alone. They were almost always accompanied by aides and very often bodyguards. In Chatelet's case al-Rashid had spotted at least one bodyguard in nearly every photo taken of him at a public gathering.

The two exceptions, of course, would be when he arrived home, or when he showed up at the apartment of his mistress—especially if Mme. Laurent told him that it was important he come to her immediately. That they had a problem needing his attention.

Madame Chatelet herself would be the problem.

FORTY

□

Parking the blue Tahoe on Thirty-eighth Street a couple of blocks north of the sprawling Georgetown University grounds, Dorestos, dressed in a jacket, jeans, and a dark green dress shirt walked down to T Street and headed east. The neighborhood here was almost completely residential. It was a little after 11:30 P.M., and the bars down on M Street were still busy, though here only the occasional car passed.

He hesitated at the corner of Thirty-seventh, which was also NW Wisconsin Avenue, All Saint's Hospital a block and a half away on a narrow side street that connected with Whitehaven Parkway NW. Traffic was heavier here, and he had to wait for the light before he could cross.

Colonel León had been taken to the hospital by ambulance with no siren or escort, which could have meant she was dead and they were merely transporting her body, or she was wounded but still alive and there'd been no siren because they wanted to bring no attention to themselves.

"The thing is you have to make certain," Msgr. Franelli had told him.

"There is the chance that they may be expecting me. The risks would be great."

"Yes, I know this. But the woman is very important to Mr. McGarvey."

"Then I do not understand. If she is so important to his search, then why don't we allow her to help—if she is still alive? Won't he find the diary much sooner?"

"Perhaps, but we do not want the Cuban intelligence apparatus to become involved. Just as we do not want the CNI butting their noses into Church business. The only outsider's help we need or want is McGarvey's."

"What if I am captured?"

"See that you're not. But at all costs you must find out if Colonel León is dead, and if she still lives you must kill her."

"I don't see how—"

"You are our finest soldier, my son, you will seek God's help and He will show you the way."

God's help, Dorestos allowed himself a bitter thought. God had never once been mentioned during his actual training exercises. Prayers were said before a mission for its success, and afterward for the souls of those who had lost their lives, but never during a battle.

There are old warriors and there are bold warriors. The Order wishes for boldness. Go with God, but remember what you have learned.

The hospital fronted on Thirty-fifth Place, but Thirty-sixth Street deadended at an expanse of trees that grew to within a few yards of the rear iron fence that was twelve feet tall, the tops of each rung ending in spikes. Climbing over it would not be impossible, though almost certainly security cameras would be trained on the entire perimeter.

Earlier in the evening, after making sure where the ambulance had taken the woman, he'd raced back out to the jet parked at Reagan National where he'd talked to the monsignor, and afterward studied the layout of the hospital on one of his databases. The fact of its existence wasn't a secret, only the fact that its patients were exclusively operators from the U.S. intelligence community was.

He'd come up with a plan to create a diversion that would hopefully last long enough for him to get inside, find the woman, make certain that she was dead, and get out. Only he knew that it couldn't work if it included his escape with his own life intact.

He packed a small overnight bag with a couple of shirts, and several magazines of ammunition for his pistol, and drove back to Washington where he checked in at the Georgetown Suites under his work name of Albert Thomas.

A half hour ago, he'd written a note on hotel stationery to Kirk McGarvey apologizing for the incident in the woods behind the Renckes' house, but that the death of Colonel León was necessary. He sealed it in a hotel envelope on which he wrote the All Saints address, and taking only his handgun and spare magazines, leaving the overnight bag behind, slipped out of the hotel, and found a taxi in a queue on M Street waiting for customers from the bars.

"I would like you to deliver this letter for me," he told the driver who was skeptical.

"Get in, I'll take you wherever you want to go, and you can deliver it in person."

"That isn't possible," Dorestos said. He held out a hundred-dollar bill. "It's not far from here. Should only take you a few minutes."

"Whatever you say, pal," the driver said. He took the money and the envelope.

"One other thing, though. I don't want you to take it up there until midnight."

"What the hell is this supposed to be, some kind of a gag?"

"Exactly that," Dorestos said. "But the money is real."

"I can't guarantee I won't be taking a fare somewhere across town. So I'll either deliver it right now, or you'll have to take your chances that I'll be on time."

Dorestos pulled another hundred-dollar bill from his pocket. "Midnight."

The driver only hesitated for a moment, before he took the money. "Midnight," he said.

Dorestos glanced at the driver's taxi license. "I sincerely hope that I have not wasted my money, Mr. Singh, three-two-eight P-L-sixteen. I believe it's called double-dipping."

Lights illuminated the rear parking lot and emergency entrance, and standing in the darkness behind a tree a few yards from the fence Dorestos spotted three cameras—one at each corner covering the fence line and one in the middle trained on the entrance. Even if someone did make it over or through the fence they would be spotted in the parking lot and tracked to the door.

If someone were watching the monitors.

The tree limbs had been cleared so that the lowest one was at least ten or fifteen feet overhead, good enough to stop someone from climbing up unless they'd brought a ladder, or a grappling hook and line. But something like that would almost certainly attract attention.

Keeping the trunk between him and the fence line, Dorestos stepped back ten yards and sprinted forward, leaping off the ground at the last moment, his big hands outstretched above his head. He easily caught the lowest branch and hauled himself up into the deep foliage of what he thought was probably an oak tree.

He remained absolutely still for a full thirty seconds, watching for any sign that someone in the hospital had spotted him, and would sound the alarm or come running. But nothing changed. The only noise was from a garbage truck on Whitehaven Parkway just to the north.

It was ten minutes before midnight and Dorestos worked his way up to a stout limb that stretched almost to the fence line, about five feet higher than the tops of the spikes where it had been trimmed back.

He waited another thirty seconds to make certain he hadn't been detected and then eased into a position from where he could see the east quarter of the front gate where the taxi driver would show up to deliver the letter. If he didn't, Dorestos hoped that the man was at peace with his god.

Early in his small-arms training, he was on the two-hundred-inch pistol range, firing a variety of semiautos, among them the SIG Sauer, a variety of Glocks, and a few other more exotic weapons of Russian and Chinese manufacture. The stress was on learning what weapons were currently in use in the field, so that if chance found him needing to scavenge a pistol he would understand not only how to shoot it, but how to fieldstrip it.

The man at the position next to his right was a veteran of a number of SMOM missions. Out of the corner of his eye Dorestos noticed that the man had turned left, carelessly holding his weapon in such a way that if it were to fire it could injure someone.

"Watch it," Dorestos said.

The priest grinned. "What's your problem? It's on safe." He raised the pistol.

Dorestos reached over with lightning speed and grabbed the pistol, yanking it up and to the right. It discharged into the air.

"Bastard," the priest said, and he came at Dorestos, who stepped to the side and laid both pistols on the stand.

He didn't remember what he said, or exactly what he did next, but in an instant the range supervisor and a couple of instructors were running his way, the priest lying on the ground, his chest caved in.

The entire incident had been recorded on range surveillance video, and Dorestos had not been reprimanded though he'd heard later that the brief film clip was being used as a training exercise. What not to do in a weapons-hot situation in the presence of an unknown enemy.

Headlights flashed on the street at the front of the hospital, and moments later the cab pulled into the driveway. The cabbie beeped the horn once.

Dorestos counted off a full twenty seconds. By now all eyes inside the hospital would be on the front gate.

He scrambled to the end of the limb and leaped out over the spikes and dropped to the ground on all fours, almost like a cat landing.

He caught a fleeting glimpse of what he thought might be the figure of someone in a fourth-floor window, but then he was across the parking area and through the door to the rear reception area and emergency room, deserted at the moment.

FORTY-ONE

◻

McGarvey watched from the front entryway as Kutschinski, his pistol out of sight at his back, walked down to the front gate.

"This your guy?" the CIA babysitter had asked.

"Not unless he's hiding in the backseat, but watch yourself. I'll back you up."

The driver got out of his cab and handed something through the gate. It looked like an envelope.

The phone on the security console in the stair hall rang as McGarvey, his pistol in plain sight, stepped outside and walked down to the gate.

The driver stepped back a pace. "Shit," he said. He turned to get back into his cab.

"Hold up," McGarvey said.

The cabbie looked over his shoulder, his eyes wide. "I don't want any trouble here. I'm just delivering a letter."

"It's addressed to you," Kutschinski said.

McGarvey took the envelope. "Who gave this to you?"

"A big guy, didn't give me his name. Said I was supposed to bring it here at midnight."

"Where was this?"

"M Street, about a half hour ago."

"How'd he sound?"

"Like a fag or a teenage girl," the cabbie said without hesitation.

It was a diversion. "Get the hell out of here," McGarvey told the cabbie, and he and Kutschinski raced back up the drive.

"Is it him?"

Ellerin was on the phone when they burst in. "Your girl called, said she saw someone come over the fence. I'm trying to get Pat but he's not answering."

"You didn't see anything on the monitors?"

"I was watching the front gate."

"Son of a bitch," Kutschinski said, and he headed for the stairs in a dead run.

"I'll clear the back," McGarvey said. "But watch yourself, this guy will know we're on the way up and he's damned good. I've never seen anyone faster."

Kutschinski didn't reply as he took the stairs two at a time.

McGarvey hustled down the corridor where he held up at the door into the emergency room and cocked an ear to listen for a sound. Anything. But except for some piece of machinery running somewhere in the distance, the hospital was silent. Even Kutschinski bounding up the stairs was so light on his feet that he made no noise.

Moving with care, McGarvey crossed to the rear stairs where he spotted two wet footprints on the tile floor just inside the door from the parking area. The priest had walked through the woods in the back and had somehow gotten over the fence when all eyes inside the hospital had been watching the front gate. Everyone except for María.

He started up the stairs, stopping at the first floor long enough to check the corridor, which was dimly lit in red from the exit signs front and back.

He did the same on the second floor, with the same results, then moved to the third just as Nurse Randall came out of one of the rooms.

She stopped short, startled when he came through the door. She started to speak but he motioned for her to keep quiet, and when she spotted the pistol in his hand she looked over her shoulder into the room.

"We have an intruder, but I don't think he'll come after you or these four guys," McGarvey, keeping his voice low, warned her. "He's after the woman, but keep out of sight."

She nodded and went back into the room and closed the door.

McGarvey headed up to the fourth floor, the corridor in near total darkness. Both exit lights had been turned off, and the only illumination came from what was probably a television set halfway down the hall in María's room.

He eased the door open. "Morris," he called softly.

The corridor remained silent.

He opened the door and moving fast, rolled left around the corner into the reception room. Pat Morris, a thin trickle of blood from a hole in his forehead, lay sprawled back on the couch.

McGarvey glanced over his shoulder but nothing moved in the corridor.

Morris's pistol lay next to the Heckler & Koch on the coffee table, the magazines missing from both weapons.

Bambridge would not have sent amateurs out here, yet it looked as if Morris had been caught totally unawares. Yet he must have heard someone coming through the door from the stairs, he must have known that his life was in danger.

McGarvey stared at the weapons for a long moment, before he holstered his pistol. He fieldstripped the pistol, tossing all the parts behind the couch. Then he removed the receiver spring from the MP7, pocketed it, and laid the weapon back on the table.

He turned and dodged his way to María's open door. He took a quick peek inside before he pulled back. The bed was empty. The bathroom door was open but no one was waiting there.

With his pistol in both hands up at chest height he rolled into the room, scanning left to right, but except for the picture on the television screen nothing moved. Nor was there any sign of violence.

María had evidently seen someone coming over the fence, had phoned Ellerin downstairs, and had presumably warned Morris that they had incoming. But she was gone and Morris was dead.

McGarvey took ninety seconds to clear each of the other six rooms on the floor before he went to the front stairwell door and opened it a crack. If the priest had gone down to the third floor searching for María he would have run into Kutschinski. No one had heard gunshots, which meant that everyone including the priest was using silenced weapons.

But the man had to have good intelligence to know what this place was, that María was a patient, and had the balls to come here to what amounted to a CIA stronghold. He either had a death wish or he was even better than McGarvey thought he was, and arrogant enough to know it.

Silently closing the door McGarvey used the house phone on the wall a few feet down the corridor to call Ellerin. But the phone rang four times, before he hung up.

The priest *was* like a shadow or a ghost, flitting over the fence, then up here to kill Morris and then down to the ground floor to take out Ellerin. The son of a bitch was pulling the odds down to his favor by eliminating the opposition one-by-one. But if he'd gotten to Ellerin, it meant he must have passed right through Kutschinski.

At the stairwell door again, McGarvey listened for several seconds before he slipped through and started down, checking each course over the railing before he proceeded.

Just below the third floor landing he spotted Kutschinski, obviously dead, crumpled in a heap, a great deal of blood pooling under his body, and spreading several steps down. His pistol was still in his right hand.

He'd come charging blindly up the stairs and the priest had been waiting in ambush for him.

McGarvey eased open the third-floor door. Nurse Randall lay on her side outside one of the rooms. She too had been armed. A 9 mm standard U.S. military issue Beretta pistol lay on the floor a couple of feet from her outstretched right hand.

What had happened here was already done with.

The four CIA officers were dead, shot while they lay in their beds, two of them with IV drips and monitor wires still attached to their bodies. Those two at least had probably been unconscious when the priest had assassinated them.

María was not in any of the rooms. Nor was there any obvious signs that she'd been here.

For a long moment McGarvey stood rooted to a spot just outside one of the rooms in which a helpless man had been murdered and he was nearly overwhelmed with an intense anger. For money? For gold, silver, for treasure? Some act like this could not be sanctioned by the Catholic Church. Nothing like this had happened, so far as he understood history, for several centuries. It was as if he were caught in the middle of some surreal dream that had begun with María León's insane plot to kidnap Louise to force Otto to come to Cuba.

For some reason he focused on the white blanket that covered the dead officer, and he spotted what were flecks of something white, something granular. It made no sense at first, until a drop of blood fell from above and he looked up as a section of ceiling tile, a small splotch of fresh blood along the seam, suddenly collapsed and María León, the chest of her hospital gown red, came crashing down on top of the dead man.

FORTY-TWO

☐

Dorestos was beside himself with rage. He had failed after all. He'd heard at least one other person scuttling around on the second floor like a mouse behind the wallboard, and yet he'd not been able to find out who it was, though he suspected it was one of the nurses.

He went to the main security console with its six monitors and pressed the button to open the gate when the woman he'd come to assassinate fell through the ceiling onto the body of one of the CIA officers. A second later McGarvey came into the frame, and helped her to sit on the edge of the bed. The front of her hospital gown was soaked with blood, but she was still awake.

McGarvey got a towel from the bathroom and placed it over the wound in her chest.

Dorestos flipped a switch for the sound.

"This'll have to do until I can get the doctor back here."

María was looking up at McGarvey. "If you had let me keep my gun I might have had the chance to end it."

"You did the right thing. But how the hell did you get up into the ceiling?"

"It was Charlie's idea," she said, glancing at the officer's body. "He even helped me climb up. He'd just got the tile back in place and had lain down when the bastard came to the room and shot him. There wasn't a thing I could do about it."

"If you had tried you'd be dead by now."

María looked up at the camera. "Is he gone?"

"I don't know, but for now you're staying put."

"Well, has someone at least called for help?"

"They're on their way," McGarvey said, and he leaned over to whisper something in the woman's ear.

Dorestos cranked up the volume, but he couldn't make out the words.

McGarvey straightened up. "He might still be in the building somewhere. I'm going to try to find him."

"Are you nuts?"

"No. I'm pissed."

"Where are you going?"

"I'm going to start on the fourth floor again and work my way back down."

Dorestos switched the view on the in-house monitor to the third-floor corridor as McGarvey walked past the nurse's body and headed directly for the rear stairs, as he unscrewed the suppressor from a Walther PPK and pocketed it. He was on the hunt and he didn't care how much noise he made.

The decision came down to flight or fight. It was possible that McGarvey would get the drop on him, and cut off any chance of escape. He didn't think that after Casey Key the man would listen to reason, and his orders not to kill the former DCI were very specific.

But he had been ordered to eliminate the woman, along with anyone else who might get in the way. Job one. His immortal soul wasn't at stake, but in the way the monsignor had put it, damnation for failure was possible.

He studied the console for a moment, and then with a few keystrokes erased the current video memory, and shut the recording system down. He stepped back, put a couple of silenced rounds into the main console, then took the batteries out of the keyboard. Turning on his heel he hurried down the hall to the emergency room and the rear stairs, where he stopped a moment to listen in case McGarvey had doubled back for some reason. But there were no sounds, so he started up, silently, taking the stairs three at a time.

Passing the second and third floors, he emerged on the fourth and retrieved the magazines of ammunition for the dead babysitter's SIG and the MP7 from under the couch, and loaded the submachine gun, pulling the slide back to charge it. But the weapon had been tampered with. The slide would not snap back into place. The spring was missing.

He looked down the corridor, the flickering light from the television still coming from the woman's room.

McGarvey had been here, and had sabotaged the weapon. Dorestos realized that he had underestimated the former CIA officer.

Laying the weapon aside he also realized that the pistol was gone as well, which left him only with his handgun and two magazines and a partial. And he understood that he might have made a mistake leaving his own MP7 behind; the extra firepower might be needed after all.

He headed down the corridor to the front stairwell, keeping low and close to the wall and moving fast, pausing only long enough to put a round into the television set.

He cracked the door open and stopped again to listen.

Colonel León was badly wounded and still on the third floor. But McGarvey presented several possibilities. He could have been aware that he was being watched. It would explain why he had whispered something to the woman. It could be that he was staying on the ground floor, waiting in ambush, or he had told the woman the truth and was already on his way up here.

Dorestos slipped into the stair hall and gently eased the door closed.

He waited for a full minute, watching the rear stairwell door through the small square window, but when McGarvey didn't appear, he started down the stairs, taking extreme caution not to make the slightest noise.

He stopped at the third floor door and looked out the window. Nothing moved, and the corridor was mostly in shadows, the only light coming from outside, through the windows in the rooms and the open doors.

"Protect me, Virgin Mary," he mumbled. He slipped out of the stairwell and raced to the room where McGarvey had left the woman, but the door was closed and wouldn't budge even though the handle moved when he tried it.

The woman had barricaded herself inside, knowing that he was coming for her. It was a trap but he still had time because he had a feeling that McGarvey had been lying when he'd told the woman that help was on the way.

The man had an ego, he would want to do this himself. It's why he hadn't called for help at the Renckes' house.

Dorestos put his shoulder to the door and it gave a couple of inches.

"Stand down," McGarvey said from the end of the corridor.

Dorestos looked up, keeping only his profile as a target. "I mean you no harm, signore," he said.

"We're past that. You killed some good people here. Innocent people."

"They were America's soldiers, and it is war."

"Between us and the Vatican?"

Dorestos was distressed. All of this misunderstanding was his fault, and he didn't know how he was going to face the monsignor. "No, of course not. We are not your enemy. Only Colonel León is."

"Why did you kill the nurse?"

"It was a mistake," Dorestos said. As was staying here any longer.

He fired two shots down the corridor, above where he thought McGarvey was standing in the darkness, and then sprinted toward the other end of the corridor, firing continuously over his shoulder.

McGarvey got off three shots, one of them plucking at his sleeve, but then he was through the door and racing downstairs, sick at heart at the disaster he'd created here, and almost believing that it might be best if he lost his life this night. Jesus would accept him, sins and all. He could feel the Lord's love washing over him. But the Order wouldn't be so forgiving.

On the ground floor he darted past the security console, out the front door and down the three steps to the driveway, moving faster now than he'd ever moved in his life.

He reached the open gate and flitted around the corner as McGarvey fired two shots, both of them hitting the tall brick wall.

In the next block he crossed over a narrow canal and threw the pistol away. The Tahoe he intended to leave behind, along with his bag at the hotel.

He used his cell phone to call his aircrew. "We leave within the hour. File a flight plan for San Juan. Do you understand?"

"Yes, sir," the pilot said.

Three blocks later on R Street he found a VW Jetta that had been left unlocked. He forced the ignition switch and drove off, wondering what would happen to him next. He'd never failed before, so he could only guess at the consequences.

But if he were given another chance he would move heaven and earth to see that McGarvey succeeded, and that the Cubans were kept out of his way.

FORTY-THREE

Mme. Laurent was not as tall as she appeared in the photographs al-Rashid had seen, but she was every bit as elegant as he pictured she would be. She came out of her apartment building at ten minutes before eight, saying something to the old doorman who smiled and saluted her. She'd made his day. There wasn't a straight Frenchman who didn't appreciate the attention of a pretty woman.

She'd gotten a half block down the street when al-Rashid got up and followed her.

Dressed in a lightweight trench coat, belted at the waist, she wore a brightly patterned Hermes head scarf, and carried a Louis Vuitton bag over her shoulder.

She walked slowly, her hips swaying. Traffic had picked up and she was a woman who knew the attention she was creating, and she didn't want to rush it. Al-Rashid almost felt sorry for monsieur the vice mayor, who undoubtedly gave up a great deal every day to have her as his mistress. And this day the man would have to give up even more.

For a block or so al-Rashid had no idea where she was headed, unless it was to find a taxi on the much busier Boulevard Malesherbes, but the doorman would have gladly called for one. On the other hand if she was to use the Metro, a station was in the park practically across the street from her apartment.

Before he approached her he wanted to make certain that she wasn't on her way to some rendezvous—either with Chatelet, or perhaps with someone else. Another secret lover?

She crossed the very busy Boulevard de Courcelles and made directly for the Metro entrance near the end of the Avenue de Villiers, which he realized would take her on a more direct route to her office.

He caught up with her just before she was about to descend in to the station. "Mademoiselle Laurent, *si'l vous plait?*"

The woman stopped and turned, curiosity, but no alarm on her oval face. Her chin was agreeably narrow, her cheekbones delicate and high, and her dark eyes very large. Her looks, figure, and bearing were movie-star quality. "*Oui?*"

"Permit me. I am Pierre Gaulette. You do not know my name, but I have some information for you that may be distressing."

She smiled. "You are perhaps a paparazzo with information to sell to me about my employer?" She looked around. "Where is your camera-man?"

"Actually I'm a private detective, who was hired not by your boss Monsieur Chatelet, but by Madame Chatelet."

Her lips tightened. "I am sorry, but I have no idea what you are talking about," she said disdainfully, and she turned to go.

"We have information about an organization that the mayor may some-how be involved with."

She turned back.

"It may be a subversive organization that has no friends in the Élysée Palace. The fallout could spread."

"What has this to do with me, or with Madame Chatelet?"

"You are the vice mayor's mistress. Madame Chatelet knows this, of course, and she has asked me to approach you as a friend not as an enemy. I am here to help."

"You're making no sense," Mme. Laurent said, and again she turned to go.

"This has to do with a great deal of money controlled by a secret so-ciety from which an extremely important document was stolen recently. The vice mayor can save himself. But naturally it would be impossible for me to approach him personally, and his wife wants to avoid a scan-dal and to keep her husband out of prison."

Mme. Laurent had gone two steps down, but she looked up, morning commuters brushing past her. She didn't look as certain as she had at first. "What document?"

Al-Rashid shook his head. "I've already said too much in public. We need to go somewhere so that we can talk. I'll tell you everything I know, including who stole the document and its current location."

Something else came into the woman's eyes but just for a moment, and then she nodded. "My apartment isn't far."

"We may have to call the vice mayor."

"You may be right, Monsieur—?"

"Gaulette."

"From which agency?"

"That will have to wait, for the moment," al-Rashid said, stepping aside for her.

When she came up he took her arm and they headed across the avenue, workday morning traffic now in full swing. She said nothing, nor did he wish to prompt her, though they could have discussed in details the plans for building a nuclear weapon and no one on the street would have paid them the slightest attention. And he had a feeling that she understood this as well as he did. Which was somewhat bothersome. Yet in his mind only another professional would not try to at least get a hint about what was happening.

The doorman's name was Henri, and face-to-face he didn't look anywhere near as old as al-Rashid had guessed from a distance. He accepted a kiss on the cheek from Mme. Laurent, but didn't ask why she'd returned, or who the man with her might be.

Al-Rashid got the feeling that the doorman's eyes were on his back as he and Mme. Laurent went down the corridor to the rear apartment. But when he turned around as she was unlocking her door, the man was looking at something on the street.

Her garden apartment was small, but exquisitely furnished with what to al-Rashid's eye looked like genuine antiques mostly from the Louis XIV period. At least one of the paintings on the wall was a Renoir and another in the corridor to the left was a Picasso—the only jarring note in the place other than an ultramodern and very expensive Bang & Olufsen flat-screen television and sophisticated sound system at one end of the living room. The garden courtyard was alive with flowers and small trees that looked almost like Bonsai. Herbs grew in a long planter box outside the kitchen door.

Mme. Laurent laid her purse and coat on the end of a couch and sat down. She took a cigarette from a silver box, and lit it with a matching lighter.

"So, Monsieur Gaulette, please tell me what this is all about. And forget the fiction that Madame Chatelet has my best interest in mind."

"I think we need to telephone the vice mayor, have him come here. Tell him that it's an emergency with his wife."

"In that case the nursing home would be the one to call. It is Alzheimer's."

"I didn't know," al-Rashid said. It was sloppy on his part. "Then we will invent another fiction to get him here."

"Perhaps I will tell him the truth. That a private detective has shown up to ask questions about a secret society of millionaires who have lost a document. And he has resorted to kidnapping his mistress."

Al-Rashid went to the French doors and looked out at the garden. "Perhaps you should." Even in the winter this would be a pleasant room. A porcelain fireplace in the corner opposite the television would be nice, especially at the holidays. He'd never had such a safe haven, and he'd never missed what he'd never had until now.

"He's bound to ask if I am in any danger."

"You are not."

"But he'll want to know about the document. You've said that you know where it is. He'll definitely want me to tell him that part. He's a very bright man, a careful man who does not make decisions quickly. Sometimes I find that trait in him charming, but at other times it's irritating. Do you know what I mean, Monsieur—?"

Al-Rashid came to the realization that what had bothered him about her out on the street was a professionalism. She was no mere mistress, or city engineer. And when he turned he wasn't surprised that she held a subcompact Glock 29 pistol in the 10 mm version pointed at him.

FORTY-FOUR

□

At All Saints, Dr. Franklin had been the first to show up, and after he'd made a quick examination of the four CIA officers dead in their beds on the third floor, and of Nurse Randall, Morris, Ellerin, and Kutschinski, he'd found the other two nurses frightened but unharmed and they'd taken María into the operating room.

Bill Callahan had arrived a couple of minutes before the cleanup and removal crew from the Company along with four babysitters from the Office of Security. All of it was low-key enough that none of the neighbors had any inkling that something unusual had happened while they'd slept.

The front gate had been closed and technicians had set up a temporary terminal to monitor and control the hospital's security measures.

Deep in thought McGarvey stood at the front door looking out the windows at the street that was quiet for now.

Callahan had been on the phone for the past fifteen minutes mobilizing a special task force that would search for the priest. They were keeping the local cops out of it because some of them would almost certainly get killed if they came up against him.

"What're the chances this guy will try to come after her again?" Callahan asked, hanging up his cell phone. "Tonight maybe?"

"I wouldn't put it past him," McGarvey said. He turned around. "That's twice the son of a bitch has gotten past me. There won't be a third time."

"You think that he's from the Vatican?" Callahan asked skeptically. He was a devout Catholic.

"Sacred Military Order of Malta."

"That's a myth."

"Tell it to Nurse Randall, who was just trying to help save lives," McGarvey said bitterly.

"If it's true he'll be able to go into any Catholic church or monastery anywhere in the world and be home free. We won't be able to touch him."

"Convenient, isn't it? But it doesn't apply to me."

Callahan gave him an odd look. "No, I suppose it wouldn't," he said. "Do you believe in anything?"

The question hurt, but McGarvey understood it. "Yes," he shot back. "Saving lives is more important to me than the sanctity of a church. And if there is a God I think He'd understand."

"I'm in the same business, Mac. Always have been. But if this guy is as good as you say he is, he must have been trained somewhere."

"The Hospitallers."

"Leaving them aside for a moment, how about the military? You said he spoke with an Italian accent. Have you asked the Italian army for help? The Ninth Parachute Assault Regiment, for one. They're like the British SAS. Could be this guy trained with them at one time."

McGarvey had turned his cell phone back on a few minutes ago. He'd missed a call from Otto. He hit the callback number, and Otto answered on the first ring.

"Are you okay?"

"My ego is a little bruised, but he did a lot of damage here," McGarvey said. "And this entire business is making less sense every step I take." He briefly brought Otto up to speed.

"Why would he kill the four guys in their beds? At least one of them was critical. And what about the nurse? There was no reason for it, unless the guy is nuts."

"Or dedicated," McGarvey mumbled. He was missing something. They all were. "Bill Callahan is here, he wants to know if we could run a check with the Italian special forces, see if someone like this guy ever trained in the Ninth Parachute."

"Checked them, along with the Fourth Alpine Parachutists, the 185th Recon Target Regiment, and their Navy and Air Force units, plus the Carabinieri special units and the State Police NOCS, their Central Security people. Some fairly close matches for size, but no one with that voice."

"His voice wasn't in any database."

"You'd be surprised, *kemo sabe*, but I have a friend in Rome who owed me a favor. He's got connections, and he won't make anything of my request, even though he knows about the SMOM."

"Why?"

"Official Rome is scared shitless of them. So goes the Vatican, so goes Italy. And the Malta order provides the muscle. All of it under the table."

"Anything else?" McGarvey asked. He glanced over at Callahan, who had stepped aside and was talking on his cell phone.

"Could be he's not coming back any time soon. I tracked a private jet from Sarasota to Reagan yesterday. Executive Charters International from London. No passenger manifest, but it filed a flight plan for San Juan, Puerto Rico, direct and took off sixty-five minutes ago, again with no passenger manifest other than the flight crew."

"Did they list their names and nationalities?"

"Yes, all Brits. But the thing is the aircraft disappeared from radar fifteen minutes ago. No Mayday, no transponder codes." The three emergency codes that a pilot could send from his aircraft included 7500, which meant the plane had been hijacked; 7600, which meant they'd lost communications abilities; and 7700, which meant an emergency—they were going down.

"No one's looking for them."

"They were outside U.S. airspace when they decided for whatever reason to change their flight plan. Happens all the time."

Callahan was excited.

"He's gone," Otto said.

"I'm not so sure," McGarvey said. "How's Louise?"

"Believe it or not she wants to know how Colonel León is doing."

"She's in the operating room. Franklin came in."

"I'll let her know. In the meantime?"

"See what's going on with the CNI, especially in Seville."

"The West Indian Archives?"

"I don't think that Dr. Vergilio told us the truth the last time. Could be we'll have to pay her another visit."

Otto chuckled. "Now why didn't I think of that?" he asked. "I'm on it."

McGarvey hung up.

"We found your blue Tahoe abandoned three blocks from here," Callahan said. "A forensics team is on the way."

"They won't find anything. But in the meantime see if anyone's reported a stolen car, or if any cabdriver has turned up missing this morning. I'll be back in five."

McGarvey walked to the emergency room and out the back way across the parking lot to the rear fence, which was tall and topped with sharp iron spikes at eight- or ten-inch intervals. Impossible to scale or leap over in the short time that Ellerin had been distracted from watching the rear monitors.

The recorders from all the surveillance cameras had been erased, though he suspected that given time Otto might be able to retrieve some of them. But this was the way the priest had come. A tall oak tree, its lower limbs pruned to within at least ten feet of the fence, was the nearest object. No ladders, no rope and grappling hook had been left behind. The priest had left through the front gate, and he certainly would not have run around back to retrieve any of that equipment.

He'd climbed the tree, no mean feat in itself, had crawled to the end of one of the branches, and when he'd seen the lights of the cab show up in front had leaped across ten feet of air, clearing the top spikes and landing within the compound.

The priest was impressive. McGarvey could think of no other term for the man's athletic prowess, or for his stick-to-it attitude.

He would come back for María. Nothing could keep him away. Unless he wasn't given the chance.

FORTY-FIVE

□

Al-Rashid sat down on a wingback chair, a heavy coffee table between him and the woman. He was seething that he had made such an elementary mistake about the vice mayor's wife, but there'd been nothing in the media about her illness. Yet he should have picked up on the fact that nothing about her had appeared in the media over the past couple of years.

None of that showed on his face. He motioned to the cigarette box. "May I?"

"Yes," Mme. Laurent said, her aim never wavering.

Al-Rashid got a cigarette, lit it, then sat back and crossed his legs. "It seems as if you and I are at an impasse now. You're not about to shoot me, at least not yet, and I'm not about to leave until your lover shows up."

"I will shoot you, though not at the moment," she said. She was collected. Nothing was apparent on her features except for a slight interest, and a hint of amusement. "But tell me who you really are, and what your interest is in whatever society you think Robert is involved with."

"It's called the Voltaire Society and from what I've been able to learn it's been in existence for a century and a half or more, though I'm not really sure what its purpose is."

"Who are you?"

"I've been hired to find out about it."

"Why?"

"My employer did not share that with me."

"You're lying, of course."

Al-Rashid shrugged. "We all do from time to time. But now that I'm here it won't do any harm to call the vice mayor. I won't hurt him, I'm not armed, and in any case you have the advantage."

"What makes you think that Robert is involved with the Society?"

"I spoke to a man last night who gave me his name. Under the circumstances I had placed him under he was in no position to lie to me."

"I don't believe you, and if you don't start making sense I will shoot you as an intruder. And believe me, Monsieur Gaulette, or whatever your actual name is, I am a very good marksman."

"I'm sure you are. He was a night watchman at a small office on the Rue Gaillon. I had been led to believe that it was the headquarters of the Society, and I went there to meet with Monsieur Petain, who I thought was a Voltaire. But he wasn't there, and the office was a sham."

"You killed him?"

"There was a scuffle, it was an accident. Believe me I don't mean any harm. I just want some answers that I think the vice mayor has. And also believe me I wouldn't dream of injuring him—I'd be a hunted man in all of France and I value my life more than that."

"I won't call him here."

"Because you love him?"

Mme. Laurent inclined her head slightly.

"Then I have wasted my time this morning. I'll have to find another way." He started to rise, but she motioned for him to sit down.

"I will not ask him to walk into a trap, but perhaps I can exchange information if you agree to leave. I know about the Society. I've heard things. But believe me I will not hesitate to shoot."

"You've already said that. But if you want a deal, then we can at least try. Tell me what you know about the group. For instance, who else is involved besides the vice mayor and Monsieur Petain, that man I was to meet?"

"First you tell me how you came to hear about it, and where you got the name Petain."

"From a man who works in the Bernar Kantonal Bank," al-Rashid said, and he watched for a reaction. "Do you know this name?"

Mme. Laurent's lips pursed only slightly. "I'm not sure. But the point is how did you come to this particular man in this particular bank?"

"That I can't say. Except that he was helpful. He led me to Petain and to the Paris office, and then to you through the vice mayor."

"I don't understand."

"It was obvious at least to me that something was going on between you."

She shook her head.

"From news photographs. You were practically grafted on to his hip in some of them. But I have only two questions for Monsieur Chatelet. What has been the purpose of the Voltaire Society?"

"To do good."

Al-Rashid laughed, though it wasn't the answer he'd expected. "Spare me. From what I understand a fair amount of money may be at stake if it involves a Swiss bank such as the Bernar Kantonal."

"If you cannot accept a simple truth then it is not my fault. But what is your second question for Robert?"

"The missing document."

Mme. Laurent said nothing.

"It is the diary of a Catholic priest who apparently went on an expedition somewhere north of Mexico City with a troop of Spanish soldiers. This would have been sometime in the early or mid-eighteen forties."

The woman was shaken, but she covered her sudden discomfort well. "What is such a thing to Robert? I'm not sure that he is a man interested in history."

"This part I'm not very certain of, but I have read some history and some of it concerned the Spanish plunder in the New World, from the early fifteen-hundreds—mostly silver but a lot of it gold."

Mme. Laurent laughed, but she wasn't sincere. "Fantasy."

"The plunder?"

"No. I too have read about caches of treasure in the mountains around Mexico City, or in Cuba, or Hispaniola. But so far as I know the only real treasure ever found to date was from Spanish galleons sunk in storms—most of them off the east coast of Florida. So, if you are after sunken treasure off the U.S. coast, what are you doing here? What does the so-called Voltaire Society have to do with it? And what about this priest's diary?"

"You admitted that you knew about the Society."

"I lied. I wanted to see how far you would go with this fantastic tale."

Al-Rashid leaned forward to put out his cigarette in the ashtray on the coffee table. "Let me tell you about this diary. In it are the exact locations of Spanish treasure that was buried in the deserts of the southern U.S., in New Mexico. Are you familiar with this fantastic tale?"

She watched him, her expression neutral, but her eyes were slightly widened.

"The diary was written in Latin, but it is in a cipher. And that is a problem for my client, and by extension for you as well as your lover."

She held her silence.

"The first name I found was for Giscarde Petain, who was blown up by the Spanish intelligence service in Florida. They want the treasure— they believe it belongs to Spain. The second name I found was for Madame Petain and her son. They would not cooperate, so unfortunately I killed them. That led me to the sham office, and the night watchman who gave me the name of Robert Chatelet, which led me to you."

Mme. Laurent's right forefinger on the trigger of the Glock began to turn white.

"Do you understand where I am going with this?" al-Rashid asked. He raised his right hand as a distraction, and her eyes followed it. "I need the code to decipher the diary, and your vice mayor is my current best hope."

"Bete," the woman said. She raised the pistol.

Al-Rashid's right leg was hooked over his left, his right foot under the coffee table. He upended the table onto her lap the moment she fired, the unsilenced shot deafeningly loud in the confines of the small living room. The bullet slammed into the tabletop, and he was on her in an instant, snatching the Glock out of her hand.

She struggled to upright the table, but he clipped her in the chin with his fist. Her head snapped back against the cushions, her eyes fluttering.

Pistol stuffed in his jacket, al-Rashid went to the door, turned the lock, and stepped aside.

A second later the doorman was there. "Mme. Laurent, qu'est que c'est?"

The woman was starting to come around, and she cried out something indistinct.

The door slammed open and the doorman burst into the hallway, a big Glock 17 in his left hand.

Before the bulkier man could react, al-Rashid closed the door and broke his neck. He allowed the doorman to slump to the floor, slowly suffocating to death.

FORTY-SIX

□

Dr. Franklin came down on the elevator, pulling off his surgical cap as he got out of the car. His gown was splattered with a little blood, but not much, though he looked as if he'd been in the operating room twenty-four hours straight. His complexion was pale, his eyes bloodshot.

A cleanup detail had Kutschinksi's body, the last of the casualties, on a gurney heading for the back door, and almost all of the blood and bullet damage throughout the hospital had been cleaned up or repaired. Technicians were working on replacing the main security console, and Tommy Newman, a new man from the Company, was on the desk. He looked anything but friendly.

"I actually like patching up our guys. But when it's all undone, and I end up working on the only survivor who happens to be an enemy agent I have to ask myself what the hell I'm doing here." He looked at McGarvey. "Can anyone tell me that?"

"How is she doing?" McGarvey asked.

"Surprisingly well. Mostly just a few pulled staples. The woman is nothing short of resilient. I only had her under a local anesthetic, and as soon as I was done she asked for you."

"How soon can she be moved?"

"Immediately," Franklin said. He glanced at Newman on the desk, and the other muscle that had come in from Langley. "Are we going to come under attack again?"

"Not if I can help it," McGarvey said. "When will she be mobile enough to get dressed and walk out of here on her own?"

"I'd say one week. But from what little I've learned about her, she'd just as likely get dressed right now and join the fight. The only way I was going to keep her here for the next twenty-four was to sedate her, and she fought me on that, until I promised that if she tried to get out of bed again she would bleed to death."

"Would she?"

"Probably not," Franklin admitted. "Now if there's nothing more for me to do, I'm going upstairs to get some sleep."

"Everything's going to be okay here, Doc."

"If you say so, Mac," Franklin said, and he left.

Callahan got off the phone with his people and he came over. "You were right about the Tahoe. The team found nothing on the first pass. But they're having it towed to the lab where they're going to tear it apart."

"He didn't walk to the airport," McGarvey said.

"No cabs missing, but a VW Jetta was reported stolen sometime overnight, five blocks from here. It just turned up in the outdoor lot at National. It looks like he's gone."

"No," McGarvey said. "Have your people check all the rental car companies, the bus line, and every cabdriver who came back into the city—anywhere in the vicinity, not just Georgetown. A tall, very fit man who speaks with a high-pitched voice."

"That's going to take a fair amount of time," Callahan said.

"Before dark. And have your people check all the motels and hotels in the vicinity. The cabdriver who delivered the letter to me was parked on M Street, near the shops."

"He'd be stupid to try to come back here," Callahan said.

"That's what he means to do, but we're going to take the fight to him before he gets the chance," McGarvey said. "Tell your people to tread with care. If he's cornered he'll fight. Just let me know where he is."

"I'll call in a SWAT team, our guys are good."

"I want him alive if all possible."

Callahan turned away and got on his cell phone to start issuing orders.

Mac phoned Otto, and explained what the FBI was gearing up to do. "His voice is going to give him away."

"What are you going to do in the meantime?"

"I want a list of all the Catholic churches here in Georgetown."

"Sanctuary," Otto said. "Just a sec."

McGarvey was at the front door. He glanced over his shoulder at Callahan, who was watching him with a pained expression on his face, but he said nothing, and ten seconds later Otto was back.

"Including the Dahlgren Chapel on the university campus, there are four of them: St. Helen's on University Avenue, Holy Trinity on N Street, and Epiphany on Dunbarton. I'm sending them to your phone."

When he got them, McGarvey said thanks and was about to ring off.

"These people take stuff like this seriously, honest injun'," Otto said. He'd worked for a Catholic diocese at the very beginning of his career, before he came to the CIA.

"I know, but I have a feeling that's where he's holing up until tonight."

"It'd be a good move on his part, if he's planning on hitting you again. But listen, there've been cases where nuns have stood as a human shield around someone who'd claimed sanctuary. And if this guy is actually a priest on orders from the SMOM, they would give up their lives to make sure he wasn't taken."

"Unless he fired first."

Otto was silent for a beat. "Step easy, Mac. If he's in a church, he'll have everything going for him."

"I'm getting out of here now. I want to take it to him this morning when he's least expecting me to come for him."

Callahan was finished on the phone when McGarvey broke the connection with Otto and pocketed his own phone.

"If he did come back and you trace him to one of the churches, call us and I'll mount a surveillance operation so tight it'll be impossible for him to get out."

"Do you want to take a chance that he'd shoot his way out and that some innocent bystander might get in the way? It happened in Sarasota. Two kids were killed when the car bomb went off."

"That was a CNI action, not his."

"They both have the same goal."

"God help me, Mac, I should throw your ass in jail right now till all of this shit blows over. Because I know damn well this won't end even if you do take this guy down. There's more to it. The Spaniards and the so-called Voltaire Society. And even if the guy who attacked here last night is actually a priest, and even if the SMOM actually does exist as a paramilitary force, or at the very least an intelligence agency for the Vatican, don't you think they'll send another operative? And keep sending operatives either until you're dead or they find what they're looking for?"

McGarvey agreed. "All I can do is take them one at a time."

"And then what?"

"We find out what the hell is really going on that's so goddamned important a lot of people are willing to kill for it."

"The treasure."

"There's more," McGarvey said.

He got his Cayenne in back and Newman opened the front gate for him. The first of the churches on Otto's list was the Dahlgren Chapel of the Sacred Heart on the Georgetown University campus. It was one of the four anchors on the quad that included Healy Hall—that was a large ornate building that housed academic and administrative offices as well as the Riggs Library and Gaston Hall—along with Old North and Maguire Hall.

Just off Thirty-seventh Street NW he turned into the campus along O Street NW, passing Gaston Hall where he parked just around the circle in front of Healy, and got out.

The campus was busy at this hour of the morning, students and faculty alike on foot, on bikes, skateboards, and even two girls on roller blades. The church was on the north side of the quad, its wide double doors closed. Above the entry was a huge ornate stained glass window in the shape of a circular triangle over which was a solid bell tower.

He hesitated. For just a moment he was back on campus in Sarasota, trying to warn the two students to get out of the way. He didn't want a repeat of that incident here, among all these kids. But he simply could not let the priest walk away to kill again.

FORTY-SEVEN

□

Al-Rashid sat on the edge of the coffee table, which he had tipped up-right, watching the woman trying to hide the fact that she was fully awake and completely aware of her situation. The side of her jaw where he had hit her had turned red and was beginning to swell. A little blood trickled from the corner of her mouth.

"Here we are, another casualty. Hopefully there will not be others because of your stupid attitude."

"It will be of no use to you for me to telephone Robert and ask for him to come here," she said, her voice awkward. "He'll know that something is wrong, and his chauffeur and bodyguard will come with him."

"I expect they will. But I also think that they will not come into the apartment of his mistress. They'll wait outside on the street."

"Henri will not be at the door. Robert will know that there has been trouble here."

"Exactly," al-Rashid said. He glanced over his shoulder at the body of the doorman. "Poor bastard saw you every day, leaving in the morning, coming home at night. He'd built up quite an affection for you, that along with his fantasies—and what Frenchman doesn't have his fantasies—finally got out of hand. As you were leaving for your office this morning, he lured you back into your apartment on some pretense and he tried to rape you. In his haste you managed to kill him by twisting his head away as he tried to kiss you. Unfortunately you were so strong that his neck broke, and he is dead. You didn't know what to do except call for Robert, Monsieur le Vice Mayor, to come help you out of a dreadful situation. The publicity certainly would not be good for his campaign."

"You're insane."

"Possibly," al-Rashid said. "Where is your telephone?"

"Robert is not involved with the Society. It is I who am the Voltaire."

"Perhaps. Where is the telephone?"

"I'll tell you whatever you want to know."

"Who has the key to the cipher?"

"I don't know."

"If you are a Voltaire then you certainly know who does have it."

"No."

Al-Rashid nodded, understanding and patience in his manner. "Your telephone."

"I don't have one," she said.

Al-Rashid hadn't seen one anywhere in the living room. He went to her purse where he found an iPhone and he handed it to her.

"I will not involve him."

"He's already involved."

"No."

Al-Rashid was on her in an instant, one hand clamped around her throat, cutting off her air, while with his other he ripped her blouse and black lacy bra away. He let go and stepped back. "Perhaps to make the situation here look more realistic I shall rape you myself."

She looked up at him, fear now in her eyes.

"I am not a gentle man, mademoiselle."

She picked up the telephone. "You will never leave Paris alive, monsieur," she said with venom. She brought up a number on the screen and touched it.

Al-Rashid pulled out the silenced Glock that he had taken from the guard at the sham Voltaire Society office and pointed it at her head from a distance of less than two feet. "With care," he said.

"Robert, it is me," she said. "There has been some trouble at my apartment."

Whatever Chatelet said caused her grip to tighten on the phone.

"It is the doorman. He's dead."

She looked up.

"No, I'm okay, just frightened. I need your help right away."

Again she listened.

"Now," she said. "He's in my apartment. Dead."

Al-Rashid snatched the phone from her hand and brought it to his ear in time to hear the vice mayor say that he would be there in ten minutes. "No sirens."

Switching off, he removed the back plate and took out the battery and SIM card, which he pocketed, and tossed the phone aside.

"There is no need for this," Mme. Laurent said. She pulled the material of the shredded blouse over her bare breasts. "I do not have the key to the cipher nor do I know who has it."

"Let's hope that the mayor knows."

"He's not a member of the Society. I've already told you."

"Yes, and you've also told me that you love him, and you would do anything for him."

A little glimmer of understanding came into her eyes, but she shook her head. "No matter what you do to me, I cannot give you information I do not have."

"We'll see," al-Rashid said.

He stuffed the pistol in his belt again then fieldstripped Mme. Laurent's gun and that of the doorman's and tossed the bullets and parts aside. Next he dragged the doorman's body into the living room where he turned it over. He unbuckled the man's belt, undid his trousers, and pulled them off along with his underwear and tossed them aside.

"You're sick," Mme. Laurent said.

"From your point of view, I am indeed sick. But such a judgment is relative, wouldn't you say?"

"The Society means no harm to anyone, only good."

"You're a charity, is that it?" al-Rashid asked. He went to the door. "Does the vice mayor have a key?"

"No," Mme. Laurent said.

He turned in time to see her fumbling with the lock on the French doors to the garden, and he was on her before she could get them open. Pulling her back to the couch he shoved her down, yanked her blouse away, shredding even more of the material so that there was little or nothing left to cover her breasts.

"Does Chatelet have a key?"

"Oui."

"Very well, then we wait for him to arrive. And the moment I find out what I need I shall leave you in peace. As I said, I do not wish to harm the mayor, and be hunted for the rest of my life. As it turns out I think that he would make a fine president."

"You bastard."

"If you try to warn him I will kill both of you. Do you understand this?"

She looked away, but she nodded.

FORTY-EIGHT

□

In the office at Dahlgren Chapel, Dorestos sat facing Fr. Alvin Norman, who'd explained that he normally celebrated mass in the Thomas Moore Chapel at the Law Center. Only a few students and a couple of faculty members were out in the nave, praying or lighting candles at the Virgin Mother's statute. Or just sitting.

"I don't think that I can help you, my son," the round-faced priest said. He was in a suit and tie, his hair white.

"It's Father Dorestos, and I have come for sanctuary, perhaps for only this day and a night."

"I'm just a chaplain."

"Then may I suggest that you call your superior, because I have something that is extremely important to the Holy Father that cannot wait. Do you understand?"

"Yes, of course," Fr. Norman said, and he started to get up from behind his desk.

"Telephone him."

"He is on his morning walk, and unfortunately does not carry a cell phone with him. But it'll be just a minute, he's somewhere on the quad."

"Go with God," Dorestos said.

The chaplain was momentarily startled but he hurried out, softly closing the door behind him.

Dorestos got up and opened the door a crack in time to see the priest scurrying down the aisle to the front doors. None of the handful of people in the nave looked up. But just as he withdrew the main door opened and a man came in. He was backlit by the sun, and for a moment as he stood on the threshold his features were indistinct. But then the door closed and Dorestos shrank back.

It was Kirk McGarvey. Somehow the man had traced him this far. Dorestos leaned against the wall, trying to work out what should have been a near impossibility.

The woman still lived, and they thought that another attempt would be made on her life. Assuming that much, it meant that McGarvey would have reasoned that Dorestos was close. Someone in or near Georgetown. In a motel under an assumed identity.

Or seeking sanctuary in a church if McGarvey had made the assumption that the Vatican had become involved. The Order.

He phoned the monsignor, and explained his situation.

"Are you certain that it is Mr. McGarvey?" Msgr. Franelli asked. He sounded impatient. It was afternoon in Malta.

"Sí."

"How did he trace you to the chapel?"

"I'm not sure unless he's somehow discovered that I work for the Order, and that I've come here seeking sanctuary."

"The Cuban woman is not dead?"

"I'm not sure."

"Tell me everything," Msgr. Franelli said.

Dorestos did so, leaving out no detail. "I plan on going back in this evening. They wouldn't be expecting me to return."

"No," Franelli said. "It is far too late for that. All that we can do now is mitigate the damage that you have already done."

"I am at your eternal service, Monsignor."

"Yes, you are, Father. Give me just a moment."

Dorestos sat back and breathed in the scent of the office, of the church. Oiled wood, mixed with the lingering odors of incense from high mass, starched surplices, maybe old books and freshly cleaned carpet runners. Places like these were the only home he'd ever known, and the scents represented order and comfort and safety to him.

Franelli was back. "The Senior Chaplain there is Fr. Carl Unger. He has his doctorate in psychology so he will be a difficult man to fool. He'll see right through you unless you are careful."

"What am I to do?"

"He'll give you sanctuary, but you will have to tell him the truth, or at least enough of it to ask for his blessings and help and God's forgiveness."

"Confession?"

"Yes. But in such a way that McGarvey will see and hear you and yet will be confused."

"I think I understand," Dorestos said.

But Franelli explained it to him.

"Do you wish to speak with Father Unger?"

"No. I leave that as well as the other to you. Go with God, my son."

"And you, Monsignor."

McGarvey was halfway up the aisle when Fr. Norman came in with another man, who was also dressed in civilian clothes. They passed the CIA officer.

Dorestos closed the door, got down on his hands and knees beside the desk, and took a small vial from his pocket and drank its contents—less than an ounce—and instantly the somewhat diluted but still strong combination of Serrano and cayenne peppers constricted his throat.

He bowed his head, closed his eyes, and clasped his hands in front of him.

The door opened, and for a moment nothing was said.

"Leave us, Father," a man said, and the door was shut.

Dorestos stayed in position for a full minute, but then he finally looked up into the eyes of Fr. Unger, the university's senior chaplain. "I am in trouble," he said. "I have come for your help."

"Yes, I understand," Fr. Unger said. He was a man of medium height with a sharply receding hairline, thick glasses, and a pleasant manner that made you want to tell him your sins. As a psychologist he was the perfect father confessor.

"Will you hear my confession?" It was hard for Dorestos to speak, his throat was constricted by the peppers.

"Yes, of course. But I am told that you are a priest. Is this a problem of faith?"

"I am a priest, but it is not faith."

"What then?"

"My order is the Hospitallers. More specifically the Sacred Military Order of Malta and I need Christ's forgiveness for what I have done."

Fr. Unger was momentarily taken aback. "I think that I understand. You are not an American?"

"No."

"Are you a fugitive from law enforcement?"

"Not yet, but I may be. I have killed a man who was an apostate. A true enemy of the Mother Church. I had orders, but it was a mistake nonetheless, and I don't know what to do. It's why I came here." Dorestos bowed his head and closed his eyes. "Please help me, Father. I don't want to offend my Church and yet I do not want to offend my God."

"I will hear your confession, my son, and afterward we will decide together what your next step should be," Fr. Unger said, and he pulled a chair around from behind the desk so he could sit near.

Dorestos looked up in anguish. "This must be outside in the confessionals. Where everyone else opens their souls."

"It's not necessary—"

"It is, for me. Please, Father."

"As you wish," Fr. Unger said.

"But I will need some help. My legs have gone numb. I think that it is probably psychosomatic. But I cannot walk. I'll need a wheelchair."

Fr. Unger looked at him for a beat, but then went into a back room and returned shortly with a wheelchair, which he helped Dorestos into.

Outside in the nave they turned left to a line of three confessional booths along the outer wall.

McGarvey stood two rows back from the front, and he met Dorestos's eyes, but didn't move.

"Here will be fine, Father," Dorestos said, raising his ragged voice.

Fr. Unger bent over. "It's okay, Father, you do not have to speak so loudly," he whispered. "I will hear you and so will God."

FORTY-NINE

☐

"Cry out and I will kill both of you," al-Rashid said from the short corridor, the silenced SIG Sauer in his hand. From this angle he could see
Mme. Laurent sitting on the edge of the couch, and their eyes met. She
was frightened, but determined.

"Leave now before it is too late for you," she said defiantly.

"Not until I get what I came for."

"Robert is not a member of the Society, I am. And I don't know who
has the cipher key you're looking for. You've wasted your time."

"I know where the diary is."

"You've already said this. But you have to know that the book is of
only historical significance to us. We have made copies."

"Who has them?"

"I don't have a copy, and I do not know who does."

"We'll see."

Someone came down the hall from the building entrance and rapped
on the door. Al-Rashid took up the same position he had before so that
when the door opened he would be behind it.

Mme. Laurent sat forward and al-Rashid pointed the pistol at her and
she shook her head.

A key grated in the lock and the door swung open.

"Adie?" the mayor said, and he came into the corridor. He spotted
her seated on the couch, her breasts bare, and the body of the half-naked
man on the floor. "My God," he said, and he rushed toward her.

Al-Rashid had half a second to make certain that the mayor's bodyguard had not come with him, before he shut and locked the door.

Vice Mayor Chatelet pulled up short and looked over his shoulder as
al-Rashid came into the living room.

"Call for help and I will shoot you," al-Rashid said, his tone reasonable.

Chatelet opened his mouth to speak, but then looked again at the man on the floor and at his mistress.

"The man on the floor did not rape the mademoiselle, nor did I. In fact other than a blow to her mouth, the only indignity she has suffered is a torn blouse. Now, be so kind as to sit down next to her."

Mme. Laurent moved over and Chatelet sat down beside her. "Is this a robbery, or do you mean to embarrass me politically?"

"Neither, actually. I'm here simply for some information, that Mme. Laurent assures me that neither of you have."

"Then go. I'll give you twenty-four hours before I report this to the Sûreté."

"I appreciate the offer, but I still need one piece of information."

Chatelet turned to his mistress. "Do you know what this man is talking about?"

She nodded. "I'm a member of a secret philanthropic society. We have some historic documents that are in code. He wants to have the key to the code. But I don't have it, nor do I know who does."

"I don't understand."

Mme. Laurent laid a hand on his. "It's not important that you do," she said. She looked up at al-Rashid. "Your contact at the bank in Bern. Is he still alive, or have you murdered him?"

"He is alive."

"Then return to him. He has the cipher key."

"Only the diary was in the safety deposit box."

"There is another box. If you give me a piece of paper and a pen or pencil I shall write the password."

"No need to write it down, tell me, I'll remember."

She recited a mix of eleven numbers and letters that al-Rashid recognized.

"You have at least proved that you are a member of the Society," he said. The password for the supposed second safety box was only two letters and one number different from the password their contact had supplied them.

"Then leave us in peace, you have what you came for."

Chatelet was confused, it was written all over his face, but also written in the corners of his eyes and his mouth was a calculation of what damage something like this incident could do to his presidential bid, and perhaps even more important where there might be an advantage.

"Before you leave—and you have my word that I will give you a twenty-four-hour head start—what are we talking about here?" He looked at his mistress, and then back at al-Rashid. "A philanthropic society for which evidently people have lost their lives over, if I am understanding you correctly. Including the unfortunate doorman. That makes no sense."

"It's not what you think, Robert," Mme. Laurent said. "Henri did nothing but try to come to my rescue."

"Nor does your whore make much sense," al-Rashid said harshly, and the vice mayor rose half up off his seat.

Al-Rashid pointed the gun at Chatelet. "I am done with the fantasy."

"I gave you want you wanted," Mme. Laurent cried.

"You gave me a clever password, which I would have to return to Bern to use. But even if it were a valid number, Interpol would be waiting for me. I want the truth this time."

"I'm telling the truth."

"No."

"I don't know what the hell is going on, but I'll give you whatever you want to make this situation disappear," Chatelet said. "For Christ's sake, Adie, give the man what he wants."

"I have."

"No," al-Rashid said.

"What is it worth?"

Mme. Laurent lowered her eyes for a moment. "More than you can possibly imagine, my dear Robert." She looked up. "It is all I have to say."

Al-Rashid stepped forward and jammed the muzzle of the silencer against the vice mayor's forehead. "The truth."

Mme. Laurent said nothing.

"Where is the cipher key?"

"I don't know."

"I will kill him," al-Rashid said. The dynamic was interesting.

Mme. Laurent looked up. "You'll kill us anyway."

"You cannot know that for sure."

"For God's sake, Adie," Chatelet said, gripping her hand.

"Robert," she said softly.

"Please."

Mme. Laurent looked away. "I don't know who of us has the key, and that's the truth. But the original is in Seville. Has been from the first."

"What's in Seville?" al-Rashid asked.

"The Archivo General de Indias."

Al-Rashid knew of this place. It was the repository of original documents from the Spanish Empire's interests in the Americas and the Philippine Islands. And this was the first thing she'd told him—other than her love for Chatelet—that had the ring of truth to it.

"That is a very large, complicated place, unless you know your way through it."

"Dr. Vergilio is the curator," Mme. Laurent said. "Or at least she was during the last trouble several months ago involving a pair of agents from the American CIA."

She'd piqued al-Rashid's interest. "What trouble?"

"I'm not sure, but it had to do with the treasure," she said. She glanced at Chatelet. "I am truly sorry, Robert. None of this has anything to do with you, or with France."

Chatelet started to say something, but al-Rashid fired one shot, driving the vice mayor's head back in a spray of blood.

"No!" Mme. Laurent screeched, and she lunged over his body.

Al-Rashid switched aim and fired one shot into the top of her head, and she fell forward, her head bouncing on the coffee table, her legs twitching violently for several seconds before her entire body went slack.

For a full ten seconds al-Rashid remained perfectly still, waiting for the sounds of alarm, but the building was quiet.

He stood up, wiped down the pistol, laid it on the floor in front of the couch, then left through the French doors into the courtyard, and through an old wooden door onto the mews and then to the avenue, where two blocks later he hailed a cab for the Hotel Inter-Continental and had a well-deserved bath and full breakfast.

FIFTY

◻

It was late in the afternoon by the time McGarvey got back to All Saints. The place had been put back together, no battle damage visible anywhere. A team of security technicians had come down from Langley and installed dual motion/infrared detectors around the perimeter of the entire hospital, including the woods at the back. In addition four heavily armed combat training officers and four of their students had come up from the Farm and stood guard.

Callahan was at the security station in the front hall with Tommy Newman. He broke off when McGarvey came down the hallway from the rear entrance. "He checked in yesterday at the Georgetown Suites just off M Street."

"He wasn't there?" McGarvey asked. He thought it was probably a dead end. The priest might have checked in, but he would not have gone back there after last night.

"No. The cleaning crew said it appeared as if he'd slept in the bed, but when we interviewed the night staff, they remembered him, high-pitched voice and all, but he'd left around ten and no one saw him come back. I just found out, otherwise I would have called you earlier. What about the churches?"

"No one would admit that anyone had asked for sanctuary, though I had my doubts about the university chapel. The father superior was hearing someone's confession when I came in, but the guy was in a wheelchair and his voice was all wrong."

"Could it have been your man?"

"Except for the voice, but he looked me in the eye and nodded. Seemed that he was relieved about something."

"He confessed his sins. A lot of Catholics feel that a burden has been lifted off their souls."

"Then they go out and do the same thing the next day."

Callahan nodded. "So what's next, Mac? It's your call."

McGarvey's instincts were humming in high pitch. His tradecraft, most of which he'd learned on the run, and his understanding of what motivated just about every son of a bitch he'd ever faced told him that the priest was coming back to kill María. The hell with the odds.

Yet all the facts pointed in the opposite direction. He'd abandoned the Tahoe and the hotel room. He had stolen a car, driven it out to National, and shortly after that the same charter Gulfstream that had brought him up from Sarasota had filed a flight plan for San Juan but then had disappeared somewhere over the Atlantic just outside U.S. airspace.

The guy was gone. Yet McGarvey couldn't shake the fact that in his gut he knew the priest was not on that plane.

"I'm going home to get something to eat, take a shower, and get some sleep," he said. He turned back to Newman. "Anything comes up give me a call."

Newman, who'd been good friends with Kutschinski, nodded and smiled viciously. "Yes, sir. I'll let you know when we stuff him in a body bag."

McGarvey stopped himself from saying that he wanted the priest alive. "See you in the morning."

He gave Callahan a nod and went back outside to his car and drove around front where he was buzzed through the gate. His apartment was less than a mile away just off Dunbarton across from Rock Creek Park. In the morning he would go for a ten-K run along the creek. It seemed like months since he'd stretched himself. He was getting a little rusty, especially after witnessing the priest's antics on Casey Key and imagining how the bastard had made it over the fence at the hospital.

Sometimes like this he felt old, but then he reminded himself that self-pity was the start of a downward spiral, especially for people in this business. The ones who lost their mental edge were their own worst enemies.

As soon as he was away he phoned Otto. "I'm on my way home to take a break. That Embraer has to land sooner or later somewhere. Track it to its destination and see if we can put some boots on the ground to find out who gets off."

"I'm already on it," Rencke said. "It's a Gulfstream V, same as the C37A we fly, with a range of right around six thousand miles—give or take. It can reach just about anywhere in South America and Europe, and it doesn't need a major airport to land. Chances are we're not going to find out until it's back at its home strip."

"Which is?"

"Executive Charters, London's Heathrow. Except that the company doesn't own an aircraft with that tail number."

"It must have come from somewhere."

"I haven't found out where yet."

"Try Malta first, and then Rome. My guess is it might be registered to a company with some sort of an arm's length connection with the Church."

"I'm on it. What about the hospital? Is María awake yet?"

"No, and the place has been closed down tight. No way he's going to get past all that firepower."

"Watch your back, Mac. This business is far from over."

McGarvey found a parking spot a half a block from his apartment, and walked back, mentally cataloging the cars and SVUs parked on the street. It had been months since he'd stayed any length of time here, yet he remembered the cars from then and as recently as yesterday, and nothing seemed out of the ordinary to him now. No out-of-state plates, no diplomatic tags, no vans with deeply tinted windows, no vehicles with extra antennas.

He let himself in, and upstairs out of habit he stopped for a long moment on the landing to listen for any sounds, or this time odors, out of the ordinary. But nothing stood out.

At his door he checked the grease spot in the keyhole, which seemed undisturbed, yet that telltale had been defeated before and in the meantime he hadn't taken the time to set another one in its stead. Sloppy, maybe, but he wasn't going around unarmed. Not since the incident at Casey Key.

He pulled out his pistol and pushed the de-cocking lever to the up position, and eased the door open with the toe of his shoe.

The apartment was small, only the living room with the kitchen and small eating area to the right, and the single bedroom and bathroom to the left. A television and Bose stereo system were on a cabinet on one side of the room, bracketed by a couple of bookcases that held, in addition to books, some photos of his wife, their daughter, their son-in-law, and Audie.

He'd taken them down and put them in a drawer in the bedroom where they stayed for months, until he could finally bring them back out and face them every time he came through the door.

His heart still ached thinking about them, but he'd become a changed man. Harder, Louise told him some months ago. Easier to get angry, sharper, less patient, more content with being a loner than ever before.

In the old days, even when he'd hidden out in Lausanne after the assignment to kill a general in Chile had gone bad, and Katy had given him the ultimatum—her or the CIA, for which he chose neither—he'd not been content to live alone. But every woman, including his wife when he'd gotten back together with her, had lost their lives because of their association with him.

Now being alone was better.

He swept the living room with his pistol, then closed and relocked the door behind him. He took a quick look in the kitchen, then went back to his bedroom.

Nothing moved, nothing was out of place. The only light was the one in the bathroom. The door was still half open as he had left it. And he started to come down.

He safetied his pistol and tossed it on the bed, then took off his jacket and quick-draw holster at the small of his back, tossing them on an easy chair in the corner where he liked to read at the odd moment.

For just a split instant he almost froze in his tracks, but then he went across the room to the chest of drawers, where he got a pair of shorts and a T-shirt that lay on top of another fully loaded Walther PPK—the one he'd taken from Casey Key—which was fitted with a silencer.

He'd caught the odor from the bathroom of sweat and the faint but distinctive smell of a pistol that had been recently fired. The son of a bitch had tracked him here, and after everything that had happened—especially the senseless murders of the four wounded CIA officers and Nurse Randall—he was glad they would finally have it out.

McGarvey moved to the left into the deeper shadows in the corner, switched the safety lever to the off position, and pointed it at the bathroom door.

"You came here because you wanted me to help find the diary for the Church," he said, keeping any trace of anger from his voice. "I'm listening."

"Does the woman still live?" Dorestos asked. His voice was ragged, but still high-pitched.

"She bled to death before the doctor arrived," McGarvey said. "It was you at the confessional."

"It was a relief."

"How do you expect me to help you?"

"The diary is the property of the Mother Church."

"What about the claim of the Voltaire Society?"

"They are the devil's handmaidens. They stole the diary."

"The Church stole the treasure from the Spanish government."

"Spain stole it from the Native Americans. The Church has been their bedrock for four centuries. We brought Jesus Christ to save their immortal souls. It was enough."

The argument was circular just as all religious debates were in the end. McGarvey wasn't an atheist—he'd seen too much senseless death in his career to be without some belief. But he had never found a religious system that fit him. Like almost every philosophy, established religions were failures in the end.

"I don't know where to begin," McGarvey said.

"Seville. But put down your gun and we will talk."

"Face-to-face," McGarvey said.

"Of course," Dorestos agreed.

McGarvey lowered his weapon, and an instant later the figure of the priest darted out from the bathroom and crossed the room in a blur, his speed incredible.

Leading the big man, McGarvey fired off four shots as fast as he could pull the trigger.

Dorestos nearly made it to the bedroom door into the short corridor, managing to get off one shot over his shoulder that went wide, before he crashed against the wall with a loud bang and went down hard.

He had fallen on his side, his gun hand underneath his body, and he tried to pull it out when McGarvey reached him. He looked up, obviously dying and obviously knowing it. But he didn't seem in much pain or distress.

"Thank you," he whispered, his voice still ragged.

"The people you killed: why?"

Dorestos's eyes fluttered. "My mother was there," he said.

"What?" McGarvey demanded. "I don't understand."

Dorestos smiled. "Go with God, my son," he said, and he died.

FIFTY-ONE

"Seville," McGarvey said to Otto just before they went into Walt Page's seventh-floor conference room of the CIA's Original Headquarters Building on the campus.

"Are we sharing that this afternoon?" Rencke asked.

"No."

Including the DCI at the head of the narrow table, Bambridge and Carlton Patterson were on his left, Bill Callahan at the opposite end, and two chairs were open on the right.

Pete Boylan, the Company's senior debriefer, sat at the far corner next to Callahan, an understanding smile on her pretty face. She was thirty-three, with short dark hair, bright blue eyes, and the voluptuous good looks and figure of a Hollywood superstar. She had worked with McGarvey on the operation that had sprung from the deaths of his wife, daughter, and son-in-law, getting wounded in a gun battle near the end.

"Mr. Director, good to see you again," she said.

McGarvey gave her a smile, but turned to the others. "None of this will be taped."

"Why is that?" Bambridge demanded.

"Because you won't like what you're going to hear, and you won't want it on record."

"May I take notes?" Pete asked.

"Sure," McGarvey said, and he and Otto sat down.

"You're no longer connected in any official capacity with this agency, so you will not be conducting this debriefing," Bambridge said.

"Marty, from what I've seen you're a damned fine DDO, but you need to guard against bombast."

Patterson chuckled. "Would you like to begin with the dead body in your apartment?" he asked. "We assume that he's the man who attacked All Saints last night."

"I'll make it brief, and you can decide the ramifications, because this is going to involve the State Department and the White House. And if it goes public you're going to have a very large mess on your hands."

Rencke had brought an iPad and he powered it up.

"That won't work in this building," Bambridge said.

Rencke shrugged. "This one will."

"A Frenchman claiming to represent something called the Voltaire Society came to see me at New College. He said that a diary that belonged to them had been stolen from a bank vault in Bern, and he wanted me to help find it."

"We've heard all that," Patterson said.

"The diary apparently pinpoints the locations of what were seven caches of gold and silver buried somewhere in New Mexico, what is now military testing grounds. Near the same place we tested our first nuclear weapon in nineteen forty-five. Supposedly the Voltaires have already emptied three of the caches, converted the metal into hard currency, and spent it."

"On what?"

"According to the Frenchman, they spent it to help democracies in trouble."

"Christ, spare us," Bambridge said.

"We uncovered a fairly substantial payment to us shortly before the Civil War. There may be others, Otto's working on it."

"Payment to who exactly?" Patterson asked.

"To the U.S. Treasury via a bank in Richmond."

"That can be researched," Patterson said to Page.

"I'll give you what I found," Otto said, looking up from his iPad. "But from what I've come up with so far someone began burying these sorts of transactions shortly afterward. There could have been more payments, but digging them out might be tough. My suggestion would be to start within the last ten years or so, to find income to the U.S. Treasury that has no line items. Not taxes, not seizures of property, not donations left by little old ladies. A few billions of dollars here and there unexplained."

"You want to sift through tens of trillions of dollars? More?"

"Yes, and you might match it with crises points, where we were cash-strapped as a nation."

"Like the bank bailouts?" Bambridge asked sarcastically.

"Where did all that money come from?" Otto asked.

"This Frenchman came to you because of your involvement with the Cuban government in the person of Colonel León, I assume," Patterson said.

"I turned him down, and as he was leaving the parking lot his car blew up, killing him, and killing two kids who were standing at a bike rack."

"And then the CNI surveillance operation on you," Bambridge said. "You've already told us that it was they who killed the Frenchman—"

"And the two students."

Bambridge nodded. "Unfortunate. But you got into a shoot-out killing all four of them. Would you care to go into more detail? I'm sure that the Bureau is most interested."

Callahan said nothing, which seemed to disappoint the DDO.

"Only three, in self-defense," McGarvey said. "The fourth was killed by the man in my apartment."

"And you maintain that this person—possibly a Catholic priest—managed to breach the perimeter at All Saints, kill four of our wounded officers in their beds, a nurse, the on-duty security officer, and the two bodyguards from Housekeeping who you'd requested be sent over to guard Colonel León, who herself had been wounded in a shoot-out behind a previously unknown safe house that Mr. Rencke maintained. We weren't able to retrieve any of this from surveillance tapes at the hospital," Bambridge said. "Does that about sum it up?"

"He was good."

"Good enough to do all of that, and still break into your apartment without your being aware of the fact until he attacked you. Yet you beat him. You took him down. You shot him to death."

"Yes."

Bambridge looked at the others and spread his hands. "You're right, I don't like any of it. Particularly the business with the Spanish government. My concern is what happens next, because from where I sit this is nothing but a fantasy that has gotten a whole lot of people killed for no reason."

Page interrupted. "Go on, Mac."

"Fantasy or not, the Spanish CNI is involved in searching for the diary to such an extent that it was willing to assassinate an agent of some society who'd come to me for help. For the treasure that Spain believes is theirs."

"And the man in your apartment?" Page asked.

Otto was suddenly busy on his iPad, his fingers flying over the virtual keyboard.

"I think that he was an agent of a Catholic order—whether officially or not I can't say—to eliminate the Spanish operation against me, so that I would be free to find the diary. The church claims that the treasure is theirs."

"The Spanish government wants the treasure," Patterson said. "As does something called the Voltaire Society—philanthropists if we are to believe the story—as does some Catholic quasi-military order, and as does the Cuban government again in the person of Colonel León. Do I have it all?"

"The priest came to Otto's safe house to kill not me, but Colonel León. And he came to the hospital to try to finish the job."

"You had a guardian angel," Bambridge said. "So why did he suddenly show up at your apartment to eliminate you?"

"Son of a bitch," Otto muttered.

"I don't know," McGarvey said, and they all turned to Rencke.

"Unless I'm smoking something and have gone more delusional than normal, someone else is after the diary."

"What is it?" McGarvey said.

Rencke inclined his head. "Share?" he asked.

"Damned right you'll share whatever you came up with inside this building," Bambridge said.

"IPads don't work here."

McGarvey nodded.

"The Frenchman who came to see Mac in Sarasota gave us a business card with the name Giscarde Petain and a phone number. The number matches an office in the Second Arrondissement of Paris—where lots of banks have their headquarters. A night watchman there was found murdered. And a couple of hours later, just two blocks away, a woman and her son were found shot to death with the guard's pistol. Their names were Petain."

"Does Sûreté have any leads?"

"They're a little busy right now, *kemo sabe*. Robert Chatelet and his mistress were found shot to death in her apartment. The doorman was also found dead, his neck broken. He was bare from the waist down, and it looked as if the woman—Adeline Laurent—might have been raped."

"The vice mayor of Paris?" Bambridge asked.

"Yeah, and a leading candidate for the French presidency."

"I don't see the connection."

"But it's there," Rencke said. "I can smell it."

"So can I," McGarvey said. "The ante has just been raised."

PART
THREE

The following days

FIFTY-TWO

The afternoon on the Harrat Rahat, which was Saudi Arabia's largest volcanic lava field between Jeddah and Medina, was brutally hot, topping 120 degrees Fahrenheit. Prince Saleh and al-Rashid rode a pair of magnificent Arabian stallions, the horses delicately picking their footing across the horrible terrain. To make a misstep here would cause them to break a leg after which they would have to be destroyed.

Which was the point the prince was trying to make. He often brought people who had displeased him out here to break their spirits. Many times he rode out onto the lava flow with a minion and came back alone.

But where the prince seemed to revel in this environment, al-Rashid endured the brutal circumstance with the same stoic indifference as he felt on the battlefield, whether it be in the city or out here.

They were dressed in Bedu white thobes, over which were sleeveless abas and kufeya headgear secured with wool ties. Al-Rashid felt only faintly ridiculous, though the traditional desert garb had been perfected over a couple of millennia to keep the desert nomads relatively safe from the sun.

The prince wore a curved dagger in his belt.

Overhead an American-made Predator drone, controlled by a Saudi Air Force unit outside Riyadh loyal to the prince, circled. At the slightest sign of trouble the unmanned aircraft, equipped with a 20 mm cannon, would obliterate any threat to Saleh.

"You have been a busy man on my behalf," the prince said. They topped a small rise and stopped where they looked out across the fantastic swirls and ridges formed by molten rock nearly eight hundred years ago. This was truly a no-man's-land.

"Yes, but I am not finished."

"I know, my old and loyal friend. But you have created some complications that have come to the notice of the king, who actually sent a minor cousin to talk to me. It was an insult considering all that I have done for the family."

"Better than recalling you to the palace," al-Rashid said.

"Better that you watch your tongue," Saleh shot back angrily. "France is not our enemy. Murdering Chatelet and his mistress was an incredible blunder on your part."

"The Sûreté has not identified the killer, nor will they."

"But the king's spies know."

"Which means you have an informer on your staff."

Saleh sat back in his saddle and looked to the east, toward Medina, the Radiant City, where the tomb of the Blessed Muhammed lay under the green dome of the Al-Masjid an-Nabawi, in an obvious effort to control his temper.

Al-Rashid followed his gaze. The prince would be dead before a drone strike could be ordered. And riding with the body, the controllers would not shoot. In was an option, one of several he always kept open.

"You may be right," Saleh said. "And if such is the case I will deal with it out here." He turned back. "It still leaves us with the incident in France. It must never be traced back to us. It was suggested that you disappear permanently."

"That can be arranged, if you wish it, my Prince. But it would leave you without my services."

"There are others with your skills."

"No," al-Rashid said simply. "If that were actually the case you would have ordered my death sometime ago. And even now you know that I tell you the truth no matter how disagreeable it may be to you." He smiled faintly. "In fact I may be the only man in the kingdom who does so. And without truth, you could not exist."

Saleh paused again for several long beats. "You can never return to France. Not to Marseille."

Al-Rashid was stunned. Among the very first lines of defense he'd created for himself was his background story as a French businessman with a home in Marseille. No one was to know for sure where he went to ground between assignments.

He had salted away a reasonable fortune of something more than twenty-five million euros that would, if the need arose, be enough to change his identity and hide for the remainder of his life. He would have to become frugal, but he knew that he could manage.

If the need did arise, his first act would be to kill the prince, but for now he kept any of those thoughts from changing his expression.

"The French will stop looking eventually, and classify the crime scene for what it appeared to be: the doorman attempted to rape Mademoiselle Laurent, who called for her lover's help. When he arrived they had a falling out as lovers often do under extreme stress, and either the vice mayor killed her and then committed suicide, or it was the other way around. Sloppy, certainly, but the French have had experience with love triangles gone bad."

Saleh eyed him coldly. "You will make a mistake one day."

"Perhaps. But I accomplished more than that in Paris, which was what led me to the woman and her lover."

"So you have said. But you did not find the cipher key without which the diary is useless to me."

"No, but I have a very good idea where I may find it."

"Back in Switzerland?"

"That is a possibility I'll leave to the last."

"Not back to Paris?"

"To the Archives of the Indies in Seville, where all the records of the Spanish plunder of the New World are kept. They were as bad as the Nazis; they kept records of all their slaughters."

"You mean to go to this archives where someone will tell you how to find the cipher key?"

"It will not be that easy because I don't believe that even they know they have it."

"You're making no sense," the prince warned. "And I am certainly not going to authorize or pay for you to go on some wild-goose chase that has the likelihood of turning into another international incident that may get back to the family."

Al-Rashid had considered the possibility that even the prince might get cold feet, and he had worked out another set of options for himself. A few billion euros did not mean much to Saleh. But it was a considerable sum of money that was of interest to the Spanish government as well as to the so-called Voltaire Society, either of whom might be willing to pay a considerable finder's fee under the right circumstances.

"I'm at your service, my Prince," al-Rashid said at length.

"Yes, you are, at the service of the Kingdom who paid for your training and your education. It is we who created you."

It came to al-Rashid that whatever message the cousin had brought from Abdullah must have been a strong one for Saleh to have made such a sudden about-face. Evidently the prince was good, but he had probably been told that he was not indispensible. He was passing the warning along.

"What about the diary and the cipher code?"

"Where is the diary?"

"In a safe place. I didn't think it would be wise for me to carry it around."

Saleh nodded. "Is it here in the country?"

"No."

"In France?"

"No."

Saleh's anger flared. "Don't toy with me, Mahd. For now you will suspend your search for the key. I want you to get the diary and bring it to me for safekeeping."

"And afterward?" al-Rashid asked, knowing for sure now what he would do next.

"I may have another assignment for you. We'll see. But in the meantime you will not return to France ever again. You will stay here as my guest."

FIFTY-THREE

□

For the next couple of days McGarvey shuttled between the CIA's surveillance and information processing center called the Watch, which was on the seventh floor of the OHB where the situation in France was being closely monitored, and Callahan's office in the FBI. The Bureau's forensics people were trying, without luck, to identify the priest who McGarvey had shot to death. He'd gone back to the Renckes' safe house.

The French had come to no definite conclusions about either the killing at the bank building or the deaths of Madam Petain and her son. Nor had they'd made connections yet between those crimes and the bloody scene at Mme. Laurent's apartment.

But the French tabloids were all over the supposed love triangle between the vice mayor, the doorman, and the mistress, for which the Sûreté had no comment.

"They're still looking for a fourth person who a passerby might have seen leaving the building from the rear courtyard about the time of the killings," Otto had told him last night over dinner at his and Louise's new safe house. "A slender man, but nothing else."

"Anything yet from Seville?" McGarvey asked.

"The CNI have taken no special notice, so they're either hiding in the bushes on the chance you'll show up, or they've not made the connection. But you're certain that the priest told you the answers were in Seville?"

"It was before I shot him. I told him that I didn't know where to begin looking for the diary. And he said Seville."

"Do you think he was lying, trying to throw you off?"

"I think that everything he did in Florida and then up here was to get me involved."

Otto shook his head. "If he'd come to your apartment to kill you, why would he give you such a clue? Doesn't make any sense."

McGarvey had thought hard about that exact thing, and the only conclusion he'd come up with was totally nuts. "Could be at the end he was ordered to kill me, but rather than that he pointed me toward Seville and then to prove that he wasn't lying committed suicide."

"Jesus," Otto said softly.

They were at the table in the kitchen, Louise seated across from McGarvey. "Only the Islamic fundamentalist crazies do that kind of stuff anymore," she said.

"He could have been the same guy at the college chapel. His voice in the apartment was a little ragged. Could be he'd taken something to change it. If it was him, he'd apparently given his confession. I just saw him for a couple of seconds, but to me he looked happy."

"Like he'd made a decision?" Louise said.

"Yeah. And Bill Callahan agreed with me. If this guy was from the Order he might just have martyred himself to push me to find the diary."

"Then isn't it likely that someone from the Order will be waiting for you in Seville?"

"I'm counting on it," McGarvey said.

He'd wanted to go back to his apartment, but the FBI had mounted a tight surveillance operation around the place, looking specifically for Cuban intelligence operatives, who by now had to know where María León was being held, and that once again McGarvey had had something to do with her hospitalization.

The Bureau didn't want him anywhere near the place, and he wanted to keep his distance from Otto and Louise in case the CNI or the SMOM or someone else traced him and wanted to try something.

"What are we waiting for?" Otto had asked. "If the answers are in Seville, let's get going."

"Soon," McGarvey had said.

He'd cleared out first thing in the morning, before dawn, and had driven over to All Saints in time for the surveillance team's shift change. Newman was back, and McGarvey made the scheduled trek around the perimeter fence with him.

"Anything we need to know?" he'd asked.

"Bill Callahan thinks it's possible that Cuban intel might mount an ops to grab the colonel, but that's fringe. They're just guessing."

They'd stopped at the back door, the woods behind the compound just beginning to take definition with the dawn. "What's your gut telling you, sir?" Newman said.

"I'm going to ask her just that before I get her out of here."

Newman was startled. "No shit, you're springing her?"

"Yeah. You guys can stand down."

The CIA security officer was wistful. "A lot of good people died here for no reason. Tell me she was the cause, and you can take her out in a body bag."

"She'll be more useful alive than dead," McGarvey said.

"If you say so, sir," Newman said, but he was skeptical.

McGarvey had waited until after breakfast was served to María, who was their only patient, and until the staff and surveillance guys were fed before he went upstairs to her fourth-floor room.

A bulky young kid with a shaved head who was a student at the Farm was seated on a chair in front of María's room, the door closed, and when McGarvey got off the elevator he pulled his pistol from a shoulder holster and jumped up. He was nervous, and when he saw who it was he visibly relaxed.

"You gave me a start, sir," he said as McGarvey came down the corridor.

"Everything okay?"

"Yes, sir, except she bitches nonstop about everything. Why I closed the door; I got tired of listening to her."

"I'm taking her off your hands," McGarvey said. He knocked on the door and went in.

María had just gotten out of the shower and was toweling off. She looked up without modesty. A small square bandage about the size and thickness of a pack of cigarettes was taped just above her left breast. She had been careful not to get it wet.

"If you've come to tell me I have to stay here another day, you might as well shoot me, because I've leaving."

"Technically you're under arrest," McGarvey said. Louise had given him a bra and panties, a pair of jeans, and a white cotton blouse, in a paper grocery bag, which he handed to her. "Sizes are all wrong, but these should do until we can get your other things wherever you've stashed them."

"In the rental car, wherever your people impounded it," she said.

"I'll send someone over. In the meantime do you feel good enough to travel?"

"Spain?" she said. "It's why I came from Havana to see you in the first place."

"But you have a lot of catching up to do before we go."

"I'm listening," she said. She tossed the towel aside and put on the panties, which more or less fit, but the bra was too small, so she laid it aside and put on the blouse. "Louise send these?"

"Yes, but I don't know why after what you put her through four months ago."

"Not me, just the idiots who worked for me. But she did it because she is a good woman."

"The Vatican is not the only organization who thinks the treasure exists and who want it."

"We do, and so does the CNI, which Dr. Vergilio warned me about. Something put them in high gear, and according to her they are seriously motivated. Who else? Your people?"

"The Company doesn't believe in it. But what's Vergilio's take? I would expect she wants it for her own government."

"You wouldn't believe me if I told you."

"Try me."

"Her father was Castilian, but her mother was a Cuban. They met on some aide program in Zaire, I think. I never properly researched it. Thing is her father died when she was an infant, and her mother raised her alone. She still has relatives in Cuba, who I've looked after."

María pulled on the jeans, which barely fit at the waist, but she had to roll up the cuffs.

"It was a priest who tried to kill you."

"That figures."

"Have you heard of a group that calls itself the Voltaire Society?"

She shook her head. "Like the French philosopher?"

"Yes. They have been in control of the seven caches of gold since the mid-eighteen hundreds. And they've already emptied three of them."

"Jesus," María said, and she came out of the bathroom. "Then it does exist."

FIFTY—FOUR

Walt Page was chauffeured over to the White House first thing in the morning at the president's behest and was immediately shown into the Oval Office. He had a reasonably good idea why he'd been called over, so he wasn't surprised to see the attorney general, Stanley Blumenthal, seated in front of Joseph Langdon's desk.

"Morning, Walt," the AG said. Neither he nor the president seemed happy.

Page took a seat and a moment later Frank Shapiro, the president's adviser on national security affairs, shambled in like an uncaged bear, closing the door and taking a seat.

Langdon picked up his phone. "No interruptions, Joyce," he told his secretary.

"We have a brewing situation on our hands that needs to be dealt with before it spins totally out of control," Shapiro said to Page.

"The incident with the Spanish intelligence officers who were shot to death in Florida," Page replied. It was what he'd expected.

"By the former director of your agency," Shapiro said. "The man needs to be kept on a leash and right now you're the only one who can do it."

"Has O'Connor briefed you yet this morning, Mr. President?" Page asked. Francis O'Connor was the president's new director of the FBI. "There've been several developments overnight."

"I got a call late last night from President La Rocca demanding the bodies of the three men and one woman who he claimed were tourists. Their ambassador has returned to Madrid for consultations and he all but suggested that our ambassador return to Washington to explain to me the delicacy of this business."

"According to McGarvey it may be worse than that," Page said.

"Here we go again," Shapiro said.

The president silenced his NSA adviser with a motion. "I didn't like what La Rocca said to me, nor did I like his tone. But I have a feeling that I'm going to like even less what you're going to tell us."

"It's complicated, sir, because there's a lot more involved than just Spain. And the four who were shot to death have been positively identified as Spanish intelligence agents. But McGarvey only shot three of them, the fourth's body was found a few miles north. McGarvey thinks he was assassinated by a Catholic priest."

The AG started to protest, but the president silenced him too. "Anything having to do with McGarvey doesn't surprise me."

"He's done good things for this country, Mr. President, and paid a very heavy price for it."

"I won't argue the fact. Nonetheless the people who've had to pick up the pieces after him are practically a legion. Does this have something to do with the Spanish treasure supposedly buried in New Mexico?"

"I'm afraid it does, sir. And it may also have something to do with the death of Robert Chatelet."

The Oval Office was suddenly deathly still. None of them had expected such a bombshell, and their reaction was the same as Page's had been, incredulity to the point of outright disbelief. The problem he faced was how to convince the president of something that he himself was having a hard time swallowing.

"You have my attention, Walt," the president finally said. "I want the situation in a nutshell for now. You can send over a written report later this morning."

"And try to keep yours and McGarvey's wild speculations to a minimum," Shapiro said. He reminded Page of an angry Kissinger, who had been a dangerous man when riled.

"It began a few days ago in Florida when a man claiming to represent an organization of international bankers came to ask for McGarvey's help finding a diary that was stolen from a bank vault in Bern. Mac turned him down and as the man was driving away his car blew up, killing him as well as a pair of bystanders. The diary, written in the mid-eighteen hundreds—before our Civil War—apparently pinpointed the locations of seven caches of Spanish treasure in New Mexico."

"Urban legend," Shapiro said.

"One that has resulted in the deaths of a number of people, and Mc-Garvey doesn't think it will end until the diary is found."

"Go on," the president said. His mood was impossible to read just then, except he seemed patient. Something this president had never been known for.

"The Bureau has definitely linked the car bombing to the CNI surveillance team that had been set up next door to McGarvey. That same evening when he went over to confront them there was a shoot-out in which three of them were shot to death. The fourth escaped. That same evening McGarvey was attacked by someone he said had a high-pitched voice, and who spoke English with a decidedly Italian accent. McGarvey has reason to believe the guy was a priest, who served as a soldier in the Sacred Military Order of Malta."

"What's become of this priest? Has McGarvey also assassinated him?" Shapiro asked.

"He showed up at McGarvey's apartment in Georgetown and there was another shoot-out," Page said. "But the night before that the priest—if that's what he was—managed to penetrate All Saints' security measures and murdered four wounded CIA officers lying in their beds, one of the nurses, and the security team."

"What was he after? Or should I ask who—" Shapiro said, but then stopped. "McGarvey was there."

"Yes, but the priest wasn't after him, he was after Colonel María León—the same one from Havana who showed up several months ago looking for the Spanish treasure. She came back again for the same reason, and was wounded in a gunfight at a safe house maintained by my Director of Special Projects. She was taken to the hospital."

"Otto Rencke," Shapiro said.

He had a long-standing love/hate relationship with the CIA, for a reason or reasons that Page had never learned. In the early days he'd been one of the architects of the office of the director of national intelligence, which most professionals in the business thought was little more than another wasted layer of Washington bureaucracy.

"Yes."

"A French banker comes to McGarvey, the CNI kills him, McGarvey kills the CNI team—all but one—who is killed by a priest, who tries to kill Colonel León, and who dies in a shoot-out with McGarvey. Is that about right?"

"So far," Page admitted.

"But you're going to tell us how all of that connects with the deaths of the leading candidate for the French presidency, along with his mistress and a doorman who according to the papers tried to rape the woman."

"We think there is someone else involved. The man who came to ask for McGarvey's help gave a phone number that Rencke was able to trace to what probably was an accommodations address in Paris. A night watchman there was killed, and the next morning we believe the pistol registered to the night watchman was used to kill the vice mayor and his mistress. It's one fact that the French authorities have not yet made public, for the simple reason they don't know what to make of it."

"But McGarvey does."

"He thinks so."

"He thinks so," Shapiro said sharply.

"You've obviously debriefed Mr. McGarvey," the AG said.

"This morning."

"Where is he at this moment?"

"I'm not sure," Page admitted.

"At the least he should be in custody until we can get this mess straightened out," Shapiro said. "What about Mr. Rencke?"

"He's gone as well."

"Vanished without a trace?" the AG asked.

Page nodded.

"And let me guess, Colonel León is missing as well."

"Yes."

The president, who had remained silent through most of this, sat forward. "Any idea who this fourth—or would it be fifth—party in Paris might be? Or what his purpose is?" he asked.

"No, sir."

"Well then, I would like to have a word with Mr. McGarvey. As you say he has done many great things for this country, and has suffered for it. I'd like to get his views on what's going on. And have Mr. Rencke come along, and the Cuban colonel."

"That might not be such a good idea," Shapiro said. "We might have to put some distance between him and this office, in case there is a French connection after all."

"I want them here as soon as possible," the president said. "This afternoon at the latest."

"But you don't know where they are," Shapiro said to Page.

"Rencke monitors any number of intelligence nets. I'll get word to him as soon as I return to my office."

"I hear a but in there, Walt," the president said.

"I can get word to them, but if they're in the middle of something they may ignore the summons."

"Even from me?" Langdon demanded.

"Yes, sir, even from the president."

FIFTY-FIVE

At the Renckes' safe house just off Dupont Circle Otto and Louise were seated around the breakfast nook with McGarvey and the star of the evening, María León, who looked pale, but not like a woman who'd been shot in the chest forty-eight hours ago.

"So the priest is dead, if that's what he was, where does that leave us?" Louise asked.

They were having drinks—beer for Otto and Louise, a Cognac for McGarvey, and a glass of rum neat for María.

"Still with the problem of the missing diary," María said.

"Which you believe will lead us to the treasure. Same story as before and it didn't work the first time. What makes you think it'll work this time?"

McGarvey was content for the moment to let them hash it out as he tried to work out all the ramifications, because nothing seemed to fit; there was no pattern to the events here and in Europe that he could see. And yet what they were facing was anything but random.

"Because there're a lot more people interested enough in it to commit murder."

"Is that why you came here, Colonel?" Louise asked, her voice and manner suddenly sharp. "From where I sit I'm looking at some serious past history with you and your fellow countrymen." She looked to McGarvey. "Call Bill and have the Bureau send someone over to take her into custody. Protective custody, whatever you want to call it. She can be deported later, or maybe set loose on the Calle Ocho. I know some people who would like that."

"I came here because my government still has a stake in what Spain stole from us."

"Save me. There's more Spanish in you than native Carib. You're no mestizo by a long shot."

"More important why did you come here just now of all times?" Otto asked. "Why not last month, or next month? And what did you come hoping to find?"

"Raul sent me."

"Who told you about the diary?" McGarvey asked, looking up. "Was it Dr. Vergilio? Are you and she bosom buddies? She calls or texts from time-to-time?"

McGarvey watched her for a reaction, and when she finally broke eye contact he got up and went to the counter where he poured another small Cognac. He stood drinking it, his back to the table, and when he was finished he turned back.

"The problem is the fifth man—and for the moment I'm assuming it's a man. He's probably the one who somehow got access to the safety deposit box in Bern—if we are to believe Monsieur Petain—and stole the diary."

"Dr. Vergilio thought the same thing," María said. "But if he has the diary then why did he take the risk of going to Paris to find someone from the Voltaire Society, which for some reason—according to you— led him to the vice mayor of Paris and his mistress? Doesn't make any sense."

"I didn't think so until just a minute ago when I realized that the diary was no good to him because he couldn't read it."

"Probably church Latin," Otto suggested.

"Translatable, unless it was in code."

"For which he needed someone from the Society to provide him with the key."

"But they wouldn't or couldn't so he killed them," McGarvey said. "Which raises two questions. If the diary was so valuable wouldn't they have made a copy? And if the people the guy confronted didn't know the key why didn't they tell him where it could be found? Shunt him away. Maybe misdirect him. Why give their lives? To save what?"

"To save it from the Vatican," María suggested.

"According to Petain, the Society has already plundered three of the caches, which means they have the key, or at the very least had it at one time. And they certainly wouldn't deal with the Vatican."

"Seville?" Louise said.

María shook her head. "Adriana would have known if it was there."

"Maybe," McGarvey said. "But without the key the diary is worthless."

"And without the diary, the key is worthless," Otto said. "So what do you suggest?"

"The CNI won't stop and neither will the Vatican nor the Voltaires. But we know something about them. We don't know anything about the guy in Paris who was willing to kill the possible future president right under the noses of his bodyguard. And I'd like to know something about him—or her—before I show up in Seville."

María's eyes were suddenly very bright. "You're going after it?"

McGarvey had thought long and hard about that over the past few days. He didn't give a damn about some historical treasure whether it was in a Spanish galleon sunk in a hurricane off Florida's coast, or buried somewhere in Arizona. Nor did he care about the deaths of the priest or of the CNI operatives—who were not much different than María in terms of their disregard for collateral damage.

It was the deaths of the two students in the parking lot at New College, the four wounded CIA officers lying helpless in their hospital beds, and the nurse. The Company security officers were a different story, however. They'd died in the line of duty, and they would get stars on the granite wall in the lobby of the OHB in Langley. He felt sorry for them and for their families, but they were soldiers who'd fallen in the field doing what they'd been trained to do.

It was the senseless murders of the innocents and the helpless that always got to him. Though a number of terrorists he had personally faced—including Osama bin Laden—had all argued that no one was innocent.

At length he nodded. "But not for the reasons you might want."

"But you need my help," María said, and it was perfectly clear that she had her own agenda, and she was willing to trade her aid for McGarvey's. "You'll have to figure out a way to get into Spain clean. The CNI catches one whiff of your presence and they'll be all over you."

"I think that we might need to go to Bern first. Assuming the killer in Paris is the same guy who managed to steal the diary from a bank vault, he'll have left traces."

"Lots of banks in Bern," Otto said. "How're going to find out which one?"

"I'm going to start knocking on doors and making noise. But quietly as if I'm trying not to be noticed."

"But you will be," Louise said, getting it. "By the killer himself, or the organization he works for. Or the CNI, or the Church, or the Voltaire Society who wanted to hired you in the first place."

"What about me?" María asked.

"You're going to stick it out here with Louise—if she'll have you—until it's time to go to Seville, if that's where we need to be."

"We'll be just peachy here," Louise said. "I need to catch up on my girl talk."

"No," María said.

"It's either here, your word on it, or I'll have the Bureau put you in a holding cell until I need you," McGarvey told her, and he didn't really give a damn what she chose.

"Cristo!"

"Maybe the holding cell would be better," Otto said, concerned.

Louise grinned. She was enjoying herself. "She can't defeat the alarm. And if she tried something she wouldn't get to the end of the block before she was nailed. Anyway, she wants what she figures is Cuba's part of the treasure, because whether she gets it or not, she'll go home a hero for trying. And there are big things on the horizon in Havana for heroes of the people."

"Nobody knows where we are for the moment," Otto said. "The first problem is getting out of the country without the Bureau or the Company finding out until it's too late."

"You're staying behind to work the Internet."

"Not a chance in hell, Mac. Where you go, I go, because I have a stake in this too. Louise and I do. Audie. Anyway, I can work the Internet from anywhere."

McGarvey turned to Louise. "Convince him."

"Nope. He's right. But how are you going to get out?"

"The Church is going to help."

FIFTY-SIX

□

The Archivo General de Indias was housed in a magnificent building begun in 1584 to hold the merchant's exchange, because of complaints from the Mother Church. Directly across the street was the Cathedral where businessmen would retreat from the heat of the Andalusian day. Catholic officials were not pleased and pressure was brought to bear on King Philip II to create a home for the tradesmen who were so vital to the prosperity of Seville.

The ornately decorated two-story building enclosed a central patio where oftentimes archives staff personal would go to eat their lunches and mingle with the few tourists who bothered to visit such a musty place that contained nothing more than five and a half miles of shelving that held forty thousand plus books of eighty million pages.

Here were all the records of the Spanish conquest and administration of the New World, including the journal of Christopher Columbus (it was from Seville he sailed down the Guadalquivir River on his voyage across the Atlantic), the records and dispatches from the first conquistadors all the way to the end of the nineteenth century, including military expeditions, numbers of indigents captured and converted or killed, detailed maps of the countryside showing all the major trails and pathways that had been used by the natives for a thousand years, sailing routes and directions not only across the Atlantic but across the Pacific to Manila. Also on the shelves was a record of every single ounce of gold or silver that had ever been mined or appropriated from the natives, and the disposition of the wealth including losses from storms as well as from piracy, theft, and graft.

Occasionally a guide would bring a small group of tourists, many of them Europeans visiting Spain via bus or boat up the river, for a tour that seldom lasted for more than an hour. The stacks themselves were open for viewing, as were the few artifacts on display, but nothing could be handled except by staff or the ocassional scholar. The offices and preliminary restoration and preservation labs were at one end of the building on the second floor and off-limits to the public.

Al-Rashid, dressed in a lightweight linen suit, was in a group of a dozen tourists, many of them Germans, but some Italians, and a couple of Americans. They'd stopped at a glass case in which was displayed a handwritten log.

"These are the logs of Cristoforo Colombo, as he was known in his native Genoa," the pretty tour guide told them. "But we know him as Cristóbal Colón, because it was the Spanish crown that financed his four expeditions to the new world." She spoke English, as a lingua franca.

An American woman was in front. "To us he is Christopher Columbus, the discoverer of our country. We even have a national holiday in his name."

"Actually he never reached the North American continent, the nearest he reached was the Bahama Islands."

Someone in the group chuckled.

"Are these the actual logs?" al-Rashid asked. He was traveling as a writer under the name Paul Harris, with a British passport, one of his several work names. His name, a brief biography, and a list of historical books he'd never written were listed in Google.

The young woman smiled faintly. "Heavens no," she said. "The actual logs are in hermetic storage as are many of the original documents from that early era."

"Will we be able to see them?"

"No, nothing from that period is available to the public, though scholars with accredited projects are given certain limited access."

"Is anything here real?" one of the Germans asked.

"Oh, yes, nearly everything from the sixteen hundreds and forward are genuine—that's to say the items that are on display. No one but staff, however, are allowed to actually remove items from the shelves."

"No exceptions?" al-Rashid asked.

The guide gave him a sharp look. "That would be up to Dr. Vergilio."

"The curator?"

"Yes."

"And how does one go about seeing her?"

"By appointment."

"I see," al-Rashid said, and he stepped back to let someone else look at the logs.

The main floor of the building was all but deserted except for the occasional staffer, and the security officer at the reception desk just inside the front doors. No one except for the tourists in the group wore identification badges on lanyards.

They had come full circle around the central courtyard back to their starting point in front, past some of the cataloging and restoration rooms, which had been surprisingly quiet. But as the guide explained very little new material was coming into the archives, and the real work of major restorations was done elsewhere.

"We'll take a fifteen-minute break now, in the courtyard where we have provided refreshments," the guide said. "There are many statues for you to see, or if you find that the morning is too warm there are places to sit in the shade."

"May we smoke?" an Italian asked.

"I'm afraid that smoking is not allowed anywhere in the archives or on the grounds for obvious reasons. You may, however, leave the building and smoke. You'll have to turn in your pass at the desk, and retrieve it when you return. But don't be late."

They went out into the expansive courtyard where the guide left them, promising to be back in fifteen minutes sharp. The Italian and a French-woman went back to the main hall and crossed to the security desk.

Al-Rashid slipped out just behind them, and as a security officer was collecting their badges, he pocketed his, crossed to the stairs, and went up to the second floor.

Bookcases reaching nearly to the sixteen-foot ceilings were arranged perpendicular to the outer walls, windows looking down onto the street between each set. A young man wearing white gloves stood on an upper rung of a ladder down one of the aisles but he was so intent on his reading that he didn't notice al-Rashid passing.

At the southwest corner of the building, several offices looked down on the courtyard. A nameplate at the last door read: Dr. Adriana Vergilio, Curador.

Al-Rashid knocked once, and went in. The tour guide from downstairs looked up from behind her desk where she was talking to someone on the phone. She said something and hung up.

"You're obviously not lost, which means that you're trespassing. Either you will give me your visitor's pass and allow me to escort you out of the building, or I shall call the police."

"I'm sorry, but this is the only way I knew how to meet with Dr. Vergilio without going through the customary appointments rigmarole."

The woman lifted the telephone. She was angry, and al-Rashid considered killing her before she could make the call.

"This is very important to her and the archives," he said. "Already several people have lost their lives, and there may be more."

An older woman, under five feet, gray hair up in a bun, her face weathered and brown from too much time in the sun, appeared at the door to her inner office. She was scowling.

"Who are you?" she demanded in Spanish.

Al-Rashid understood her. "In English, please," he said. "My name is Paul Harris, I'm a writer of historical fiction mostly, but I've come across an incredible story that I think a number of people have lost their lives over. At least that's what I was told."

"By whom?"

"A Frenchman who came to see me at my home in Greenwich. Claimed he was from an organization called the Voltaire Society, and he was in a fight for his life with some Americans. Maybe from the CIA."

The tour guide, her mouth open, had not yet dialed a number.

"It's all right, Louisa," the woman in the doorway said.

"Dr. Vergilio, I presume?" al-Rashid said.

"Yes. And I have been expecting you or someone like you to be showing up."

FIFTY-SEVEN

McGarvey and Rencke drove to the Georgetown University Dahlgren Chapel, parking in back and walking around front. The church was empty, but they found the office where McGarvey had seen a priest in civilian clothes coming out with the man in a wheelchair.

They knocked once and went in, finding themselves in a small anteroom, the receptionist's desk empty. The door to the inner office was open and the same priest in civilian clothes looked up from his desk.

"Father Carl Unger?" McGarvey asked.

"Yes, may I help you?"

"It's about the priest whose confession you heard yesterday. He's dead."

"Dear God in Heaven," Fr. Unger said softly, but he didn't seem surprised. "May I be told how it happened?"

"He came to a hospital here in Georgetown where he murdered four men in their beds, a nurse, several security officers, and would have killed another woman, herself a patient, except that she managed to hide herself."

The priest turned away, gathering his wits, and when he looked back his eyes were filled with a very great sadness. "I didn't know."

"I think you knew something. In fact I think he told you who and what he was when he confessed."

"You were here in the chapel?"

"Yes, but I didn't recognize him because he was in a wheelchair. What did he tell you in the confessional?"

Fr. Unger shook his head. "I can't reveal that. Not to you, not to anyone, even to the police if that's who you are."

"But you must if the confessor tells you about a crime he's going to commit," Otto said.

"Are you a Catholic?"

"I was. Did he tell you that he had come here to kill people?"

"No."

"But he was troubled," McGarvey said.

"You met him?"

"Three times. He said that he'd been sent here to protect me."

"He told me that, though he didn't say who it was or why," Fr. Unger said. "May I ask who you gentlemen are, and what your business with Father Dorestos was?"

"I think he worked for the Hospitallers. The Sacred Military Order of Malta. He came here to convince me to help find something that belonged to the Church. And last night he committed suicide in order to make me believe that he was telling the truth."

It was almost too much for the priest and he started to rise, but McGarvey motioned him back.

"We work for the Central intelligence Agency, and you won't believe the problems that your Father Dorestos has stirred up coming here, except that seven people lost their lives in Florida—two of them innocent young students who were not involved. That's in addition to the others last night, and the priest himself, and most likely six more in Paris including the vice mayor and his mistress, and a mother and her son."

"The butcher's bill has always been high for the Mother Church," Otto said bitterly. He'd walked away from the Church years ago under bad circumstances—of his own doing—but he'd been left with a scar. "And what the Vatican doesn't need right now is another scandal. Pederasty is terrible, but murder is worse."

"I don't know what you want from me. Why have you come here?"

"For your help, Father," McGarvey said "We want to prevent any further bloodshed."

"I don't understand."

"Father Dorestos was a Hospitaller. Someone sent him here with orders to direct me to search for something."

"Search for what?"

"A diary that was stolen from a bank vault in Bern. The point is none of what happened over the past days need never to have happened. I'm ready to help—we're ready to help—but my government doesn't want us to get involved."

The priest was at a loss. "What can I do?"

"Contact the Hospitallers—the SMOM, and find out who directed Father Dorestos. Tell them their man is dead, and that we would like to come to Europe to discuss what needs to be done."

Fr. Unger shook his head. "I'm just a college chaplain and a scholar. I'm not involved in things like this. And in the first place even if I thought I could help, I would have no idea who to call."

"We need to be flown out of here on a private jet as American priests," McGarvey said. He laid two passports on the desk—one for him and one for Otto—under the work names of Rupert Mann and Michael Rosenberg. "Whoever you contact in Malta will know how to check these to make certain there are no holds or queries."

Fr. Unger made no move to touch the passports. "I'll have to ask you to leave," he said.

"We'll wait just outside by the confessionals."

"We want to help the Church," Otto said, and he and McGarvey got up and left.

Back out in the nave they sat down in one of the pews about halfway to the entrance.

"You lied," McGarvey said.

Otto got out his iPad and accessed one of his search engines on a CIA mainframe at Langley. "The Church has been doing it for a couple of thousand years, it's used to hearing lies." He nodded toward the confessionals. "It's all about redemption. Raise hell all week, but come Saturday you can confess your sins, do a penance, and on Sunday go to mass with a clear conscience because the slate has been wiped clean, so on Monday you can start all over again."

"It's better than Islamic fundamentalists killing people and expecting to go straight to paradise as martyrs."

Otto looked up. "Even murder can be forgiven by Jesus through a priest in the confessional."

An image of Fr. Unger seated at his desk came up on the iPad. It looked as if he was typing on a keyboard just below the frame of view, and he was agitated.

"He's found a number on Skype and he's calling it now," Otto said. "It's European." He brought up another program on a split screen. "Three-five-six. It's the dialing code for Malta."

"Hello, this is Father Unger, I'm the senior chaplain at Georgetown University in the United States. I need to talk to someone about Father Dominigue Dorestos."

"Of course, Father," a man with a heavily accented Italian voice replied in English. "Please wait."

Otto split the screen again so that they were seeing Fr. Unger on one side, and on the other a man in a monk's robes with a tonsured haircut. The monk was seated in what appeared to be a small office.

The screen froze for several seconds, until the monk's face was replaced by the image of another man, this one much older, with a broad forehead and wide serious eyes beneath a normally cut head of hair. Nothing other than his image from the shoulders up was visible.

The man spoke, his English nearly without accent. "You have news of our son, Father Dorestos?"

"I'm afraid that I have bad news for you, I have been informed that Father Dorestos is dead. He may have committed suicide."

The man on the split screen had no reaction. "Who told you this?"

"Two men are waiting outside in the nave at this moment, waiting for me to call someone to say that they are willing to help with the mission Father Dorestos came here to accomplish."

"Did they say how they meant to help?"

"They've given me passports, in different names. The CIA has forbidden them to become involved, so they want us—your order—to provide them with a jet out of the country."

"To where?"

"They didn't say."

"We have a jet standing by at Reagan National Airport. I will alert the crew. Tell them that they may come to the airport at any time within the next two hours. If you give me the names and numbers off their passports, I will also alert the airport authorities."

"I will tell them."

"One more thing, Father, ask them to bring Father Dorestos's body with them if at all possible. Even as a suicide he is our son."

FIFTY-EIGHT

The day was bright, the sun streaming through the windows, and yet Dr. Vergilio's inner office seemed stuffy because it was crammed with books, manuscripts, papers, scientific journals, and many maps showing current archaeological projects around the globe. But the woman was anything but stuffy.

"Be brief, Señor Harris, I am a busy woman," she said.

"Would you like to check my background?" al-Rashid asked.

"No, because I think that everything you've come to tell me, and everything else about you, is almost certainly an elaborate lie. So let's just get on with it. You said that a Voltaire came to see you in England."

"Yes, about two weeks ago. He identified himself as Giscarde Petain and wanted to hire me for a job of research. His organization had lost a very rare diary that was a record of a Spanish military expedition from Mexico City to what is now New Mexico in the United States."

"Señor Petain was murdered a few days ago, and his wife and child were killed just two days ago in Paris."

"Yes, I saw both stories in the news. It's why I decided to come here."

"For what?"

"Answers."

Dr. Vergilio gave him an appraising look. She was irritated. "Do not play games with me, Señor Harris. As I've said, I have expected you or someone like you to come here asking damn fool questions about caches of Spanish treasure, the locations of which are supposedly pinpointed in this diary you were told about. But it's not true. It is a lie." She waved a hand at the books and maps in her office. "Millions upon millions of words and maps and reports—detailed reports. Mind-numbing bureau-cratic documents. And nowhere have I ever found direct evidence of

Spanish treasure in the United States except at the bottom of the ocean mostly around the coasts of Florida. The *Nuestra Señora de Atocha* being the most famous, of course. One of its salvaged and restored cannons is downstairs."

"I'm not familiar with the story," al-Rashid said, though he was. He wanted to keep the woman talking, betting that she would make a mistake. A hint, even the slightest of references to a cipher key was all he needed.

"I thought that you were an historical writer."

"Of fiction. But my expertise is in research, including the Spanish Thirty Years' War. Mention was made of financial losses that forced the crown to borrow money, but I pursued the war more than its financing. I told that to Monsieur Petain."

"The *Atocha* sank in sixteen sixty-two off the Florida Keys in a storm, and she was carrying so much gold, silver, and other treasure that it took two months to load it aboard. And that, Señor Harris, is no urban legend. It is a fact that an American treasure hunter by the name of Mel Fisher managed to find the ship and recover the gold and silver, and a few of the cannons."

Al-Rashid held his silence. The woman was worked up.

"In fact the contents of that ship belonged to Spain, if for nothing else than its historical value. Yet we got nothing."

"Except for the cannon."

"You came looking for answers."

"Yes," al-Rashid said. "Petain told me that the diary had been stolen but that it would be of no use to anyone because it was in code."

Dr. Vergilio was suddenly very interested though she tried to hide it. "Did you find the diary?"

"After I learned of Petain's death, I backed off. But when his wife and child were murdered my curiosity began to get the better of me. So I came here to find out if you could tell me anything about the diary or about its code. I thought that perhaps with my investigative journalism background and your archaeological resources here at the Archives we might make a good partnership."

"And you would share the treasure with Spain?"

"Urban legend," al-Rashid reminded her. "In fact I'm not a treasure hunter, I'm looking for a good story to tell."

"I'm sorry that you came all this way, Señor Harris," Dr. Vergilio said, getting to her feet. "There were journals from many Spanish military expeditions to the New World, of course. Most of them are here in the Archives. But none of them were ever written in a cipher or any sort— most of them were written in Spanish, and some written by priests or monks in Latin. Of those many of the originals are in the Vatican's library."

Al-Rashid remained seated. "I'm sure that what I have come looking for is in the Vatican's archives, but those collections are closed to someone like me. From what I understand a priest managed to join an expedition to New Mexico, and the diary he kept—in code—was stolen by the Voltaires before he could return to Rome."

"And you came to tell me that it was stolen from the Voltaires?"

"Yes."

Dr. Vergilio held out her hand. "Give me your passport."

Al-Rashid handed it over, and the woman went to the door and gave it to the tour guide. "Find out who this man is, please, before you return to your group," she said, and she came back to her desk. "Are you an intelligence officer with New Scotland Yard or MI6?"

"Just a writer onto what I think might become a good story. Murders, intrigue between the Vatican, the Spanish government, almost certainly the U.S. government, and some sort of secret society that I'm assuming was either began by or at least named after the philosopher Voltaire." Al-Rashid shrugged depreciatingly. "And throw in a secret diary written in a mysterious code and an ancient treasure buried somewhere, and I can't miss."

"The treasure is a myth."

"One that someone is willing to kill for."

"People have been killed for a lot less."

The tour guide was back in under a minute. "One hundred twenty thousand hits on Google," she said, handing the passport back to al-Rashid. "Mr. Harris shows up on the third page in a Wikipedia article, which describes him as a minor British novelist, six books to his credit, most notably one published three years ago under the title *Trouble in Paradise*. Formerly a journalist with the BBC, and before that with Reuters. Oxford. Parents deceased, no wife or children."

"Thanks, Louisa, but no more strays, please."

"I'll try."

When the young woman was gone, Dr. Vergilio gave al-Rashid an appraising look. Her attitude had changed. "You have my attention, Señor Harris, what exactly is it that you want?"

"The diary, for starts."

"I haven't the faintest idea where it is."

"Petain told me that it had been in a bank vault in Bern. He suggested that I start there."

"And did you?"

"No, I wanted to talk to you first. If the diary is in a code, I suspect that the cipher may be somewhere here, but hidden."

"It's not here, I've already told you."

Al-Rashid suppressed a smile. She believed enough in the treasure stories and the diary that she had already searched the archives. "Maybe it's in some of the documents from that military expedition. Could be in plain sight, unrecognizable for what it was without the diary in hand."

"Or it could be in the Vatican's archives, which is more likely."

Al-Rashid shrugged. "In which case I'd have to try Rome. But for now I'm betting that if I can come up with the diary, we'll find the cipher key here."

Dr. Vergilio's eyes widened. "Do you already have it?" She was excited.

"No. But I have the name of a man in Bern. I think he might be a good lead, but as I said I wanted to come here first to see if we could make a deal. You and I working together." He laughed. "You can have the gold— I'd take a finder's fee—but what I'm after is the story."

Dr. Vergilio laughed too. "I don't believe a word you've said, but in actuality I have nothing to lose. Bring the diary here, and we'll see if we can find the cipher key if one exists."

FIFTY-NINE

□

As soon as the Gulfstream had taken off from Washington National Airport and reached its cruising altitude of thirty-five thousand feet above the Atlantic, Otto powered up his laptop and connected via a National Reconnaissance Office satellite to his mainframe at the CIA. He'd worked through the night and when McGarvey woke from a couple of hours of sleep he was grinning.

"I think I came up with a lead on the guy who may have swiped the diary from the bank in Bern, and then did his thing in Paris just a few days ago. But it gets even better, and you're not going to believe how."

The attendant brought McGarvey a cup of coffee. "I'm told that you wanted a little brandy in it, sir," she said.

"You needed a pick-me-up," Otto said after the attendant went forward. "This guy—if it's our man—goes by the name of Bernard Montessier and lives somewhere in Marseilles. He runs a small international legal affairs consulting firm with only a secretary."

"How in the hell did you come up with that?"

"Tedious but simple. It's what my little darlings back home are so good at," Otto said.

His little darlings, as he called them, were his specially designed search engines that piggybacked on thousands of computers—most of them government or university mainframes—without leaving any traces. Multiplexing to vastly increase the speed and scope of his search algorithms, he could scan millions of terabytes per second of information, from nearly an unlimited number of sources simultaneously.

"I looked at everyone who had traveled by air or train to Bern in the past two weeks, and compared those names with arrivals by air or train to Paris over the same period. I also took a look at rental car records on the off chance that he might have landed elsewhere and driven across borders."

"And you came up with Montessier?"

"Actually I came up with a hundred twenty-seven names, half of which I dumped because of their ages. But then I went looking for little anomalies. The odd bits that seemed not to fit any sort of a pattern."

"And?"

"Bernard Montessier. You'll never guess where this guy has been during that time, and going back three years—all I could come up with in only a few hours. Jeddah, Saudi Arabia. All the dates match. He flies from Marsellies to Jeddah, then from there to Bern, and from there back to Marseilles and then Jeddah again, and to Paris just three days ago."

"Any background?"

"No. Wherever he lands no one by that name shows up in any hotel registries—at least not at the bigger hotels where he would most likely stay. When he travels it's always first class."

"He's either staying with someone in those cities, or he's using a work name," McGarvey said.

"But there's the kicker. After Paris he showed up yesterday in Seville. Now there's no way in hell that can be a coincidence. Bern for the diary, Paris for the Voltaires, and Seville for the archives."

"He got the diary and now he's looking for the cipher key."

"Bingo. But in the meantime he runs home to Mama in Jeddah for orders."

"Does the Company have any assets on the ground there? Someone who might have heard something? Maybe mention of someone flitting in and out? Meeting with someone?"

"Operators like that, if Montessier is our guy, don't come cheap. So whoever he's working for in Jeddah most likely belongs to the Royal family. I can check our NOC list."

"See what you can find without alerting Marty," McGarvey said. "I'm going to warn María to watch her step in case you're right about Montessier."

"I have a passport photo you can send to her, if she's not already in the air."

María had been set to leave for Seville about this time to meet with Dr. Vergilio to pave the way before McGarvey went to talk to her. There was no telling what his reception would be, especially if the CNI got wind that he was in the country.

He tried her cell phone but it was only accepting voice mail, so he called Louise, who answered on the fourth ring.

"Are you guys in Malta yet?" she asked.

"About an hour out," McGarvey told her. "Has our guest already left?"

"Dropped her off at the airport a couple of hours ago, but I waited to make sure she got through security okay."

She was traveling under her DI work name of Ines Delgado. Otto had checked before they left, and had found no flags on her Spanish passport.

"I tried to reach her cell phone, but she must have turned it off."

"Trouble?"

"Possibly. Call the airport in Madrid and have her paged. Tell her to call you. I'm sending you the passport photo of Bernard Montessier, who Otto thinks might be the guy who swiped the diary from Bern, and who might have been involved with the murders in Paris. He showed up in Seville yesterday."

"Peachy," Louise said. "Bern, Paris, and now Seville. Can't be a coincidence."

"No."

"Send me the picture. If she doesn't answer the page she'll turn her phone back on sooner or later. Maybe once she gets through customs in Madrid."

"Where is she staying in Madrid?"

"She wouldn't tell me."

"You've done your part, Louise. Now it's time for you to hunker down, maybe go down to the Farm to be with Audie."

"Here in town Marty doesn't know how to get to me. I'm going to stay put in case someone else interesting happens to show up."

"Watch yourself."

"Take care of Otto for me," she said.

"Will do," McGarvey said. "I'm sending you the photo."

When it went through he broke the connection and looked up. The attendant was at the head of the aisle, looking at him. She was smiling pleasantly.

"Would you like another cup of coffee, sir? Or perhaps something to eat?"

"How soon to Malta?"

"Fifty-five minutes."

"I'll wait."

Otto turned his computer around so that McGarvey could see the screen. A photo of a large, hulking man with long curly hair and a thick salt-and-pepper beard filled half the screen, while the other half displayed details about his background. At the present he was the only NOC in Jeddah—most of the others were in Riyadh. He was posing as an engineer for the Swedish firm Andresen Pumps, specializing in "fluid solutions for oil and water." His name was Bren Halberstrom, and he'd been in place for six years.

"Do we have contact information?"

"Yeah, but it could be dicey for him if someone is paying attention, which is a real possibility. The Saudi intel people are pretty good."

McGarvey didn't want to put the man's life at risk for no good reason, yet people had died. "Anything in his file about recalling him?"

"He's made three requests in the last eighteen months to call it quits."

"It's time for Mr. Halberstrom to come home," McGarvey said, and he dialed the man's sat phone number.

SIXTY

□

Al-Rashid sat drinking coffee and reading the English language *International Herald-Tribune* at a small sidewalk café just up the street from the Alcazar fortress and within sight of the Archives. He was dressed in an open collar white polo shirt, jeans, and a black blazer.

Last night the streets downtown had been filled with a mob of people angry about Spain's latest austerity measures. The riot police had come in and beaten back the crowd with batons and tear gas, and the people had fought back with Molotov cocktails, bricks, and in at least two instances with guns. The story, along with similar protests in Greece, had made the front page because two police officers and four protesters had been seriously hurt. Dozens of others had been arrested.

This morning the area still smelled like gasoline and the sharper, irritating odor of phenacyl chloride, the major component in the tear gas the police used last night. Workmen were still on the streets cleaning up debris, and others were installing window glass, though many merchants had decided to board up their windows. The *Tribune* was reporting that further rioting was likely in the coming days.

A sharp unease had settled over the city, and this morning even the desk clerks at the upscale Gran Melia Colon hotel seemed gloomy though they tried to hide it.

"Are you checking out, Señor Harris?"

"Not at all. I've worked in Baghdad, Kabul, and Tripoli, so I understand violence. But last night the crowd was foolish."

"But then it is a matter of money. Pardon me, but it is the common family man who has the most to lose, and he does not understand the government's claim that we are a nearly bankrupt nation, despite our palaces and museums and—"

"History?" al-Rashid suggested. He didn't know why he was going on with the silly man because he'd always found stupidity to be boring.

"Precision!"

"Actually I've come to rent a car for the next several days. Will you arrange it?"

"Certainly. Do you have a model in mind?"

"Maybe a little sports car. Something fast. I'm going out in the country to see the sights."

"It will be here within the hour. I'll just need to see your driving license and passport, of course."

Al-Rashid handed them over, and after an excellent breakfast of croissants and cheese, he'd picked up the dark blue BMW Z4 convertible in front, and had driven back to the Centro area downtown where he'd gotten lucky with a parking spot just around the corner from the Archives.

Around nine o'clock Dr. Vergilio showed up on a Vespa motor scooter and slowly circled the building before pulling up on the sidewalk and parking just across the street from the Cathedral.

She seemed cautious to al-Rashid, almost as if she expected to see the rioters still lurking somewhere around a corner, ready to do damage to her Archives, which had come out unscathed so far.

He waited for a full fifteen minutes after she went inside before he paid his bill and walked back to where he'd parked the car. Traffic was normal for a workday, and once he was away from the Centro section of the city he headed north to the Barrio de la Macarena, which was a huge neighborhood covering most of Seville's historic section. Here were market squares, churches and convents, little gardens and pocket parks, plus Dr. Vergilio's apartment on the ground floor of an ancient four-story building just one block off the river.

Parking a block and a half away, he walked past the building. A tall archway enclosed by tall iron gates, open at this hour of the day, gave access to a narrow cobblestone walkway that ran straight to an outdoor courtyard at the rear of the building. Just inside the gates an old woman sat on a wooden chair smoking a cigarette and cleaning mushrooms with a brush. No one else was around, and back here only the occasional car passed on the street.

Al-Rashid turned around and walked back to the woman, who looked up curiously when he appeared at the open gate.

"May I help you?" she asked, her voice raspy from years of smoking.

"Yes, please, Señora," al-Rashid said in his rudimentary Spanish. "But I am looking for the building of Dr. Adriana Vergilio. I was told this was the address."

"Yes, this is the correct number. But she has already left for the Archives."

"I was just there. I must have missed her."

"Well, she'll be there by now."

"But I haven't the time. May I leave a message for her with you?"

The old woman hesitated, but then shrugged. "I am an old woman with a terrible memory. So if it is complicated you will have to make the time to return to her office."

"I'll write it down. If you have a pencil and a piece of paper."

The woman sighed, but put her cigarette in a small tin can at her feet and led him into her apartment, where she got a pad of paper from a small table beneath a wall phone.

Before she could turn around, al-Rashid was on her, breaking her neck, her body convulsing once before she went limp.

He carried her into the bedroom at the rear of the small apartment, and covered her with the blanket, arranging her body with her head turned away from the window so that it would look as if she were merely taking a nap.

He checked at the front door to make certain that no one was around, and he got her chair, the bowl of mushrooms and brush, and the tin can and brought them inside. A set of seven keys were on hooks next to the phone. He took the set marked AV, and again checking at the door to make sure that the passageway was still empty he went back to Dr. Vergilio's place and let himself in.

Standing just inside an entry vestibule, al-Rashid listened for any sign that someone might be here, or for a dog or some other animal, but the apartment was silent and he went the rest of the way into a very large living room.

Tall bookcases, with a wooden ladder on brass rails, lined three walls. The shelves were overstuffed with books, most of them very old. More books and piles of newspapers and magazines were stacked on the one couch, and on a big wingback chair. Books were stacked in the corners, on the coffee table in front of a second wingback chair, beside which were even more books.

A large map of the New World, which looked as if it had been drawn by hand a very long time ago, was framed and hung on a wall between a pair of windows, the heavy drapes drawn.

A small kitchen with a two chairs and a butcher block table were to the left just beyond a dining room, the table of which was piled with maps and what appeared to be a half-dozen expedition journals, these in modern field notebooks. The cover of each was marked with a date, starting in November 12, 1984, along with what were likely the names of archaeological digs Vergilio had been on, in various spots around Mexico City and north.

Al-Rashid quickly leafed through them, but nowhere was New Mexico, or Cibola, or the Mother Church, or treasure mentioned. If she had been looking for the gold—which she claimed did not exist—there was no evidence here.

A short corridor led back to a bathroom and two bedrooms, one of which was used as a filing room mostly for maps in long flat drawers. Nothing here gave any hint of an expedition or expeditions to anywhere near the U.S. border.

The corridor's walls were covered with dozens of framed photographs showing Vergilio and others out in the field at various digs. None of the photos were captioned, but most of them appeared to be in dense jungle settings out of which had been hacked clearings where trenches were being dug by hand. In one shot, a younger Dr. Vergilio, a broad-brimmed hat in hand, stood atop a small Aztec or Mayan ruin looking down at what had to be more than a hundred workmen ringing the pyramid and looking up at her. She had a broad smile on her face. Triumphant.

More books were stacked beside her bed, and on the nightstand, and even on the floor beside the tall, ornate wooden wardrobe.

For a long moment or two al-Rashid stood very still, his head cocked to one side, trying to absorb the place, trying to see Dr. Vergilio working here alone every night. There'd been no television in the living room and none here, only a small radio on a shelf in the kitchen. Here was not a home; it was nothing but an office away from the Archives. She worked all day downtown then came back here to work more.

He walked back out into the corridor and looked at the photograph of Vergilio standing atop the pyramid, a broad smile on her face. The only time she was free to enjoy herself was out in the field.

Turning, he looked in the map room again, then walked back to the living room and into the dining room and kitchen.

She had written several books. It was all here in her apartment; all the journals and maps and references that she would need.

But there was no typewriter, and more important there was no computer.

Al-Rashid smiled. The woman was hiding something.

SIXTY-ONE

The same sort of aluminum coffin used to transport the bodies of American soldiers killed in the field was taken from the hold of the Embraer by two men, who loaded it onto a wheeled cart and brought it over to a waiting hearse.

McGarvey and Otto, who'd been told to remain aboard, watched as a tall man in jeans and a military styled khaki shirt, the sleeves rolled up and buttoned above the elbows, accompanied the casket from the plane and before it could be loaded into the hearse he blessed it.

When it was aboard and the men drove away, the man in the jeans turned and came back to the airplane.

He hesitated just inside the hatch and asked the crew if they wouldn't mind waiting outside for a few minutes. They agreed and left.

The interior of the Gulfstream was laid out with several very large and plush leather seats on swivels all within reach of a highly polished cherrywood table. It was obviously used to transport VIPs, and was fitted out with a luxurious bathroom at the rear, and a small but complete galley, including a credible wine stock, just aft of the cockpit. A flat-panel television dropped down from the ceiling, and in the armrest of each chair was a telephone. The plane was equipped with its own sophisticated communications system.

The man sat down across the table. "Gentlemen, thank you for bringing home the body of our son," he said, his English nearly accentless.

McGarvey recognized him from the Skype call Otto had intercepted. "Monsignor Franelli, you must know the circumstances under which he died."

"Father Unger told me that he committed suicide, which is a terrible crime for those of our faith. Do you know the circumstances of his death?"

"He was in my apartment, and I was forced to shoot him."

"Pardon me, Señor McGarvey, but that would not have been possible under normal circumstances. He was much younger than you, and in superb physical condition. If he'd wanted to defend himself it would be you who was dead."

"I know. He was waiting for me when I came home, and he could have killed me the moment I walked in the door. But he didn't. He told me that he'd been sent to help me find the diary. I told him that I didn't know where to begin."

"You lied."

"I wanted to see what he would tell me."

Msgr. Franelli nodded. "Did he mention Seville or Bern first?"

"Seville."

"Then why have you come here?"

"To deliver Father Dorestos's body to his controller and to find out why the Order came to me for help. What do you think that I can do for you, that your soldiers and trained assassins can't?"

Msgr. Franelli's lips pursed. He was irritated. "Certain restrictions have recently been placed on the Order."

McGarvey sat forward. "Bullshit. Your priest killed a Spanish intelligence officer in Florida."

"You killed the three others."

"But I didn't kill four helpless men in their hospital beds, or an unarmed trauma room nurse whose only job was to help save lives, not take them."

Msgr. Franelli held McGarvey's gaze. "Mistakes were made. Father Dorestos was not completely stable. Terrible things happened to him when he was young, and by the time he came to us he was a damaged soul."

"That you used," Otto said angrily.

The priest turned to him. "You're Otto Rencke, a computer genius, I'm told, who once worked for the Church until you were excommunicated. I think for some sexual dalliance, so don't judge lest you yourself are judged."

"But then there has always been that element within the Church that condoned murder and torture to further its own aims and its own power. The Spanish Inquisition comes to mind."

"Strictly speaking at the hands of the Spanish government."

"*Tribunal del Santo Oficio de la Inquisicion espanola.*"

"Yes, established by Ferdinand II of Aragon and Isabella I of Castile. The king and queen of Spain, if I might remind you, Señor Rencke. Play with your computers but leave the history of the Church to us."

The priest had a sharp edge to his voice and his manner, and McGarvey realized all at once that the man was being defensive because he was frightened. "You sent Father Dorestos to the States to help me. It wasn't meant to be an assassination mission."

"We weren't sure who was watching you, though I suspected it was Spanish intelligence. They want the treasure, which they believe belongs to the government, and they were willing to kill for it."

"What can you tell me about the Voltaires?"

Msgr. Franelli's temper flared. "They are apostates."

"It is their diary."

"Our diary, written by one of our priests who went on the second Spanish expedition to find the gold and silver."

"A treasure that the Church stole from the Spanish authorities in Mexico City."

"It's a moot point, Mr. McGarvey. The treasure, if it exists in your New Mexican desert, is being claimed by a host of people, all of whom are ready to kill for it. My Order was merely trying to direct you."

"The man who was killed in the college parking lot was a Voltaire who came to ask for my help. His wife and son were murdered two days ago in Paris."

"Yes, I know. Their souls will also burn in hell."

"Was it one of your operators in Paris who did it?" McGarvey asked.

"No."

"Who then? Do you have any ideas?"

"Not the Spaniards. It is some someone else, but we're not sure who."

"Another treasure hunter?"

"Presumably. The Cuban government is interested. Maybe the same agent who you worked with several months ago."

"No," McGarvey said.

Msgr. Franelli was about to say something but he stopped, and cocked his head. "You know who it is?"

"We have a possibility."

"Are you going to tell me?"

"I want the use of this jet and crew for the next few days."

"In return for what?"

"Your Father Dorestos was correct. The answer is in Seville."

"At the Archives. But what answer?"

"We think that the diary was written in code, and the cipher key is either at the Archives in Seville, or in a vault in the Vatican."

"It's not in the Vatican, I can tell you that much. If it were I would not have sent Father Dorestos to help you."

"You need the diary itself to make the cipher key worth anything."

"You'll have to trust me that we do not have the key. But I agree that the diary or the key alone are worthless."

"And then what?" McGarvey asked. "If we find the diary and the key and we make the translation, then what?"

"We find the treasure."

"It does not exist," McGarvey said.

"If that's the case, then why are you doing all of this? Why are you risking your lives?"

"You wouldn't understand."

"Try me."

"For two innocent kids who were in the wrong place at the wrong time," McGarvey said. "But we're also here for help getting to Seville."

"The aircraft and crew are yours for as long as you need them. But the Spanish authorities will place you under arrest the moment you step off the plane."

"Which is how you can help," McGarvey said, and he told the monsignor what he had in mind.

SIXTY-TWO

□

Al-Rashid drove back downtown where he parked a couple of blocks from the Archives and walked to the Cathedral directly across the street from where Dr. Vergilio had chained her motor scooter to a light pole.

Cleanup efforts were still going on, and police were setting up barricades, blocking the streets leading from the open space of the Murillo Gardens where the crowd had gathered last night, and from where they had marched to the Archives, the Cathedral, the Alcazar, and the Hospital de los Venerables.

Killing the old woman manager at the apartment building had been a necessity, though once her body was discovered any further cooperation with Dr. Vergilio would be impossible. But he'd needed to search the good doctor's apartment on the chance she had taken records of the second Spanish military expedition to New Mexico. She hadn't, nor had she left her computer, which could only mean that the cipher key, if it existed at all—and now he thought it did—would be in the Archives.

He had considered breaking in and looking for the expedition's documents, but merely finding the right files and then interpreting them would take too long. Perhaps weeks, even for a trained historian. But Dr. Vergilio would know exactly where they were shelved. All she needed was the incentive to get them.

He telephoned her office and she answered on the second ring. "Hello." She sounded harried.

"Good morning, Doctor. This is Paul Harris. I'm calling you about the diary."

"Do you actually have it?"

"I will by this evening. It's coming by courier."

"From where?" Dr. Vergilio demanded.

"Out of the country, but we'll need to meet as soon as I have it. Perhaps first thing in the morning in your office?"

"No. I don't want to wait that long. We can meet tonight."

"The police are expecting another riot tonight, so maybe someplace else would be better."

"Someplace neutral, Señor Harris."

Al-Rashid smiled. "You still do not trust me?"

"Of course not. In any event before we can make any sort of a deal I'll have to see the document to determine if it's genuine or merely a clever fake. And believe me that will take less than one minute."

"And the cipher key?"

"For that you will have to trust me. But I can guarantee you your story and the Archives will certainly pay you a finder's fee if it's the real thing."

"That's all I ask," al-Rashid said. "You can expect my call between six and ten this evening. We'll meet in the Cathedral across the street from you."

"That's hardly a neutral spot," Dr. Vergilio objected.

"On the contrary. With a riot most likely going on, and armed police officers everywhere, the Cathedral will be the safest spot in all of Seville for us to meet."

"As you wish."

"Bring the cipher key."

"I don't have it," Dr. Vergilio said.

Al-Rashid pushed the end button, pocketed the phone, and stood for a long half minute staring at the Archives, and the centuries-old secrets it held.

He started to turn away when a taxi pulled up at the rear entrance, and an attractive woman with long dark hair, wearing jeans and a fashionable white top, got out, and went inside. He got only a brief glance of her profile, but something about her self-assured manner, the way she walked, the way she held herself erect, almost with a military bearing, struck him. She was not the usual visitor to the Archives, and it bothered him that he should know who she was, and did not.

He walked away, reaching his car that was parked well outside the police control zone. Traffic, both vehicular and pedestrian, was as normal as was possible under the circumstances of the blocked roads. But the people seemed to be taking it all in stride.

His cell phone rang as he settled in behind the wheel. He expected it might be Dr. Vergilio calling him back, but the caller ID was blocked. It was Prince Saleh from Jeddah.

"Where are you at this moment?" the prince demanded brusquely.

"Seville."

"Do you have the cipher key yet?"

"Tonight. But you didn't call to ask me about that. Is there trouble?"

"There may be," the prince said. "But you've actually found it? Where?"

"Tell me about the trouble."

Saleh hesitated for only a moment. "I got a call a half hour ago from General Abd al-Yasu." The general was the head of the General Investigative Directorate, known as the Mabaheth, which was Saudi Arabia's interior police and internal security agency.

"I'm listening."

"A man who has been identified as likely agent of the Central Intelligence Agency got a phone call on his cell phone, after which he began making inquiries about me."

"This has happened before," al-Rashid said. "You are a very high-profile man, near the top of the Americans' watch list."

"Yes. But never in connection with your Montessier persona."

Al-Rashid's grip tightened on the cell phone, and he looked out the windshield at the buildings on either side of the street, and in his rear-view mirror at the people and the traffic. All of it seemed normal. But if the CIA knew his work name, had his description or even a photo, and if they had somehow traced him here to Seville there might even now be an assassin's rifle trained on him.

But that wasn't possible. Not so soon. And yet the dark-haired woman entering the Archives through a rear door bothered him, though he didn't know exactly why.

"Do you have this man in custody?"

"The order was given but he had left his office and he was not at his home. He's disappeared."

"What is his name?"

"Bren Halberstrom. He traveled under a Norwegian passport."

The name meant nothing to al-Rashid. "Do we know who called him?"

"It was from a cell phone but the number was blocked, although the general believes that the call originated in Malta."

For just a moment al-Rashid was at a loss, but suddenly it struck him. He held the excitement from his voice. "Was the call recorded?"

"It was encrypted. The technical people don't know how it was done, because Halberstrom's phone was not capable of encryption, though how the general's people knew this is beyond me. The fact of the matter is that someone has made a connection between you and me."

"Do you wish me to withdraw?"

"I've thought about it. But what do you think?"

"The CIA makes random sweeps from time to time, looking for the stray bits of intelligence. This Halberstrom may have been nothing more than a Norwegian businessman who cooperated with the CIA, or more likely he was a deep-cover agent, maybe stationed in Jeddah merely to watch you. Such a possibility should not come as a surprise to you."

"No, of course not. But what about you?"

"I'll either have the cipher key tonight, or it will have been destroyed. Either way I'll be leaving first thing in the morning."

"Your name has come up, the airport may be watched."

"I won't be taking a commercial flight out of here. I've made other arrangements."

"You know what's at stake."

"Yes, I do," al-Rashid said, but he was certain that Prince Saleh did not.

"Then go with Allah."

Al-Rashid ended the call. Halberstrom was almost certainly a CIA NOC. The call had come from Kirk McGarvey. And the fact that it had been placed from Malta made it a very real possibility that the Catholic Church was not only involved in the search for the diary, but had agreed to help.

Which still left him with the mysterious dark-haired woman.

SIXTY-THREE

□

María León showed the pass that Dr. Vergilio had given her several months ago to one of the security officers who'd happened be near the rear stairway as she started up. He smiled nervously but nodded.

"Looks like it was a big night here," she said to him in Spanish.

"Sí, señora, and tonight promises to be just as bad or perhaps even worse."

"Was any damage done to the Archives? I didn't see any from the outside."

"Oh, no. The police were mindful, and whatever the people think of our government, they have respect for history. They weren't hoodlums."

"Let's hope that their regard for this place holds. Is Dr. Vergilio here?"

"Yes, she arrived earlier. Shall I escort you up?"

"No, that's not necessary. I know the way."

The guard nodded and left.

Upstairs María walked down the corridor past the stacks, a couple of researchers at work, until she reached the doctor's suite of offices, but instead of going in she turned and sat at one of the small tables by a window looking down on the street. If anyone arrived or left the offices they would pass by in plain sight.

In Madrid just after she'd passed through passport control and picked up her single bag, she'd been paged. It had been Louise needing to reach her before she caught the flight to Seville.

"Mac and Otto were in Malta, but by now they're on their way to Gibraltar. I'm sending you a photograph. Hang on."

A moment later what was obviously a passport photo came through. She did not recognize the man. "Who is he?"

"We don't know his real name, this was from a French passport under the name Bernard Montessier. Otto is sure it's a work name. And he's pretty sure that this was the guy who managed to swipe the diary from the bank in Bern. Apparently he's a hired gun of a Saudi prince in Jeddah. A big money player."

"Do we know anything about him?"

"Just that he was in Bern when the diary went missing, after which he returned to Jeddah. From there he went to Paris where Otto thinks he killed the vice mayor and his mistress and most likely several others—possibly Voltaires."

"He's looking for the cipher key, and anyone who doesn't cooperate gets killed," María said. "Nice."

"Thing is it's likely that he's in Seville for the same reason you're headed there, so Mac says for you to watch your back. He and Otto should be there later this afternoon or early this evening."

"I'm not armed."

"I'm sure that you can arrange something," Louise said dryly. "You have more connections in Spain than we do. Especially right now."

She'd made one call to the Special Interests Section duty officer at the Cuban embassy on Paseo de la Habana in Madrid where she'd explained who she was and what she needed. And when she arrived at the airport in Seville a man waiting with his taxi opened the rear door for her.

On the seat was a small package, the contents of which were a Glock 29 subcompact pistol, a silencer, and three spare magazines of 10 mm ammunition. She'd loaded the pistol, screwed the silencer on the threaded muzzle, and put it and the extra magazines in her big shoulder bag. She ordered the driver to take her to the Archives and when they'd arrived she paid him the standard fare. Nothing else was said between them.

During the cab ride into the old city she'd phoned Manuel Campos, her new chief of staff at DI headquarters in Havana, and sent him the photo of Montessier. "He's evidently a player, though probably not French. A freelance for a Saudi prince in Jeddah. Find out who he is."

Sitting by the window now, her telephone chimed softly. It was Campos. "He's a French importer/exporter with an office in Marseilles, but beyond that he comes up clean. Almost too clean."

"Do you have an address?"

Campos gave it to her.

"Keep digging. Because if he's who we think he is, he's probably been

involved in any number of incidents. He'll have left footprints somewhere."

"I'll keep on it," said Campos. "The president called earlier this afternoon asking for a progress report."

"What did you tell him?"

"Not that you were wounded. How are you doing, Colonel?"

Campos had risen from a working man's family in Havana, but he
had none of the Hispanic male macho attitude toward women, or at
least he'd never treated her that way. So far as she could tell his com-
ments were always truthful, on the mark, and sincere.

"I've been better, but I'll live. The doctor was damned good."

"Watch your back," he said, and rang off.

It struck her as curious that he would use the same boyish American
expression as Louise had used.

Dr. Vergilio, dressed in baggy khaki slacks and a short-sleeved safari
shirt, passed by the two stacks, her head down. She was in a hurry, and
her concentration was elsewhere.

After a moment María muted her cell phone because she did not
want to be disturbed at this point, then got up and went to the end of the
stacks in time to see the doctor disappear between another set of bookcases one-third of the way to the other end of the building.

She waited a little while longer before she went down the corridor,
pulling up just at the edge of the aisle that Vergilio had gone down for just
a second before she peeked around the corner.

Vergilio was up on a ladder pulling a leather-bound box about six
inches thick from a top shelf. When she had it she started down, but it
wasn't until she had reached the bottom and had turned that she noticed
María standing there, and she reared back.

"Is everything okay?" María asked.

"I wasn't expecting you so soon, you startled me."

"I came early because I found out something that you must know. It's
important."

"Tomorrow, Colonel."

"Right now. This could mean your life if you reveal the cipher key."

"What are you talking about, what cipher key?" Vergilio asked. She
held up the box. "You mean this?"

María inclined her head. Either the doctor was a damned good liar or what she'd fetched from the top shelf of the bookcase did not involve any cipher key.

"This is Pope Alexander VI's Papal Bull dividing the New World between us and Portugal. A researcher in Leipzig wants copies."

"You have assistants," María suggested, not believing her.

"Easier for me to do it myself. I know where practically everything is located here."

The lie hung in the air between them

"We need to talk."

"Not today." Vergilio was stubborn. "You have no authority here, Colonel. Nor does Cuba have any rightful claim to whatever may be discovered from the Ambli diary."

"Without the information from my father's journals in Mexico City before the revolution you would be nowhere. I thought that we had an agreement to find the caches for their historical value and then let our governments decide what came next."

"Leave or I will call the police."

"No you won't," María said. She pulled out her cell phone, brought up the photograph of Montessier, and walked back to where Dr. Vergilio stood clutching the book box to her bosom, her eyes wide, her expression angry.

"Leave . . ."

María held up the phone. "Has this man been here?"

Dr. Vergilio wilted. "His name is Paul Harris."

"He's almost certainly an assassin, and likely the one who managed to steal the diary from a bank vault in Bern."

SIXTY-FOUR

☐

They'd finally gotten out of Malta about an hour ago and were in the air en route to Gilbraltar's North Front Airport. Otto was on his computer trying to find out if there'd been any unusual occurrences in Seville overnight or anytime today, and McGarvey took out his Vatican passport that Msgr. Franelli's people had made for him.

It identified him as Fr. Robert Talbot, a special emissary from the Pope. Otto had been given a similar passport with his photo under the work name Fr. Bruce Ringers, also a Papal emissary.

"Three murders overnight in Seville in addition to the riot on the streets," Otto said, looking up.

"Not unusual for a city that size," McGarvey said.

"A husband stabbed his wife and the man he found in bed with her then called the police. And two hours ago an old woman was found dead in her bed by one of the neighbors. At first they thought she'd died of a heart attack, but when the ambulance crew arrived to pick up the body they found that her neck had been broken."

"A burglary?"

"The woman was the manager in the building where Dr. Vergilio has an apartment."

"Montessier," McGarvey said.

"Looking for the cipher key in the doctor's apartment. If he found it he'll be gone by now."

"If he found it," McGarvey said, and he tried telephoning María but she didn't answer.

Otto was watching. "Are you trying to reach her?"

"She's not answering."

Otto pulled up one of his computer programs that linked with a powerful telephone search engine at the National Security Agency, entered María's number, and a half minute later her phone came up. "It's switched on, but she probably has it on mute."

"Could be she's in the Archives right now and doesn't want to be disturbed."

"We'll ask her," Otto said, and he entered a couple of commands on his virtual keyboard, and a couple of seconds later her phone started ringing.

After four rings it went to voice mail.

Otto sent another set of commands and María's phone started ringing again. "She's at the Archives, but not on the ground floor, I think. The altitude function doesn't work very well for small elevations."

María's phone went dead. She'd shut off the power.

"Insistent, isn't she," Otto said, and he sent another set of commands, switching her phone back on. "This time she'll have to pull out the battery to shut down."

The call went through and this time María answered on the second ring. "Who is this?" she demanded in Spanish.

"It's me," McGarvey said. "We have to talk right now."

"I'm in the middle of a situation."

"You're in Doctor Vergilo's office on the second floor of the Archives, but unless someone is pointing a gun at your head we need to talk. Now."

"Just a minute."

"This isn't something that you need to keep from her, so put it on speaker phone. Otto is here with me."

"Where are you?"

"Should be in Gibraltar in a couple of hours, and Seville an hour or so later. Make it six or seven."

"Otto might get past passport control, but you won't."

"Both of us will. Can Doctor Vergilio hear my voice?"

"Yes," the woman answered. She sounded subdued.

"Has Colonel León told you about Bernard Montessier, the man who we think managed to get his hands on Ambli's diary?"

"Yes. He came to my office this morning and identified himself as a Paul Harris, a British writer of historical fiction. We checked him out on Google and he seemed legitimate to me."

"We don't know what his real name is, but he is an assassin, hired by a third party who wants the diary and the cipher key."

"I know nothing about any such key. I've already told Colonel León as much."

"If you told that to this guy, he almost certainly believes that you are lying. Have you heard from him again?"

"No."

Otto was monitoring the call, and he'd brought up another of his sophisticated programs, this one a stress measure algorithm. He turned to McGarvey and shook his head.

"You're lying, Doctor," McGarvey said. "This man will not hesitate to kill you. This morning he killed the woman who managed your apartment building."

"My God," Dr. Vergilio said. "Why? There was no reason for it."

"He needed to search your apartment and he wanted no witnesses. What did he find there?"

"Nothing."

"Literally nothing?" McGarvey insisted.

"Nothing," she repeated.

Otto hit a key on his computer. "How about the laptop with the book you're writing about the diary and the key?" he asked reasonably.

"I keep it with me—" Dr. Vergilio said, realizing her mistake immediately.

"I think that he's contacted you again, and told you that he had the diary and he would share it with you if you would provide the key."

"Cristo," she said softly. "He called and told me that the diary was coming by courier tonight—sometime between six and ten. He wants to meet me across the street in the Cathedral."

"You agreed?"

"It may be impossible. The police are expecting another mob of rioters tonight."

"But you agreed to the meeting?"

"Yes."

"To which you will bring the cipher key?"

"I do not have such a key," she said.

McGarvey gave Otto a questioning look, but Otto shrugged. It was impossible to tell if she had lied.

"He'll expect it," McGarvey said. "Are you willing to risk your life?"

"I don't give a damn about some treasure buried in your desert, though Madrid is desperate. I want the historical record. I want completion of something I've worked my entire life on. Do you understand scholarship, Señor McGarvey? Do you know what it means to have questions without answers? Have you any conception about the moment of discovery—when you find a glimmer, just a hint of something that could possibly point you in the right direction? Do you know the meaning of ecstasy? Or its opposite, that of profound loss?"

"I do."

"Then how can you ask if I'm willing to risk my life? Of course I am."

"For what gain?" Otto asked.

"Knowledge," Vergilio said.

"María, are you armed?" McGarvey asked.

"No. I didn't think there was any need."

"Tonight, if we are late, I want you and the doctor to lose yourselves in the mob. Don't try to barricade yourself inside the Archives. It won't work. This guy is too good. If he could crack a bank vault, he certainly won't have any trouble getting inside a museum."

"If we give him what he thinks is real, he'll give us the diary—or at least a copy."

María was playing both ends against the middle. It was obvious to McGarvey. She had her own agenda, her own intel, and she'd come to the states for no other reason than to use whoever she could to get to this point. No way was she going to back off now.

"We'll be there as soon as we can," McGarvey said, and he broke the connection.

"She's lying," Otto said. "But Doctor Vergilio wasn't at the end."

"Doesn't matter," McGarvey replied, resigned. "They've got a real chance of getting themselves killed tonight."

SIXTY-FIVE

☐

Al-Rashid drove across the river, and headed south into the commercial section of the city, with its docks and cargo ships in sight of the soaring Puente del V Centenario looming over the railroad swing bridge that squatted over the water. He'd plugged the address he'd been given by one of his contacts in Madrid into the car's GPS and followed the directions to a small building in the warehouse district.

The types of men he'd dealt with over his career—the ones who could supply weapons, explosives, or just about anything else illegal under the laws of most countries—always seemed to live in the seedier sections of any big city, where anonymity was easy to come by. They were almost always under the radar and nearly impossible to find unless you knew where to look.

He parked in the rear and went through a steel door into a large workroom, about twice the size of a two-car garage. Workbenches and power tools and supplies—everything from lengths of steel pipe, rebar, rolls of wire, and bins of miscellaneous nuts, bolts, screws, and other odd bits— filled nearly every available square foot of floor space. Along a back wall were four tall metal cabinets secured with large combination locks, and in a corner two very large gun safes.

Stairs went up to a balcony on the second floor. A short man with an enormous belly, wearing filthy jeans and a black leather vest, tattoos covering most of his chest and arms, came out of a door, a shotgun in his hand.

"Who the fuck are you, and what the fuck are you doing here?" he said in guttural Spanish.

"A man with money come to purchase something from you. A friend in Madrid gave me this address."

"Who is this man?"

"Señor Garbajosa, and he warned me that although you could help, to watch my ass because you are a cheating son of a bitch."

"Did he give you my name?"

"The Supplier."

The man laughed. "Son of a bitch." He came down the stairs, the shotgun cradled in the crook of his arm. "You may call me Miguel, for now. Let me see your passport."

Al-Rashid handed it over, and Miguel stepped back just out of reach and briefly looked at it. "Paul Harris. You sound like a Brit, but this is a forgery. Damned good, but a fake nevertheless. Is your money counterfeit as well? I would not be happy if it was. I would have to kill you and fence the bills for whatever I could get. Not my specialty."

"American dollars."

Miguel nodded. He returned the passport, and held out his hand.

Al-Rashid took a one-hundred-dollar bill from his jacket pocket and handed it over.

Miguel stepped back again and raised the bill to the light so that he could examine the water marks, leaving himself open for just a moment, long enough for al-Rashid to step to the left and snatch the shotgun.

"You bastard," Miguel said.

"I don't like guns pointed at me," al-Rashid said. He unloaded the shotgun, tossed the shells across the room, and laid the weapon on the workbench to his left. "Nor do I like the men who do the pointing. Do we understand each other?"

After a moment, Miguel pocketed the bill and nodded. "What do you want?"

"A handgun, semiautomatic, no lighter than nine millimeter. A silencer, and three magazines of ammunition."

"Do you have a preference? A Glock? A SIG? I can give you a Beretta. It's only nine millimeter, but it's accurate and easily suppressed."

"The Beretta will do. And I'll need four one-kilo bricks of Semtex and pencil fuses. And an accelerant, but not liquid."

"You're going to destroy something, then to make sure you're going to burn it down, and you're expecting some resistance."

Al-Rashid shrugged.

"The Guardia will be all over this, so I'll need to know what you're going to hit, when, and why?"

"It'll be tonight, downtown, during the riot. But that's all you need to know."

"I have to cover my own ass."

"Do you have what I need?"

A shrewd look came into the man's eyes. "That will depend on the money."

"Name a price."

"Fifty thousand."

"Do you have what I need?"

"Do you agree to my price?"

"Actually I was prepared to pay more, but you haven't answered my question."

"Normally an order like that, especially during these difficult times, could take several days, up to a week. But you want these items this evening."

"I'll be here at seven."

"Sixty thousand."

"Seventy-five thousand," al-Rashid said. He pulled two banded stacks of hundred-dollar bills from his jacket pocket, and laid them on the workbench beside the shotgun. "Ten thousand as a down payment. I'll bring the rest this evening."

"Agreed," Miguel said without hesitation.

Al-Rashid turned and started to leave, but then turned back. "Do not cross me, Señor Meolans. I found you here, I could find you anywhere."

If the man was surprised that al-Rashid knew his real name, he didn't let on. He glanced at the money on the workbench. "Seven sharp," he said.

Back at his suite in the Gran Meliá Colón, al-Rashid ordered a couple of Heinekens and a small plate of tapas for a late lunch. While he waited for room service to arrive he phoned Prince Saleh.

"Any word on Halberstrom?"

"He's disappeared. Where are you?"

"I'm getting ready to leave Seville tonight. It's too bad your people didn't find the American. I would have liked to know why he suddenly started asking about you."

"Do you have the key?"

"I will by this evening."

"And then you will bring it to me," Prince Saleh said.

"Of course," al-Rashid said, and he hung up. He went out on the balcony that looked down on the busy Calle Canalejas, and watched the traffic. The hallmark of his tradecraft had been precision from the beginning. Attention to details. Awareness of even the smallest, most insignificant of details. The stray van parked across the street, the Vespa in his rearview mirror, a man's eyes—the way they looked, what they were seeing, and the reactions in them.

Not many men in his profession—what he had come to accept as a fixer, which was a more civilized term than assassin—lived to retire. He had set aside something under forty million euros, and his retirement was something he had thought about for the past several years. But each year the prince had come up with something new, something needing fixing, and he'd always been generous with his rewards.

Time to get out now? he wondered. Already the risks he had taken were mounting to unacceptable levels. And tonight the situation could easily spin out of control.

One last fix, and then he would leave.

But it was the dark-haired woman he'd seen going into the Archives that bothered him. The Voltaires, he understood. The CNI of course, along with McGarvey and the CIA, also were understandable.

Which left who?

The room service waiter came. Al-Rashid signed for the bill, added a few euros in cash, and when the man was gone, he called for his car to be brought around, and he went downstairs.

SIXTY-SIX

María rode pillion on Dr. Vergilio's Vespa back to the apartment building. The uniformed police were still there, along with an evidence van
and several plainclothes detectives. They were stopped at the open gate.

"You may not enter," a cop told them.

"I live here," Dr. Vergilio said. "What has happened?"

A few civilians were watching from across the street. A second uniformed police officer came over.

"Let me see your identification," the first cop said. He was a nervous,
skinny kid who looked like he was still in his teens.

Dr. Vergilio dug out her driver's license from her backpack, and
María handed the cop her passport. She still had the pistol in her shoulder bag, but leaving the Archives she hadn't wanted to go anywhere
unarmed.

The second, much older cop came over. "What is going on here?"

The young cop handed over the IDs.

"I'm Dr. Vergilio, I live here."

"Yes, I know," the older cop said. He looked at María's passport, then
compared the photo with María's face. "Ms. Delgado, what are you doing here?"

"Dr. Vergilio is the curator of the Archivo General de Indias. I'm here
searching the records with her gracious help."

"Sí, but what are you doing here?"

"Someone phoned and said there were police at my building," Dr.
Vergilio said. "I have valuable books and maps in my apartment."

"I came as a friend," María said.

"Wait here," the older cop said. He went through the gate to the open
door into the manager's apartment.

A moment later an older man, in civilian clothes, who was tall, very dark, and suave looking, came out, took the driver's license and passport, and came back to Dr. Vergilio and María, and handed them back their papers.

"I am Policía Nacional Detective Lieutenant Zubaro. I'm sorry to say, Doctor Vergilio, that something dreadful has happened here. Do you have personal knowledge of Mrs. Vallalpandro?"

"Yes, she is the building manager."

"We know that. But are you aware of any family, or perhaps friends—men friends?"

"Lady friends here in the neighborhood, but I believe that she was childless and her husband passed away years ago."

"No nephews, nieces?"

"Not that that I am aware of," Dr. Vergilio said. "What has happened here?"

"The poor woman was murdered sometime this morning."

"My God."

María stiffened. Vergilio was not a very convincing actress, and the detective's eyes narrowed a little.

"In fact I was just about to telephone your office," he said. "There didn't seem to be a robbery in Mrs. Vallalpandro's apartment, nor in any of the others. We looked at yours, naturally, because yours was the only place that contained anything of real value."

"Was anything missing?"

"Frankly, we cannot tell. It is why I was about to telephone to ask you to take a look."

"I have a lot of historical documents."

"Would any of them be worth stealing?" the cop asked. "By that I mean to ask, is there anything in your apartment that, say, an antiquities thief might be interested in?"

"Probably."

"Then my question is: Why aren't these items kept at the Archives?"

"I often work at night," Vergilio said. "It is more comfortable to do so in my own home."

The cop stepped aside. "Leave your scooter here, and I will walk with you."

María walked with them through the gate back to Vergilio's apartment, half expecting the detective to stop her. But he said nothing until they got inside.

"We touched nothing," he said.

"I appreciate that," Vergilio told him, obviously distracted.

María hung just behind the cop, as the doctor went immediately into the second bedroom where she opened several of the map drawers and examined the contents of each.

"Is there anything missing?" the lieutenant asked.

"Not yet," Vergilio said. She turned and brushed past them and walked back out to the dining room, where she looked at several files in thick accordion folders.

For several long moments she stood almost as if in a trance, before she went to her bedroom, where she idly flipped through several other files, and a couple of rare books. When she was done she turned to the cop.

"Nothing has been disturbed," she said.

"And nothing is missing?"

"No. I doubt that he was here."

María winced inwardly, careful to keep her expression neutral, but she stood just to the left of the detective, and she could see that he had reacted to the mistake.

"He?" the cop asked. "Do you know who may have killed your building manager, and left no mark of searching for something here?"

Dr. Vergilio shook her head. "I don't understand what you mean. I have no enemies. I'm just a simple archaeologist."

"Famous in certain circles lately."

"What does that have to do with someone coming here to commit murder?"

The detective shrugged. "There is a row of keys in Mrs. Vallalpandro's apartment. For the apartments. The only key missing was for yours. So whoever killed the poor woman was here. Something here was his motive for the crime. And you said 'he' as if you knew someone who might do this thing, and why."

"I don't know. It was just a figure of speech. Isn't it usually men who commit such crimes?"

"That is true," the detective said. "But then there are exceptions." He glanced at María, who held his momentary gaze.

"Nothing was disturbed here," Dr. Vergilio said, digging herself a deeper hole in front of the cop.

"We know he took your key, so the natural assumption is that either he is a very careful professional who doesn't leave traces of his comings and goings, or you are lying, or both."

"I am not lying!" Dr. Vergilio shouted. "Nothing was disturbed here. Beyond that I know absolutely nothing, except that after last night's riot right outside of the Archives and now this horrible crime I am shook up and frightened. You cannot imagine what an inestimable loss it would be for Spain if the Archives were to be seriously damaged."

"I understand," the detective said sympathetically. "But you must also understand, Doctor, that I am trying to do my job, which among other aspects is assuring your personal safety. Someone wants something that you have, and I think that you know who it is, and I think that your life may be in danger. Please help me to help you, and Spain's priceless treasures."

Dr. Vergilio shook her head. "I need to get back to my office. There may be another riot tonight and I want to prepare my security people and staff."

The detective stepped aside. "I will provide an escort for you."

Outside they passed through the iron gate to where the Vespa was parked when María spotted a man in the crowd across the street. She only caught a momentary glimpse before he turned and walked away. But she was almost certain that it was the man whose passport photo McGarvey and Otto had sent her.

"Is it possible for us a get a ride back to the Archives?" she asked the detective. "I don't think Dr. Vergilio is up for driving her scooter back just now."

"It's not necessary," Vergilio protested, but the detective disagreed.

"I think Ms. Delgado may be right," he said.

SIXTY-SEVEN

They landed at Gibraltar's International Airport in late afternoon, and taxied over to a private aviation terminal where they were picked up in a Land Rover by an older man with a badly pockmarked face in the black robes of a priest, who identified himself as Father Aguero.

"It was probably a very good idea that you are entering Spain from here, rather than flying to Madrid first," the priest said. "Monsignor Franelli thought it would be best."

"I'm known in Spain," McGarvey said.

"But not as a representative of His Holiness."

"Do you know about our mission?"

"No, nor do I wish to know. I'm here simply to get you across the border without being searched, and then take you to your hotel in Seville."

They drove to the border crossing where they stopped at the back of a line of a half dozen other cars, a couple of them taxis. When it was their turn, a passport control officer in uniform came over. "Father," he said respectfully. He looked at McGarvey and Otto in the backseat. "May I see your passports?"

They handed them out the open window, and the officer studied both. When he looked up, he nodded. "Do either of you have anything to declare?"

"No," McGarvey said.

"You're an American."

"Cleveland Diocese, actually," Fr. Aguero said.

"Their business here?"

"They are emissaries from the Pope, but their mission is classified. You understand, señor."

The officer was getting suspicious, and the priest lowered his voice. "His Holiness will be making a visit to Spain, specifically to Seville in six months. These gentlemen are here to begin making the arrangements." He shrugged. "In the present climate one cannot be too careful."

Spain, like many other countries on the Continent, was beginning to have a Muslim problem—not with law-abiding people, but those with ties to Islamic militant groups. Elsewhere there had been threats on the Pope's life.

"I understand completely," the officer said. He handed back the passports. "But why didn't you fly directly to Seville?"

"That's the other part of the secret mission. His Holiness wants to visit here first and then make a pilgrimage, if you will, by motorcade." Fr. Aguero shrugged. "Sometimes the will of a Pontiff is not for us to understand."

The border guard nodded. "Go with God, then," he said, and stepped aside so that they could pass through.

Once clear of the border crossing and past the rows of condominiums and tourist attractions on both the Mediterranean and the Bahía de Algecira sides of the narrow peninsula at the town of La Linea de la Concepción, they headed north to the N340 at San Rogue and then east until they reached C339, which was a narrow country road with very little traffic.

The day was waning, and Fr. Aguero kept glancing in his rearview mirror, as if he expected to pick up a tail.

"Anyone following us?" McGarvey asked.

Otto was on his computer getting them hotel reservations and arranging for a car in Seville.

"Not so far. Monsignor Franelli suggested I take this route rather than the main highway so that if we were followed from Gibraltar it would become evident almost immediately and we could deal with it."

"Are you in the Order?"

The priest glanced at McGarvey's image in the rearview mirror. "No."

"Just a parish priest?"

"Something like that."

Otto looked up. "We're in," he said. He turned the computer so that McGarvey could see that they had a two-bedroom suite at the Gran Meliá Colón, under the names Joseph Burton and James Schwartz.

"Anything on the police net we need to know about?"

"They're setting up for another night of riots in the Barrio de Santa Cruz."

"Lots of places in which to get lost," McGarvey said, thinking of how he would do it if he were Montessier. The area had been the old Jewish quarter and was a rat warren of narrow, twisting streets and alleys.

The riot would provide a diversion, but if his mission was to get the cipher key from Dr. Vergilio he would need something more than that. Something more compelling, something that would force her to bring the key in exchange for the diary.

They went through several small forests that were broken up by small farm fields, some of wheat and some of grasslands for cattle. But most of the eighty miles or so up to Seville was open land of scrub brush and near deserts, until just south of the city the first olive groves growing up the hillsides started to appear.

Fr. Aguero held his silence. He was on a mission for the Church that he neither liked nor disliked. He was merely following ecclesiastical orders.

Traffic picked up a little after five when they reached the N334 highway outside of El Arahal, which turned into a divided highway about ten miles outside of the city, and Fr. Aguero began to relax a little.

"What hotel do you wish to be taken to?"

McGarvey told him, and twenty minutes later they pulled up in front of the grand hotel, and a bellman opened the doors for them and took their single bags. Otto hung on to his laptop.

"Thank you, Father," McGarvey said to the priest through the open driver's side window. "This is important. Lives are at stake."

"They very often are with the Order."

McGarvey stepped back and the priest drove off without looking back.

Seville smelled like Spain—olive oil, fish, maybe sardines, wood smoke, in the distance the spice saffron, and just now a hint of burnt gasoline and something else, maybe vinegar, maybe tear gas left over from last night's riots.

Otto went ahead up the stairs into the central lobby under the stained glass dome, and checked them in while McGarvey picked up a house phone. "Paul Harris, please."

"One moment, sir," the operator said. The room number rang several times, before the operator came back. "There is no answer, sir. Would you care to leave a message?"

"Yes, please. Tell him that an old friend is in town, and would like to meet with him for drinks sometime this evening. Here in the hotel."

"Shall I say a time?"

"Let's say, eight. Tell him I have the key. He'll understand."

"Yes, sir."

McGarvey hung up and went to the front desk and handed his passport to the clerk, who took an impression, and then handed it back.

They took their bags from the bellman, McGarvey gave him a generous tip, and he and Otto went upstairs. When they were in their suite, McGarvey checked the windows, which looked down on the street, traffic light at this hour. Later tonight things would pick up, especially if a riot materialized down in the barrio near the museum.

Otto had connected to one of his programs back at Langley.

"He's here," McGarvey said.

Otto looked up, his eyes round.

"In the hotel. The bastard checked in under the Paul Harris name he gave Dr. Vergilio."

"Arrogant."

"Yeah," McGarvey said. "He thinks that he's the smartest guy in the room. And probably the toughest, because if anyone catches up with him, he's sure that he can take them down. He's evidently never failed before."

"What are we going to do?"

"Show him the error of his ways."

SIXTY-EIGHT

□

Al-Rashid finished an early dinner of filet of sole, with a good potato salad and a half bottle of a local white wine he'd never heard of downstairs at the hotel's El Burladero bar and restaurant. It was just before six-thirty when he signed for the bill. On the way out he passed a house phone, and for no reason he could think of, picked it up and asked if he'd had any messages.

"Just one, Señor Harris, about twenty minutes ago. Would you like to hear it?"

"Yes, please." The prince would have called his cell phone, not the hotel.

The voice was unmistakably that of an American. An old friend, he said, but al-Rashid didn't know who it could be, until the key was mentioned.

". . . would like to meet with him for drinks sometime this evening. Here in the hotel."

"Shall I say, a time?" the operator asked.

"Let's say, eight. Tell him I have the key. He'll understand."

It suddenly came to al-Rashid that it was Kirk McGarvey, who had most likely got the Harris name from Dr. Vergilio, but the Americans knew that he was in this hotel too soon.

"Will there be anything else, señor?"

"No," al-Rashid said, and he headed outside and went down the block and around the corner to an underground parking garage where he'd left the BMW, preferring to keep it there rather than with the valet for just such a circumstance.

Leaving the ramp he crossed to the broad Calle de San Pablo, and from there crossed the river on the Isabell II bridge and reached the Port of Seville's warehouse district fifteen minutes later, well before the time of his appointment with the arms supplier Miguel Meolans.

He parked a half block away pulling between several stacks of shipping containers, rising twenty-five feet or more. The area was nearly deserted, which he found odd, unless the dock workers were heading toward the Murillo Gardens for tonight's riot. It made sense because it was the working man who was bearing the brunt of the austerity measures.

He telephoned Dr. Vergilio at her office. "Do you know who this is?"

"Yes, do you have it?" she asked. She sounded excited.

"I'm on my way to pick it up now. Has the crowd begun to gather yet?"

"A few people are showing up, but the police are already here. Why don't you come to my office?"

"No. We will meet at nine across the street in the Cathedral."

"It may be too dangerous," Dr. Vergilio objected, but al-Rashid cut her off.

"For you, if you do not bring the cipher key."

"That wasn't our agreement."

"It is now. And, Adriana, do not tell anyone—not the policeman you spoke with outside of your apartment, and especially not Mr. McGarvey who is at the same hotel where I am staying."

"There was no reason for you to kill my building manager to merely search my apartment," Dr. Vergilio shot back angrily. "You found nothing, because nothing is there."

"You took your laptop with you. Really very clever. Bring it tonight."

"I do not have the cipher key."

"You're lying, of course. But tell me who the attractive dark-haired woman is? The one who was with you this morning at your apartment?"

"Just a friend."

"Trust me, if something goes wrong, no matter what, I will kill you. The only reason you're not dead yet is because you have access to the key. But I still have the diary, and if you won't cooperate I'll find someone to decrypt the thing. Who is the woman?"

Another woman came on. "My name is María León, I'm a colonel in Cuba's intelligence service, and I'm here for the same reason you are. Is it possible that we could make a deal?"

Who she was did not come as a very big surprise. "What do you have that I might need?"

"Kirk McGarvey and his friend Otto Rencke, who is the special projects director with the CIA. I'm here with them, and I can divert them from you."

"There is no need."

"If you believe that, Mr. Harris, then you would be making the greatest mistake of your life."

Al-Rashid chuckled. "You sound as if you are in love with him."

"*Puta,*" she swore.

He'd hit a mark, which did come as a surprise. "I have the diary, Dr. Vergilio has the cipher key, and you promise to divert McGarvey in exchange for what?"

"A copy of the journal and of the key. Some of that treasure belongs to us, and my government means to claim it in the international courts. To do that we need proof of its existence in the United States."

"Nine o'clock across the street in the Cathedral," al-Rashid said. "And Colonel?"

"*Sí?*"

"If McGarvey is anywhere close I will kill you."

Al-Rashid shut off his cell phone, and headed around the corner to the rear of the building where the arms dealer had his office, workshop, and possibly even his apartment on the upper level. The trash-filled alley was barely wide enough for a forklift to pass, and in any event the warehouses here were more or less off the beaten path, away from the more up-to-date bonded facilities.

The battered old steel door was unlocked and al-Rashid went in, finding himself to the left of the gun safes, just beneath the wooden stairs up to the balcony. One of them was open, and from where he stood he saw a dozen or more assault rifles in racks from the middle up, and twice as many pistols below. Shelves on the bottom two feet contained boxes of ammunition, and a couple of bins the contents of which he couldn't make out.

The shop was mostly in darkness, the only light coming from outside through a row of dirty windows near the ceiling. But there was enough for him to spot a man on either side of the front door, their backs to him. Neither of them was Meolans.

Al-Rashid crept to the open gun safe where he picked out an old Generation One Glock 17 pistol, and a box of 9 mm ammunition, and keeping his eyes on the two men loaded the weapon's seventeen-round magazine by feel. When he was finished he slammed the magazine into the handle and racked the slide back.

The men at the door turned, pistols in their hands, and al-Rashid fired five times, shoving both men backward against the front wall in sprays of blood.

The silence afterward was gloomy.

"I thought that you might try to rob me," al-Rashid said. "But now that the odds have been evened, I still need the things I contracted for."

He figured that the arms dealer was upstairs on the balcony, shotgun in hand just like earlier today.

"I have the remaining sixty-five thousand dollars, if we can come to an arrangement."

"Your things are on the table in the middle of the room," Meolans said from directly above. "Leave the money, and take them."

Al-Rashid fired seven rounds up into the balcony floor, walking the rounds left and right.

Meolans cried out twice and fell to the floor with a heavy thud.

Al-Rashid waited for a full half minute until blood began dripping from the holes in the floor, and then went cautiously out to the stairs and took them slowly up to the landing.

Meolans lay on his side, the shotgun a couple of feet away, blood streaming from an oblique wound in his chest, and from two in his groin. He was in a great deal of pain, yet he tried to reach for a pistol in his belt beneath his leather vest.

"Actually it's a bloody wonder that you lasted this long in the business," al-Rashid said, and shot him in the forehead at nearly point-blank range.

He went back downstairs, wiped the pistol clean, and laid it on one of the workbenches. The Beretta, silencer, spare magazines, and the Semtex and pencil fuses had been set out in a neat row, along with two clear plastic bags, each about the size of a small loaf of bread filled with a coarse gray powder. The bags were marked "Mg." Magnesium dust that burned with an intense white light. The perfect nonliquid accelerant.

But Meolans had laid out the things only for show, for bait, because he'd not provided anything to carry the things in.

It only took al-Rashid a couple of minutes to find an old canvas haversack into which he loaded the things after first checking the pistol to make sure that its firing pin hadn't been removed, the bullets to make sure they were not blanks, and the Semtex and fuses to make sure that they were genuine.

He checked at the front door to make certain that no one was coming to find out about the gunshots, and then let himself out and went back to his car.

He would be on the road before ten this evening, heading for the border with Portugal. By morning he would be in the air for Jeddah, a man finally wealthy enough to disappear.

Before he drove off he made a call to a contact in the CNI.

☐

SIXTY-NINE

McGarvey let Otto drive the rental Fiat 500L, but as he had expected the crowds radiating out from the Murillo gardens made it impossible to get any closer than a couple of blocks from the Archives. They pulled down a narrow side street and parked with two wheels up on the sidewalk.

"I want you to get down to the Archives as quickly as you can," Mc-Garvey said. "But don't take any chances, do you understand?"

Otto nodded. He was a computer genius, not a field officer, and had never pretended to be one.

"If you get into a situation that looks dicey, make a one eighty and get the hell out of there."

"Where will you be?"

"Around. But so will Montessier. I want you to try to talk Vergilio out of meeting with him. But no matter what goes down, I want her out of the Archives. Anywhere but there or the Cathedral."

"What if she refuses?"

"Get the hell out of there and call me."

"How about María? She has her own agenda, which means she'll do whatever it takes to get the diary and the key. She's already got a deal with the doctor, but she might try to make another deal with Montessier. And you know damned well that she's armed. Probably got a gun from her people at the Cuban consulate here."

"I'm counting on it. With any luck she'll provide a diversion for me."

They were standing by the car, a few people passing by on foot, a couple of them holding signs protesting cuts in teachers' salaries. They seemed determined, even angry.

"Whatever you do don't push her," McGarvey warned emphatically. "You know what she's capable of. Deliver your message, and then get the hell out of there with or most likely without Vergilio. Whatever happens call me."

They separated in the next block, Otto heading directly toward the Archives while McGarvey angled around to the Alcazar fortress, which was a massive Moorish castle that nowadays served as a part-time residence of the royal family. It, along with the Cathedral and the Archives, made up a UNESCO World Heritage Site.

The gathering crowd flowed around the buildings, gathering on the narrow streets that were blocked by the police to motor traffic surrounding them. No one seemed to be in charge of the mob, and there was no sense of a front line. But many of the people chanted the same slogan— something to the effect of returning to the old days—thus the second night of gathering in the city's historical district.

Most of the sidewalk cafés were still open for business, though the antiques stores and souvenir shops were closed, their metal security shutters down. Young people were crowding around a fountain in one of the small plazas; some of them sat on painted tile benches and played guitars. Just like those in the cafés, the people not on the streets marching were observers not participants.

McGarvey more or less went with the flow of the crowd until he found a spot at a café within sight of the Cathedral and the Archives, just in time to see Otto show up and go inside.

He was one row of tables back and in a corner under an awning as much in the shadows as possible. It would be difficult for someone passing on the street, or even someone nearby in the Cathedral or at one of the windows in the Archives, to spot him. But he could almost feel the presence of Montessier, who planned on meeting Dr. Vergilio sometime this evening. The guy was a pro; he would show up early to make sure that the opposition hadn't taken up positions to wait for him.

But from what little McGarvey knew of the woman, and from what he knew about María he didn't think that any force on earth would stop them from making the rendezvous. And it was almost certain that María would be the one hiding in the shadows to wait for him. If she did it, it was very likely that she would get herself and the doctor killed.

Unless Otto could talk some sense into them.

The waiter came and he ordered an espresso. Two minutes after he got his coffee his phone chirped.

"Otto?"

"No, Monsieur McGarvey, this is not your associate Monsieur Rencke, but my name is no importance, except I am on the board of directors of the Voltaire Society, and since you are in Seville I assume that you are on the track of the man who managed to acquire the diary. For that we wish you *bon chance*."

"The vice mayor was a member?"

"The woman was. And as you have found out our office in the banking district was a sham, nor did Madame Petain and her son have any importance to the Society."

"How did you get this number?"

"We have contacts in the United States, but believe me when I assure you that we are not your enemy."

"Neither am I your friend," McGarvey said. "The diary you claim is yours was stolen from the Catholic Church."

"Yes, the Order, who meant to plunder the fortune for itself."

"A fortune that doesn't belong to them or to you."

"Who then?"

"Native Americans and Caribs."

"Almost all of whom are an extinct people. To whom do you suggest the treasure belongs today? The Church who stole it from Spain? Spain who stole it from the natives?"

"Or you?" McGarvey asked.

"Yes, us. Because we have done good with it, and will continue to do good providing the Saudis do not get their hands on the diary and the cipher key and plunder it first."

"What does Saudi Arabia have to do with this?"

"The man you have identified as Bernard Montessier and who I presume you've traced to his travels to and from Jeddah, we think works for a member of the Saudi Royal family. He is a finance minister, who controls an immense amount of wealth, and not merely from oil revenues, but from other dealings in the international arena. He would like to get his hands on the treasure; it is why, we suspect, that he contracted Montessier to find the diary and the cipher key."

"Do you know Montessier's real name?"

"Unfortunately we have not been able to learn it, though by now you must realize that he is a professional, and a ruthless man. If he manages to get the diary and the key there will be little we could do to stop him. At that point it would be up to your government."

"It comes back to why should I help you?"

"Because you are an honorable man—"

McGarvey cut him off. "Bullshit. I want the real reason."

"You have found out that the Society made a substantial payment to your government through a bank in Richmond, Virginia, before the start of your country's Civil War. Without its help for the Union it is possible that the war could have been lost, or at the very least have dragged on for years shattering an already precarious economy. We sent the money to help your democracy. As we have at other times of crises."

"I don't believe you."

"Why? Because you no longer believe in altruism? Even though your stated motive in pursuing this matter was to avenge the needless deaths of those two students? Or because Monsieur Rencke could find the records of no other payments? Though I assure you more were made: During the First World War, and the second, and Korea—though not Vietnam because we believed you were wrong. You have not been able to find the traces because we have a banking system in place that screens such transfers."

McGarvey wasn't accepting any of it, and he said so, and yet he could detect no artifice in the Frenchman's voice, only an apparent sincerity.

"You have become a cynic, and rightly so considering your past. But think about America's role in the world—especially in the Western hemisphere in the last two centuries. People don't immigrate to China, or Saudi Arabia, or Iran or Iraq. Poor Mexicans don't usually head south to Guatemala, Belize, or Honduras—they cross the Rio Grande by the tens of thousands to find a better life for their children who when they are born in the United States automatically become citizens."

"I know the history of my country," McGarvey shot back, when two men in plainclothes got out of a dark car and crossed the sidewalk directly toward him. He broke the connection, enabled the password protection, and laid the phone on the table, his hands in plain sight.

"Señor McGarvey," the taller of the two said politely. He held up his credentials wallet, while the other shorter, squatter man remained a step behind and to the left. "I am Captain Eduardo de la Rosa, of the Centro Nacional de Inteligencia. You are under arrest, charged with murder."

SEVENTY

□

María went with Dr. Vergilio across the broad corridor through the stacks to a window on the opposite side of the building that looked across the street at the Cathedral, colored lights already illuminating its façade and bell tower. At just a few minutes before eight the crowds had grown dramatically, but so far it didn't look as if any confrontations with the police had begun. A lot of people carried signs, and even up here they could hear some of the chanting.

Vergilio stepped directly in front of the window to get a better look, and María pulled her back.

"Bad idea," María said. "If this guy wants to take you out you don't have to make it easy for him."

"Our meeting isn't until nine."

"He's here already, believe me."

Vergilio gave her a sharp look. "He's not going to do anything to me as long as he thinks I have the cipher key to trade with him."

"But you do, and so long as you hold out he'll bargain."

"But I don't have it. I've been telling you and McGarvey and anyone who wants to listen that I simply do not have the key. Never did."

"Then what use would the diary be to you?"

"Not much beyond the historical record. The government will probably be interested, though. And they'll make copies and bring in the encryption experts, all in secret of course." She shook her head and looked María in the eye. "When I was younger I would have fought for the rights to make an expedition to New Mexico, fought my government, the U.S. government, anyone I could. But now?"

"A lot of people have given their lives for this."

"A lot of people's lives were taken."

They'd left the office doors open, and they heard the distant jangle of a ringing telephone. Dr. Vergilio turned away from the window and walked back across the corridor, María right behind her.

The Archives was deserted now, only she and the doctor, plus three security people downstairs were in the building at this hour. But the three were old men, only here to keep the tourists in line. The real security tonight was the police presence outside, and mission one for them, so far as she understood it, was to protect the Archives, the Cathedral, and the Alcazar from harm by the mob.

She reached the office right behind Vergilio as the doctor picked up the telephone.

"Sí?"

María tried to gauge Vergilio's reaction, but the doctor only seemed a little perplexed.

"I don't know a priest named Ringers. If he wants to see me tell him to come back in the morning. We're closed now. And when he's gone make sure that all the doors are locked."

María held up a hand.

"Just a minute," Dr. Vergilio said, and she held her hand over the telephone's mouthpiece.

"Can you bring up an image on the security cameras downstairs?" María asked.

Dr. Vergilio brought up the program on her desktop computer, and Otto Rencke stood at the security desk looking up in to the lens.

María wasn't much surprised. "Send him up," she said.

Dr.Vergilio relayed the order and hung up. "Do you know him?"

"He's a friend of McGarvey's."

"I'll send him away," Dr. Vergilio said, and she reached for the phone.

"No. I have a better idea."

Otto showed up at the door a minute later. "We thought you might still be here," he said. He came in, and looked around. "Neat place."

"Is Mac with you?" María asked.

"He's watching the Cathedral, I suspect waiting for the guy you know as Paul Harris to show up."

"Won't be there for another hour," Vergilio blurted.

"That's what he told you, but it's a good bet he's already there, or somewhere very close."

"So it's going to be a shoot-out between them?" María asked.

"If it comes to it," Otto said, and he blinked. "Because sure as hell if you go over there and try to get the jump on him with whatever weapon your embassy supplied you with you'll get yourself and Dr. Vergilio killed."

"You don't give me much credit."

"And you're not giving this guy his due. He's a professional gun, probably working for the Saudis. He's already killed the vice mayor of Paris and his mistress, along with the wife and teenage son of the Voltaire who came to see Mac in Florida. The one the CNI took out."

"But he has the diary," Dr. Vergilio said. She was angry.

"He won't give it to you," Otto said. "Think about it. This guy was the one who killed your building manager. Broke her neck, according to the cops. If you bring him the cipher key, he'll kill you."

"*Puta*, I don't have it!"

Otto grinned. "I'm not a whore, or even a son of a whore. If he believes you, he'll kill you, and then break in over here and steal your laptop. The one he was looking for at your apartment."

Vergilio instinctively glanced at the computer where she'd laid it atop a pile of papers on the credenza behind her desk.

"Yes, that one," Otto said.

"What do you suggest?" María asked.

"Mac wants both of you to get out of here right now."

"To the Cathedral?"

"Anywhere but there. Go down to the train station, or even a police precinct station, but just get the hell away from here. And take your laptop with you."

"It contains no cipher key!" Vergilio shouted. "And I'm not leaving the Archives, not with that mob outside, except to go across the street."

"They're not here to harm this place or the Cathedral or the Alcazar. Anyway, there are enough cops out there to make sure nothing happens tonight."

"I want the diary."

"He won't give it to you, and you'll end up dead," Otto said. "And so will you," he told María.

He turned away and took an iPhone from his pocket.

María pulled the Glock from the waistband of her jeans, and pointed it at him. "I won't allow you to call Mac."

"Shoot me and the guards downstairs will hear it."

"If need be I'll shoot them as well."

Dr. Vergilio's eyes widened in surprise. "What are you talking about?"

"You and I are going to meet with Señor Harris. You're going to give him your laptop, after we load a flash drive with the cipher key, just in case. But when he produces the diary I will kill him and we'll come back here and make copies."

"If she gets her hands on the diary, she'll kill you too," Otto said.

Dr. Vergilio stepped back. "You're both so stupid. I'll tell you for the last time, I do not have the cipher key."

"Close the office doors," María said.

Vergilio was confused.

"Now," María said.

"Don't you understand what's going on?" Otto asked.

But Vergilio went past him and closed the outer door into the corridor and then came back and closed the inner door to her office.

"Toss the phone on the floor," María told Otto.

Otto did it.

"Are you armed?"

"You know Mac well enough to know that he doesn't much trust me with guns."

"Call the guards," María told Vergilio. "Tell them that you spoke to the police, who want all of us to leave once they've locked up."

Dr. Vergilio did so, and even though she was the curator it took her a minute to convince the man she was talking to to do as he was told. She hung up. "They're going," she said.

María switched aim and fired one shot into the woman's forehead, sending her sprawling backward against her desk.

SEVENTY-ONE

□

Al-Rashid had worked his way down the street between the Cathedral and the Archives in the middle of the mob, which he estimated to have grown to at least ten thousand people or more in the last half hour. He'd picked up a protest sign someone had dropped, and no one, including the police, paid him any attention—his was just one face in a sea of faces. Even the haversack he carried elicited no attention.

About twenty minutes earlier two men had gotten out of a car in front of a sidewalk café and moments later they led a man in handcuffs from the restaurant, stuffed him in the backseat, and drove off.

He'd been too far away to make out who it was they had arrested, and he decided that in any case it wouldn't matter. Whoever it was, he was out of circulation for now.

The problem of getting into the Archives was twofold. The first were the security guards inside, and a few minutes after eight three of them came out of one of the side doors, checked the lock, and walked away.

The second issue was the police, but none of them seemed to be paying any attention to the building, only to the mob. But a civilian carrying a sign and taking the time to pick the lock would stand out.

He turned and started after the three guards, who almost immediately split up and walked in three different directions.

The largest of the three, the one who'd locked up, headed left directly past the Cathedral and made his way through the mob, bucking the flow until he reached the nearby Avenida de la Constitución, where he passed through the police barricades and headed straight across toward the river.

Al-Rashid discarded his sign, and keeping his head down, crossed the police line and hurried across the broad avenue until he caught up with the guard a half a block later just at the entrance to a very narrow side street that was already in deeper shadows. Traffic here was almost non-existent and at the moment no pedestrians were about, and all the shops were shuttered because of the demonstration.

"Señor," he said softly.

The older man turned around. His face was broad, his hair beneath his cap white. He wore dark trousers and a coat with the Archives insignia on its breast. "Sí?"

"I have a pistol beneath my jacket and if you call for help I will kill you."

The old man stepped back in alarm. "Is this a holdup? I have nothing of any value."

"We'll see. Down the alley, please, and you will come to no harm. I promise you."

The Archives' guard backed up a step, and looked around, but no one was here.

"Please," al-Rashid said politely.

Resigned, the old man shuffled around the corner and into the alley. About fifty feet in, he stopped and turned, his eyes widening when he spotted the silenced pistol in al-Rashid's hand. "What do you want?"

"Take off your jacket."

For several beats the guard was confused, but then he realized something and he raised a hand.

"Your jacket or I will kill you. Be quick about it."

The guard reluctantly took his jacket off and held it out.

Al-Rashid took it then shot him in the heart. The man fell back, dead before he reached the cobblestones.

Stuffing the pistol in his belt, he dragged the body ten feet farther down the alley and manhandled it behind several trash cans before any blood could leak onto the cobbles. Because of the effects of the suppressor the bullet had penetrated the heart but had not exited out the back.

He found a ring of keys in a trousers pocket, but not much else. No weapon, nor had he expected one.

A car passed on the street they'd come down, but no one was around, no alarms had been raised. Al-Rashid put the old man's jacket on, walked to the opposite end of the alley, and headed back toward the far side of the Alcazar by a completely different route.

The crowd had not turned ugly yet; no one had started throwing

Molotov cocktails like they had last night. The police stood their ground, but did not offer any sort of provocation.

Al-Rashid reached the plaza where earlier kids had been playing guitars and singing, but it was mostly empty, only stragglers arriving to join the mob. In five minutes he was back at the Archives, where he went up to the side door and waved at the nearest cops, who merely glanced over but then ignored him.

The door lock was old, and of the keys on the guard's ring the largest one was the most obvious, and he was inside the building, in ten seconds, immediately locking up.

For a long time he stood stock-still in the deeper shadows away from the windows, listening for sounds, any sound that might indicate someone was still here. But the Archives building was deathly still, the only noise coming from the low murmurs and occasional laughter of the people outside.

Their silence was unexpected and somewhat ominous as if it were the calm before a very large storm. He had counted on more noise to mask the sounds of any trouble he might run into here.

At the far corner of the first floor, a large area was filled with long steel cabinets, slender drawers filled with maps starting in the fifteen hundreds. He opened several of the drawers at random, took out the maps, all of them protected by clear plastic sleeves and dumped them in a pile. He took a brick of Semtex out of the haversack and laid it on the pile of maps. He stuck one of fuses into the plastique but did not set the time. Then he spread several handfuls of the magnesium dust accelerant around the area. The fire when it started would be very bright and hot.

Walking around the long open corridor to the opposite corner that looked back toward the main stairs, he pulled armloads of books from the dozen or so tall stacks and dumped them on the floor, making another pile of what he knew had to be priceless material. He set another brick of Semtex with a fuse and spread more magnesium dust, then headed to the second floor noiselessly, taking the broad marble stairs two at a time.

If it came to it, which he expected it might, he would set the fuses and step back out of the blast radii. His intent here was to cause enough damage and make enough noise so that Dr. Vergilio would come on the run to save the one artifact she valued the most, which was almost certainly the cipher key for the diary. He was indifferent to the damage, though he didn't consider himself callous enough to bother destroying the entire Archives, though if it happened he could see himself walking away with an untroubled conscience.

Upstairs he went to the side of the building that looked across at the Cathedral. The street was packed with people, but from his vantage point he could see the entire front façade of the large building, including its bell tower and its main entrance and the iron gates that were slightly ajar.

Dr. Vergilio had taken the bait, she was already there. He was sure of it.

Her suite of offices occupied one corner of the building. He walked to the opposite corner, and pulled a large number of books from the stacks and piled them on the floor in front of a window that would be clearly visible from the Cathedral. He laid another brick of Semtex on the pile and inserted a fuse but did not crimp it.

Halfway back to the offices, he piled another twenty or thirty books in front of a window, and set his last brick of Semtex and acid fuse but no accelerant. If he was caught up here he didn't want to risk a large fire.

It was quarter to nine, and by now the woman would be getting nervous. Somewhere with her would be the Cuban intelligence officer he'd seen at the doctor's apartment and had spoken with on the phone. She would be somewhere across the street in the Cathedral, but watching from a safe distance for him to show up.

She would come on the run with the doctor, but separately, when the fires started, and he would kill her. Once Dr. Vergilio had retrieved the cipher key, he would kill her and take it.

When the fire department arrived, he would continue his masquerade as a security guard and slip away into the mob.

He looked down at the Cathedral. Fifteen minutes.

"Do you mean to destroy this place for the key?" María asked from behind him.

SEVENTY-TWO

□

The police station housed in a squat unattractive building across the river from the Jardines del Guadalquivir had been nearly deserted when McGarvey was brought through a rear sally port and taken immediately to a small interrogation room.

His pistol, cell phone, Vatican passport, and everything else in his pockets had been taken from him, but once he was in the windowless room furnished only with a metal table and two chairs, all bolted to the concrete floor, the handcuffs were removed.

The arresting officer, Captain de la Rosa, sat down across from him. "You are working for the Vatican police now?"

"No," McGarvey said. In less than a half hour the situation was going to come to a head, and he needed to get the hell out. "Nor am I working for the CNI, who wanted me dead."

"On the contrary, Señor McGarvey, Spain is not your enemy."

"In that case give my things back and let me out of here."

"You shot four of our people to death, you son of a bitch! You're not going anywhere!"

"Then let me talk to someone in authority. Someone from the CNI. Before it's too late."

"Before what's too late?" de la Rosa asked. McGarvey's pistol, spare magazines, and silencer were gone, but his cell phone was on the table. The cop picked it up and pushed several buttons. He looked up. "Nothing."

"Seven-seven-Q-nine."

"Is this going to blow up in my hands?"

"I'm expecting a call. The phone is password protected."

De la Rosa entered the numbers, and immediately the phone chirped.

He answered it. "*Sí?*" After a moment, he shook his head. "No one," he said.

"Put it on speaker phone," McGarvey said.

After a moment the cop did it.

"I'm in a police building not too far from you," McGarvey said. "What's your situation? We're on speaker phone."

"Are you under arrest?" Otto asked.

"Yes."

"You need to get out of there post haste, *kemo sabe*, 'cause the shit is about to hit the wall at the Archives."

"What happened?"

"Dr. Vergilio is dead, María shot her. She means to make the rendezvous herself, with the doctor's laptop, which she thinks contains the cipher key. Or at least she's going to offer it to Montessier as such."

A very tall, ascetic-looking man, thin with wide eyes, a severe white sidewalls haircut, beak of a nose, and a long angular face, came into the room. He was dressed in a crumpled suit and white shirt but no tie. He seemed angry.

"Who is on the telephone?" he demanded. "Is it Señor Rencke?"

"Yes, and I expect that you may be Major Prieto, from the sound of your voice, and from the images Mac's phone is picking up."

De la Rosa reached to shut it off, but Prieto waved him away.

"Dr. Vergilio I know, but who is María?" the CNI officer asked.

"Colonel María León, Cuban intelligence. She's here looking for the same thing you're looking for. The diary," McGarvey said. "Any sign of Montessier?"

"No," Otto said. "After she sent the guards away, she shot the doctor and told me to leave. It was a present, she said, to Louise and Audie."

"Where are you exactly?"

"In the crowd about twenty yards from the front entrance to the Cathedral. The iron gates are open. But listen, Mac. A guy wearing a security guard jacket showed up and went inside."

"Montessier?"

"That's what I figured. He was carrying a haversack."

"Christ," McGarvey said. "Keep your head down, we'll be there in a few minutes."

Otto canceled the call.

"You're not going anywhere," Prieto said. "Who is Montessier?"

"He's an assassin working for the Saudi government, maybe for a member of the Royal family. We think that he managed to steal the diary from a bank vault in Bern. But it was written in code, and he came here looking to make a deal with Dr. Vergilio for the cipher key. At this moment he's inside the Archives and unless I miss my guess he's going to destroy the place rather than let the key fall into the wrong hands."

"Whose hands?"

"Yours. The Vatican's. Mine."

"But you're working for the Vatican."

"Despite what it looks like, no. I'm working for no one. But, Major, unless you get your ass in gear you're going to lose a lot of priceless historical documents."

"Send a couple of your men over to check it out," Prieto told de la Rosa.

"Almost everybody is doing crowd control," the cop said.

"Then you go."

"If he goes over there alone he'll wind up dead," McGarvey warned.

"Take your partner."

"They'll both die," McGarvey said.

De la Rosa got to his feet, but he looked uncertain.

"Then what do you suggest?" the major demanded.

"Get me down there right now, and watch the doors and windows to make sure he doesn't get past me."

"You're a murderer!" Prieto roared.

"Self-defense. Your people shot at me first when I went to ask them why the hell they had me under surveillance."

The major knew that it was not a lie and McGarvey saw it in his eyes.

"I have a car and driver outside," Prieto said. "We'll go."

"What about me?" de la Rosa asked.

"Organize the people already down there to watch the Archives as well as the crowd. Now, move it!"

"Better call the fire brigade to stand by," McGarvey said, pocketing his phone.

Prieto nodded, and on the way out McGarvey's pistol and spare magazines were returned to him.

Outside they got into the back of a black C-class Mercedes and the major told the driver to get them as close to the Archives as he could, as fast as he could.

Traffic was light this far away, but McGarvey didn't think they would be able to get within a block or two of the place by car. He phoned Otto.

"I'm on my way. Anything yet?"

"No, as far as I know he and María are still inside. It's possible they're making a deal, because if the cipher key does exist—though Dr. Vergilio swore up and down that it didn't—it'll be on her laptop."

"Once he finds that out he'll kill her."

"If he actually has the diary, I think she means to kill him. And she's not bad."

"Are you still in the mob?"

"Yeah, a little closer to the Cathedral entrance. But it looks as if it's going to get ugly around here pretty quick. Don't dawdle."

"No," McGarvey said, and he hung up.

"What about your Vatican passport?" Major Prieto asked.

"It was one of their soldiers from Malta who took out one of your people in Florida. Like you he was sent to help me look for the diary. They still hope that I'll find it and the key and share it with them."

"Will you?"

"I'll share it with anyone who wants the damned thing. Let your people work it out, along with the Cubans, and the Voltaire Society— one of whose people your agents killed in Sarasota. Along with two innocent students."

Prieto didn't turn away. "I'm truly sorry it happened that way."

"Your surveillance team weren't sorry."

SEVENTY-THREE

□

Al-Rashid held up at the end of the stacks, the Beretta in his right hand, a little blood seeping from the flesh wound high on his left arm. He hadn't thought that the bitch would fire. She wanted the diary above everything else and she was evidently ruthless enough to do whatever it took.

"We can still make a deal, if you have the cipher key," he said.

"I have the key," María said from somewhere to the right, down the corridor in the direction of the offices. "But you said that you didn't bring the diary with you."

"No, but it is very close at hand. Produce the key and I will produce the book."

"The deal is no longer that simple, Señor Harris, or whatever your real name is."

"What are your terms? I am listening."

"We each have something that the other wants. But you came here intending to kill me and Dr. Vergilio."

"Only if you couldn't provide the key."

"You're a liar."

"Your terms?" al-Rashid said. He laid the pistol on one of the shelves, and began pulling books just below eye level and quietly laying them on the floor. "What do you propose?"

"Throw out your pistol and we'll go get the diary."

"I won't do it. There'd be no reason for you not to kill me."

"There's every reason in the world. I want the diary and you're the only one who can lead me to it."

Al-Rashid had cleared about two feet of books from the shelf, exposing the row face in, on the opposite shelf. "I'll take you to the diary, what's to prevent you from killing me?"

"We'll meet someplace public, where neither of us will have the advantage, for the exchange."

Al-Rashid picked up his pistol. "What did you say?" he asked, but before she could answer, he shoved the books on the opposite side off the shelf.

María stood just beyond the end of the next stack, and al-Rashid fired three shots in rapid succession.

She fell back with a cry and fired four shots in return, all of them slamming harmlessly into the spines of the books on either side of the opening, before she disappeared around the corner.

The building fell quiet, except for the noise of the crowd outside. They had begun chanting something about fair wages, fair prices, fair humanity. Like most mob-led slogans, this one made no sense to al-Rashid.

"You missed," María called from around the corner.

"Perhaps I'll go over to the Cathedral and meet with Dr. Vergilio after all," al-Rashid said. He was becoming frustrated. Job one was killing the Cuban bitch. "Perhaps she'll be a little more cooperative."

One of the bricks of Semtex landed on the floor at the end of the stack not five feet away from where he was hiding. He stepped back reflexively until he realized that the acid fuse had been removed.

María laughed. A moment later the long, thin pencil fuse landed a couple of feet away from the plastique and two seconds later it popped off like a flare.

"Cristos! My aim was off. Maybe I'll get luckier next time."

Al-Rashid reached around the corner and emptied the Beretta's fifteen-round magazine. He ducked back, ejected the spent magazine, slammed another in the handle, and charged the weapon.

"Tell you what, I'm getting out of your way for the moment," María called. She had moved farther down the corridor. "You might want to take a look in the doctor's office. I'll wait for you downstairs, and we can get serious about our options. The deal is still possible."

Al-Rashid eased to the end of the stacks and looked down the corridor just as the woman disappeared down the main stairs. He waited another ten seconds then made his way after her, stopping just short of the landing. Again he was just in time to see her disappear around the corner into the gloom.

A few drops of blood had dripped on the first step, and more two steps farther down. She had been hit, but not badly.

He glanced down the corridor in the direction of Dr. Vergilio's suite of offices. The outer door was open, and he suspected that some sort of a trap had been laid for him. But he knew that she was downstairs, and even if she'd found a second brick of Semtex and had placed it in the office, she would have had no idea how much time to set on the fuse.

In any event she wanted the diary, and she meant for him to see whatever was waiting for him in the doctor's offices. She was using whatever it was as a bargaining chip.

And he figured that he knew what it was.

Glancing again toward the darkness at the base of the stairs to make sure she hadn't come back, he sprinted down to the open office door. A few more drops of blood had fallen on the tile floor, which didn't make sense unless she had been hurt earlier. But again there wasn't much of it, so her wound was slight.

He eased around the corner, and swept the small outer office with his pistol, but nothing moved. Nor was anything or anyone behind the door, nor did he see anything that would indicate she'd laid a trap for him.

At the door to the doctor's inner office, which was also open, he hesitated before he looked in.

Dr. Vergilio, a small hole in her forehead, lay crumpled on her knees, her head back against the front of the desk. The Cuban had shot the doctor at close range, but it made no sense unless she'd taken the cipher key for herself because the doctor had refused for some reason at the last minute to cooperate.

Back out in the corridor he returned to the head of the stairs to listen. But the only sounds were those of the crowd outside.

He turned on his heel and sprinted noiselessly past the stacks he had hidden behind to the rear service stairs that he took cautiously to the ground floor, where he held up again. Tall book stacks lined the rear corridor, framing the back door that opened onto the side wall of the Alcazar. To the right were display cases and around the corner toward the front were the rows of map cases and one of the bricks of Semtex he'd set.

Someone in that direction was talking. It was the woman and she sounded urgent.

Al-Rashid crept to the corner and made his way almost to the map cases, when he spotted María crouched behind one of them, her attention to the right, toward the main staircase. He slipped behind the last of the book stacks.

". . . I don't know where he's hiding, but I'm telling you he killed Dr. Vergilio, I saw her body with my own eyes."

Al-Rashid ducked back just as María turned and looked over her shoulder, a cell phone to her ear.

"I was hiding just around the corner and soon as he left I checked on her, but it was too late."

She had to be talking to McGarvey. It was very possible, even likely, that he was the man arrested at the sidewalk café because of the tip al-Rashid had called to the CNI. But if that was him, it meant he'd been released. Or at the least had convinced someone to get back here. Time was running short.

"Yes, Otto's right, he's wearing a guard's uniform. But he's gone now."

Al-Rashid had eased around the corner intending to shoot her, but he stopped.

"Listen to me, goddamnit, I'm across the street in the Cathedral. I followed him over. And I talked to him. I have a flash drive on which I downloaded the cipher key from Dr. Vergilio's laptop. I told him we could make a trade, the key for a copy of the diary."

Al-Rashid didn't move.

"Of course we weren't face-to-face. He would have killed me, and taken the key. I told him that I'd wait for the copy."

The woman was playing both ends against the middle.

"I don't know where it is, but he said he would photograph the key pages with his cell phone. He's supposed to be back in ten minutes. And no, I don't want you barging in over here, for all I know he never left. He could be hiding somewhere inside the church to take the photos. I want you guys to back off. I don't want another shoot-out. I want the diary."

Al-Rashid watched as she pocketed her phone and he stepped out from around the stacks. "I'll have the flash drive, if you please," he said.

SEVENTY-FOUR

□

Two blocks out they stopped at the edge of the crowd, got out, and headed the rest of the way on foot. Prieto was talking on a handheld radio, ordering the police to keep a close eye on every door and window of the Archives and the Cathedral.

"She could have been lying about where she was," he said when he finished the transmission.

"That's possible," McGarvey said. "You and your people take the Cathedral, I'm going into the Archives. But I'll need one of the cops to help me get in, because I'm sure that it's locked up."

Prieto relayed the order. "Someone will meet you at the front door."

"Tell him not to go inside, because if Montessier is there your man will find himself in a shoot-out. And I want the guy alive. He's probably hidden the diary somewhere and if he's dead we may never find it."

Prieto gave that order as well. "We don't know what he looks like."

McGarvey brought up the passport photo on his phone, showed it to Prieto, and then sent it to the major's cell phone.

At the police line Prieto held up his open credentials wallet and they were passed through.

Before they separated the major gave McGarvey a hard look. "I have a feeling that you're lying to me, that the Cathedral is a ruse. You want to take the bastard yourself."

"Just in case, watch yourself."

"If you find what you're looking for don't run, señor, because wherever you go I will come after you."

"You already tried it in Florida."

Prieto nodded tightly. "The next time it won't be a simple surveillance mission."

McGarvey angled left, working his way through the surging crowd that was starting to get ugly. A lot of the demonstrators held bottles half filled with gasoline, the necks of which were stuffed with rags.

In some spots the people had got to within fifteen or twenty feet of the police line, and the cops in the riot gear, batons at the ready, clear Lexan shields up, were clearly nervous. The chanting had grown louder and more urgent than earlier.

A cop in riot gear was waiting at the main door of the Archives. He had a Heckler & Koch MP7A1 slung over his shoulder by a strap. The small weapon, which could be used either as a pistol or as a submachine gun, carried a ninety-round magazine of 4.6X30 mm ammunition, the same as the older MP5, Room Broom.

"Señor McGarvey?" he asked. He was a sergeant.

McGarvey nodded. "I need to get in right now: do you understand English?"

"Yes, but the door is locked. I don't have the key."

"Shoot out the lock."

The cop hesitated.

"Do it!" McGarvey shouted.

The cop reluctantly unslung the MP7, switched off the safety, and fired several rounds into the lock.

McGarvey pulled his pistol and shoved the door open with his foot. "Stay here," he told the cop, and dropping to the tile floor just inside, he rolled left so that he would not be framed by the lights outside.

Except for the crowd noise the interior of the museum was quiet. Behind him the door slowly swung closed. To the left were display cases, straight ahead beyond the reception desk the main stairs led up to the second floor, and down the long corridor to the right low cabinets were lined up in precise rows and columns.

McGarvey lay quiet for a full minute, absorbing the sounds and smells of the place. It dawned on him that he was smelling something other than the dusty books and records, something modern and even sweet. Perfume. Chanel. María.

Someone to the right called out, but softly, the voice ragged.

"Kirk."

McGarvey got to his feet, and sprinted down the corridor, making as little noise as possible, all his senses alert for Montessier.

María lay on a pile of what looked like manuscripts or maps, all of the pieces encased in plastic sleeves. Black dust, what almost looked like gunpowder, was spread all over the place. Blood streamed from wounds in both shoulders, both knees and her chest, just above her left breast. She was in a great deal of pain.

"No," she cried. "Stay back." She tried to move, but couldn't because of her wounds.

"I'll get an ambulance."

"No, get back now."

McGarvey looked over his shoulder to make sure that Monstessier wasn't standing in the shadows nearby, waiting to kill both of them.

"Please, Kirk, get away before it's too late," she said, her voice only a whisper. She was desperate. "I'm lying on a brick of plastique and he's cracked the fuse. It's going off any second now."

McGarvey holstered his pistol and went to her.

"No," she moaned.

"Easy," he said. He moved her aside as gently as possible, but still she whimpered in pain.

The Semtex was a one-kilo brick, an acid fuse stuck in one end. McGarvey yanked the fuse out of the plastique and a split second later it sparked, burning his fingers as he tossed it away. "Jesus."

María said something in Spanish that he couldn't quite make out.

"I'll get help."

She tried to reach for him but she couldn't move her arm.

McGarvey took her hand in his. It was icy cold. "It'll be okay."

"He's still here," she whispered. "He took the flash drive with the key. But he can't get out because of the cops."

"Where is he?"

"Upstairs, I think. Be careful—" she said, and she died in mid-sentence, all the light going out of her eyes, her chest rising and then falling as if she was a tire that had been punctured.

McGarvey stared at her face for a long time. Hers had been an uneasy life, yet she was a product of the Cuban state. She was her father's daughter, had been even before she had come face-to-face with him on his deathbed just a few months ago. A liar, devious, a manipulator, a user, a sociopath, a killer.

Now that she was dead he felt some pity for her. Some sorrow.

Whatever she deserved, this wasn't it, and yet he knew that he was being a maudlin fool.

On the roof, al-Rashid had spotted McGarvey appear out of the crowd and with the help of a uniformed cop shoot his way through the front door. He glanced at his watch. The digital timer was more than one minute past zero, and still there had been no explosion from below.

The woman could not have moved her arms to defuse the Semtex, so it had to have been brave McGarvey. The champion of the underdog. Yet Colonel León was an intelligence officer of an enemy state. It made no sense to his way of thinking.

His plan was for the explosion to occur, and when the fire department showed up he would descend to the ground floor where he would pretend to be a victim. Once outside he would discard the guard's jacket and walk away. He had the diary, and now he had the cipher key. Once he delivered them to Prince Saleh, he would be paid and he would disappear into the woodwork. Maybe Thailand. Maybe even the Czech Republic where life after the Russians had become good.

All that had suddenly changed. First he would have to deal with the problem of McGarvey, and then he would have to set the fuses on the remaining two bricks of Semtex.

Only a small delay.

"You shouldn't have left the ladder down," McGarvey said from behind him.

McGarvey, crouched on the second to the top rung of the wooden folddown ladder, his head and shoulders just above the access door to the roof, hadn't expected Montessier to simply throw down his pistol and turn around.

"Ah, Monsieur McGarvey. You found the woman, and disarmed the plastique. How clever. And now you have me. So what's next? Will you shoot me, or will you arrest me? Or are you open for a deal? Anything you need or want?"

"The flash drive you took from Colonel León."

Al-Rashid reached into his pocket.

"Easy."

He took the flash drive out of his pocket and tossed it down. "And the diary too?"

"Yes."

"I don't have it on my person this evening, but I've already made a copy and sent it to my employer. Surely you must have guessed that by now."

"Put your hands together behind your head and lace your fingers together."

Al-Rashid did as he was told, but slowly, measuring each movement.

McGarvey climbed the rest of the way up. He was less than ten feet away from the man, an easy shot even under the poor light conditions. He took out his cell phone. "María was willing to make a deal, so why did you shoot her?"

"I had no use for her. She had the cipher key and I took it. Except for you my work is finished here. I merely need to get out of this building."

McGarvey dialed Prieto's number, but there was no answer and after four rings he called Otto.

"Yes?"

"I have him on the roof of the museum. Major Prieto is in the Cathedral, tell him to get over here now."

"You might have to hold on for a bit. It's starting to get ugly down here. What about María and the doctor?"

"They're dead."

"Hang on, Mac, we'll get to you."

An explosion below on the street lit up the night sky, followed immediately by a volley of gunshots.

Al-Rashid turned to look over the railing at the edge of the roof, and in a flash leaped over it and disappeared.

By the time McGarvey reached the edge and cautiously looked over, al-Rashid had already climbed down to the level of the second-story windows. A shot from this angle was impossible, because if he missed he would hit someone on the street below that was shoulder to shoulder with people—most of them men, but many of them women and even a few children.

Al-Rashid, hanging on with one hand, fired six shots up, all of them slamming into the stonework, a piece of which caught McGarvey in the jaw as he ducked back. The caliber was small, almost certainly María's pistol, a Russian-made 5.54 PSM, with only an eight-round magazine.

"You won't get out of here alive," McGarvey called.

Al-Rashid fired two more shots, and a moment later the sound of a lot of breaking glass came from just below.

McGarvey looked over the edge again, but al-Rashid had disappeared through the second-floor window.

Unless the assassin had a spare magazine the pistol was dry.

Al-Rashid got to his feet and raced out to the corridor and headed in a dead run to where the wooden ladder from the roof came out of the ceiling in one of the restoration rooms adjacent to Dr. Vergilio's office.

He held up at the doorway and looked inside. He'd expected to see McGarvey climbing down the ladder, but the man wasn't there.

Getting away from the museum was contingent on two things: First of all he had to eliminate McGarvey and then he had to set a fire.

"A deal is still possible," he called.

"You're not leaving here tonight," McGarvey said from the shadows to the left. "I want you alive."

"Then you'll get your wish," al-Rashid said. He fired three shots into the darkness, and ducking behind a cabinet fired two more shots in the same direction, when something slammed into his shoulder.

He turned in time to see Otto Rencke, with a pistol in hand just a few feet down the corridor, a cop with an MP7 a few feet behind.

Otto fired a second shot, catching al-Rashid in the mouth, driving him backward before he could switch aim and return fire. A third shot entered his brain through his right eye, and he fell back dead.

"Mac?" Otto called.

McGarvey stepped out of the shadows in the corner, blood dripping from his chin. He held his left hand over a wound in his right arm. "Damned good shooting."

"Louise said I ought to practice up a bit if I was going to continue to hang around you."

The cop had come to the open door, but he just looked from Otto to McGarvey and to the body on the floor.

"What about Major Prieto?"

"No way I was going to make it across to the Cathedral, so I figured it'd be better if I came here and lent a hand. Did I do right?"

McGarvey nodded. "You did right."

Back in their suite after dinner Otto spent a couple of minutes on his computer and then headed out the door. "Be back in a flash," he said.

McGarvey, his arm in a sling, was on the balcony watching the night traffic. It was just about eleven in the evening and Seville was coming alive. Party hour here usually didn't get into full swing until around midnight, and the riots seemed to have come to a sudden end for no known reason, and Spain was ready to have some fun again. At least for now.

The CNI had cleared them to leave first thing in the morning after forty-eight hours of intense questioning. Montessier had carried no identification, the flash drive they'd retrieved from his body was blank, and his encrypted phone had been sent to headquarters in Madrid for examination.

Major Prieto had cleared their release with someone very high in the government. No one wanted the politically embarrassing situation to continue to spin out of control. Crimes had been committed by the CNI on American soil, and by Americans on Spanish soil. Never mind Cuba, and no one was willing to talk about the so-called Voltaire Society. Spain wanted the problem to disappear.

No cipher key existed, because the diary that was supposedly stolen from a bank vault in Bern was a myth. The entire operation had been a failure from the start; intelligent men chasing after a will-o'-the-wisp, so intently that lives had been lost for no reason.

"Do not come back to Spain, señors," Major Pietro had said to them at the end.

Otto had first called Louise to tell her that everything was fine, that he and Mac were okay. She would have Audie brought up tomorrow, and in the meantime Otto arranged for a CIA aircraft to pick them up. It was at this moment over the Atlantic inbound for Seville's San Pablo Airport, and would be touching down around 7:00 A.M.

McGarvey went to the minibar for another beer, when Otto came back, a big smile on his face. He was carrying a small leather-bound book that looked very old.

"No one who knew that Montessier was staying here under the name of Paul Harris was left alive," he said. "No ID on the body, no hotel key card, nada."

"You got in?"

"Four-oh-seven. I hacked the hotel's computer, switched our room number with his, then called the front desk and told them that I had lost my key, so they made me a new one."

"To four oh seven."

"Bingo," Rencke said, and he began to hop from one foot to the other like he used to do in the old days when he was excited. "I was there two minutes ago and found this tucked in a pocket of his suitcase." He held up the book. "The arrogant bastard didn't think that anyone would find him and come looking."

"Jacob Ambli's diary?"

"Yup."

"No good without the key."

Otto's grin widened. "I figured it out on the way up in the elevator," he said. He opened the diary to the first page, and began to read, slowly, but in English:

"For the Sanctified, Caesarean, Catholic Pontiff, the Bishop of Rome, his holiness Gregory XVI, our Sacred and Blessed Pope."

Otto looked up. "And it goes on for an entire page and a half about grace, and peace and that kind of crap, along with a list of all of Vatican's holdings, including those most recently saved souls in the New World—all of it in his name, of course.

"Then there's a couple of more pages about Mexico City, about the Spanish military expedition to Northern Mexico under the orders of the SMOM, and signed Yr. Most Obedient servant Father Jacob Ambli."

Otto looked up again. "From there it's mostly sketch maps and daily logs. I haven't read it all."

"Is it in plain text after all?"

"No, it's Latin, but encrypted. Easy enough to sight read if you know the trick and go slowly. Two keys. First is that it's a substitution cipher based on the Fibonacci chain of numbers. Our military used to use it for their crypto machines back in the sixties."

"Never heard of it."

"No reason, unless you're a geek like me. A mathematician by the name of Leonardo Fibonacci came up with it just as a curiosity—though it's been used for lots of stuff—especially in the past forty or fifty years in electronics. It starts out with the number one, then one again, then two, then three, then five, then eight then thirteen. You just have to add the previous two numbers to come up with the next. Add three and five to get eight. Add eight and five to get thirteen."

McGarvey was following him. "What's the second key?"

"Figuring what number in the chain to start with—it's a different starting point for each sentence, and then always subtracting just enough so that the resultant number never gets above twenty-three—that's how many letters are in the ancient Latin alphabet."

McGarvey had never seen Otto happier, except when he and Louise were with Audie.

"You just have to do the addition and subtractions in your head as you go along, and then figure out a few of the substitutions, and after that it's a piece of cake. So now what? Do we take this home with us?"

McGarvey had known the answer almost from the beginning, and he shook his head. "Photograph the pages on your iPad, and include the explanation of the two keys and send it to everyone. The Vatican and SMOM, Spain, Cuba, our people—Callahan will want to know if all of this was worth something—and the Voltaire Society."

Otto held up Jacob's diary. "What about this?"

"We'll have the hotel deliver it to the Archives after we've left Spain's airspace," McGarvey said. "That's where it belongs." He got the Heineken and opened it. "And then we're finally done."

"Yeah, right," Otto said. "Until the next time."